# Becoming
# Beautiful
### Despite being
## Bullied and Abused

# Becoming
# Beautiful
## Despite being
## Bullied and Abused

CARMALITA JEAN JONES

**TATE PUBLISHING**
AND ENTERPRISES, LLC

Published by Tate Publishing & Enterprises, LLC
127 E. Trade Center Terrace | Mustang, Oklahoma 73064 USA
1.888.361.9473 | www.tatepublishing.com

Tate Publishing is committed to excellence in the publishing industry. The company reflects the philosophy established by the founders, based on Psalm 68:11,
*"The Lord gave the word and great was the company of those who published it."*

Book design copyright © 2015 by Tate Publishing, LLC. All rights reserved.
*Cover design by Nikolai Purpura*
*Interior design by Mary Jean Archival*

Published in the United States of America
ISBN: 978-1-63449-683-4
1. Fiction / Coming of Age
2. Family & Relationships / Bullying
15.06.05

# Contents

# A Letter of Thanks

I, Carmalita Jean suffered through numerous hardships in my lifetime, that's true. However, many beautiful people have also crossed my path along the way. For those wonderful, caring people I would like to say thank you. It was because of you and your generous, loving spirit I was able to go forward into my life's adventures and fulfill my purpose.

Thank you for the concerned friends and family who took care of my basic needs such as food and housing without expecting anything in return. Your generous, kind ways were much appreciated.

Thanks for my spiritual friends I've encountered along the way that helped me become closer to God and who accepts me as I am.

I thank God for loving me when I could not love myself, for never giving up on me, and for sending both earth and celestial angels to guide me through the rough patches. Thank you for the many gifts you have bestowed to me such as my keen mind, sensitive spirit and my artistic talents. Thank you God for gracing me with an abundance of love in my life. You are indeed an awesome God and worthy of all my love and praise!

Thank you my husband for accepting me and loving me through good times and bad. You've been a strong, supportive redwood tree to me. Thank you for putting up with my intense emotions, my moods, my physical and mental limitations. You know me, love me and accept me as I am and for that I am truly grateful.

A hearty thank you goes out to my various professors. The psychology classes helped me to understand the reasons why I acted and often reacted the way I did. That knowledge benefited me a great deal. Thanks to the wonderful art teachers and creative writing teachers. Through them I have learned to express my inner most emotions through love and creativity and not through hateful destructive means. You helped me keep my heart and soul alive.

Thanks to all the counselors that I have seen throughout the years. They've helped me unlock the door to my mind and to release the incredible pain that laid deep within the recesses of my troubled heart. If it weren't for you, I probably wouldn't be alive to write this book and so I am extremely grateful to you.

Thanks to my daughter Rosa. It was through your birth I was finally able to learn how to love…truly love. Once I learned how to love, God blessed me with the love of a good man.

It was because of you I started to do better in my life. I didn't love myself enough to want to do those beneficial things for me. I did them for you, at least I did at first. Although you were unplanned by me, you were planned by God. He sent you to me for he knew my love for you would turn me around. I have completely changed my life because I loved you so much. I shed the activities of the past that belittled my personal integrity and poisoned my spirit, mind and body. I started this incredible transformation all because of the love of a child…you.

# Prologue

The following story is based on the life of Jeanie, a lovable but troubled girl. The selected words and ideas in this novel are not meant to shock, horrify or degrade Jeanie for she has endured enough hardship in her life. Although much of what this budding young woman had experienced was not pleasant, this story is meant to enlighten not depreciate the human spirit.

Despite what the universe had thrown at the main character, she always had the courage and stamina to continue on in her life's path. There may have been times when she felt like giving up but nevertheless her inner strength kept her forging forward in life. Although our purpose isn't always clear, as is the case of Jeanie's, still if one proceeds with love, kindness and fortitude, eventually everybody gets what it is they seek in the world.

Jeanie is readily depicted as a sensitive person who had a lot of love to give but didn't know how to give or receive it. Throughout the book the reader will see a similar pattern emerging with Jeanie. Early on in years, through no fault of her own, the young vulnerable girl fell into the victim role. Once being placed in that role, it was easy to see why and how the young lady subconsciously chose the people she included in her life.

Although much of Jeanie's life and loves had been viciously cruel, the dreamer kept forging on. Despite the overwhelming obstacles Jeanie encountered, she felt certain that out in the vast universe was a place where she would be loved and accepted for being herself.

Even though many of Jeanie's thoughtless actions created havoc in her life, she was still a good, beautiful person deserving love…including God's love. Although she had made her share of mistakes and crawled in the shadows of her own misconceived beliefs, the girl still had a lot to give to the world. It took her much time to realize that.

As you read the troubled tale of this lost child remember that the path for some is not as easy as they are for others. Rather than condemn Jeanie for the journey she had taken along the way, try to understand why she took the roads she did. Gaze within the eyes of this sensitive soul. By doing so, you may be able to fathom how the girl formed her perceptions, and how she dealt with the deep emotions and her ill conceived conceptions the way that she did.

Delve deep within the lost lady's complicated mind to see beyond her actions. Look within her confused, over sized heart and you will see the girl as she really is…sensitive and zany with a strange logic all her own. The world didn't make sense to Jeanie's perplexed mind so it was up to her mind to create the kind of world in which she could comfortably and sometimes not so comfortably live in.

Despite the tough life this wayward woman traveled, she still deserved to be appreciated and loved, though there were times when she thought not. Since Jeanie's need for acceptance and love was so strong, she continued to search for a way to satisfy to those inner needs. Despite what the universe was teaching her about the unpredictability and fickleness of people, she still sought their approval and love.

Mixed emotions about where she fit into the world coupled with a low self esteem made Jeanie's life struggles even harder. Still, despite all of what she's done and where she has been, she has developed into a strong, spiritual, giving person.

Enjoy the most personal gift Jeanie could give to the world... her life's story. Read it with an open mind and an open heart. Try to understand the journey the sensitive soul traveled and the many obstacles she encountered throughout her life. The various barriers may have slowed the growth of her delicate soul but the delays did not stop her from achieving her life's purpose.

May God guide you gently on the path you're meant to be on as well. Feel the universal pull in your heart guiding you towards the magnificent things available to you such as love, acceptance and purposeful living.

Jeanie's search for love and belonging did finally become actualized. May your inner most desires become an actualization for you as well.

# CHAPTER 1

# Little Jeanie

"Damn it!" Jeanie cried as she hung up the phone. "That stupid get away truck couldn't even leave the city never mind go cross country!" Jeanie knew that once again her ignorance shone through.

"I never should have spend so much money on that used piece of crap."

The only reason Jeanie laid down a thousand dollars on that old truck was because she thought it had a rebuilt engine recently put in it. There was a shiny, blue painted engine under the hood. It surely must be a rebuilt engine, she thought. Jeanie remembered questioning the previous owner about the trucks engine. The man jokingly gave a vague answer to her inquiries and left it at that.

Nearly a lifetime at the automotive school couldn't get that old truck kicking again, the trusting girl thought. She already depleted her bank account trying to fix up the brown rust eaten, money gobbling piece of machinery and all for what? Nothing. Two days after she drove it out of the automotive school, the brown bomb died again. A terrible banging noise sounded from the engine.

"Uh oh, that doesn't sound good. What's this going to cost me?" the down hearted girl whimpered.

Since Jeanie had been out of work for several months due to an automobile accident, she didn't have the money to fix the truck up. Still, after the truck graced her driveway for three weeks, she decided to bring it to a local shop to get the low down on what the problem was. The crankshaft in the engine was bad and the truck could possibly have broken rods too. It would cost at least another $900 to get that fugitive from a junkyard moving without the aid of a tow truck.

"I've got to cut my losses," Jeanie told herself.

After terminating the phone call from the automotive shop, she placed an AD in the local paper to sell her rust bucket. She also placed a huge for sale sign made of plastic shelving paper on the truck's windshield and attached it with packaging tape. Carmalita Jean spend $1600 on the truck already and barely put 60 miles on it, yet the sign on the truck read for sale $900 or best offer. Hopefully, best offer would be at least $700, she hoped. She would lose her shirt on that truck, but she wasn't about to lose her britches too!

Jeanie's money was nearly gone. Her hope for a bright future she envisioned for herself and her daughter was almost gone too.

"Why did I move out here in this godforsaken city?" she cried. "Why did I drag my little girl so far away from our family and friends to follow a dream?" Jeanie was perplexed. She couldn't decide whether she was being a visionary or a fool. Was it indeed a stupid move coming down here? "How can I be so smart yet do so many stupid things?"

Jeanie ran to her bed tucking her face into the pillow. "If I had the nerve. I'd drown myself," she said to herself.

That feat wouldn't be difficult to do. The little lake, she routinely visited rarely had any visitors early in the morning. She could swim out in the middle of it and let her legs sink below her body. Soon her chest, with the weight of her heavy thighs would become under the water. After her chest was submerged, it would only be a matter of seconds before the crystal water flooded into her mouth and relieved her of her last remaining breath. All the sorrow and pain that life thus far brought her would be eliminated too. If she could just fight the instinct to kick her feet as she started to sink then maybe she would succeed in her plan to destroy her miserable life.

Jeanie cried harder as she shook the terrible image from her mind. "No, that's not what I want to do. I want to live. I don't want to die. God oh why, oh why have things gone so badly since I've been here in Arkansas? I've tried so hard to do right. I've tried so hard to succeed. Why haven't things gone any better for me?"

Jeanie remembered how hard she struggled in college all those years while she raised her little girl all alone. The teary eyed idealist thought for sure the bachelors degree, she earned from the New England college would carry her far.

"At last, I'll be able to get a decent paying job where I can properly take care of my fast growing girl. I won't get rich being a social worker, but that's okay. Money isn't everything. No it isn't. I want to help people. I want to make a difference in someone's life."

How ironic the little pauper thought. She chose to study human services in Massachusetts, because she wanted to help others, but right now she couldn't even help herself. Jeanie knew that her depression was getting worse and worse. Months ago, the doctor put her on antidepressants, but they did not seem to do much good. So she quit taking them. Jeanie didn't feel enough of an improvement emotionally to counteract the nausea she felt after swallowing those blue pills. It just didn't make sense to keep taking something that made her body feel so bad. Anyway, Jeanie was sure that the depression she felt didn't come from a chemical imbalance. No, her state of mind was bought on by her environment, her situational stresses. Her negative state of mind was surely caused by all the unpleasant factors in her life which she had no control of.

A stupid auto accident, put Jeanie in physical pain. It also created further money problems. It definitely wasn't her fault though. She was riding with a friend when his vehicle was hit from behind and then to the side. The car didn't suffer great damage, but Jeanie's back and neck got a double whammy from the two different impacts. The chiropractor's adjustments helped but it would time to mend the muscle damage. It would take time for her body to heal, but eventually it would heal. Too bad all the multitude of Jeanie's psychological pain couldn't be repaired that fast.

It seemed that she no sooner fixed one part of her broken psyche when another almost forgotten injury jutted out it's ugly head into Jeanie's consciousness. Isn't that the way life is. She would forget the things she wanted to remember and remember the things she wanted to forget. There were so many aspects in Jeanie past life that she wanted to permanently forget, but her mind wouldn't let her. No matter how deeply she shoved those memories into the bottomless trash heap of her mind, they would eventually resurface. These phantoms didn't always reappear in the girls mind when it was convenient for her either. Sometimes little everyday things would trigger an almost forgotten memory and all those floating feelings would randomly bombard her mind.

The depressed mother cried harder as she shook away all those images of her colorless body being swept away by the water's currents. As despondent as the injured lady was, she considered herself fortunate. She could've been hurt far worse that she was. She's glad she wasn't though for who would've taken care of her daughter? Yes, it was the knowledge that her little girl depended on her and her alone that ultimately kept the grieving woman from putting her suicidal thoughts into action.

Rosa, Jeanie's daughter was the primary reason why she endured the many obstacle that were thrown at her. She worried about her girl. However, sometimes she even wondered if she would be better off without her. Maybe Rosa would be happier if she had rich parents and lived in a huge mansion on a hill. They do live on a hill now, but their residence wasn't a mansion. No, but it was still home. Yes, thank God for their little rent house. Thank God that even though she currently had no income, she wouldn't be destitute and living on the streets. Jeanie knew that despite her joblessness, her and Rosa would still have a place to live. She may eventually be without electricity and using her free weekly newspaper as toilet paper, but at least she wouldn't be homeless. Thank God for subsidized rent.

Jeanie didn't think that she would ever have to rely on government help again when she left Massachusetts with a bachelor's degree. Jeanie was a single mom raising her child on welfare when she started college. Attending college was difficult enough, but it was even harder because Jeanie was an older returning student. The good study habits that were learned in high school were forgotten. Jeanie had to relearn such necessary skills as time management and speed reading. The girl also had to learn to take tests without becoming catatonic with fear.

It was so important to the hard working scholar that she did the best that she could in her studies, for she felt her life depended on it. The girl would often go without the sleep that her body needed to study for the multitude of tests she routinely took. There were times when she went to school sleep deprived due to her anxiety or because her tiny tot had a restless night. Due to Jeanie's emotionally distant family, she basically had the task of raising her difficult child alone, void of the important emotional assistance needed to keep her life in balance.

Struggling with the finances were rough. Jeanie became quite efficient with the meager amount of government money which was allotted her. She lived most of her life on a shoestring, so she knew all the tricks necessary to survive on barely nothing. What was really rough for the emotionally distraught gal was the struggle she had with raising her young, strong willed child by herself. She attended school full time, and put in many hours at her work study job in between classes so time was scarce. She still had homework to do after Rosa went to bed as well as all the multitude of household tasks to maintain a decent home.

Although Jeanie had a series of long-term relationships throughout her college days, Jeanie was basically on her own. The stressful home environment caused severe strain on both the mother and daughter. Still, Jeanie endured many years in her emotional hellhole so that she could achieve her dream of being financially independent.

Jeanie was tired of being poor. She was tired of living on government handouts. She wanted to do things to make her feel good about herself. For years it seemed that the rebellious, foolish girl did everything she could to foster self hate.

It took the birth of her daughter Rosa to encourage Jeanie to forget and forgive her wild foolish past with all her mistakes and sorrows. Carmalita Jean knew long before her daughter was born, that she had to forge a different path for her life now. She found a way to cut through the thicket of her scarred heart through her psychology courses. While studying the things that helped her, she learned how to help others. The girl who thought she wasn't smart enough for college, graduated with honors. Even though she was a little older than most other college graduates, she was smart and responsible, compassionate and sensitive. Jeanie was sure that it would only be a matter of time before she obtained a good paying job in her field of study.

Unfortunately life doesn't always turn out as planned. Living in Arkansas wasn't all strawberries and cream as the little miss dreamed. Life in the sunny state was more like quicksand and cherry pits. Jeanie had worked a variety of low-paying service jobs for five years. She believed with all her heart if she just got some experience to go with her gold lettered diploma then her life would turn around.

Jeanie however felt like an alien living in a foreign land. She didn't know anyone in the job field that could help her get ahead start on her career. She didn't come from a well-known reputable family, nor was her daddy a Congressman who could pull a few strings for her. The bright, sensitive girl knew that starting life out in the natural state would be difficult, but she never dreamed it would be like this.

Things were starting to get better in Jeanie's life, financially at least. She was finally hired for a position where she could use her use her human services degree. At last a job with good pay and good benefits. After five years working diligently towards her goal of achieving independence, it was finally becoming a reality.

For a couple of short months, Jeanie worked long and hard at her newly acquired job. The energetic, positive employee worked like a fool to be efficient at her position as a social worker/ activities director. However, that postiton position zapped much of Jeanie's physical energy and psychological strength. She was hired just as the facility was about to under go state inspections. It was stressful! Still she was bound and determined to stick with the job. She loved the residence at the nursing home. She felt loved and needed in return. It was a long time since she felt such emotions anywhere…from anyone including her own teenage daughter

Even though Jeanie was a pretty girl, she hadn't had a boyfriend for quite some time. The last man, she went with physically abused her body and psychologically tore up her mind. James didn't portray himself in that manner when Jeanie first met him. No, he was sweet and gentle, smart and creative. The lovesick woman child fell head over heels in love with James within a few months time. The two of them even talked about getting married. Although no engagement ring was given to Jeanie, she introduced the young man to everyone as her fiancé.

For a couple of short months, everything was perfect in Paradise…seemingly. There were little occurrences that may have given Jeanie clues to the type of person this man really was. However at the time she was too blind to see them. Jeanie's teenage daughter, Rosa told her mom in no uncertain terms what she thought of James. The frustrated mom just thought that Rosa was being jealous and disagreeable. Now Jeanie wished she paid more attention to her daughter's perceptive observations.

Jeanie could remember going over some of her poetry while waiting for her beloved. When James finished getting ready for their night out, he walked over to where Jeannie sat. As the young poet read her written words memories flooded her mind. Heartfelt emotions unwillingly came pouring out in the form of salty tears. Instead of being compassionate and concerned, this self-centered immature man gruffly told the sensitive tear struck Jeanie she had to quit carrying on. Untouched by her emotions, James hurried her out the door. It was true that they planned to go somewhere, but they could've gone to dinner at their leisure. There were no reservations to keep or friends waiting for them. The fact was that James was so wrapped up in his life and his feelings that he had little regard for anyone else's. Jeanie could see that now. Too bad she couldn't see it then.

"Yup that was one more abusive, jerk of a boyfriend I managed to get involved with," Jeanie said disdainfully to herself.

"Why is it I get involved with so many assholes?" It was clear, even to Jeanie who had become a master at hiding things from herself. "Oh yes, Slugger."

# CHAPTER 2

# The Hills Had Eyes

Jeanie met Slugger when she was sweet sixteen. She went walking downtown one early fall evening with no destination in mind but with one objective…to score a bottle of booze. The pretty, long haired youth saw a group of guys hanging along the street corner while on her walk. Being an attractive, sexy young lady, the whimsical lass decided if she took the time to flirt with the guys, maybe she could con one of them into getting her a bottle of wine.

Wine was the girl's liquor of choice. Daddy used to give her and her sister a shot of it on Christmas eve. Jeanie used to think that her parent gave her that sweet spirit so she wouldn't stay awake all night and go into a hyperactive frenzy when Santa and his reindeer magically appeared in their living room. Of course now she knew that it was given to her and her sister Deana for an entirely different reason. That small amount of cordial given them was to keep them asleep. Mom and Dad didn't want their two girls waking up in the middle of the night to view the chaotic scene of them assembling the boxed bikes and laying out the array of presents that Santa was supposed to have left.

Yes, just thinking about those magical, mystical nights made Jeanie long for the comforting memories of those yesteryears. In those days Jeanie head was filled with enchantment and dreams. Life was magical and mysterious. Life was carefree and calm. There was safety felt in predictability and in the open fields which she roamed. There was no way to bring back any of those positive feelings of yesterday after all the garbage she's gone through. She would just have to comfort her raw emotions in another bottle of wine.

Bingo! With a little eye batting and smiling a pretty girl could get herself almost anything Jeanie thought to herself. Yes, the brown haired girl had really turned into quite a knock out since she lost those twenty five pounds. Sometimes, being pretty could be a disadvantage also.

Yes, sometimes being attractive could be outright dangerous. At times through no fault of your own, you get the wrong kind of attention. You just happen to be at the wrong place, at the wrong time. That's exactly what happened one afternoon two years ago on Hickory Hill.

For the past year the slightly overweight teen would walk an hour every day to help her lose weight. She was tired of feeling ugly and awkward. The shy, sensitive girl longed to become someone different. Someone better. Someone much prettier.

It was bad enough being the child of a poor, single mother but to have a body like this was totally unacceptable. Jeanie felt such hatred for herself and the circumstances of her existence. The gal wanted to be accepted and loved so badly, she felt like crying. Often times while alone in her room she did.

Jeanie was trying hard to change her image. She had lost a good portion of the weight she wanted to lose. That made her feel good. Maybe she could also find a part time baby sitting job and earn a little money. Then she could buy some pretty clothes. Her mom was living on government assistance and barely had enough money to cover the necessities like rent, utilities and food. Things like pretty clothes for her young teen daughter was on the bottom of her list of priorities. Jeanie knew that and accepted that fact.

Jeanie thought it would be easier to be loved and accepted if she was pretty. Since the girl learned about nutrition in home economics, she knew how to lose the extra pounds she harbored for years. In order to change something she didn't like, she had to have some idea of how to make those changes. Well, she found out how and she was doing it. Jeanie didn't shed those pounds through crazy diets and pills. No, she did it all on her own by cutting out all junk food (in other words everything that tastes good) and increasing her exercise. At last, she found the key to shedding that ugly fat. Maybe if she was no longer chubby, she wouldn't feel so ugly inside.

Jeanie started liking the way she was beginning to look. It was getting people's attention. Jeanie finally got her first boyfriend this past week. She was thirteen years old. Although this age seemed young for her mother, it seemed very old for this shy gal. All the popular girls her age had boyfriends. Ever since those girls could walk practically, they had a significant other doting over their every whim. Of course Jeanie was not one of those lucky girls. She wasn't one of the pretty ponies because until recently, she was saddled with too much weight. Well that extra weight was nearly all off now. Things were going to be different in her future. She just knew it. Yes, things were definitely going to be much different.

All the dreams of having a beautiful life crumbled that fateful day she met Mr. Martin on the hill. Jeanie remembered seeing him walk by her secluded house in the country on several occasions. Although they never talked, he seemed nice enough. The naïve girl wasn't the least bit afraid of him when he approached her on the hill that afternoon.

Jeanie regularly walked up and down that long hill as part of her exercise regimen. It was a nice peaceful walk. There she gazed in wonderment at all the pretty wild flowers and enjoyed the shade provided by the canopy of trees around her. While she strolled along that route, she often saw pink Ladies Slippers and Lilies of the Valley. Her own family's back yard didn't grow such beautiful specimens. Jeanie also enjoyed stopping at that large piece of petrified wood that was nearly at the top of the hill. There she routinely rested against the moss covered, rocky tree and watched the energetic little squirrels play their racing games. Once the fastest squirrel climbed all the way up that big pine tree, he would look down at the others still on the ground. Jeanie couldn't decipher squirrel language but she's pretty sure the fast, fur ball was taunting the others. Sorta like saying "Na Na Nana Na."

Mr. Martin walked towards Jeanie in a friendly, easy way. He was soft spoken and very polite. He wanted to tell her something he said. The man went on to tell her how he had been watching her lately and how pretty he thought she was. Jeanie was flattered. She was not used to anyone telling her how pretty she was except her Dad. She had no idea what all the sugar coated conversation was leading up to. She was after all very naïve and had led a very sheltered secluded existence thus far.

Mom didn't teach her anything about life. She had to learn about the birds and the bees out of a medical encyclopedia. Back in the late 60s or early 70s people in general didn't teach children about the dangers of strangers. They weren't warned about the unpredictable, terrible things that sometimes happen to people... especially little girls. Since the gal was so naïve she didn't think anything of it when Mr. Martin approached her. Up until that day she only saw Mr. Martin as a lonely, harmless old man.

It was at that point when Jeanie realized how very alone she was out there, where she was standing. There wasn't a house for at least half a mile in either direction. The road she was on was very rural with minimal traffic. The chance of a vehicle coming down that road at that particular time was minuscule. Of course cell phones back then were nearly nonexistent if they existed at all.

Mr. Martin was also aware how isolated they were for he started to become bolder in his approach to Jeanie.

It was near Jeanie's favorite resting place, that large piece of petrified wood, that the friendly neighborhood drunk took advantage of the shy quivering girl. As he kissed her, she could taste the sour brew that had recently passed his lips. She could feel his strong hands around her waist as they slowly reached up to cup her breast.

At first the frightened girl couldn't move. She was paralyzed with fear. She just stood there while the snake's clammy hands touched parts of Jeanie's body that were innocent and pure. Rather than race the squirrels down the road, she stood frozen like a statue, unable to get her legs to move.

After a couple of minutes, Mr. Martin loosened the grip he had around Jeanie's waist. It was then that she found the courage and stamina to flee from the ugly scene. She ran down that long steep hill like the devil himself was after her soul. No, that devil was after her body and she would be damned if he was going to do anything else to it.

Only after Jeanie was safely home did she take a moment to catch her breath. She tried to tell herself that what Mr. Martin did wasn't that bad. He didn't rape her. He didn't touch her down there. He might have if she didn't run. Thank God she was finally able to run. Still she felt very upset over what had happened. She felt dirty. Very dirty.

If only Daddy was there to help her. He's so far away now that him and mom had gotten divorced. Still, she thought, how could he have helped her? Even if he was home with Mom, he wouldn't have known she was in trouble. She could've screamed bloody murder and nobody would have heard her. Not where she was. She was all alone out there. All by herself with no one there to help her. As it turned out, she wasn't alone after all.

Jeanie didn't know that her newly acquired boyfriend was en route to see her that afternoon. As her body was being succumbed by Mr. Martin's powerful hands, her friend hid in the woods and watched. Since Carl didn't see Jeanie resist the tall, shadowy man before her, he just assumed that the scared and now scarred Jeanie wanted what Mr. Martin had done to her. Nothing could be further from the truth. Jeanie had never been so frightened by anything in her young life. The catatonic child was aware of what was happening to her body but she did not have the power at first to resist the predator's advances.

That painful day still burned like a fire inside Jeanie's fragmented heart. Of course she couldn't tell her mother or sister what happened.

"What happened is my fault," the frightened girl cried. "I let Mr. Martin touch me. I'm a filthy, bad little beast."

All the soap in the world couldn't wash Jeanie's body clean that night. The imprint of Mr. Martin's hands appeared on the tearful girls body in ghostlike outlines. Jeanie could no longer look at herself in the mirror without feeling disgust over what happened. The scarred child just wanted to forget what occurred on the hill. However, she had difficulty getting her mind to focus on anything other than the horrible experience. Jeanie thought that perhaps the activities at school would at least be a gentle distraction for awhile. Perhaps within the steel walls of the junior high classrooms, Jeanie could lose herself.

"Perhaps if I really get into my books and study hard I'll gradually forget what happened," Jeanie said to herself. Unfortunately, she was not allowed to forget and heal.

The following day the classmates who usually looked beyond the invisibly shy girl started tormenting her with derogatory names. At first the innocent miss didn't know why. However after much thought, she came to the conclusion that it must be because of Carl. He must have been on the way to see her that day. He was out there on the hill the afternoon Mr. Martin accosted her. All she knew was the following day after the attack, the rumors and the subsequent bullying started. There was nothing she was able to do that would make things better. If only she knew she wasn't alone and helpless, she would have screamed and mustered the courage to run before anything happened.

In Carl's eyes Jeanie wasn't screaming or running so she must've wanted what Mr. Martin did to her. It was bad enough realizing that Carl saw the whole ugly scene but it hurt Jeanie even more to find out that he was the one telling everyone what he supposedly saw. Jeanie never thought that Carl could be so cruel. He was as much a monster as the drunken scoundrel that violated Jeanie's innocent body that day.

"Sex Pot! Sex Pot!" Jeanie's tormenters would callously scream at her. Besides the name calling, many of the teen boys would poke at her and pinch her on or near her private areas behind the teacher's backs. Although Jeanie was still a virgin, she felt like a little slut.

"Hey Carmalita want to eat a banana?" Jeanie knew what kind of banana they were referring to. She wasn't that naïve. If she was, then she might not have been so offended. Yes, if she was more naïve or even perhaps a little slow, she could believe they were merely offering her a piece of fruit for dessert. Sometimes she wished she was too stupid to realize what filthy, derogatory words were being directed at her.

Everyday for nearly three years, Jeanie's school days were pure torture. All through the day she heard Sex Pot! Sex Pot! Those torturous words weren't just coming from the hormone driven boys either. Jeanie was well aware the other girls were talking about her behind her back. They would look her way, point and giggle. A few would even call out some snide little comment about her being a little whore. Their hurtful comments bore an even bigger hole in Carmalita Jean's heart.

The boys were more physical and aggressive in their tormenting. Their sexually explicit poems, prodding, body language and the cruel sexual pictures that were passed to her made Jeanie sick.

Jeanie only told one person, her best friend what had really happened that day. The only thing that Annie would say was

"Don't tell anyone." Is it any wonder why Jeanie thought the truth about what happened that day was worst then her classmates assumptions

The distraught girl believed that everything that happened on the hill was her fault. "It's all my fault. I'm a no good little whore!" Jeanie cried. She wanted to die. Inside it felt like she already had.

Jeanie couldn't escape the overpowering emotions created by her calloused classmates emotional taunting. She didn't know how to deal with the incredible amount of anxiety that threatened to short circuit her sensitive spirit. She felt like she would lose her mind if she didn't do something to defuse her life's trauma.

Jeanie quietly observed how her mother handled her frustrations and anxiety. Soon, the girl started following her guardians' example. Yes, Mother taught her well. When things got tough and the whole world seems rough…eat.

So despite how she struggled in the past to lose weight, Jeanie started once again turning to food as a means of coping with all the verbal garbage that was being thrown at her. Crunch. Crunch. Munch. Munch. Chew away the anxiety. Swallow away the pain. Cradle that inner baby with all the love she could give her. No one knew how much inner turmoil the young lass suffered. After the eating sessions Jeanie felt incredibly guilty. Now, she had even stronger negative feelings to combat. She started gaining weight again too. Now she was going to be a fat ugly Sex Pot. Jeanie buried her face in even more ice cream and chips.

In one of her eating marathons Jeanie's gut was so extended that she involuntarily threw up. She discovered she felt better after she threw up. Her stomach was nearly flat after getting sick too. The various name calling antics still made her emotionally sick, but at that moment she did not feel physically sick like she did.

The overwhelmed girl thought about what just happened. Her anxious mood began to relax a bit as she pondered over what she just realized. For the first time in ages, she smiled. She may not have learned how to cope affectively with all the name calling and poking she endured during the day but at least now she had a way to prevent herself from getting fat again.

Jeanie had become very adept at hiding her inner pain. She had to hide the pain her peers inflicted on her daily or the piranha would have devoured her entire soul. The gal had to hide those extreme feelings from herself as well, if not her mind would've retreated within a big black hole never to be found again.

"That's it. That's what I'm going to do," Jeanie said to herself. "When I eat too much and begin to feel guilty about my overeating I'll just make myself throw up. At least I won't grow into a giant hog!" Well that was one problem solved. Just one of many. But was it really a way of handling all the inner turmoil Jeanie endured everyday?

There were times when the gal would feel guilty about her puking sessions. Jeanie knew making herself sick the way she did was just plain sick. It wasn't an activity she did a lot. She didn't mostly because it was a secret activity. Her bulimia, like her molestation was something to hide…something to be ashamed of.

When Jeanie was home she spent a large portion of time hid in her room muffling her sobs within her bed pillow. Sometimes she wrote down her feelings in her journal. It felt good to verbally express the deep seated pain she suffered through. However, it did nothing to change what was going on in her life. It did nothing to stop the relentless teasing of her cruel classmates. Her writings did ease the discomfort of her nearly destroyed psyche somewhat. At least temporarily.

If only Jeanie could get a respite from the bullying at school even for a little while, she would be grateful. Carmalita Jean would be happy if for just one day she didn't hear someone calling her Sex Pot or pinching her arm, waist or leg. She wasn't some over ripe fruit there for the plucking. Like their verbal assaults weren't causing her enough pain. Those prodding boys just kept poking her like a Thanksgiving turkey. She felt like a holiday turkey the day after the feast. All the goodness within her was gnawed away and all that was left of her now was a hollow shell.

Jeanie kept the secret of her bulimia from her family as well. Her mother rarely left her alone and her sister didn't venture far from the house either. Jeanie had to plan her throw up party. There were times though when she couldn't control her anxiety. There were times where she couldn't quiet her mind by thinking of something else or escaping in the wondrous world of one of her fiction books. There were times when she wrote in her secret journal and felt worst afterwards instead of better. During those times her anxiety was so elevated that she became completely out of control. She was like a big brown dog that hadn't had a meal in a week. That poor starved animal would eat anything in sight. She would eat everything in sight. Jeanie's gorging and subsequent purging went rampant at times.

There were some days when Jeanie thought she could cope in her hell away from home. Some days were better than others. She remembered one day in particular which she thought would be better than most. The bright girl had gotten positive recognition from her English teacher and she readily absorbed his soul feeding comments. He commented how wonderfully insightful her book report was. Jeanie beamed from her head to her toes. The lowly girl's spirits picked up tremendously for just a minute…before someone in the back row snidely shouted out "Sex Pot" Of course everyone laughed. After that, the only thing Jeanie could hear the rest of the day was the cackling and giggling from the girls in class. Once again Jeanie had to hide her feelings. She plastered on a stone face and pretended that their dirty little name calling didn't hurt her. Oh but it did hurt her. Her inner pain was indescribable. But she knew she had to hide it. She had to pretend that their cruel words didn't matter. She couldn't let those around her see just how much they had hurt her. Her classmates seemed to get so much pleasure in inflicting the pain. She couldn't let them know that every time they poked fun at her, they chewed off another piece of her heart.

During the day the distressed girl became a walking zombie, totally void of emotions. That was the only way for her to handle things. If she couldn't physically climb under a rock and hide, she had to find the next best thing. She had to find a place to hide within her mind.

During those extreme days of torment Jeanie had absolutely no control over any of the food she consumed. In the past her purging was limited because of the immediate presence of her family. Since she could no longer plan her gorging sessions, she had to think of a way to get rid of the excess calories before they became permanently glued to her butt. She had to use her ingenuity to find a way to cover up that sick behavior. One day she discovered how. If she went into the bathroom and opened up the bathtub faucet full force, it would muffle most of her toilet bowl singing. She thought she hid her special way of keeping thin from her mother, for her parent didn't say anything when she exited the bathroom. She was wrong.

Her mother thought at first that her pre-teen daughter had just gotten the flu or worst yet, was pregnant. However, after hearing her girl wrenching her gut in the bathroom sporadically for several months, her stomach remained flat. Since her daughter probably wasn't pregnant, something else must be wrong. Jeanie's mom decided that she needed to see a doctor for her affliction. Jeanie needed a doctor all right…just not that type of doctor.

After a series of tests, her family physician decided that the out of control girl merely had a nervous stomach. Actually Jeanie's entire nervous system was breaking down due to all those days of verbal and emotional abuse. Jeanie couldn't tell the doctor what was really wrong. Once again she felt like a dirty, stupid girl. Jeanie helped herself to a bowl of ice cream when she got home. She stopped at one bowl though. She had to learn how to minimize her overeating. She had to minimize her throwing up sessions. She didn't know what kind of tests the doctor might order next.

Jeanie assumed most of her school teachers heard and saw what was going on in the unruly classroom. Still, no one said anything to the children who shouted those heart murdering words at her day in and day out. No one did anything on her behalf. They seemed to care more about teaching their lessons than preserving the soul of a wounded child.

After months of the taunting, Jeanie plotted how she would end her life. She just couldn't live like that anymore. She used to like school a long time ago. Her mind was a blank slate when she started school seven years earlier. After the shy girl felt safe without her mother at her side, she opened up her heart and mind and thoroughly got into whatever lesson was being taught at the time. She enjoyed learning about the many different things her teachers taught. Her professors opened up new worlds to Jeanie. Through them Jeanie learned the power of words from the great literary masters. She looked up to her knowledgeable elders with awe and wonder. Although the girl still enjoyed learning new things, she couldn't stand to be in school. Just the thought of going to school and facing the mean mouthed kids made her sick. Just the thought of facing another day in that torture chamber made Jeanie nauseas.

Jeanie feigned sickness at least once a week to escape the impending emotional torture. Her mother though, became wise to her daughter's feigned sicknesses. There were several days when the girl made up her mind that she wouldn't go to school that day no matter what. Since she couldn't hang around the house while her mom was there, she would just outright skip that day. It was on those days she disappeared in the woodsy trail that meandered behind her former home. Often, she hid out in the old shed that still sat on top of the upper fields of her former residence. There she spent the day writing in her journal or reading. Even though the shed was dirty and weathered with age, Jeanie felt at home in it. Her father built it years ago when they lived there as a family. Even though her father was nowhere near, she felt his presence in the planks of the walls. After the day warmed and she no longer wanted to physically stay in her wooden cocoon, she would lay under that beautiful oak tree that grew near the shed. She'd lay on top of the soft green moss hid under the magnificent tree's shade and tried to clear her mind of all the confusion and pain that cluttered it. Obviously Jeanie skipped school as often as she could to avoid the daily humiliation and to retreat to her safe house.

Before Mr. Martin's approach on the hill and the ugly rumors with the subsequent name calling, Jeanie was a good student. She diligently studied her lessons every day. She thought about finding a way to pay for her college education because it was obvious she couldn't get any help from her financially strapped mother. She loved the little animals and it was her plan to become a veterinarian one day. My how things had changed.

Now Jeanie spent every hour she could away from the school she used to love. She wrote in her journal often but kept it's written pages unread by anyone but herself. In between expressed outpourings of her heart, she silently plotted her suicide.

It was a good thing that Jeanie didn't have access to any sleeping pills or the money to buy any or her life may have ended on any number of those torturous days. Eventually it would come to a point where her shredded heart could bear no more and she would seek out the means to destroy herself. That day wouldn't come until much further down the road.

How Jeanie hated it when the cruel classmates called her Sex Pot. She hated it even worst when they made those sick rhymes from her name. Oh how she hated her first name. Carmalita. Why did her mother ever name her that? They didn't live in Mexico or someplace even remotely close to Mexico. She used to have kids make fun of her name before that horrible incident on the hill just because it was different. Her name wasn't the only thing different though. She was different. What she didn't know at the time was that those differences were the things that made her most beautiful.

Still during the years of thirteen and fifteen and a half, Jeanie's life was pure hell. She used to be teased because her name was weird. Then after her parents broke up, she expressed the tensions she felt by eating. That act of course didn't make things in her life better. All that eating made her twenty pounds heavier than she needed to be. Besides having a strange name, and being a lard butt, Dad left Mom dirt poor. Carmalita Jean didn't wear rags, but the clothes she did wear either did not fit her right or they were stained or just plain ugly. Jeanie was picked on way too much before that sickening scene with Mr. Martin and the awful rumors and name calling that followed.

Jeanie's grades were naturally falling along with her attitude and attendance. There were many times when she was sent to the office for acting out some of the anger she harbored. It was actually a blessing when she was sent to the guidance counselor. At least there, she didn't have to listen to those mean names tossed at her. No, for awhile the girl felt emotionally safe from all the bullying that tortured her throughout the day. For awhile, she felt safe. For awhile, she felt someone cared.

The emotionally troubled girl started seeing Mr. Raleigh on a regular basis. She talked to him about how she felt all alone in the world. She would tell him how much she wanted to be loved and accepted. She even told him about her parents recent divorce and the effect it had on her. It made her cry when she told him about that last argument her parents had. How she saw her father pack up his bags and leave. Jeanie thought her love for her Dad and his love for her would keep him there in the household. Obviously it didn't. He looked right past his eleven year old girl like he didn't see her. Her dad picked up his bags and opened the door, never to return home.

All the things Jeanie told her counselor were tough to say, tough to acknowledge. Still, she never told him about what happened on the hill. She never told him about how her classmates bullied her and what they said, or how they poked her. One guy even poked her in the knee with a lead pencil. It took a long time for that mark to heal in Jeanie's skin. It took even longer to heal the pain inflicted in her heart created by all those years of being bullied.

Jeanie told Mr. Raleigh about many of her problems and concerns but she didn't want to tell him about the teasing regarding her name or her peers favorite name for her "Sex Pot". She was afraid if she did, he would ask her why he thought they called her that and she surely didn't want to tell him. Carmalita Jean didn't want Mr. Raleigh to think she was a whore too.

On one particular bad day at school with more tormenting and teasing than normal, Jeanie walked a mile or so home with the intention of putting a stop to her miserable life. Along the walk home she stopped at the local pharmacy. She had recently gotten some gift money so she thought that she would use it that day to put her suicide plan into action.

While laying on the flowered cover of her twin bed Jeanie dreamed of what it would be like to be someone else. Just for a few minutes she thought about how different her life would've been if she were born to different parents. Yes, it would've been nice to have been born to rich parents. Then she would be wearing real nice, well fitted clothes. She would probably be in a different school as well where all the rich snooty kids hung out together. If she didn't like the school or someone picked on her, all Jeanie would have to do was whimper a little. Since she would be a privileged, loved child, Mother or somebody would beat the crap out of whoever bothered her. Yes, Jeanie thought her life would've been so different, so much better if only. Jeanie shook off her fanciful dream and dried her eyes.

"But my life is not like that. It'll never be like that. Before Mr. Martin touched me on the hill I was invisible most of the time. No one hardly talked to me. I wish I could go back to being invisible. Being totally ignored by those around me. Anything would've been better than this. Anything!"

It was then that Jeanie took the sleeping pill bottle out of it's cardboard carton. She opened up the bottle and looked at the blue pills and started to cry. She wondered if the medicine in that small pill bottle would be enough to kill her. She didn't want to become merely sick. She emptied the entire contents in her hand and stared at them. As she held the two dozen pills in her hand, she uncontrollably cried hot tears of hopelessness. Then the girl looked at the destiny in her hand and thought about something. All those pills barely filled her hand. Those few pills probably weren't enough to end her miserable life. Knowing her luck, they would probably just destroy her brain cells. She cussed at herself for being so stupid, then she cried some more.

After much thought, Jeanie slowly put those intended death drugs back into their container and threw them in the trash. To keep her mother from finding them, she hid the opened carton between a used sanitary pad wrapped in newspaper. Then, for a moment Jeanie thought about the big butcher's knife on the kitchen counter. She wondered how she could bludgeon herself enough with one big jab to thoroughly accomplish the job of ending her miserable life. The distressed girl erased that thought from her head almost the instant it popped in. She decided cutting herself would hurt too much if she didn't die right away. Besides that would make an awful mess for her mom to pick up. That wouldn't be right. Instead of reaching for the knife, Carmalita Jean reached for a pen instead and wrote this poem

Wheels of Life

Engulfed in sadness
and I know why.
All there is for me
to do is cry.

The music playing
turns my heart.
The sadness fading slowly
as I think of a new start.
Hang my head lowly.
Listen to the music
claiming my heart.

Think of life
as a rotating cycle
spinning like the spokes
of a moving bicycle,
until it comes to a sudden stop.

Then the day is gone
with night ending with it.
I see the light of dawn.
Dusk has faded.
Is my eternity gone?

The wheels haven't stopped turning.
Life has to go on.

In Jeanie's next counseling session she told Mr. Raleigh about her thoughts of suicide and what she had done. Maybe she wanted affirmation that her life was worth living and that she had a lot going for her. She couldn't remember the reason why she told her counselor and friend. She just remembered that she did. Jeanie however didn't see him as a friend at all when he informed her that it was his duty to tell her mother about her troubles including the suicide attempt.

When Jeanie went to see Mr. Raleigh in his office the next day the receptionist told her that he was in there with someone's mother. Jeanie held her breath and quietly listened to the voices in the next room. She hoped the person in there with Mr. Raleigh wasn't her mother, but it was. It broke her heart to hear her mom crying like that. Those tears were for her, the girl thought. Her mom hadn't shown much emotions since her dad moved out. Still, there she was, crying over her. Jeanie was happy when she realized that her mother did indeed love her. She was really sorry that she hurt her though. Real sorry. After Mr. Raleigh's breech of trust (to her) the emotional, shell of a girl limited her conversations she had with him. He was just looking out for her, but Jeanie didn't see it like that. She just saw him as one more person who had let her down.

Eventually after 2 ½ years the derogatory comments and the hurtful name calling ended. Jeanie had lost an additionally ten pounds and let her dark lustrous hair grow down to her waist. She had grown to be quite pretty and started to get some positive attention from some of the older boys in the high school.

One day when one overly annoying classmate tried to tease her with the name Sex Pot, Jeanie just smiled at him and said "Yes I am awfully sexy aren't I."

Even though she still didn't like that nick name, that little comment on her part helped end that particular nick name. It's ironic she thought "Now that I really am sexy as hell, that name doesn't bother me as much."

Now that Jeanie had stood up to the bully and let him know that the name calling didn't bother her anymore, the name calling stopped. Maybe she should have done that a long time ago, the girl thought. Unfortunately when a person is treated like they're just good for one thing, that's what they come to believe about themselves. What a person believed about themselves was what they often would become.

Although talented and smart Jeanie only saw herself good for one thing. After all, the guys Jeanie went out with all treated her like she was just as stupid bimbo. Good for nothing…except sex. She learned that lesson well with the guy she lost her virginity to nearly two years after that scene on the hill.

Jeanie met Golden Rod at the high school she attended. The exact way she met him she forgot. She wished she could forget him altogether. She was only going with the boy a month or so before their first and last sexual escapade. Since Jeanie was wearing his class ring and they had been together for what seemed a long time, she thought this guy really liked her. Maybe even loved her. The poor love starved girl gave her all to the young horn dog and what did she get…screwed! Physical and metaphorically. The painful night still lingered in her mind.

Unlike guys, the first time a women has sexual intercourse it's generally painful. Even in Jeanie's drunken state she cried. The physical pain that Jeanie felt that night could not be compared however with the emotional pain she felt afterwards.

The heartless creep who took Jeanie's virginity never even called her after their night of passion. He apparently got what he wanted from Jeanie, so why bother to continue on in the relationship. The chase was over. He won the gold cup. Game over!

"How could he do that to me?" the shaken girl yelped. Yes, how indeed. Unfortunately similar behavior continued to arise from other uncaring wolves. Just when the vulnerable naïve girl thought that one particular guy was different, she would once again be used and discarded. This uncaring behavior from her dates caused the sensitive girl to become even more distraught.

Jeanie felt like an old rag doll with all the stuffing coming out of it. Still, despite the two legged wolves she encountered, Jeanie continued to date. Repeatedly the under loved, misunderstood girl allowed the boys to use her body so that she could get what it was that she wanted…affection. Jeanie usually waited until she dated a fella two or three times before she opened up her heart and her legs to him.

Not every guy Jeanie went with wanted to wait until the second or third date before he got his sexual gratification fulfilled. There was an occasion when she went to the lake with a boy she liked instead of going to school for the day. Stupidly Jeanie figured that the two of them would do a little necking and maybe some petting and that was it. Wrong. The creep ended up forcing Jeanie, yes date raping her there in his relatives lake house.

The strong oversexed teen overpowered the shaken girl until he got what he wanted. Jeanie couldn't fight him off. Although she tried to kick the boy off her, she gave up after several futile minutes. She exhausted all her strength trying to fight him off. It was no use. He was bigger than her and so much stronger. It was early spring, still pretty cold, so there was no one around to help her. There was no one around to hear her screams.

After that day Jeanie's face would burn every time she saw the horny toad in the school halls. Jeanie held her breath when her period didn't come on time two weeks after the rape.

Jeanie didn't feel good about herself. She really believed that she deserved to be date raped.

"I lead him on. It was wrong of me to lead the guy on and not let him do anything," Jeanie would say convincingly to herself. Jeanie was just thankful that her period did finally arrive. The emotionally unbalanced girl had enough problems, she definitely didn't need to have a baby at her young age.

Despite how most of the guys treated Jeanie, the sensitive soul felt that in order to be somebody, a girl had to have a guy in her life. Jeanie remembered how it felt not to have a boyfriend. She felt like a nothing. She was nobody of value. Nobody worth talking to. No one worth loving. Is it any wonder the broken girl from a broken home fell for the guy she met on the street that night she was looking for booze. Is it no wonder she fell head over heels in love with Slugger.

# CHAPTER 3

# Slugger

Slugger viewed Jeanie's bronzed, angelic face and immediately took a liking to her. The girl was young and sweet, slim and beautiful. Jeanie wore a halter top on this warm fall day and flaunted her tiny, waistline.

Slugger was a good looking guy himself and could get just about any girl he wanted but at the time he wanted Jeanie. Still he tried to play it cool by combing his wavy brown hair with his hand. He planted on a coy devil may care smile and gazed her way. The tight pants he wore hung down low, well below his hips. His shirt draped across his muscled masculine chest. Usually all he had to do was peer his penetrating blue eyes in a girl's direction and they would melt. This fine filly may not be melting while she approached him however she certainly looked hot. Slugger's whole devil may care attitude shown through his impish eyes. His x ray vision worked overtime. The more he looked at the pretty young thing before him, the more he wanted her.

Jeanie provocatively wiggled her hips as she pranced towards the stud before her. Her well fitted blue jeans accentuated her curved young body, leaving little to the imagination. Carmalita involuntarily moistened her lips with her tongue anticipating the conversation she would strike up.

Jeanie's rosy cheeks blushed as Slugger cracked an off the wall comment about life in the "Big" city of Windsock. Yeah, out in the very rural town you either had to make your own excitement or let yourself die of boredom. At least the local pub offered live entertainment for those brave enough to enter the premises and didn't mind inhaling the screen of smoke.

The local recreation center was a good place to hang out if you were into sports. Jeanie was into jocks…not so much sports. She only attended the local games so she could see all the fine male specimens flaunt their flags in tight clothes while they ran for the touch down, or the bases or whatever.

Talk about unfrocking the jocks with her eyes, made Jeanie smile. She had already made a home run with Slugger, the soccer champ in her mind. Wouldn't it be nice to make that handsome hunk of man hers she thought. I wonder if he kisses as good as he looks?

Even if he isn't interested in going out with me seeing I'm only 16, I bet he'll at least buy a bottle of booze for me, Jeanie thought confidently to herself.

No doubt the hormones flied high between them. It didn't take much idle talk to convince Slugger to purchase some wine for Jeanie. After obtaining the fruity cordial the man gladly handed the bottle over to the beautiful brunette before him. Jeanie giggled at her new friend's off the wall observations. Both of them chuckled as one of pub's patrons staggered out of the bar and nearly fell on his face.

Jeanie cradled the glass burgundy bottle in her hand while laying out the hook. Slugger was quick to pick up on her hint and asked the pretty schoolgirl for a date. They continued their idle talk for a minute or two before Jeanie excused herself and briskly walked away. She gave Slugger her phone number. Whether or not he would call was out of Carmalita Jean's control. Still, she hoped he would.

It was definitely an ego booster for Slugger to capture the attention of a pretty young thing like Jeanie. The fact that she was but sixteen didn't phase him a bit. She acted much more mature he reasoned, plus the way she filled out those pants made him pant.

Jeanie did a little heart dance. She was totally thrilled that she could turn on such a sophisticated older man. "Imagine Slugger being interested in me!" smiled Jeanie.

A couple of days after the chance meeting with Slugger, he called to make arrangements for their first date. She would have gone with him the first night they met, but her and the bottle of booze already had other plans. Tonight though, all her plans were centered around Slugger.

Mr. All American was a few minutes late picking Jeanie up. She was beginning to wonder if the muscular man had changed his mind. Ten minutes after the hour she heard a robust knock at the door. No one was expecting company except her, so confidently the girl opened the door without looking in the security peep hole. Jeanie quickly introduced Slugger to her mother before she sprinted to the door. She didn't want her mother to give the sexy guy the third degree. No, if he had to stand there and be grilled by her parent, he may take off running. She didn't want her mom to ask such personal questions as…"where do you live, who are your parents, where do you work or worst yet…how old are you anyway?"

The couple's first date together was spent at a local pizza parlor. Between mouthfuls of oozing mozzarella cheese they made small talk. First dates can be so awkward Jeanie thought to herself. Despite a few tense moments between bites, she had a good time with the local soccer hero. Yes, both Jeanie and Slugger were equally charmed with one another.

After dinner the two of them went for a walk down the town's nearly deserted streets. It was a tad cool that time of night. Still, just being close to Slugger warmed the girl right up.

At 9:30 on a week night nearly everybody in the town had shut themselves up in their cocoon like houses. Except for a couple of bars, nearly everything was closed down for the night. Beneath the street lights the duo walked hand in hand down the isolated streets of Windsock. A few well thought out words were sputtered between them in an attempt to further charm their date mate. Although Jeanie was turned on by this older man, she was determined not to let things go too fast. Since Slugger hadn't been in school for several years, he probably didn't know about her bad reputation. So far he had treated her like a lady because he didn't know better, the unsure lass told herself.

"Maybe, just maybe I could get this man to be with me for more than a night or two. I need someone to be with me, to love me to hold me. If only I could get someone like Slugger to want me," Jeanie repeatedly told herself, "then my life would be so much better."

Jeanie's need for love and affection guided her actions through out her young life. Although she knew that her mother loved her, little attention or affection was exchanged between them. Carmalita had one slightly older sister but they were worlds apart. The only person she felt some type of bond with, was her dad.

Like Jeanie, her dad, Leif was artistic and sensitive. He could understand her since she was most like him. However, since her parents divorce five years ago, she hardly saw him at all anymore. Usually once every twelve months dad would make the long voyage north to see his two girls. Although her dad tried, he couldn't very well squeeze in a year's worth of time and attention in one weekly visit. Through out the remainder of the year the grieved girl would camouflage the hurt she felt inside. The sensitive poet felt like an orphan after the physical abandonment of her father. Her mother was so depressed about him leaving that she remained in a protective shell for years.

Jeanie felt the psychological abandonment from her mother. The young girl wanted to help her mother climb out of the depression which weighed her down. However Jeanie had all she could do to keep her own emotions in check. Besides she didn't know how to talk to her mother, so she didn't. Of course they made small talk, but they didn't really talk about anything of importance. Basically mother and daughter were strangers.

As if the divorce itself wasn't hard enough on Jeanie, that chance encounter with Mr. Martin tumbled her world. She no longer felt safe in it. The security she felt in her poor, detached family was taken away. Jeanie's mom and sister remained in their tacky little trailer, but that didn't feel like home. Worst of all, that wonderful hill she used to walk up was no longer a safe place (as if it ever truly was). Since she could no longer get her exercise going up and down that stretch of road, she resorted to dancing. The nervously, energetic gal would spend a hour or so every day disco dancing to The Beatles or The Rolling Stones.

Still Jeanie needed to refresh her soul in the great outdoors. Thank goodness they lived fairly close to a lovely, but small park. Jeanie always did feel more comfortable outside. She felt like part of the great universe when she was outside without any outer walls. When it wasn't raining or just outright cold, she loved sitting on one of the benches under the leafy oak tree. Most of the time Jeanie was able to enjoy her moments in the great outdoors alone. Only occasionally a child invaded her space. When that happened, Jeanie would pull herself away from her thoughts or her book and watched the youngster frolic in the sun without inhibitions…without fear. To think, she used to be like that once. She used to be full of joy and wonder. Those days ended long ago. Those days were gone forever.

The days of joy ended and the torturous days of her adolescence started. Jeanie happily escaped her taunting peers in the quiet beauty of the park. The nature lover smiled as she followed the little chipmunks that chattered among themselves climb down the tree besides her. They seemed to be playing peek a boo between the rocks in the stone wall fence. When she watched the birds soar in the sky, her heart became filled with peace. She felt at one in the world, like she truly belonged. That was a great feeling. Too often Jeanie felt like she didn't belonged anywhere.

Since those rumors started Jeanie's life became unbearable. The shy, awkward girl went from being invisible to being "Sex Pot". Rather than being shunned and ignored, she was ridiculed and verbally beaten everyday. What little self esteem she had disintegrated.

The only good thing that came out of all that torment, was that she lost a few pounds. Since she was poked fun of regularly, She couldn't eat in the cafeteria. That would give the tormenters another reason to make fun of her. Those calloused creeps didn't need another reason to pick on her. Jeanie became extremely hypersensitive to her peers laughing and ridiculing. She would think every time someone was laughing, they were laughing at her. Often times they were. The tell tale snickers and the looks they made told Jeanie that indeed they probably were.

"Slugger doesn't know anything about me. That's good!" Jeanie thought. "Maybe he'll take his time with me. Maybe he'll treat me like something other than a piece of meat." That optimistic attitude lasted only a short while unfortunately.

The first date ended with Slugger walking the brown haired beauty to the doorstep. There, the handsome athlete gave Jeanie one long, passionate kiss. How nice, she thought smiling. Before the blushing girl could open the door to her home, Slugger asked her for another date. She didn't have to think about the answer. "Why yes. Of course".

The second date with the soccer player started out about the same way. Another pizza date. "The man knows what he likes," the lass thought "and he likes me!"

After devouring their pepperoni pizza, Slugger escorted Jeanie out to the car. Tonight he thought the two of them would go to the local make out spot. Slugger parked his beat up Chevy under a tree overlooking the river. There were a few other vehicles parked in the vicinity but everybody kept a good distance from each other. After all people needed to have their privacy. Most of the lovers out there at Rolling River were high school students with no place of their own to go. Slugger unfortunately was still living with his family, so it would be awkward to go there and do their snuggling with his parents watching.

The make out spot was indeed a popular hang out. Many girls lost their virginity in the back seats of their boyfriend's car there. No doubt about that. Still, the schoolgirl thought that Slugger only brought her there to kiss and cuddle. She felt that he really liked her. Surely he wouldn't push her into anything that she didn't want to do even if they were at Rolling River.

The naïve gal spent most of the night pulling Slugger's hands off her breast while guarding her other private areas.

"Dam it! I thought you liked me. I thought you really cared!" cried a mystified Jeanie.

"Ah come on baby. You know you want it. I know you've done it before. Come on! Do it with me!"

The evening ended with Jeanie in tears but her integrity intact. Heated and annoyed, Slugger brought Jeanie home. Much to her surprise, Slugger called her the next night. He even apologized to her.

"Wow, I guess he really does like me after all," Jeanie sheepishly said to herself. Despite how things ended the night before, she agreed to see him the following night. In her eyes Slugger proved something to her…that he really did care about her and not just for what he could get off her. Since Jeanie was sure that she was not just another conquest to Slugger, she agreed to go to his friend's house to make out and whatever came up.

The night ended with the two in bed together. This time Carmalita Jean felt different after having sex because she felt genuinely cared for. Slugger continued to hold the love starved girl and kissed her even after the sexual act was over. He showed a gentler side, one she never expected to see from him since he portrayed himself as such a rough and tumble guy.

Within a month's time Jeanie and Slugger were going steady. She proudly displayed her boyfriend's class ring around her neck. It hung across her chest like a holy cross. It was given to Jeanie the same night Slugger declared his love to her. To Jeanie it was as much a symbol of love as a wedding band. The ring showed the world that she was somebody. She felt very special because she was loved by this popular, handsome man.

Since Slugger started going with Jeanie, he got himself a little apartment so that they could spend many hours, several times a week loving each other. Jeanie snuck off to a local clinic to be put on birth control pills. God knows she didn't want a baby at this young age. With Slugger, the girl had a pretty full social calendar. Just about every weekend they would go dancing in a night club. Whenever someone would try to check Carmalita's ID, Slugger would become irate. He'd make snide remarks to whoever tried to card her saying such things as "I'm twenty two years old. Do you really think I would go with some teeny bopper?" Back in those days, the drinking age in Massachusetts was eighteen. Jeanie definitely wasn't eighteen. She didn't even have a fake ID stating she was. Still the doormen would let her in the clubs. She drank a little, but didn't go over board, at least not usually. Slugger sometimes went a little over the top in his indulgence. However, it didn't bother Jeanie, at least not at first. As long as the party animal sobered up a bit when it was time to leave the club, she was alright.

No doubt, Slugger was good to the young lady. Of course they had their share of arguments but nothing major that couldn't be forgiven and forgotten the next day. Things went fairly well between them…at least for the most part. When Jeanie had a pregnancy scare, things definitely changed between them.

Since Jeanie couldn't see a doctor right away to be put on birth control pills, her and Slugger just tried being careful. Neither one of them wanted a child at that time. No kind of birth control was fool proof. The rhythm method definitely wasn't as reliable as birth control pills, so often couples would find themselves in an awful predicament. Unfortunately to the couple's dismay, the sixteen year old girl became pregnant.

Jeanie didn't want to have a baby that young. She was just a child herself. Despite her serious hatred of school, Jeanie wanted to at least complete high school. Slugger was young and wild himself and definitely didn't want to be encumbered with a child either, so they decided that Jeanie should get an abortion. Since the girl was still in the first trimester, she would get the simpler, less brutal one.

That day in the abortion clinic was awful. Just the waiting in the halls and the antiseptic smells were enough to make her nauseas. When the medical personnel wheeled her into the procedure room, Jeanie was shaking inside. The anesthesiologist just barely put the mask over her face when they inserted the suction tube inside her uterus and hooked up the noisy machine. Jeanie was fully awake and conscious of the extreme pressure and tugging. She felt like someone was ripping out her intestines with a vacuum! She cried, but she dared not wiggle afraid that it would cause her more pain.

After the procedure was over, Jeanie cried even more. The girl had never before endured such pain. The calloused nurse who tended to her looked down at the tearful young girl and merely said…"If you were having a baby, it would've hurt a lot more."

The young lady already hurt so much inside that no words could describe it. The physical pain was excruciating, but the inner pain she felt inside hurt even more. Even though the baby growing in her wasn't very big, it was still a developing human being. Still, she wasn't going to carry a baby all those months then give it away to someone like a stray animal. The girl knew if she had it, she would never want to give it up. However, she also didn't want to give up her unencumbered life with Slugger or the remainder of her youth. Some say Jeanie took the easy way out by having the abortion. However, what the girl went through that day was far from easy.

The weeks following the abortion were hard on Jeanie. It would take awhile for her body to heal and even longer for her mind to come to terms over what happened that day. For the month immediately following the procedure, Slugger was exceptionally kind and loving towards Jeanie. She definitely didn't let him touch her again until she knew for certain that her birth control pills were working. Once in awhile Jeanie would hear a rumor in school about her being pregnant, but she quickly told people that she merely had a kidney infection and that she definitely wasn't pregnant.

Although things weren't perfect with Jeanie and Slugger, their relationship together was better than anything the girl had been into previously. The two really seemed like a great match. Jeanie was a little shy and quite submissive. Slugger was outgoing and domineering. Their personalities seemed to complement each others.

Friction between the couple started to rise between them during Jeanie's junior year in high school. That was when the dynamics of their relationship radically began to change. Jeanie started to grow out of her shyness. Being with Slugger for the past year greatly improved Jeanie's self esteem. Since she started to feel better about herself, she became more verbal. Slugger didn't like the girl Jeanie started to become. He liked her better when she was a quiet, shy, play pretty. Slugger was used to having his way in their relationship. He determined where they would go, who they would visit and what movie to see, etc.

Situations dramatically changed when Jeanie started asking things of her man. When she voiced her preference as to where she wanted to go for dinner or how they should spend their Sunday, Slugger became angry. The girl had become a threat to Slugger's authority. He could no longer call all the shots. He didn't like that. He also couldn't dominate her behavior or her mind any longer. "He definitely didn't need some woman telling him what to do!"

At first just cruel words were exchanged between them. Then the shouting matches began "You're noting but a little whore!" Slugger would sling at Jeanie. "You're nothing but a loser. Miss Carmalita Jean. You're a miss in life. You missed the boat."

Jeanie once again began to feel badly about herself. She made a mistake of telling her boyfriend how other guys treated her in the past and how their actions made her feel. Little did she know that Slugger would use that painful knowledge to hurt her.

The sometimes charming guy would fling the soul tearing memories at her like a weapon. A stab in the heart with a butcher knife would have been less painful. Slugger knew just what to say to hurt Jeanie. He knew just how to keep Jeanie the whimpering, fragile schoolgirl he could dominate and control.

The verbal assaults took it's toll on the fragile heart of Jeanie. There were several times when she threatened to break up with the bully but he would beg her not to. The tough guy would even break down and cry thus melted the heart of the easily swayed gal. The handsome athlete would treat Jeanie better for a few days. However the guy would go back to his old abusive ways within a few weeks time.

Eventually Jeanie got sick of Slugger's lying words and fiery tongue. "That's it. No matter what you do or so say, I'm breaking up with you!" screamed Jeanie one night. "I don't need you and all the grief you give me. I don't need you at all."

Jeanie ran towards the pain chipped door of Slugger's apartment. She was almost there when Slugger body slammed her from the right side. Shocked and bruised, her limp body lay almost motionless beneath the weight of her larger boyfriend.

"I'm not going to let you go unless you say it's all right between us. I love you so much. I'm not going to let you go...not ever!" Slugger screamed at Jeanie. Then the man started to cry. It wasn't the false whimpers and tears that he had displayed earlier. Salty drops ran uncontrollably down his face. Slugger sincerely sputtered out "I'm sorry." He reached his hand down to the gray tiled floor where Jeanie sat and gently helped her to her feet. "I love you so much! Please don't leave me!" He held onto his girlfriend strongly yet passionately, kissing her forehead and her tear streaked face. "Oh baby. I've never loved anyone as much as you. I don't know what came over me. It'll never happen again. Please forgive me!"

Jeanie's heart melted to see her strong boyfriend in such a weakened vulnerable state. "Yes, I forgive you. I won't break up with you. I love you." Jeanie tenderly proclaimed to her boyfriend. The evening ended with an incredibly passionate night. The pretty brunette never had a guy care so much about her. "He lost control. He just lost control. It won't happen again!. He won't push me down and hurt me like that any more," Jeanie convinced herself.

Unfortunately, Slugger didn't keep his word. However it didn't occur until after several months since the first act of aggression. After that short reprise, the domineering, abrasive man once again got physically violent with his young girlfriend. By that time, Jeanie was practically living with Slugger since she didn't really have a home of her own anymore.

Jeanie's mother had recently gotten remarried and moved out of state. Although she was officially living with her older, domineering sister, she didn't like being there. Naturally, she spent most of her nights and days in Slugger's apartment. Slugger's not so bad Jeanie thought. He can be quite nice to her.

"Maybe Slugger will turn around," Jeanie told herself. She hoped her comforting words were true. He had to love her. Most of the time he treated her well. Yes, he had to love her!

Unfortunately, Slugger lost his temper with his girlfriend more times then she cared to remember. Each time he would strike her, the attacks got stronger and more violent. Many of the times he lost control over his temper he was drunk. Still, that's no excuse. There was no reason for him to hurt her like he did.

There were times when he would push the terrified girl on the floor and repeatedly slam her head against the hard tiles just because she said something he didn't like. Slugger had turned into such a woman hating brute. His sarcastic remarks degraded women in general. They made Jeanie snarl her lip in disgust. There were times when she wouldn't go to school for days because the black eye she got from her "lover" couldn't be covered up with makeup. No matter how much green eye shadow Jeanie put around her eye lid, the blackness and swelling showed through.

Even though Jeanie hated what Slugger did to her, she really believed she deserved the beatings. After the fights, the whipped girl would make excuses for his brutish behavior.

"He had a bad day at work," Jeanie would tell herself. "If only I was more understanding things would be better. If he didn't love me as much as he did, he wouldn't lose his temper with me. I should just be quiet and let him say what ever. After all words can't hurt that much." Even the gullible girl herself knew she was lying. She remembered only too well those two and a half years of name calling her peers at school subjected her to.

Jeanie looked down at the engagement ring Slugger gave to her several months earlier. All the girls in school were envious of her. She was engaged before any of them were, and to such a popular, handsome guy. They all thought she was so, so lucky. They even treated her differently.

Rarely were ugly rumors and derogatory names uttered toward Jeanie's direction anymore. All those past memories seemed like a nightmare now. It's hard to believe that fat, ugly kid in seventh grade was her. Carmalita had disassociated herself so much during those turbulent years that she could hardly associate herself with them. In a way, it seemed those mean spirited things happened to someone else. Those experiences seemed to belong to a different person, someone who lived in another lifetime.

There were times when Jeanie was quite content being with Slugger. Even though she didn't like soccer, the girl really liked soccer season. It was during that time of the year when Jeanie had Slugger's apartment all to herself several evenings a week.

Sometimes when Slugger would go out she would wait up for him. In the foul mood he'd been lately, she surely wouldn't that night. She silently rejoiced when he announced he would be going out. The times he was gone, the apartment was all hers. She could be free to be herself without panic or fear. Jeanie could put on the music she liked and dance to her heart's content without anyone telling her to change the song or to bring him a beer.

With the mood Slugger was in when he left that evening, Jeanie arranged to be in bed, hopefully asleep when he came home. She knew that if they lost the game, he'd be in an even worst mood and take it out on her. The girl didn't even want to be awake if they won. Either way, Slugger would undoubtedly come home plastered. She figured it would be in her best interest to feign sleep in order to avoid a confrontation with the man. Sometimes the little scheme worked. Most of the time however it did not.

Slugger would often go out with his buddies after the soccer games and get rip roaring drunk. After being out with the guys most of the night, he would go home totally inebriated. The guy's body would be sticky and stinky with sweat. His breath tasted like stale beer. His hair would have the lingering aroma of second hand smoke. Yuck! Better aromas come out of a dirty kitty box! Still the player would come home and expect sex while in his stinky, drunken state. Jeanie learned quickly enough to let the man she hated and loved have his way with her most of the time She would do practically anything Slugger wanted to do just to avoid a confrontation. However sometimes, no matter how softly

Jeanie walked around him, Slugger's explosive temper went off like a bomb.

Despite her shattered self esteem and domestic difficulties, Jeanie graduated from high school. For a while she didn't know whether she was going to graduate or not for she skipped more days then was allowed. However the smart girl always made up her work and did well in her lessons while she was in class. The principle ended up letting the bright girl graduate with her class despite his reservations.

Many years ago before the molestation by the petrified tree, Jeanie wanted to be a veterinarian. Now she only thought of getting married young and having children. Jeanie definitely didn't want to go to college...not anymore. She had enough school to last a lifetime.

At this point in her life Jeanie's main ambition was to change Slugger from the brute he'd become back into the nice guy she fell in love with years ago. She underestimated how big an undertaking she was making at the time.

Just a month after Jeanie graduated from high school Slugger once again became violently angry with her. The bruises she received from her aggressor hurt every time she attempted to breathe. That was it for the disheartened young lady. That night when Slugger was out getting drunk with his friends, Jeanie got someone to go to his home and gather her belongings. She was determined not to go back to that abusive creep. She had about all she could take! Now that she was out of high school, there really wasn't anything keeping her there.

Jeanie called her estranged father in Arkansas and talked to him for several minutes. She told him that she broke up with her boyfriend and that she wanted to go down south to live with him. Her dad was thrilled at the prospect of having his favorite daughter join him in the sunny south. Less than a week later, Jeanie's father came pulling up into her sister's driveway with a large blue van. Carmalita Jean hugged her father. It had been nearly a year since she had seen him. She missed him terribly. That day he was her savior. He was her way out of the life of abuse she so desperately wanted to escape from.

That day Jeanie and all her worldly possessions embarked on that long trip to Arkansas. Though she was a trifle scared, her heart was full of hope for a better tomorrow. She would be starting life over again in a new, unfamiliar place with a father she barely knew. Many adventures were sure to await her. Her move would undoubtedly bring about many changes and challenges.

# CHAPTER 4

# Oh Arkansas

With much patience Leif loaded all of Jeanie's things into his van. Yep, the excited girl and her dad along with all her worldly possessions were Arkansas bound. Jeanie had briefly visited the sunny state a year ago when her dad first moved to Arkansas. She remembered how nice it was to go canoeing in the middle of April. Up north, there was still snow on the ground until May. Jeanie hated the cold weather and cold people of her small Massachusetts town. She was certain that she made the right decision to move down south with the father she loved so much.

Leif was a dark, handsome man with a rugged build. He was also a very busy man. He owned and operated a ceramic mold business in an old restored building in the town of Seven Springs. His work took up a great deal of his time. The two of them shared a little time together but what time they had together was strained. Jeanie wasn't the little virgin Mary that her dad told everyone she was either. Disappointment showed in the man's brown eyes the first time a profanity slipped out of her mouth.

Jeanie's childhood vision of her dad was distorted as well. Leif was not the sensitive, strong man who could do anything. What ever happened to that all powerful man who could plow through any and all problems without flinching an eye? Jeanie still thought of her dad as some sort of superhero. Most dads were heroes to their daughters when they were young. However Jeanie never got a chance to let go of this image when she was younger since he was rarely seen. The man was seen even less after that chilling day in the fall eight years ago.

That was the day the 11 year old girl woke up early to hear her parents loudly arguing. Their curious daughter snuck out of her bed and peeked into the living room where she heard the commotion. She didn't remember exactly what was said to whom. However she remembered vividly the actions that followed that terrible argument.

The curious girl sat silently on the rug on that cool fall morning and silently eavesdropped. Her little face peered sheepishly around the corner to observe the scene from behind the wall. She just hoped she wouldn't get caught. Apparently, they were so enthralled in their conversation, they didn't see nor hear their daughter. Jeanie was glad of that. She didn't want them misdirecting their anger at her. It was then that the family she knew would be gone forever.

In great dismay little Jeanie watched her dad collect the dust covered, beat up suitcase from under the bed. He ransacked his drawers and shoved crumpled up garments into an open vinyl, coffin. Remnants of shirttails and fragments of socks hung over the sides of the over stuffed suitcase. With one quick motion, the clothes eating monster chewed up Jeanie's future memories of her dad in one quick snap.

Before that ultimate argument, Jeanie knew that her mom and dad were having marital problems. Not long before this terrible argument Jeanie thought her dad tried to tell of his impending departure from the family through a song on the radio. She had difficulty hearing the lyrics over the strong beat. Basically the song stated that Dad would continue loving his child even though he's not living at home anymore. Only then did she realize how important it was for her to listen to that song. Leif was indeed trying to tell her something.

Still, the beautiful dreamer never believed her dad would leave the family…Especially her. "If daddy loves me as much as he says then why would he leave me?" Jeanie cried silently to herself.

The girl watched in disbelief as her dad grabbed the keys to the family car. Without looking back, he walked out the door with his dusty, gray suitcase in hand. Jeanie watched through blurry eyes as her dad speeded out of the driveway and out of her life.

For awhile her dad came on a weekly basis to see Jeanie and her sister Deana, but that was short lived. Her dad had financial problems and thought the best solution for him was to move to a far-off state and start life anew. With over 1000 miles between them, Jeanie rarely saw her beloved father. That hurt Jeanie more than anything.

Despite her dad's temper and his quick hand, Jeanie dearly loved her father. She idolized him. Before the divorce, she would go to his ceramic studio on Saturday and make things while he taught his class. There she would sit for hours painting her figurines. Carefully she added that special detail and color to make her specific art pieces unique.

That weekly visit into her dad's world made the sensitive girl feel connected to him. That was important for Jeanie because she felt so disconnected from the rest of the world. That time together made Jeanie feel like she belonged somewhere, even though she was a chubby, socially awkward child. Yes, back when Jeanie was 11, her dad was her hero. She quickly blocked out all his shortcomings in her mind and almost made him into some kind of a God.

Now that Jeanie was 19, she quickly saw how things really were with her dad. He was human! Imagine that. The idealized life Jeanie had envisioned she would have with her father slowly faded away. She thought when she joined him in Arkansas, they would once again share many days doing the art work they both loved and engage in intimate conversations such as how she felt about this or that. Unfortunately she was wrong.

Jeanie was lonely. She knew that her dad couldn't take time out of his busy work schedule to continuously cater to her. No, it was up to Jeanie to make her own excitement.

Jeanie made the acquaintance of several young men in the area. Her dad had hired a local youth to work in his shop making ceramic molds. The bright eyed boy quickly spread the word to his friends that there was a pretty new girl in town. Within only a few days a half a dozen boys hung around the old school house all trying to win Jeanie's fancy. It didn't take her long to find a cute country boy among the crop of visiting guys to be her new boyfriend.

Jeanie smiled, and thought assuredly, "Now I have someone to do things with and show me around!" That was important to Jeanie for she did not have her driver's license, never mind a car.

Jeanie's idea of having fun at that tender age was getting drunk, dancing, and of course having sex. Just before the girl left new England, she bought a large quantity of liquor. She was of legal age to drink in Massachusetts but not in Arkansas. So before Jeanie left that state, she made a trip to the local liquor store. She bought enough booze to fill one of her large suitcases. The sophisticated teen selected a variety of liquors and wines that she liked with the hopes that she might find a sweet guy whom she could share her treasures with.

Prior to the trip south, Jeanie was excited about living with her dad, but she was also very nervous. She had always been a little hyper but her anxiety significantly increased due to the external forces she was unable to control in high school. She always tapped her foot when she sat at her desk or else wiggled her leg. Sometimes she would tap her pencil. Those behaviors obviously drove anyone near her crazy and of course didn't help with her popularity. Jeanie's nervous disorder never did go away.

There were times when she would get so anxious, she couldn't think straight.

Jeanie was naturally scared of her big move to the sunny south even though she knew that it was something she had to do. Still, an adjustment in her lifestyle would have to be made. She did not know what kind of privileges and privacy she'd have with her father. The girl was thrilled when she saw the little haven her dad prepared before her arrival.

It was obvious the teen's cool dad remembered what it was like to be young. Leif wanted his daughter to feel comfortable in her new surroundings. He also wanted her to have a little bit of privacy, after all Jeanie was now a young lady. So, he's securely stationed his travel trailer on the north side of the main building where he resided. That little trailer became Jeanie's place of refuge for almost a year. Inside that tiny, wheeled vehicle was a bed and a bathroom, as well as a dining table and chairs. It was like a mini apartment for Carmalita Jean.

Jeanie pretty much had her privacy when she wanted it. Still her father kept a watchful eye on his sexy, nearly grown daughter. Jeanie spent many a night with the first cowboy she dated. He would leave early in the evening, park his car down the street and walk back to Jeanie's trailer.

Jesse was cute and sweet. Jeanie was as turned on by his country accent as he with her northern dialect. She liked the way his black cowboy hat rested against his brow. He liked the way she filled out her short shorts. It wasn't long, before Jeanie fell madly in love (or lust) with the sandy haired fella.

Despite the attention she got from Jesse, Jeanie was quite lonely. She desperately needed to feel loved. The girl knew Jessie cared for her, but he wouldn't say those three magic words. She did feel wanted and desired however. She felt cared for and comforted when she was in Jesse's arms. So, the two of them became intimate after only a few weeks of going together. Leif probably surmised that something was going on sexually with the two, but didn't know how to approach that delicate subject. So, he chose not to say anything at all

Leif had other things on his mind besides his wild daughter. He had many financial problems. Although he was an intelligent man with a variety of artistic talents, he was not very good at handling his finances, He knew if his small business was to survive, he had to work long and hard. The many orders he needed to fill would bring the much needed money to pay the accumulating bills.

The first couple of months following his daughter's arrival, Leif worked many long, hard days. He had to work quickly and often to produce the large mass of ceramic molds needed for his accumulating orders. After Leif manufactured the molds that were necessary, he would fill up his van and deliver them. He repeated the cycle every six months or whenever he had enough ceramic molds to deliver. He had to make his trips as cost effective as possible.

The energetic artist planned to make a trip across country delivering his orders within the next few weeks. It was important for him to finish producing this last big order before he started his long trip to Washington state. With determination and stamina Leif barreled on towards accomplishing his mission.

Besides making the planned deliveries, Leif wanted to stop at several different places along the way. He wanted to show his travel deprived daughter some of the magnificent, natural creations that God created in this earth. Jeanie was anxious to see them too.

Although Jeanie didn't want to leave her newly acquired boyfriend, she was excited about seeing parts of the country she had only read about in books. Maybe, father and daughter could open up the lines of communication also. After so many years of being apart, Jeanie and Leif seemed like strangers. Neither one of them knew what to say to the other one. The awkward moments experienced during the long trip were relieved only by the occasional interruptions to take pictures, eat, and make deliveries.

Except for an occasional catnap in a rest area, the teen's dad never slept. Money was very scarce. Leif just couldn't afford the luxury of a hotel during their trip. Jeanie understood that and learned to sleep somewhat comfortably in the bucket seat of her dad's over packed van. After several days cooped up in the blue van, the last of the ceramic molds were delivered. The two of them ended their trip visiting one of her uncles in Washington state. Up until that day, she had only seen pictures of Uncle Rodney and his family.

While visiting her unknown family members, Jeanie felt she was part of one big family. After her parents divorced, there was a major split in the extended family. Mom didn't visit any of the relatives on dad's side of the family anymore. Jeanie guessed her mother wanted to forget she ever had a life with Leif. It wasn't enough for her mom to be divorced from her father. No, she had become divorced from his entire family as well.

"Even though the trip was long, it was rather nice, especially seeing Uncle Rodney and everybody!" Jeanie enthusiastically told her dad. Jeanie sure did miss Jessie though. She couldn't wait to get back to him in Arkansas.

Several unfortunate things happened the week following Jeanie's return to Arkansas. Jeanie surmised those two weeks away from her honey might throw a wedge between them. She was right. Their flaming desire for one another definitely cooled. Still they continued seeing each other for another month. Jessie even gave Jeanie driving lessons. He was certainly sorry he did that though.

Jeanie's inexperience driving didn't mesh well with the winding mountain road Jessie chose for her driving lesson on one particular night. They were involved in an automobile accident while Jeanie was driving. Except for a few bumps and bruises, no one got hurt. However the vehicle definitely got hurt. It turned out to be a costly driving lesson! Jeanie's massive mistake cost her honey much money. Jessie and Jeanie's relationship never fully recuperated from that error. Their rocky romance completely withered away after that night. The beautiful brunette and the country cowboy were no longer a kissing couple the week following the incident.

Jeanie drowned her sorrows in the last remaining bottles of booze she stowed away. Her drunken isolation caused even more distance between her and her dad. Leif knew Jeanie was hurting inside over the breakup of her boyfriend. They both hurt over the rumors that immature cow poke spread about his treasured daughter. There was nothing to do but ride out the waves Jeanie thought. However she didn't want to ride out the storm by herself.

Jeanie had been residing with her dad now for five months. Although she courted guys occasionally, she really didn't have any girlfriends. That wasn't such a great loss to her though for she could get along better with men anyway. There was something missing from the confused girl's life though. She didn't have someone whom she could talk to and chum around with. She didn't have someone that just wanted to be with her because he or she liked her. Jeanie's life changed dramatically when she met Gina.

Gina was a lot like Jeanie's in many ways. They were close in age. They were both bouncy brunettes with a zest for life. They had similar interests and similar personalities. They both had endured and learned hard lessons from the school of life as well. Gina was a sounding board for Jeanie. Jeanie was a sounding board for Gina. For the next several months you couldn't see one girl without seeing the other. Together, the two of them crashed parties and broke hearts. They learned a lot about life and they learned a lot about themselves.

Although the two of them had a blast talking, partying, and enjoying their young lives, the two of them lacked direction and motivation. Neither one of them would go anywhere in their low wage service industry jobs. Nor were they getting serious about any of the guys they dated. There was one fella Jeanie liked for more than a friend, but he already had a fiancé. He made it clear that she could never be more than a fun night away from his old lady. Jeanie wanted more than that!

"Forget him. Who needs him!" Jeanie sarcastically said.

"Yeah," Gina agreed. "Who needs any of them!"

Both girls tried to convince themselves they didn't need the love of a man, but they both knew they were lying to each other and to themselves.

Jeanie wanted desperately for some sweet guy to love her. She wanted to get married and have babies. Out of loneliness and depression, the dreamer once again initiated contact with Slugger in the form of letters.

At first the letters were casual, like two friends merely touching bases. Jeanie liked the idea that Slugger still cared about her. She needed a man to care about her in the worst way. It made the young girl feel good that she still could find a man who'll want her for more that a few hours or a couple of days. She did not know if she would ever go back with him. After the way he treated her in the past, what made her think that he had changed.

Communication between the two were friendly but light for a month or so. Jeanie continued flirting with her ex-boyfriend without ever getting real serious. She felt more comfortable at that moment keeping him at arms length. Only during the last month of living with her dad Leif, did Jeanie seriously consider returning to Slugger.

Something was creating an even bigger chasm between Jeanie and her father lately, but she didn't know what it was. She thought their lack of closeness was because she wasn't the pure virgin he wanted her to be. She was sorry she disappointed him, but she was tired of being what other people wanted her to be. After all. She was nearly a grown-up. Surely, she should be allowed some freedoms such as who she wanted to spend time with and how she chose to spend that time.

Leif along with his neighbors and friends found out early on that Jeanie was just like any other red blooded American girl with certain social needs. After several months together, she thought that her dad had started to accept who she was. After all, he didn't give her any flack about going out with the guys she liked anymore. At first Leif thought that no one was good enough for his daughter, but now he didn't flinch an eye when she brought a less than conventional man to their residence. No, something preoccupied her father's mind. The girl's curiosity would soon be satisfied much to her dismay.

Jeanie's handsome, artistic dad had been sidetracked from his work and everything else lately. He spent much of his time away from his home and his daughter. Leif was obviously distracted by something, but Jeanie had no idea what it could be. She was curious what her dad was up to but she never directly asked him for fear of being reprimanded. She felt that he would tell her, when he wanted her to know. Still, Jeanie wondered what was going on. He seemed so secretive about his life and his new love. She would soon know why.

One Saturday evening Leif put on his best pants, shirt and vest in preparation for a night out of town. While Leif was dressing, Jeanie answered a knock at the door. Much to her surprise, one of Jeanie's ex-boyfriends was at the door all snazzed up too. They left together without saying much to Jeanie before heading to Little Rock. The perplexed girl didn't think the day she bought Jerry home that he and her dad might like to go clubbing together. It seemed so unlikely. Jerry was a little older than Jeanie, but he certainly was nowhere near her dad's age. It kinda bugged the girl too. Why would Jerry want to spend so much time with her dad and not with her? She didn't find out the answer to that question until later that week.

Jeanie knew that Jerry held some feminine characteristic, but she didn't hold it against him. Actually, she liked the fact that he was gentle, soft spoken and not pushy in the least. Obviously, her dad did too. However, he saw something in Jerry that Jeanie was blind to. The girl's exboyfriend didn't want to continue dating her because he was confused about his sexuality. Jerry was either bi-sexual or gay. Still, the naïve girl would not have come to that conclusion on her own. She just thought that he was a gentle person.

The week after Jerry and Leif went clubbing, he pulled his daughter into his private quarters for a talk. Rather than being lectured for doing something she shouldn't have done, Leif disclosed something that totally blew her mind.

That was the day Jeanie's father openly admitted to her that he was gay. Obviously, this awkward conversation was very hard on both Leif and his daughter. Jeanie's dad couldn't even tell his little girl those hard facts without crying. He felt ashamed for the kind of things he hid from his daughter. However, he couldn't continue to be untrue to her. He couldn't continue to be untrue to himself. He hadn't realized he was gay until he had been married to his wife (Jeanie's mother) for several years. That was one of the reasons he left the household…that and for financial reasons. Despite the feelings Leif hid within himself, he hadn't actually come out of "the closet" until he had been divorced for several years.

Leif wanted Jeanie to know the truth about who and what he was. He needed approval and acceptance as much as his daughter did. He hadn't planned on telling his daughter at that time, but he just couldn't hide his inner turmoil any longer.

Leif was experiencing deep, overwhelming emotions that he could no longer hide. He had fallen so madly in love with Jerry that he could barely think of anything else but him. However, Jerry could not reciprocate his love and he was devastated. He was so emotionally distraught that he couldn't sleep, he couldn't eat, he couldn't think. As spiritually drained and physically exhausted as he was…he couldn't work. All he could do was cry.

Jeanie didn't know what to say or how to react. She was in shock. Jeanie regrets acting momentarily statuesque. The girl was so overwhelmed by what her father unveiled, that she just couldn't speak. She wanted to run and hide, but she didn't. She just stood there and listened to her strong, masculine father empty his heart to her while uncontrollably weeping. Jeanie could feel the intensity of his pain but she didn't know what to do or what to say to alleviate the painful emotions that crushed her father's susceptible heart.

That difficult disclosure was something Leif wanted to discus with his daughter for some time, but didn't know how. Their not so close relationship became even more strained after that day. She didn't know who her father was in the least anymore, as if she ever did. The sensitive, artistic man Jeanie knew as her father lived a double life. Jeanie couldn't help but feel betrayed. She also felt extremely hurt that her dad who she loved so much, would rather spend time with her ex-boyfriend than her.

Naturally, it didn't take the small minded town's people long to discover the truth about her father's sexual identity. Rumors started flying about shortly after Leif and Jerry broke up. She didn't know who or why the person started the vicious rumors. Whatever the reason, Carmalita Jean and her father openly suffered for their lack of sensitivity and discretion.

Everybody in that small southern town seemed to know her and her father's business. Soon, neither Jeanie nor her dad could walk anywhere without hearing loud voices brazenly criticize their way of life. Jeanie was the wild child where as her dad was just a plain old pervert! The towns folks ostracized the both of them. Soon neither one of them felt welcomed. They remained in that little town for barely a month following the rumors before Jeanie and her father both actively sought another place to live. In the final weeks prior to their departure they both felt the strain of being on a chopping block. Verbally, they were both eaten alive.

Both father and daughter handled their anxiety and depression in different ways. Leif openly mourned his lost love through endless crying. Jeanie sought nurturance and pseudo love through the many different guys she dated. She never took a shining to any of them like she did Jesse. Besides, she started having the same problem here as she did in her earlier life in Massachusetts. Jesse's waggling tongue made Jeanie into a whore which of course made him a Casanova. How cruel Jeanie thought. She couldn't believe that she once cared about him!

Gina though, continued to be a friend to Jeanie. She didn't care what the others around them talked about. She wasn't the least judgmental of Leif's sexual orientation. She and a few other open minded, young people couldn't care less about what the majority of the town's people waggled their tongues over. Jeanie was thankful that she was able to enjoy the company of a few friends that accepted her and her dad just as they were. As wonderful as her friends were, none had the financial means to take care of her basic needs, until she could take care of them herself. So, she couldn't stay with any of them when her dad moved onto another location elsewhere. Hell, they had all they could do to take care of themselves. All but one of her buddies lived with their parents. They were all young adults trying to find their way like she was.

Jeanie knew that soon she would have to worry about where she would be living. The girl could live with the ugly rumors circulating around town if she had to. However, her dad was being crushed with financial troubles too. His steamy affair with Jerry took too much time away from his work. It also took much of his money. Jeanie's sure that the two ended their relationship because of the combination of Leif's financial problems and the ugly rumors. Shortly after the two broke up, Jerry moved in with a distant relative in another part of the state. He couldn't take the emotional beatings any more than Jeanie could take them when she was thirteen. The distraught girl wished she had the option to move someplace when she was being eaten alive. She wanted to move in with her dad then, but her mom wouldn't let her. Of course her mom didn't know why her daughter had wanted to move away. Just like Slugger didn't know the real reason why she wanted to move back to Massachusetts to reawaken their romance.

Since his affair ended, Leif was devastated. He totally went to pieces. He couldn't work. He couldn't eat nor sleep. For a month following the break-up, the sensitive artist climbed further and further into an abyss...one that he could not climb out of. He was just an empty shell of a man. The emotional pain of an ended relationship was tough enough on a person, but it didn't help her dad emotionally to be carved up daily for dinner because he was gay.

Back in the mid 70s, people did more than frown at someone if they strayed from the norm. In the southern Baptist town, people were very religious. They didn't call it the Bible belt for nothing. However those religious fanatics were very hypocritical. They obviously didn't follow God's Golden Rule: Do unto other's as you would have others do unto you.

Before Jeanie left for Massachusetts, the towns people totally disemboweled her beloved father. Despite his different sexual preferences, Jeanie thought the world of him. No matter what he was or who he chose to love, nothing could take away her love for him. Nothing!

It was obvious father and daughter could no longer live comfortably in Seven Springs. Jeanie's father planned to move far away. He wanted to make a new start. Jeanie would have to also.

Now, the letters to Slugger became intense. She told her ex-boyfriend, the man she both loved and hated, that she wanted to give their relationship another try. He had told her several times how sorry he was about how he treated her in the past. He insisted that he would never, ever strike her again. Jeanie believed him. She had to. Her life was falling apart. She didn't know where to go and she didn't know who to turn to. She wanted to be loved and comforted. Despite Slugger's flaws, Jeanie knew that he loved her. So, it was decided, she would return to Slugger. Jeanie hated leaving Gina, but she knew that she had to go. The girl didn't feel she had a lot of options. Unless she moved quickly, her world around her would collapse.

Leif obviously was blessed with extremely strong emotionss just like his little girl was. Jeanie wished she could be strong for her dad, but she couldn't. The girl had a hurricane churning inside her as well. Rather than being there for each other during those turbulent times, Jeanie and Leif retreated to the solitude of their own bedrooms alone. They spent most of their waking days crying and reminiscing over past times when their lives were happy and their loves were new.

Jeanie felt helpless. She couldn't erase the image of seeing her distraught father in such emotional pain. Up until that point she believed that only young people such as herself could love so strongly. Leif's whole world had collapsed. He lost his love and soon he would lose his house in the bankruptcy proceedings. Within a short time Jeanie would have to return to Slugger. She just hoped that she was making the right decision.

Leif didn't know the circumstances involved in his daughters breakup with Slugger. If her dad did, he wouldn't have brought Jeanie back to Massachusetts. The two depressed souls rode 1800 miles back to the northern state with barely a word uttered between them. While Leif delivered Jeanie back to the arms of her previously abusive boyfriend, he prayed aloud to God. He openly cried during the entire journey. Leif mourned over his lost love. It saddened him that he could no longer be a good father to his wild child. He cried even louder over the fact that he was a gay man stuck in a harsh, judgmental, straight world. He wanted to die. His wish almost came true.

Jeanie's dad drove almost non stop for 30 hours before they arrived in Massachusetts. There, Leif delivered Jeanie to Slugger the savior. The two men worked quickly to unload Jeanie's possessions. Leif hated to see his daughter merely living with a man, but he knew that he could not take care of her. He couldn't even take care of himself at that time, not financially nor emotionally. He also knew Jeanie didn't have the education or skills to take care of herself at the present time either.

71

Leif wanted to say their good buys quickly. He didn't know when he would see his daughter again. That tore at his heart even more the further the two men got in their unpacking. Jeanie tried to talk her troubled father into staying for a while to rest, but he refused. She found out the next day that her dad had a terrible auto accident. It occurred only a couple of hundred miles south from where he dropped off Jeanie. Although the wreck totaled his leased van, he was all right. For that, she was thankful. God was indeed merciful! Still Jeanie felt terrible when she thought that her dad got involved in that accident bringing her back home to Slugger. If he would have been seriously hurt, she would never be able to forgive herself.

"What kind of daughter am I?" Jeanie said to herself. "I should've insisted he rest on the couch for awhile! I'm a selfish uncaring person...that's why"! Jeanie tucked her head into her shoulder in shame and cried.

# CHAPTER 5

# Lost Loves Lost Hopes

Jeanie was hoping the life she wanted with Slugger would be better the second time around. Unfortunately, it was not. At first they both walked on tip toes trying to rebuild their rocky relationship. The honeymoon period between Slugger and Jeanie didn't last long though. Within a few months time, Slugger was going out frequently with his friends and getting drunk. It was funny how some things never changed. Why did Jeanie ever think that a leopard could change it's spots. Still, even in his drunken state Slugger maintained control over his overwhelming desire to strike Jeanie…at least he did for while.

The imprint of their previous time together had left a scar on the both of them that was difficult to erase. Although Jeanie felt she loved Slugger, she could not put her trust in him. It was undoubtedly hard for her to forgive and forget the mistakes of the not so distant past. Slugger had hurt her so much, both physically and emotionally. No one could really blame the shaken girl for being cautious with her heart now.

Despite Jeanie's reservations about how life with Slugger would work out, she hastened to do what ever she could to make their house a home. The little upstairs apartment was decorated with all the personal touches that added flavor and individuality to the homestead. Even when she worked full time, she alone kept the house clean. The little homemaker did all the cooking as well. She didn't mind the household chores. They kept her busy while her fallen sport's hero chilled out in the other room.

After one particular day after Jeanie tidied up the house, she hit the streets in search of a job. Having nothing but her high school diploma the disheartened girl took whatever job she could get. She really didn't like to work in the hot factory doing the repetitive tasks given her, but she didn't feel she had a choice. She had to work someplace. Unfortunately, without additional education or skills, it was difficult obtaining a job. It was even more of a challenge finding employment in a small town.

"Oh well," Jeanie said to herself. "It's not as if I'm going to be doing this forever."

Jeanie truly believed since Slugger had done a good job at controlling his temper, it would only be a short while before they got married. After marriage of course came children. She hoped to have many beautiful dark-haired children. They'd all be little carbon copies of her and the man she loved. Through her children, the young lass thought that her life would finally have purpose. After all, isn't it every woman's desire to have children, to carry on the family's name and heritage. It was imprinted onto Jeanie's inner core that it was her duty to her man and her ancestors to bring forth new life into this world.

Jeanie's dream of having a happy home with Slugger was short-lived. So was her vision of becoming his wife and bearing his children. Halfway in their first summer together as a new couple, things started to go downhill. The shouting matches once more began. She was embarrassed to think that her downstairs neighbors undoubtedly heard the entire argument. So she avoided her potential friends as much she could. Jeanie felt ashamed.

She thought that it was a woman's duty to keep harmony in the household. Obviously, she failed that role miserably.

It was only a few weeks after the shouting matches began again when the pushing and shoving started as a well. The violence Slugger inflicted on the lonely, socially isolated girl, took its toll on her. She wanted to leave, but she felt trapped there. She didn't have a good paying job, nor anyone she felt she could stay with for a while. So, she put up with Slugger's occasional bullying. She kept hoping things would get better, but she wondered if they ever would.

Jeanie hated her job in a factory and was glad when she got laid off a short time later. Much to her dismay though, she hadn't worked there long enough to collect unemployment benefits. The financial strain of living on Slugger's paycheck put even more stress on Jeanie's relationship with him. Slugger wasn't shy about letting Jeanie know that she had to get another job and quickly. After a week or two searching for a local job without success, Jeanie took a bus to the small city just a few miles south of Windsock.

The displaced worker walked the streets in Harden practically all day. She really didn't want to go home to Slugger without a good job prospect, at least. Just before Jeanie was about to give up on her job search, she walked inside a small café for a beverage. Jeanie's eyes lit up as she noticed a help wanted sign posted in the window. She readily made out the application and was immediately hired as a waitress.

Jeanie had to take the nine o'clock bus out of Winsock to go to Harden five days a week. From the bus stop, the determined girl walked a mile to the café. It seemed like a lot of trouble, but it was worth it. The one major glitch in working those twenty miles away however, was Jeanie's transportation home. Her work schedule didn't end until six at night. Unfortunately, the last bus headed for Winsock stopped running an hour before her shift ended. This forced Jeanie to depend on Slugger for transportation home from work every night.

Although Slugger didn't like the idea of driving thirty minutes each way to pick up his girlfriend from work, he did it anyway. Except for a small amount of pen money, Jeanie gave all she earned to Slugger to help cover the bills. She didn't mind though, for she enjoyed working as a waitress. She loved helping people and the job wasn't nearly as boring as her previous job was. When it wasn't busy and she was all caught up on the cleaning, she made idle chit chat with the patrons too. The shy girl started to relax somewhat around people. She felt a sense of satisfaction from her job too. Working there definitely helped the insecure girl build her people skills as well as her self-esteem.

Most of the time Slugger was right there at six o'clock when Jeanie's shift ended to pick her up from work. There was a time or two when he was 10 or 15 minutes late. Overall, her boyfriend was reliable. There was a time, though when he was over 45 minutes late. Everybody had gone home and she was left alone on that isolated street in Harden. It was late fall with daylight quickly fading. Jeanie waited and waited for Slugger, but he was nowhere to be seen. The girl didn't know what to do. They didn't have a phone, so she couldn't call him. She had no friends to speak of either that could offer the young lady assistance. Jeanie was in a panic! She knew she had to get back to Winsock somehow. It was almost dark and soon it would be much colder too.

Carmalita Jean reluctantly put out her thumb. She figured the only way she would get home that night was if she bummed a ride from someone headed in that direction. The naïve girl routinely hitchhiked several years ago. Slugger talked her out of that unsafe practice. After all there were a lot of nuts out there. She was reminded of that fact that very evening. unfortunately.

Shortly after Jeanie put out her thumb, a young guy stopped to give her a ride. She flashed her pearly whites at the man and asked if he was going to Windsock. After nodding yes, Jeanie opened the door and got into the vehicle.

The two of them hadn't traveled more than a couple miles down the streets when the car slowed down. The vehicle started swerving to the left onto a deserted dirt road.

Jeanie yelled, "Hey where are you going?" She knew where the car was headed for she'd gone parking there before with one of her old beau's. The road only went one place and that was to the cemetery. Panic overtook the bewildered girl as she watched the disheveled man's glazed eyes glare at her. The evil grin on his face told of his intentions clearer than his lack of words. Jeanie knew she had to do something. She was about to be raped and murdered if she didn't do something.

The frightened girl had to get out of the moving car fast! In one quick motion, she grabbed her purse with the left hand and opened the car door with her right hand. As her body leaned against the car door, she pulled the handle. The door opened widely and out she rolled out of the impending death mobile. The tearful, naive waitress felt her body slam hard against the asphalt pavement. Blood trickled from her scraped knees. Her palms were scratched and bleeding as well. She was all prepared to run into the woods on the opposite side of the road in an attempt to hide from monster. Fortunately she didn't have to. The car directly behind them stopped and offered the injured girl his assistance.

The concerned man who stopped to help Jeanie did what he could to comfort her. Teary eyed, the poor hitchhiker told her terrible story. Although the man was originally only driving a short distance up the road, he traveled a few extra miles and brought Jeanie to a safe haven. He didn't want to place her in harms way again. Only after the frightened girl was dropped off at the local police station, did she calm down.

Not knowing, who else to call, Jeanie called her boyfriend's dad. Within a few minutes, Slugger's dad was at the station to bring the scraped up, uniformed girl home. Slugger was naturally concerned about the untimely event of the evening. Although he was sorry that the horrible event happened, he insisted he drove to Harden to pick her up. Since she was not in front of the café when he reached it, he just went back to Windsock and his drinking companions. Jeanie explained to her man that she could not wait forever for a ride she wasn't sure was coming. He wasn't the most reliable person in the world. He was famous for being a little late picking her up when they were going out for an evening. Still how could her fiancé leave her alone on the darkened sheets of Harden with a clear conscience? Slugger was late getting to the café because he lost track of time while out drinking of course. How typical Jeanie thought. She knew where she ranked on his list of priorities.

Despite the couple's not so perfect relationship, Jeanie stayed with Slugger. They were together this time now for over six months. Except for some loud words thrown at her and an occasional push, Slugger was more or less in control this temper. Maybe things weren't so bad here Jeanie thought. When she looked around and saw all the pretty things around her including a nice big color TV, it was difficult convincing herself that she would be better off leaving Slugger. After all, how many other girls her age lived as nice as this? Yes, looking around the apartment, one might think Jeanie had a life of comfort. Inside her heart Jeanie didn't feel comfortable at all.

It was right around the string of holidays between Thanksgiving and New Year's when Jeanie's nightmare was resurrected. Sluggers drinking was getting more and more out of control. She started to get more and more repulsed by his sick sense of humor and his drunken mannerism. The smell of liquor reeked from the pores of his body. A slimy film coated the man's lips and tongue. It was in one of Slugger's drunken stupors that he once again started his rampage of terror.

Slugger came home late that night wanting sex from his sleepy eyed girl. Jeanie was in no mood for sex especially with a man that smelled as bad as he did that night. Why, an old Billy goat smelled better. She didn't want his sticky hand groveling her perfumed body. She did not want the sickening taste of stale beer to be in her mouth. The thought of kissing someone like that made her nauseous. Jeanie pushed away Slugger's sexual advances. She was determined to stand her ground!

"I'm not your little plaything, "she shouted! "You can't go out all night with your friends, come home rip roaring drunk and expect sex from me! I'm not your little puppet!"

Life would have been so much easier that evening if Jeanie went along with Slugger's agenda. Fighting a battle of wills that night probably wasn't the smartest thing to do. However, this behavior had been going on for weeks now and Jeanie had about all she could stand.

"Why you little bitch. I'll show you who's the man of the house!" Slugger shouted as he raised his big hand towards the now cowering girl.

The force of his hand left the angry lass crying. Jeanie screamed back at the bully which only added fuel to the fire. The muscular man lunged at Jeanie. He definitely had the physical capacity to strangle the life out of her. Although he was mad enough to do it, Slugger stopped just short of the act. Jeanie gasped for breath as she held her reddened neck.

After his angry little demonstration, Slugger stormed out the door slamming it as he left.

Jeanie surely didn't want to be there when her abusive boyfriend returned. Since she lacked friends and didn't want to wake her sister at 2 am, Jeanie remained there in Slugger's house. Not knowing what else to do, she silently sat shivering in a corner. Fully dressed and alert she waited in the darkness until the sun came up welcoming another day.

Jeanie was thankful that her so-called boyfriend hadn't come home that night. Maybe he realized in his drunken state that he'd be capable of doing great harm to his girlfriend if he returned. Jeanie thought that he just went someplace and finished off another six pack before he passed out on his friend's floor. Right now she really didn't care where he was. As soon as daylight shone through the curtains, the shaken maiden put on her winter gear and barreled out the door.

A turtleneck covered up Jeanie's reddened neck. Her sister Deana had limited knowledge about the emotionally charged fights Jeanie had frequently with Slugger. However, the girl never let her sister know the full extent of the abuse she regularly endured. She hid that detail partially out of shame. She believed that Slugger became unglued because of her. She was the one at fault. True, the girl could be a little mouthy sometimes. Still, she didn't deserve all the abuse that was doled out to her.

Jeanie spent a chaotic day at her sister's house and weighed her options. She could probably stay with her if she had to, but she didn't want to. They didn't get along any better than they did when they were younger. Although they no longer kicked each other or pulled each other's hair, they weren't any closer than they were in high school.

"I'd be just as miserable here," the confused girl said silently to herself. Transportation would be a problem too for she didn't have her own car. That would mean she would have to quit her job. She didn't want to do that. She liked her job and she liked the people who frequented the place as well as her co-workers. "Damn," I guess I'll have to make peace with Slugger," Jeanie told herself sadly. The disheartened girl left her sister's house and returned to Slugger's apartment.

Jeanie arrived at her "lover's" home that night with a wind burnt faced and frost bit fingers. She licked her chapped lips as she put the key in the front door. Slugger's car was in the drive way. He had been waiting for her. What would be his reaction to her tonight she wondered?

When Jeanie walked into the living room, she could see Slugger sitting on the sofa waiting for her.

"Where have you been?" he questioned her.

"At my sisters," Jeanie murmured.

As the giant mass came close to Jeanie she shuddered. She didn't know what to expect. Slugger tenderly approached his beaten girlfriend and wrapped his hand around her reddened face.

"Oh baby, you're so cold," he's told her with concern in his voice. He took the knitted afghan that laid in a pile on the couch and gently wrapped it around Jeanie. As he placed the warm blanket around his girl, he pulled back the turtleneck sweater. There he saw the tell tale marks from the previous nights terror.

Slugger looked into Jeanie's war torn face and started crying. He seemed genuinely alarmed that he inflicted that pain upon his girlfriend. Tears poured from the man's remorseful eyes.

"God strike me dead if I ever do anything to hurt you again! I'm so sorry. I'm so sorry honey. I'll never do it again I swear. I'll never do it again!"

Slugger and Jeanie both began crying.

"I wish we could just make these bad times go way," whimpered Jeanie. Slugger just shook his head in agreement.

Things had to change Jeanie thought. She surely couldn't continue living like this. Usually after one of Slugger's fits of anger, he was really good to her for a month or so. At least Jeanie felt that her life would be somewhat peaceful for a while. She had better enjoy these times while she could.

The rest of the holiday season went without a cross word spoken between them. Yes, that brief month Jeanie felt truly happy inside. She was even beginning to believe that maybe, just maybe that choking episode shocked Slugger enough to stop his abusive ways. She hoped and prayed that it was so.

Jeanie's life appeared to be on the right track. She had a job she liked. Her and Slugger were getting along so well lately it amazed her. The shy introvert even made a girlfriend at work. Perhaps her life had straightened around. Perhaps not.

It was a cold Saturday morning in mid-January. The sidewalk outside was still glazed over with ice. A few local customers braved the elements to visit their favorite coffee shop to indulge in a friendly cup of hot brew. Although Jeanie had been into work for awhile, she was still trying to warm her insides with a hot cup of tea. She gripped the steamy mug with her hands thankful she didn't have to wait out in the snow for a city bus that day. Part way during her break, Jeanie got an unexpected phone call from her sister. Her life would be changed forever after that day.

Deana's voice was barely audible. Jeanie put down her tea and listened intently as to what her sister had to say. She never called me out here, she thought. Deana's voice was solemn but she was quick to tell the news.

"Carmalita Jean, is that you?" the voice inquired. "I don't know how to tell you this," Deana paused, "Dad is dead. The sheriff found his body last night. He was shot and robbed."

Tears flooded Jeanie's eyes. She somehow knew what her sister was going to say before she said it. Jeanie had a dream the night before that her father was dead. The dream seemed so real. She was happy when she woke up and realized that she was asleep and that she merely had a nightmare. Unfortunately, the events of that dream was all true. Her father was dead! Jeanie remembered how real the event felt in her dream state and how unreal it felt now.

Everyone at the café knew tragedy had struck the young girl's life. She balled like a baby and her knees buckled from under her. Jeanie's friend rushed to her aid. Between tears and sniffles, the quivering girl told her concerned coworker about her father's death. Jeanie couldn't stay at work. How could she concentrate on what she was doing that day when her head felt like jello. She called Slugger's dad and asked him to relay a message to his son. Within thirty minutes Slugger was at the coffee shop to bring his weeping woman home.

With Slugger's help Jeanie was able to get the first plane out to Louisiana. The brave nineteen year old voluntarily took on the family burden of tending to her father's remains. She should... after all, she was closest to him. Unfortunately there was a lay over in New Orleans which extended the journey. Jeanie always wanted to go to New Orleans but not under these circumstances. This particularly mournful day was not at all like the joyous celebrations of the Mardi Gras.

Jeanie had to spend that first upsetting night following the knowledge of her father's demise alone, in a hotel room. Slugger made arrangements and paid for his girlfriend's accommodations as well as the plane tickets. He didn't want her sleeping in the airport lobby for nine hours while she waited for the next plane out to Shreveport, Louisiana. She had to stay someplace until she caught the next plane out to Shreveport the following morning. Jeanie wished that Slugger hadn't started her plane trip the day he had. He meant well, but how she wished she didn't have to spend that first night all alone. She needed someone there to comfort her and at that time…she had no one.

In moments of extreme stress, Jeanie resorted back to her pattern of overeating and purging. That night all alone in the hotel, she was like an alcoholic that had fallen off the wagon. She felt so, so bad. Food was her only way to comfort herself at the time. It didn't help that she had just smoked a marijuana cigarette to calm herself. Naturally after she got high, she got the munchies. When she got the munchies, especially in her current state of mind, she uncontrollably ate and ate and ate. Still, no matter how much she ate, she could not erase all the inner pain and turmoil she felt inside. There was no way to erase the events of the past two days. There was no way to escape the fact that her father, the only person who she felt truly understood her and loved her was dead. After she got through with her bulimic purging, she cried uncontrollably while huddled in a fetal position on the roughened hotel's bedspread.

Jeanie had no one there for her. How she longed for Slugger's comforting embrace at that time. He'd been really nice to her during that traumatic time. He offered to buy the plane ticket and the motel room for he knew how important it was for Jeanie to be there for her dad. However, he made it clear that she would be paying him back for the trip money out of her anticipated income tax refund. That's ok, he would have expected it anyways, she told herself. Still, how she needed someone's arms around her. In her time of need, she had no one.

A friend of her dad's greeted the pale faced girl at the airport and offered her a place to stay while Jeanie tended to her father's needs. While in a catatonic state the speechless, young girl forced a smile towards the kind woman. Patsy had befriended her father several months before his untimely death. She was probably his closest friend down there. The compassionate woman was happy to help the distraught girl. Jeanie was thankful for any kind of help she received in this stressful time. Patsy's patience and love was what got the hurting child through the next few days.

The morning after arriving in Shreveport, Jeanie went to the morgue where her father's body remained. Much to her surprise, someone else was also there to view the permanently silenced body that was once her father. Leif's younger sister, Lily had traveled from Pennsylvania to visit Leif for the last time. Lily smiled gently at Jeanie, as she walked out the gray walled room inside the morgue. All she said to Jeanie was, that her brother looked peaceful.

Leif's hard shell like body laid motionless on the sheet covered gurney. The pungent odor of embalming fluid burned Jeanie's nose. Still, she forced herself to look at him. Stunned, the shaking girl removed the sheet, that covered him. She bit her lip as she looked down on his blue tinged body. He looked so different. All expression was wiped from his face. If it wasn't for his coloring, it almost looked like he could just get off that slab and walk away. Jeanie could not remember when her father looked so peaceful. Leif was shot while he was sleeping so no horror from that ungodly act of violence was imprinted on his face. The only tell tale evidence that something awful happened to her dad, was that one lousy bullet hole, which blemished her father's smooth face.

Jeanie reached down to feel her dad hand, the very hand that held hers not too long ago. The same one that taught her to draw. The same one she held when they went to the circus together when she was seven.

Jeanie's small fingers carefully reached over and touched her dad's left eye. There was a tiny hole no bigger than the tip of her pinky just over Leif's left eye. Her hero and protector was gone.

Jeanie stumbled out into the adjacent room. With her hand over her mouth the sensitive child muffled the sobs that escaped her lips. Patsy's reassuring hand reached out to touch Jeanie's shoulder.

"Leif's with God now," the sweet lady said in a gentle tone. Jeanie just nodded. With a bowed head, Jeanie closed her eyelids and allowed a few salty trickles to run down her face. That was the only escape her own tortured soul allowed her. The grieved girl was carefully led to the exit and into Patsy's car.

Jeanie's cordial hosts lightened the burden of the time spent in Louisiana. She didn't see Lily, her dad's sister again since that day in the morgue. Of course her aunt didn't know where Jeanie was staying either. Although things were definitely not pleasant, they could have been a lot worse. The solemn girl was happy that she didn't have to go through this horrible ordeal all alone. Patsy was there for her. Thank God for Patsy.

The second full day in Louisiana was harder on Jeanie emotionally than the first. That was the day Patsy brought Jeanie to her dad's mobile home in the country. That is where the crime took place. That was where Leif inhaled his last breath. The heart sick girl was shown the crimson stained bed where her father's life was stolen from him. The strong smell of dried blood sickened the girl. The trailer smelled of death. Jeanie didn't think anything would be able to erase that horrible odor from her consciousness.

She didn't think that she would ever be able to erase, the bloodied bedroom scene from her vision.

Although Carmalita Jean had access to everything Leif left in the mobile home, the grieving girl, took only a handful of her dad's personal belongings. She wanted to remember him alive and vibrant. Jeanie held onto the strap of her father's camera and smiled as she remembered the first time she visited him in Arkansas. He took so many pictures of her that spring. She was the moon and the sun to him that week. How much attention she was given those eight days. So much love was bestowed on her during that time. On the bookshelf near the camera were the treasured photos from his life. They were all neatly displayed in a gold bordered photo album. Without hesitation, the girl grabbed onto them and held the book to her chest as she remembered some of the special times they shared.

Jeanie walked over to where the stereo was located. Gently she reached into the box that held her father's favorite records. Months before she was delivered back into the hands of Slugger, Jeanie and her dad shared a wonderful hour dancing to those lively tunes. They disco danced around the kitchen like fools. A smile crept across the girl's face in fond remembrance of that day. How handsome and sexy Jeanie thought her father was. He didn't look bad for man of 44. She often kidded him how she would go out with him if he wasn't her dad. Yes, she was that attracted to him.

On the table in the living room laid her dad's eyeglasses. Jeanie carefully picked up the metal frames and gently put them in her coat pocket for safekeeping. How she wished she could view the world as her father had. Since he was an experienced artist, he had an eye for beauty. He savored the magnificent images he captured with his eyes, often putting them on film. How she wished she had her dad's way of seeing the world. How she wished she had his talents.

The last thing Jeanie grabbed as she left Leif's earth home was a tall clay urn. Her father carried it around for years. The brown, rough edged vessel Jeanie knew well. Leif told his daughter on several occasions that when he died, he wanted to be cremated. Afterwards he wanted his ashes placed in that particular urn. It was up to her to make sure his last wishes were carried out.

Jeanie didn't cry until she got back to Patsy's house. She tried so hard to act as a brave girl should. Jeanie's body may have matured to that of a young lady, but inside she was a still frightened little girl. Only when she was all alone in her room, did Jeanie open up the flood gates of her heart. She cried more than a handful of tears. She cried for her dad who was shot down in his prime. She cried for Rex, her father's dog. The poor thing had to be put down after going crazy when he smelled dad's blood. If only Leif had let Rex stay inside the trailer rather than the fenced in yard, he may still be live. Jeanie cried for the miserable abusive life she endured. Jeanie's life wouldn't be easy, especially now. Her knight in shining armor was slain by a dragon. Who would be there to rescue her now when her world falls apart? No one!

The last two remaining days of Carmalita Jean's trip were all a big blur. She remembered going to the funeral home to make arrangements for her dad's cremation, but she didn't remember the details concerning that trip.

Jeanie always thought the first legal paper she would sign would be a marriage license. How wrong she was. Jeanie signed the papers to ensure her dad's charred remains would go to her home in Massachusetts. She couldn't even remember what the funeral home looked like or who she talked to an hour later. Emotionally, the bewildered girl had shut down. Her body was moving, but her mind was on another planet. Perhaps it was for the best. The distraught little thing had about all she could deal with for now.

With a big hug, Patsy left Jeanie at the airport's gate and scurried back into her car. The grieved girl hurt so much inside. It felt like someone put a branding iron to her chest. She wondered if or when the dull, throbbing ache inside her heart would go away. Already she missed her dad. When the chips were down, she could count on her daddy. Now she had no one to count on, no one to rescue her when things got really bad.

Just three weeks before his demise, Jeanie told her dad. She wanted to live with him again. He was all ready to send his daughter a plane ticket to Shreveport to join him in his new residence too. However her and Slugger made up once again. Now she wished she would have been there with him.

Jeanie believed that her dad would never have picked up a hitchhiker on the highway if she lived with him. He would not have jeopardized his daughter's security and allowed the poor bum into their home. The kind man would not have fed the louse either. The sheriff told Jeanie that the murderer's fingerprints were found on the glasses and silverware and the guest bed was overturned.

Surely her dad would not have given this murderous man a place to stay for the night if she was there. Her father's kindness was repaid by shooting him in the head. While her poor dad laid motionless in his bed, the scoundrel pulled the diamond ring off Leif's left pinky and stole his wallet with $200 in it. The villain so wanted to possess those few earthly things that he brutally murdered her father.

Jeanie felt that she should have joined her dad in Louisiana when she was supposed to. None of this would have happened if she was there. She wiped a river of tears off her reddened face. If dad had picked up a hitchhiker that day and she was with him… then they both would be dead. Emotionally Jeanie was dead. She felt nothing but numbness inside now. "Oh why couldn't I be dead too?" Jeanie said herself in between sobs.

When Jeanie arrived at the Boston airport, she became even more despondent. She knew Slugger would be waiting for her. She should be happy to be coming home to the man that paid for this necessary trip, but she wasn't. She didn't know what the future would hold for the both of them. Things were going pretty well for a while before she made that unplanned trip. Still, she was sure Slugger's good behavior wouldn't last much longer. That was how the pattern had been so far. The man would treat her good for while then he'd go back to being an abusive asshole. To expect changes this far into their relationship was too much to hope for. Jeanie knew by now how unpredictable Slugger's actions were when he went on his predictable drinking binges.

The first few weeks Jeanie was home, Slugger was as kind and patient with the distraught mourner as he could possibly be. After a month's time, though, his patience with Jeanie was about all used up.

"How much longer you going to carry on with this? For Christ's sake Carmalita Jean, he's dead! Give it up already!" Slugger told his lady in an insensitive, sarcastic tone.

This made Jeanie even more angry. She would try to put on a stiff upper lip, just to pacify him. After she exchanged a deadly, silent glance at Slugger, she walked back into the kitchen to busy herself. The girl would do just about anything right now to avoid a fight.

Things were more tense lately for the couple's relationship. Their bedroom life was in shambles as well. Jeanie routinely took Slugger's sexual advances without a battle. He enjoyed being the master of her body. However, she didn't allow him to touch her elsewhere. There was a steel door around her heart and mind that no one could touch now. Even though Jeanie didn't get much out of the sex act, she did enjoy the hugging and kissing. The orphaned girl didn't feel so alone when she was in Slugger's strong arms. Slugger may not be the greatest thing since sliced bread, but she had to admit that he hadn't been that bad lately. Just when she was beginning to feel that maybe there was hope for the guy after all, another abusive encounter shook Jeanie back into reality.

It had been several months since Jeanie's dad made his transition into the other plane. Although the recent wounds surrounding her dad's death were ever present, the young lass was getting better at coping with them. The promise of a new start this year was prominently budding. Yes, spring was trying to make its debut in the northern states. Most of the snow melted and the temperatures usually rose above freezing during the day. Only a few glistening patches of snow remained in random clumps of grass. Jeanie was happy about that. She didn't like those white flakes or the cold. Most of the winter, she hibernated inside her home. If it wasn't for work, Jeanie would not have gone out of the house at all.

Jeanie's little job at the café turned out to be a blessing. It was a type of therapy for the shy girl. It helped turn the introverted gal around. She felt a little more at ease when she talked to people. She wasn't nearly as self-conscious as she previously had been. Jeanie and Pam, the other young waitress at work grew to be good friends. Still, she didn't know about the type of life, Slugger and Jeanie had at their home in Winsock. That part of Jeanie's life was carefully guarded. She was ashamed of their turbulent life together. Inside Jeanie still felt that she was being a bad girlfriend when Slugger lost his temper and hit her. Jeanie thought that something she did was so terrible that it justified Slugger hitting her. She felt that it was her fault that there was such disharmony in the house.

Jeanie was used to the role of the peacemaker. She acquired that role as a child. When young, she tried to keep her parents from their arguing matches. Jeanie unconsciously carried out that behavior into her adult life. Although she played that role often, she could not seem to keep the peace in her current home life with Slugger.

Jeanie's depression and anxiety hadn't eased up since she came back from her trip from Louisiana. Her emotions always seemed to be hanging on the edge. The flight or fight response was fully engaged. Unconsciously, Jeanie was preparing to do one or the other with Slugger. She just didn't know which reflex would surface and she didn't know when she would have to use it.

On one particular day, situations between the two became extremely tense. It was the typical spring evening. Jeanie was in the kitchen cooking supper when Slugger announced that he was going out with friends to play cards that night. Ok, his mistress nodded in acknowledge. Without raising her head, she carried on with her household chores. Jeanie made up her mind that after she did the dishes, she would get out her favorite magazine and thumb over it's glossy pages. In between leafing through the latest copy of Seventeen, she would watch some of her favorite TV shows. Since it was a weeknight, she didn't think her man would be getting home too late or get home too drunk. After all, he had to get up early to go to work the next day. Also, he stated he was sluggish from going out the night before, so he doubted he would be home late that night.

Jeanie waited up until 10:30 before deciding it was time for her to go to bed. She didn't want to feel fatigued at her job the next morning. The half waken girl was startled into consciousness at 1:00 am. She laid in bed and waited for Slugger to stumble into bed with her. Suddenly, she heard a loud bang and heard Slugger cussing loudly. He no doubt banged his leg on the coffee table in the living room. Jeanie tried to ignore the drunkard's cursing, but it was hard to do. Slugger was definitely in a bad mood now the girl thought to herself. She was in a bad mood now herself. Once again, the girl had to put up with her drunk boyfriend's shenanigans.

"Could you try being a little quieter. I'm trying to sleep." Jeanie shouted from across the room. Immediately, the sleepy eyed maiden knew she should have kept her mouth shut.

Slugger barreled into the bedroom with fire in his eyes.

"What did you say to me, woman!" he shouted at her.

"Nothing," Jeannie sheepishly said as she tried to hide her head under the blanket. She hoped, if she silently hid under the covers and didn't say anything else to rile him, maybe he would leave her alone. Wrong!

The brute's left hand swept under the blankets and pulled Jeanie's head up under the blankets. The right-hand of the out-of-control monster struck her left cheek, sending pain all the way down her neck. As she gazed into his bloodshot eyes, the girl knew that she could not stay there much longer. No, she had to move out of Slugger's house. She had to escape from this torturous life.

Jeanie looked into the mirror, the following day. Maybe if she used enough of the bronze liquid makeup, she could cover up the bruising. Maybe no one at work would be able to see the handprint across Jeanie's face. As drunk as Slugger was the night before, he could've done much more damage to Jeanie's body. Jeanie felt lucky she got off with light punishment. After that one good slap, the shaking girl was able to calm Slugger down enough to avoid what may have been a terribly explosive night.

In between customers Jeanie talked to Pam about possibly getting an apartment of her own. Her salary was meager though, so the distraught girl knew that she couldn't afford much. Still, after the little waitress got her next paycheck, she got a one room apartment across the street from the café.

The following day, when Slugger was out with his friends, Jeanie enlisted the aid of her brother-in-law. Together they gathered what few things belonged to Jeanie and stashed them in cardboard boxes and trash bags. Within a few minutes all remnants of the girl's life were removed from Slugger's house. She wrote him a short note and placed it on the living room table next to his house key.

Jeanie felt so relieved to be there in own apartment that night. She thought about what Slugger would do when he came home. How he would react to the note concerning her departure. She was glad that he wasn't there in the same room with her that night. Despite the unfamiliar noises around her, Jeanie was at peace. At least for a little while.

Unfortunately, the small furnished apartment Jeanie rented didn't have its own bathroom. She had to go down the hall to relieve herself when the need came. During the first night there, she had quite a fright. As the girl was on en route to the community bathroom, she bumped into an elderly man. He stumbled towards her smelling of beer. When he followed Jeanie as she walked down the darkened corridor, the paranoid girl started to cry and run. When she approached her landlord's apartment, she pounded on the door. Jeanie stood there at his door, trembling. Much to her delight and surprise, she discovered that the man who scared her, had disappeared down the hallway.

Within a few minutes, the landlord's squeaky door opened. He could see that the young girl was frightened. When Jeanie recalled the recent events, the landlord just flashed a half smile and calmly said "Oh that's just Ernie. He lives here. If you're going to come to me like a scared little girl over every little thing, then maybe you shouldn't be living here." Jeanie's face flushed as the man closed the door to his apartment. After taking care of business, Jeanie rushed back to her little apartment in tears. What did she get herself into?

Since the following day was Sunday, the restaurant was closed which meant that she didn't have to work. She was thankful for that, for she was very tired. The poor young thing didn't sleep well after the Ernie incident. "What am I going to do?" Jeanie said to herself as she walked the deserted streets of Harden.

The following day Jeanie gladly went back to work at her place of employment. Being there took her mind off all the disturbing events of the previous weekend. The young waitress didn't like living at the place she had now but at least she felt safe. Sort of. At least her ex-boyfriend didn't know where she lived. However he did know where she worked.

When Jeanie was about to get off work that night, she saw a familiar car parked inches from the front door of the café. It was Slugger's car. She was sure of it. Jeanie walked with her head bowed, as she left the restaurant. Maybe he won't see me, she silently wished. Naturally, he did. "Jeanie where have you been? I've missed you!" Slugger told the girl as he slowly walked towards her.

"I've moved out Slugger. I'm not going to put up with you hitting me anymore. I'm not going to do it!" Jeanie shouted as tears poured from her eyes.

"Let's talk about it honey. Let's just talk about it. Do you want to go out to dinner?" Her ex-boyfriend asked.

Jeanie really didn't want to go back to her dumpy little hellhole of an apartment and eat stale crackers for supper. Reluctantly, she agreed to go with him. Even though Slugger pressed Jeanie hard to return with him that night, she refused.

"I don't know," Jeannie told her estranged boyfriend. "How do I know you'll change? I can't keep living with you the way it's been. I just can't do it!"

Slugger bent his head in shame. He actually showed remorse for how badly he treated Jeanie. She didn't refuse him when he asked her out to dinner the following night as well.

After work, Slugger was there at the little restaurant to pick Jeanie up. He was clean-shaven and neatly dressed. He could be quite handsome when he dressed up, Jeanie thought. Why he even smelled good that night. Slugger was wearing some of the cologne she had brought him for Christmas. He presented the tired waitress a small bouquet of flowers. Jeanie smiled at Slugger as she accepted the slightly wilted carnations.

"Thank you. That's awfully sweet to you." Jeanie told him as she reached for the bouquet.

Slugger reached over and gave her a hug. "I miss you honey," the man said, almost weeping.

During the romantic spaghetti dinner, Slugger and Jeanie talked and talked. They held hands and flirted with each other. They exchanged breadsticks and smiles. Before the evening had ended, Slugger had swept the girl back onto cloud nine. She readily accepted his invitation to return to Windsock with him. They stopped by Jeanie's little apartment and got what few items of hers was there. She returned the key to the landlord. Luckily she only paid by the week. From there, the couple departed for home.

Life was fairly peaceful for the first month or so following Jeanie's return. The two of them walked on egg shells to avoid any kind of confrontation. There was a certain tension in the air that was felt but never openly discussed. Jeanie started getting nervous whenever she sensed the growing surge of anxiety swimming around inside.

It was during this period of silent uncertainty that Jeanie resumed contact with her girlfriend of Arkansas. They exchanged letters rapidly and rescued their ailing distant relationship. It turned out that Gina was also working as a waitress. Maybe, Jeanie thought, she could get a job working with her. Gina also had a small but cute apartment not far from where she worked. Jeanie missed Seven Springs and the few friends she found there. The young lady smiled as she remembered the fun times that the two of them had. Life was so carefree and easy. How Jeanie envied Gina's life. She appeared to be so happy. As for herself… she had moments of happiness, but nothing really stable. No, her happiness and security depended on Slugger. Slugger did provide Jeanie with a comfortable home, but unfortunately he also provided her with an occasional beating.

For years Jeanie conned herself into believing that Slugger would change. He obviously loved her. After all, he didn't have to provide her with a home. There were many times he was actually nice to her and considered what she wanted. Since the man did love her so much, surely he would make the changes needed to save their dying relationship. Wanting to make changes and actually doing them was a hard undertaking for Slugger. Still, those changes had to take place or he would surely lose her.

Jeanie shook her head as she thought about the terrible pattern of abuse the couple was stuck in. "If he ever strikes again, I'm leaving for good, and I'm never coming back!" Jeanie said convincingly to herself. She meant every word she said, that time!

Jeanie placed her girlfriend's current letter in the bottom of her clothes drawer to hide it from Slugger. He probably wouldn't like it if she resumed writing to a friend so far away. Slugger was so controlling and so suspicious. She surely didn't want to give him another reason to strike her...not that he ever needed one.

Another week or so passed since Jeanie made that silent pact with herself, when another argument broke out in a household. It all started over something so small, that she couldn't even remember what it was. Slugger wasn't even drunk that time. He had a beer or two, but he definitely wasn't drunk. Despite his fairly sober state, the angry out-of-control man pushed his girl several feet into the porcelain vanity. A stream of pain circled her lower abdomen as she slowly lowered herself to the floor. All the while Slugger yelled at her to get up.

"You're not hurt that bad! Get up bitch!" Jeanie mustered all her strength and courage to get up off the floor for fear Slugger would strike her again. After the weeping girl stood up, the tyrant walked back into the living room as if nothing had happened.

Jeanie cautiously stood up while still in the bathroom. She could feel something trickling down her legs. As she sat on the commode, she felt the pain start again. It seemed to be radiating from deep inside her stomach region. She bent her head and lowered it to observe where the blood was coming from. Crimson liquid spurted out from her vagina. In horror Jeanie quietly sat still. She didn't want anyone to hear her except God.

"I wonder if I'm having a miscarriage?" the beaten girl said to herself. The bleeding stopped almost as fast as it started. The throbbing pain from down-under stopped as well. The thought that she might be having a miscarriage stopped. The idea that she may be pregnant didn't. She hadn't taken her birth control pills for those few days she left Slugger. She might indeed be pregnant.

That afternoon, when Sluggers was at work, Jeanie gathered up a few of her clothes. She was determined to move out of Sluggers domain once and for all. However, she didn't know where she would go. Since she had no money or friends there in Windsock, the bewildered girl sought refuge in the cool, moldy basement of her abusive boyfriend's apartment building. She thought that she could sleep there at night and go upstairs to watch TV and eat when Slugger was gone. That plan worked well for only a few days. Slugger changed locks on the door the third day after Jeanie's left. From then on, the homeless girl could no longer live comfortably when Sluggers was away. Obviously, she had to find other accommodations.

Jeanie went to her sister's house for help that morning. When the girl discovered she could no longer get into Slugger's apartment to refuel and keep warm, she knew she had to do something. Unfortunately Jeanie's stay was short-lived. The first afternoon at Deana's house Jeanie spilled her guts to her sister. It was then Carmalita Jean told her sister that she was probably pregnant. She wanted acceptance and love from her, instead she got chastised and condemned for being so careless. Jeanie muffled her sobs. When the shaken girl was questioned as to what she was going to do about the unplanned pregnancy, all hell broke loose. When Jeanie told Deana that she planned on getting an abortion, the girl was kicked out of her siblings home. Her sister didn't care that she had nowhere else to go. Nor did she take into consideration Jeanie's plight. Her fetus may have been damaged by Slugger's hand. Even if her unborn child was not damaged, Jeanie didn't have a good man in her life to take care of her and her baby. She didn't have a job, or any way of taking care of an infant. She couldn't even take care of herself at the time. So how could she take care of a child? In many ways Jeanie with still a baby herself...inside.

It was during that time that Jeanie sought the help of an elderly man she befriended several years earlier. King was a very sweet man, but he was over twice Jeanie's age. Still, the kindly man had a real soft spot in his heart for Jeanie. When the bewildered girl went to his house and told him of her dilemma, he was all too ready to help her. The soft hearted man gave Jeanie a place to live with no strings attached. Most guys would've taken advantage of a homeless girl under those circumstances, but King did not! He was a total gentleman, the whole time. He supplied Jeanie with her basic needs of food and shelter. He also gave the girl the much needed moral support that her family could not give her.

It hurt Jeanie that both her mother and her sister turned their backs on her when she told them she wanted an abortion. The girl's mom helped her get the first one. Jeanie figured she did that because she was just sixteen years old and was still a kid then. Just because Jeanie was now twenty, it didn't mean she was mentally or emotionally ready to be a mother. Some people adopt out their unwanted babies. Jeanie could not do that. She couldn't bring herself to nurture a child inside her womb only to give away, for she would always wonder about it. Right now, the 11-week-old embryo was only the size of a tadpole. It was hard to think of it as being a growing baby...but it was. Although Jeanie loved children, right now wasn't the time for her to bring one into the world. Although King offered to marry the young waif, she declined his offer. She thought of King, strictly as a father figure. She couldn't see him as anything other than that.

King respected Jeanie's wishes and continued to help her any way he could. The guy even made arrangements for Jeanie to get an abortion in Boston. As if the man hadn't done enough, he bought the confused girl a bus ticket and gave her $300 to take along on her trip. Jeanie cried. She couldn't recall when anyone had done anything so kind and unselfish for her. This man was truly a King!

With much sadness, King brought the emotionally distraught girl to the bus depot and said goodbye to her forever. Jeanie said goodbye to Massachusetts and so long to Slugger. She looked out the window and remembered so many wretched memories of events she'd rather forget that happened there in Windsock.

It will be wonderful to be in Arkansas again, Jeanie said to herself. She couldn't wait to leave this area and all the awful past behind. Soon, she would be with Gina again. She couldn't wait! Jeanie gazed quietly out the window of the bus as she thought about how different her life was gong to be. There were so many changes coming her way. Yes, so many changes. Jeanie fell asleep on the bus with a smile planted on her face. She was so sure her life would be so much better now!

# CHAPTER 6

# Dancing Fool

After riding in the bus for almost two days Jeanie arrived at Seven Springs. Since Gina did not know exactly when Jeanie would be coming south, she wasn't there to greet her at the bus depot. That's all right Jeanie thought. I'll just take a taxi over to her girlfriend's apartment and surprise her.

When Jeanie arrived at her friend's apartment she excitedly knocked on the door. As soon as the door opened and Gina recognized who was there, she shrieked with happiness. The two bosom buddies bounced up and down with joy. They hugged each other so hard that it's a wonder ribs weren't broken in the exchange of affection.

"God it's good to be back," Jeanie stated enthusiastically. "I missed you."

Gina nodded her head in agreement. "Me too."

In between Gina's work schedule, the two girls ran the streets of Seven Springs. Life for them was one big party. Gina knew all sorts of fellas since she had lived in Seven Springs most of her life. She was only too happy to introduce Jeanie to them. When the two babes went to the local lake, they were certain to meet even more guys. Guys with money! Guys with boats! Guys with pot!

The dinner table of life was one big smorgasbord. The two girls never dated the same man more than twice. Life was always interesting and fun. Never routine. Jeanie got her intimacy needs met with whoever she found attractive at the time. Back in those days Aids was practically nonexistent and basically unheard of. Jeanie thought that as long as she had her birth control, she could do what ever she wanted. She didn't have to pay the price for her insatiable lust. Only until much later did she realize how wrong she was.

In some ways Jeanie missed being with somebody who cared about her. However when she thought about her ex-boyfriend and how he showed his love for her, those ideas quickly vanished. thoughts of being more than casually involved with a man just didn't appeal to Jeanie at the time. Who could blame her after what she had been through.

Just two months after Jeanie reunited with Gina, situations started to change…money wise. Gina lost her job and Jeanie spent nearly all the money King gave her before leaving Massachusetts. Jeanie tried getting a job in a small town of Seven Springs, but the only job she could obtain was as a dishwasher. She absolutely hated that job! She didn't show up for work after the first day. Out of pure disgust and desperation Jeanie got the bright idea that her and Gina should hitchhike to Shreveport Louisiana to try to get back her deceased dad's things. There was $200 in his wallet when the sheriff found his murderer, as well as his one carat diamond ring. Jeanie couldn't get those items back earlier, for the police told her they were being held for evidence. It had been several months since his death. Surely, they could release her dad's personal affects by now she thought.

While en route to Louisiana, the two brunette bombshells got a ride from a very cordial trucker. As luck would have it, he was passing right through Shreveport. Sometime during the trio's conversation, it was mentioned how much Gina and Jeanie loved to dance. Why back in Seven Springs they danced all the time. That was about all they did at night, dance, get drunk and of course have a merry time with their man of choice.

"Hey." explained the helpful trucker, "I know where you can get a good paying job that's fun. Since you girls like to dance and party all night, I'll bet you make good dancers. I know a guy at one of the local clubs in Bossier City who would be happy to hire a couple of foxy babes like you!"

Jeanie and Gina looked at each other and unanimously shouted "Yeah!" That was all trucker Troy had to hear.

"Say girls if you'd like I'll drop you off at Saks and you can talk to Larry today. Why you could be making money tonight."

That's exactly what they did. The two girls went to the club and were hired on the spot. All they had to do was wear some cute, sexy little outfit and dance. The dancers would get on the stage in rotation with the other girls and shake their booties. In between their dancing gigs, they would be waitress. While they waited on customers and brought them their drinks the girls also hustled drinks. Dancers kept so much money per drink they got their patrons to buy them. Their drinks were watered down, with barely a thimble full of liquor in them. They were extremely expensive too. One Champagne cocktail would cost five dollars. In 1976 that was a lot of money for one mixed drink. That watered down cocktail was the girls drink of choice, for they got to keep a dollar from each drink their patrons bought them. The guys at the club didn't mind buying the girls a drink or two. When the guy bought drinks for the dancers, the dancers would give their undivided attention to the man buying them for a few minutes while they drank it. Then of course the guys got to see the dancing beauties up close. The guys enjoyed the looking and the flirting. The dancers enjoyed the money they would get for their dancing, flirting and drinking.

Jeanie's friend Gina quickly shed her bathing suit top. Although it was encouraged, it was not a requirement. Her friend got so many tips when she did that. Of course Gina was very well endowed. Jeanie was not, so she chose to keep those few scant clothes on. Although Jeanie had been with many, many guys, she was still a little shy up there on the stage. She just wasn't ready to bare her boobs at that time. She was happy just bringing home whatever money she made without doing that!

For awhile both girls enjoyed working at the club. It was fun. There wasn't any hard work involved. However, it had its drawbacks. Often when a guy would spend $20 or more on drinks on one particular girl, he would expect certain favors. Jeanie didn't like to feel obligated to be with someone just because he bought her a few drinks. So…she would float around all night being careful no one guy bought more than two champagne cocktails. When she made up her mind which guy she wanted to be with that night, she would stay with him exclusively until the bar closed.

Yes, while Jeanie worked and danced at the club, she had many different boyfriends. Life then was carefree and exciting. For a awhile it was just what both bouncy girls needed.

When Jeanie and Gina first went to Bossier, they didn't know anybody in the area. Obviously, they had to sleep somewhere. To aid the girls in accommodations, the nightclub's manager brought them to a local hotel room and introduced them to Jenny. He reasoned that it would be much cheaper to split the hotel costs three ways. That arrangement would help out all three girls. Jenny had a car too so their transportation problem to the club would be solved as well. Unfortunately that expensive hotel ate up much of their money the first couple of weeks.

After that time, Gina and Jeanie pooled their saved income and rented themselves a cute, cozy house not far from their job. The two wild things had a blast at their place of employment. All they did was dance all night, deliver mixed drinks and flirt with the customers. It was hard to believe they were getting paid good money for having such a fun time. Some of the other girls who worked there did other things on the side but that was their bag. The two quickly learned that one of the perks at the club as dancers was that guys would fight among themselves to see who would be with their lovely lady of choice that night. Jeanie and Gina just ate up the attention they received.

About a week or so after their arrival in Bossier City, Jeanie thought it was about time she approached the local police about collecting her father's personal items. Jeanie and Gina went to the police station one sunny morning and inquired about getting Leif's ring and a wallet back.

The police said they couldn't give back the $200 they found in the wallet for no one could prove who the money belonged to. The ring however was given back to Jeanie but four out of six prongs which held the gemstone were broken. It wasn't discovered until the following day that the stone had been replaced with a fake. Jeanie couldn't be sure whether the police made the switcheroo or the man who killed her father. Either way, the one carat diamond like stone that was in the ring now was virtually worthless. This fact made Jeanie extremely angry, but not nearly as angry as what the police also told her. Her father's murderer had been released from prison. Although his fingerprints were found all over the trailer, and her dad's wallet and ring were found in his possession, he would not pay for his crime. Even though Greeson held many of her father's personal items, the police couldn't hold him. The guy got away with murder because of some legal loophole. Jeanie was devastated.

The girl had so much anger festering inside her heart. Between the bullying she encountered growing up, her abusive long-term relationship, and now this. She was beyond ballistic! Often she conjured up ways in her mind to torment or kill those who had wronged her. She would never do any of those things of course. Even though she was an irresponsible little pothead, she wasn't insanely stupid! Still, it was nice thinking about serving justice where justice should be served.

She didn't feel it was right the way her peers bullied her while growing up. It surely wasn't right the way Slugger mopped the floors with her all those years. It most definitely wasn't right that Greeson got away with murdering her father. If her dad wasn't a poor, gay guy, Jeanie felt that the police would've made sure the sucker who killed him would have rotted away in a damp jail cell for the rest of his life, never to see the sunlight ever again!

A few months after their arrival in Bossier, Jeanie and Gina started growing apart. The energetic dancer started to get tired of the bar scene. She was sick of the dirty old men pinching her butt. She was sick of their vulgar language. They treated her like she was a whore, although she definitely wasn't. Memories flooded her mind of her earlier adolescent days at school. At least in the clubs she was getting paid good money for listening to the patron's dirty, derogatory comments. Still, she didn't like it any better there then in junior high. She was treated poorly then and she was being treated poorly now. Although Jeanie was happy with the money she made, she certainly wasn't happy with her job. Gina was content to stay in the club to dance and hustle drinks, but Jeanie was not!

The pretty woman didn't see anything wrong with dancing in itself, it was just the atmosphere. Of course how should she expect to be treated prancing around in a string bikini that left little to the imagination. One night Jeanie decided not to show up for work. She just couldn't handle the games anymore. Of course she got fired. That's ok Jeanie thought to herself, I'll just get a job as a waitress someplace. Besides, she did manage to save some money while she was working at the club. So, to hell with them!

It was during that time that Gina and Jeanie decided to go their separate ways. The fact that they worked different environments and two different shifts was bad enough. However, the most out standing factor which influenced the split up of the bosom buddies was a guy factor. That's when the old green-eyed monster came into play. Fireworks started when the man Jeanie had been dating wanted to be with Gina.

"That's it. I'm moving out!" Screamed the angry female. Jeanie couldn't wait to move out on her own. She was sure life would be so blissful now that her sexy little sister wouldn't be stealing her dates. She didn't count on how lonely her nights would be after her date mate decided he was bored with Jeanie.

Being alone and dateless was bad enough. When Jeanie lost her job at the café where she was a waitress, financially life became rocky. For the two weeks that followed her job loss, Jeanie did nothing but sit in front of the TV and eat.

"Screw friends! Who needs them?" Jeanie said convincingly to herself. Although she tried denying her need for friendship, particularly Gina's friendship, inside her heart was crying.

Jeanie was alone in body and spirit. Money was running out as well. Jeanie knew that she had to do something fast. Even though the depressed lass gained 12 pounds, she was still an attractive lady. Despite how she felt inside about the sleazy clubs, Jeanie knew she could always go back to work in one of them as a dancer if she had to.

It wasn't long before Jeanie started dancing at the clubs again. There was a multitude of clubs on the strip. When she would get sick of the bar scene and all the sleazy guys…she'd quit. She'd live off her earnings for while. When she became broke again, she'd find another club to work in. She repeated that job hopping pattern for eight months.

Sometimes in between dancing jobs, Jeanie would go to the local discos and dance. It was different for Jeanie when she danced there. She was just like every other girl. She didn't feel like a plum ripe for the picking in the discos. After all Jeanie was dancing with her clothes on. The provocative brunette had the time of her life flaunting what she had at the discos. All the sexy girl did was flirt, dance and cuddle with one hunky guy after another. As the evening progressed, Jeanie would settle down with one chosen guy to be with for the remainder of the night. On this particular night, Jeanie sought out a tall, dark and handsome guy to be with her. After the couple hung around and danced for a while, he asked the girl if she wanted to go for a drive or something. Sure. Why not.

Topper mentioned in their drive that he wanted to get some pot to smoke before they went to his place. Since pot was Jeanie's drug of choice, she was only too happy to help him score.

Jeanie asked Topper to drive over to one of the local clubs for she knew someone that hung around there who had lots of connections. Sure enough, Stony was at the bar drinking his screwdrivers and watching the dancers. Stony said that he knew where they could get some pot, but he would need a ride to his friends house. Of course, Topper agreed to take Stony to his friends house to score a bag of pot for himself and his gal pal.

So the three compadres went to the local dealer's house to score some reefer. Stony went in to see his friends alone. He was in their house only a short while when he came out looking disappointed. Turned out that his friends didn't have anything to sell that night. However, he gave the two a complimentary joint with the promise of having the desired marijuana tomorrow. That would have to do Jeanie thought

The three puffed on the fragrant herb while driving Stony back to the nightclub. As topper pulled into the parking lot to let Stony out, Jeanie mentioned she had to go to the bathroom.

"I'll wait right here," Topper told the smiling girl.

That smile quickly left her face! When Jeanie approached the front door of the nightclub, she turned around to see where her fella had parked. God knows she didn't need to be wandering around in the dark while she tried to find his vehicle. When Jeanie turned around to locate the guy's car, she saw something that put her into shock. Donald had police license plates on his sedan!

"Oh my God! What have I done?" Cried Jeanie. When the stunned girl walked towards the car, Topper drove off. "Now what do I do? I don't have transportation of my own," cried the little pothead.

Although Jeanie tried to find Stony, it was to no avail. He had already left with somebody else. I've got to warn those people.

"They are going to get in big trouble, and it'll all be my fault!" Tears flowed uncontrollably from the distressed girl's eyes. It was rather ironic that it took the effects of a marijuana cigarette to enlighten Jeanie as to what was going on around her.

Since Jeanie didn't have her own car, she'd automatically put her thumb in the air to hitchhike a ride out to the dealer's house. Not long after the topsy turvy girl put out her thumb, when a young curly haired man stopped to give her a ride. Nervously the girl told Curly what had just happened and how badly she felt. She couldn't let that nice young couple get busted because of her.

Unfortunately, Jeanie had a terrible sense of direction. It was even worse when she was high. The poor, good hearted girl couldn't for the life of her figure out what direction Stony's friends lived. She wasn't familiar with that part of the city. She didn't have a clue how she could warn the dealer of their upcoming bust. She felt horrible!

It was after the two of them rode around a while that Jeanie became aware of a most unusual scent in the car. Almost smelled like cloves. Strange, Jeanie thought. Now why would anyone have cloves in their car? All thoughts concerning the strange scent quickly vanished when the cordial young man asked Jeanie if she wanted to go to his place to smoke another joint. Sure, Jeanie quickly answered. Although she was already high, she surely couldn't refuse a free toke.

Upon arriving at Curley's house, Jeanie noticed another car in the driveway. "Oh it's just one of my roommates," Curley said matter-of-factly.

Upon entering the huge living room, a fair, handsome man caught Jeanie's eye. His name was Raphael and he was certainly a work of art.

After the small group finished smoking the Columbian weed they shared, Jeanie spent a few minutes getting acquainted with her surroundings. She became increasingly uneasy as she looked at the furnishings in the room. On the wall was a weird poster of a goat's head in a stew. Jeanie felt very anxious as she looked at it but didn't know why. No, only after several minutes did she realize why she felt so ill at ease in the company of her newly acquired friends.

Within a few minutes another person joined them in the living room. As Jeanie looked over to where the newcomer sat, she was struck with terror. The man had red eyes. His eyes weren't bloodshot. No. The irises of his eyes were deep maroon red! There were no colored contact lenses back when this occurred in the mid seventies. There was no explanation as to why this particular man would have red irises.

Jeanie only looked into this strange man's eyes for a second. Still, she could feel him tugging at her soul with those penetrating eyes.

"Oh God!" Jeanie said to herself in a panic. "He's trying to pull my soul right out from my body!" Jeanie quickly pulled free of the man's piercing gaze and walked outside crying. She didn't know what to do. She didn't know exactly where she was. She didn't know how she would get home. What she did know was she didn't want to be in the same room with the man with the scary eyes. She didn't even want to be in the same house with him.

Raphael walked outside to where the confused girl stood. Jeanie sensed that he was good and only wanted to help her. The bewildered girl looked at Raphael and cried.

"I don't want to leave this earth yet. There's so many beautiful things here. I don't want to leave them behind. There is so much more I want to see. So much more I want to do. I love nature and all its beauty. I love sunrises and sunsets and the rainbows that bring color to the sky." As Jeanie cried, Raphael placed his arms gently around her trembling shoulders.

As the angelic man held her he said, "Some people are basically good and other people are basically bad and you Jeanie…well you are right in the middle."

For that night Raphael was the protector of Jeanie's soul. He guided her past Curly. He walked with her past the chair where the scary man with the red eyes previously sat. Raphael led Jeanie past the Satanic, goat head picture, and walked her into his bedroom. The sweet, tender man held Jeanie tightly as she rested her head on his shoulders. While fully clothed all the protective man did all night was hold the distressed girl. She laid there wide eyed all through the night and allowed her angel to comfort her.

Jeanie was afraid to close her eyes. She was afraid to go to sleep. The shaken girl's head remained on Raphael's shoulders all evening. She didn't leave his bed or his presence until she saw the sun shine through the window. She survived the night. She was alive to see the dawn of a new day. Jeanie quietly moved her head off the protective shoulders of Raphael and walked out the door without uttering a word of thanks to the sleeping angel. She naturally bummed a ride home. Yes, it was good to be home. Although her place was small, dumpy and sparsely furnished…it was good to be home.

The incident that surrounded Raphael and the scary man with the penetrating red eyes left Jeanie quite bewildered. She wouldn't soon forget what happened that night. Despite the evening's warning, Jeanie proceeded to go back to the wild, reckless life she had previously led.

As usual when the money situation got rough, Jeanie once again sought employment at one of the clubs as a dancer. She had been working at that particular club now for a few weeks. Out of loneliness and the need to save money, Jeanie moved into a small house with a dancer she befriended there. The two of them had many interesting and unpredictable adventures at their place of employment. Jeanie remembers one incident in particular.

The lively lady routinely dated the guys she met at the club. Although most of them only wanted the emotionally needy girl for one thing, that was ok by her. They gave her affection and she gave them sex. Not a fair trade. Still, it was better for Jeanie to be romanced by a stranger, then to be alone. The last thing she wanted to be was alone at night, without someone to hold her…someone to comfort her. When it started getting late in the evening, the wanton girl would set her sights on one of the men at the club and stay with him exclusively until the bar closed.

During the last hour before the club shut it's doors for the evening, Jeanie hung around one person exclusively. That someone was who she planned to be with for that evening. That young, horny man bought Jeanie several high-priced drinks and expected her to give him a night of sex. Jeanie probably would have left with her previously chosen man if it wasn't for the handsome, bearded man who had walked into the club just before it closed.

A fair, young man with light brown, wavy hair and a most serene smile entered the bar. When he sat right next to Jeanie, she knew he was the one she was meant to be with that night. The man looked like the pictures Jeanie had seen painted of Jesus Christ. She was instantly drawn to him.

Needless to say the guy she was previously with who bought her all those high-priced drinks wasn't at all happy with the way the evening was ending. The drunkard was irate when Jeanie left with Jesus' twin. He followed her to his car and started pounding on the her date's hood. Chris pulled a gun out of the glove box and stepped out his car while holding the gun barrel down. He didn't actually point the weapon at the bar patron, but he wanted the troublemaker to know that he had one just in case he needed it. After a matter of minutes, a police car pulled up alongside Chris' car. Since he didn't actually threaten the other man, he was just given a verbal warning and allowed to leave the scene unshackled.

That night Jeanie spent her time with Chris. The couple talked and kissed half the night. Chris told Jeanie in one of their serious conversations,

"I recently broke up with my girl friend. She got herself pregnant after I told her I didn't want kids. I like children. I just don't want to bring them up in the world as it is now. Some people think that by having children they achieve immortality. I guess it's important to them to leave something on this earth behind to prove they were here. Do you feel that way too?"

Jeanie looked him in the eyes and without even thinking she told him "No."

Chris casually placed the loaded gun he had in the car earlier on the headboard of the bed the two of them shared. They had a very intense, sexual relationship. Afterwards both Jeanie and Chris meditated. Some strange thoughts kept popping into Jeanie's head while she meditated.

If she was to reach the astral plane, this man would probably shoot her in the head. By destroying her body, her soul would be released. Jeanie wondered if that was the only way she could be free of all her troubles. Maybe if she was dead, she would find peace. So far her life had been anything but peaceful for her.

Being more nervous than hungry, Jeanie got up after several minutes and prowled through Chris' home searching for something to eat. She found a box of macaroni and cheese and fixed it up the best she could without butter or seasoning. After eating the whole pan full, Jeanie craved something sweet. She left what may have been her final resting ground and walked to the local convenience store. She had to have her junk food fix. From there, she hiked home all the while trying to sort out the evening's events. She couldn't help but wonder what would have happened to her if she stayed with Chris. Jeanie was too scared to go back to find out, so she continued walking in the direction of her home.

It wasn't long before the girl returned to the nightclub scene. It wasn't long before this sensitive idealist got good and sick of the dirty comments and prodding. Once again she quit her place of employment. One more time the despondent dancer lived off the money she made from her last job for a week or two. That little vacation away from that place would help her forget about all that crap she had to put up with working there. Sooner or later though she would always return to work as a dancer at another club on the Bossier strip.

Life was just one up and down battle to Jeanie. She didn't know what she wanted but she knew what she didn't want. She was sick of the nightclub scene. She was sick of hustling drinks. She was sick to death of being with guys who didn't give a damn about her.

That New Year's Eve she spent at the night club dancing for tips. However at 2 a.m. the next morning when the club closed, she went home alone. The girl cried hot bitters tears while she listened to her girlfriend and her long-term boyfriend make love through the paper thin walls that separated their bedrooms.

It was shortly after New Year's when Jeanie started getting a terrible bout of depression. Usually, when the sensitive soul got depressed, she could at least function. Now she had all she could do to get out of bed and face the day. Jeanie got so down that she could no longer drag herself to work. The girl was aware of her loneliness. It drilled holes in her heart. She was aware of her emotional pain but she didn't know what to do to stop the excruciating pain from completely gnawing out her heart. Alcohol didn't even make the pain go away. Sex did for while, but in the morning even if she was still lying next to someone, the pain inside would once again come barreling in. There was nowhere to go, no place she could run…to escape the deep emotional despair that was slowly destroying her.

Jeanie could understand why she had been feeling a lot worse lately then she had in her recent past. It was almost one year now since her father was murdered. Just thinking about what happened to her dad made the distraught girl cry. Jeanie knew she had to get out of town the following weekend. She couldn't be anywhere close to where the horrible crime took place. She knew if she stayed there in Sin City, she would go insane.

Thankfully, three days before the anniversary of that tragic day in January, Jeanie got an invitation to go to New Orleans. Naturally, the girl jumped at the prospect of leaving the area her dad was murdered in. So, with just the clothes on her back, Jeanie jumped in the car with Ben and Sonny. She met the two men when she first came to town nine months ago. She dated one of them a few times in the past. She was sure Ben probably expected Jeanie would be his little toy for the weekend. Jeanie would be content to play that role just so she could escape from this location. The two guys promised her a good partying weekend. That was just what Jeanie needed to get out of the solemn mood that was threatening to destroy her shattered spirit.

## CHAPTER 7

# A Week To Remember

The trio arrived in the New Orleans area later on the same night. While en route to their destination Jeanie and her friends enjoyed each other's company. With all that pot smoking and kidding around the girl soon began to forget about how badly she was feeling inside.

As long as Jeanie was getting high, perhaps she wouldn't have to face how miserable she had been since her father died. The lonesome girl felt like an orphan. Although there were many miles between Jeanie and her father throughout her teenage years, she felt a certain bond with him. She may have looked like her mother but she had many of her father's personal characteristics. They were sensitive and artistic with a passion for life. When he died the year before, Carmalita Jean felt that a part of her had died. The grieved, shocked girl became even angrier at the monster who shot her dad when he was released from prison.

Jeanie lost all faith in society...all faith in the justice system...all faith in God. If there was indeed a God, why did he let this horrible thing happen to her dad? He may have had his flaws, but he was a good loving man. He even studied the Ministry and for awhile was a preacher at a little Southern church. What good had Leif's faith in a loving God gotten him? It got him nothing but a bullet in the head when he tried being nice to a fellow human being. That was his reward for being good, for being kind, for being loving.

"Dad didn't get what he deserved!" cried Jeanie. "I didn't get what I deserved on that hill eight years ago either! I didn't deserve to be beaten on a regular basis by someone who supposedly loved me. I definitely didn't deserved to be bullied on a daily basis from my lovely classmates either!" Unfortunately those incidents happened. There was no denying the pain they caused Jeanie and how her life had changed for the worse following them.

Ben, Sonny and Jeanie were welcomed into the small apartment of their friends in New Orleans. Upon entering the condo, she was immediately hit with the unmistakable smell of pot. A person could get high just breathing the smoke filled air! Everyone seemed to be passing joints. Jeanie was quick to get in the midst of the action. The little lass was getting stoned out of her mind and she liked it.

After Jeanie smoked a little more pot, she began to open up to some of the friendly strangers around her. Weed had been jokingly referred to as character for it tended to open up one's personality. Often people become less inhibited when they're under the influence of pot. She was no exception.

Jeanie liked being high. When she was high, she felt at ease in her world. She felt it was all right to say what was on her mind without being afraid of what people thought. When the girl was high, the carefree girl was happy to laugh, to feel, to be!

When the social isolate was straight, she had a totally different personality. Jeanie had a tendency to withdraw into her little shell. When she was straight, she didn't like to be around many people. She was intimidated by people. She didn't trust them. Too many people had let the sensitive girl down. When straight Jeanie questioned who her friends were. When she was high... she didn't care.

The crowded apartment in New Orleans where all the parties occurred belonged to two young men, Jimmy and Jim Lee. Jimmy was the sociable one with all the friends. Jim Lee was a loner. Occasionally Jim Lee would peak his head into the living room to make a limited appearance. Most of the time when home he stayed by himself in his room and listened to music. Being a loner at heart Jeanie was immediately attracted to Jim Lee.

In between quiet times spent with Jim Lee, Jeanie had a good time with her partying friends in the other room. The group of friendly strangers talked about everything. Some of the topics of conversation Jeanie remembered being involved in was littering, wasting water, getting high, eating habits and yes even sex. Her group of earthy friends were heavily involved with the health of the ecological system as well as themselves. Despite their heavy smoking, they were good moral people who genuinely cared about others and the things around them. One of the girls who was part of the partying club made a reference to Jeanie's wild promiscuous ways.

"It's really not good for someone to have sex with every body they meet, you know dear," the long silken hair lady said matter-of-factly to the stoned girl. That fact hit a really big nerve with Jeanie. In her heart she knew what her friend said was all true.

Another girl who Jeanie just met minutes ago walked up to her and said, "You don't just love one person. You love everybody."

Jeanie did indeed have genuine love for people, but she was sure that was not what her new friend was referring to. It undoubtedly meant that Jeanie had sex with two many different partners. That may be true…but so what? What harm was she doing by having sex with a variety of men?. After all…the sex was consensual. Still it wasn't right to spread the honey too thin.

Jeanie had sex with so many people because she craved so much affection and couldn't find anyone who wanted to stay with her for more than a few short days. Although Jeanie wanted to have a beautiful true love to call her own, she didn't have any idea how to sustain a healthy relationship. It's quite sad to think that the poor underloved sweetie was responsible for much of her own misery. If she looked inside her heart long enough, she would have realized that. Still, admitting one's shortcomings was hard. Trying to overcome the obstacles keeping one from happiness was harder still.

Jeanie could see how having relationships with so many different people was harming her character. The girl hurt so much inside already, she didn't need to inflict anymore poison darts into her heart. She tried to calm the throbbing pain within by having sex with her harem of men…but it didn't work. The terrible feeling within may have been temporarily erased from the distraught girl's mind through the sex act. Still, the horrible hollowness which engulfed her heart afterwards created an even bigger chasm inside her being. Every time Jeanie gave her body to another uncaring thrill seeking man, she lost a little more of herself. It's true Jeanie wasn't hurting others through her wild ways. No, she was hurting herself.

There was only one bedroom in the apartment of Jeanie's New Orleans friends and it belonged to Jim Lee. Everyone who remained at the party that first night slept on the floor. Jeanie slept on the carpet in the living room herself. Human bodies were sprawled across all the chairs, couches and much of the floor space. Jeanie was thankful that she didn't have to get up to go to the bathroom that night for she surely would have stepped on someone.

The following morning Cheryl, one of the girls who stayed there often, gathered up some laundry to wash. The sweet, honey haired lady offered to put Jeanie's clothes in the washer as well. Since Jeanie didn't have any clothes other than what she had on, she was thankful for her friends kind offer. While waiting for her blue jeans and T-shirt to be laundered, the half dressed dancer lounged around in a loosely wrapped robe. Jeanie was going to remain in Jim Lee's room until her clothes were returned to her, but she heard some excitement going on in the next room.

Curiosity prompt the girl to open the bedroom door and enter into the filled living quarters. Eight people were clustered around the 19 inch TV. Two of the visitors sat actively engaged in a game of TV tennis. After watching the action for a while Jeanie thought it looked like fun and that she wanted to play. It proved difficult holding on to the robe with one hand and the control knob with the other. At first the brave beginner did a great job at the challenging game but slowly Jeanie's skills started slipping.

Ben said to the girl in a playful manner, "You're going to lose it!"

Jeanie wasn't sure if he was talking about the game or her loose robe. Not knowing what to do Jeanie joked with her friends while trying to hide her crimson colored cheeks.

Yes, Jeanie was fast learning one of the important rules of life. If something hurts you or embarrasses you, laugh it off. Even if it feels like your guts are being ripped out…laugh it off. Can't let anybody see how vulnerable you are inside. Hide your sensitivity, your personality. Hide from everybody…including yourself.

That was the main reason Jeanie kept herself sky high on pot or booze. Being afraid of other people was one thing. Being afraid of herself, her emotions, her thoughts, was something Jeanie could not handle. She felt so weak inside. So unprotected…so vulnerable.

There was no one in the world to be strong for Jeanie. Basically, she had to be strong for herself. However, she wasn't strong for herself. Now, that her beloved dad was dead, there was no one in the world to rescue her now. Jeanie felt betrayed by the world. She gave up on hope. She gave up on God. She gave up on herself.

Ben and Sonny left for Bossier City two days after their arrival. Jeanie liked being with her new friends so much that she chose to stay. As happy as she was there, the carefree girl didn't care if she ever went home.

The misplaced misfit finally had a place where she felt at home. It was fun getting to know her kind, newfound friends.

The carefree girl also started to spend a good deal of time with Jim Lee, the loner. Since the two of them became more than friends, Jeanie naturally went from sleeping on the hard floor to sleeping on top of Jim Lee's soft bed. She liked the guy, but he was hardly ever home. When Jim Lee was on the road, Jeanie spent a great deal of time conversing with the other people who routinely visited the household.

Cheryl was closest to Jimmy, (Jim Lee's roommate), and she took the role of mother to all. The young caring lady cleaned and cooked like a typical mother would. Eventually Cheryl and Jeanie shared the household duties. Jeanie didn't mind helping out. She wanted to feel like she earned her keep. After all, it wasn't right to keep taking without giving something back.

Since Jeanie had a lot of time to herself, she spent the majority of her time singing and dancing. The guys at the apartment had a variety of music to choose from and Jeanie loved music. This place had to be her idea of how heaven must be. There she was with people who loved her and treated her like family. She didn't have a lot of responsibilities or stress. Jeanie did a small amount of work there, but mostly she just had fun. She hoped fervently that the good times there would never stop. Still, like it or not change happens. All sorts of changes would occur just when she would least expect it. That evening was no exception.

The night started out like any other night. The living room was filled with people and everybody was smoking one joint after another. Jeanie began to feel really airy, so she decided to try to meditate. The girl walked over to the table in the other room to tend to her spiritual needs. A tall youth sat at the table already, and was in deep meditation. Much to Jeanie's amazement, the man used a mirror to meditate.

"Why are you gazing into the mirror that way?" the perplexed girl asked.

The man smiled a big toothy grin towards Jeanie's direction. "When I look into my eyes, I can see my soul."

After a few minutes, the elaborate looking mirror was offered to Jeanie. She reluctantly picked it up and held it close to her face. She tried looking beyond her brown eyes, deep within the glass… but she could see nothing, only red glazed eyes. Either she wasn't high enough or she didn't have a soul. Without giving the scene anymore thought, Jeanie put down the mirror and returned to the living room to smoke another joint.

After listening to another hour of partying jam music, Jeanie decided she needed some quiet time. Silently, the girl plopped down in the corner of the carpeted room. She sang "The Stairway to Heaven" silently to herself. While she sat there gazing at Jimmy's relaxed body draped over the chair, Jeanie had a vision. She saw a crown of thorns magically appear on Jimmy's head like the ones Jesus wore on his head the day of his crucifixion.

Jeanie thought she surely must be hallucinating, but then maybe not. After all marijuana does increase one's sensitivity. Perhaps the enlightened girl envisioned Jimmy as being the figure of Christ for he was so Christ like in nature. Jeanie was certain that she subconsciously put the feelings she felt towards him into familiar images. She probably related Jimmy to Christ because he was so good, so gentle, so honest and true.

Jeanie shook off the weird vision she had concerning Jimmy being Christ. That whole night had been so strange. First that peculiar young man at the table and his fixation of seeing his soul to his eyes and then this strange vision. Jeanie thought it was unusual that she had so many thoughts concerning God since she'd been down in New Orleans. Up until that week she had convinced herself that God didn't exist. However, what could she make out of the strange things happening around her? Stranger things than that was going to occur before the night was over, only Jeanie didn't know it at that time.

Jeanie sought out a different place to meditate after that strange vision of Jimmy with the thorns over his head. The girl chose to sit in a lotus position directly behind the easy chair which

Jimmy sat previously. She would not be in anyone's way there, the dazzled girl thought. The chair muffled the light and created an unusual atmosphere as well. As Jeanie closed her eyes, a crescent moon appeared in her mind. Suddenly a strange feeling came over her. It felt like her spirit was being pulled away from her body. Thinking that she must surely be dying, panic overcame the frightened girl. Tenseness took over Jeanie's previously relaxed state and her spirit plunged back into her body as though it was made of lead. Something strange was going on here, but Jeanie was clueless as to what it was.

After losing all ideas of meditating for awhile, Jeanie returned to her partying friends. While relaxing on the leather like sofa, she engaged in a conversation with Cheryl. The sweet, mother like girl convinced Jeanie that it was time for her to return to her home.

Cheryl made the energetic woman /child feel better about her dancing career. "There is nothing wrong with dancing," she told her in a convincing tone.

There may not be anything wrong with the dancing itself, but the atmosphere wasn't the greatest. Still, Jeanie decided she wouldn't feel so bad about herself performing in the clubs. They would at least offer the girl an honest way to make money until she found herself a more suitable position. It wouldn't be so bad returning now especially since she'd shed some weight on her purification diet. She regained some of the self-esteem she had lost when she gained those few pounds. She also regained the vitality that she had lost.

Cheryl's conversation quickly changed from Jeanie's dancing career to something the girl kept carefully hidden from all. Out of the blue, Cheryl began talking about Jeanie's abortions. How would Cheryl know that about me? Jeanie thought. She hadn't told anyone in New Orleans about it. The two guys she came down here with surely didn't know. She wasn't proud of what she did, so very few people knew that about her. That memory, along with several others, were buried in the past along with the other family skeletons. Gina, her girlfriend in Shreveport knew about her abortion as well as her past life with Slugger. However Gina did not know the guys Jeanie came down here with, and she hadn't told anyone else those secrets. How could Cheryl know that about her?

Jeanie felt so bad, that she struggled hard to keep the tears back as they welled up in her eyes. She dabbed them with her finger as they slid down her reddened cheeks.

"I can't take care of a baby. I can't even take care of myself!" The shaken girl replied. Cheryl nodded her head, and gave her friend a knowing smile. She showed the distraught girl much understanding. She accepted Jeanie unconditionally. She didn't judge her. No. She didn't hold the pitiful past against her.

Although Cheryl was close to Jeanie's age (about 19 or 20) she started to think of her friend as more of a mother. Cheryl was a beautiful, all knowing mother figure, perfect in every sense like the Virgin Mary.

As if Cheryl wasn't filled with enough surprises, she changed the conversation once again. The subject this time was Jeanie's father. She knew Jeanie was physically attracted to her dad. Jeanie however nearly choked, when Cheryl asked "Did you ever go to bed with him?"

"No! He was my father!" Jeanie quickly shouted.

"Love," Cheryl smiled "is eternal. Perhaps your father was to be your soul mate. You want someone just like you…just like your father don't you?"

Yes, that is what Jeanie wanted, but how did she know that? How did this woman know all the things about Jeanie that she did? Just who was she anyway?

Cheryl's conversation ended with the arrival of a tall, scrawny character named Bert. Now Bert liked Jeanie a lot. He liked her much more than she liked him. Although Bert was quite nice, he was physically unappealing to Jeanie. When he asked her out, she was stunned. Since the sensitive girl didn't like to hurt people's feelings, she couldn't very well say "No, I don't want to go with you because you're too ugly". No, that would be too cruel. Instead Jeanie explained how there were some people she wanted just for friends. She told him that she didn't want anything to come between their friendship, so she didn't think they should go out together. Jeanie was relieved when Bert dropped the subject and stopped coming on to her.

Cheryl, Jimmy and their followers were truthful people who abhorred lies. Yet, when Cheryl later approach Jeanie about her earlier conversation with Bert, she told her friend the truth.

Jeanie looked Cheryl in the eye and told her, "I didn't want to hurt his feelings, so I told him a lie."

"Yes, at times little white lies are acceptable, especially when these lies saved the feelings of another human being," Cheryl sweetly reassured her. Jeanie smiled at her friend for she knew she did the right thing telling that particular lie.

The next morning, Bert came over to the apartment to share in the companionship of his friends. Jeanie was alone in the kitchen cleaning up the breakfast dishes when Bert struck up a conversation with her. Jeanie explained to her likable buddy that she wanted to go home, but didn't know how she would get there. She had no money of her own nor any transportation. Bert offered to take the misplaced waif home if she would help him clean his apartment.

Bert's apartment was an absolute disaster! Jeanie looked around in amazement. It was hard for her to believe that anyone could live in such a mess. There were two sinks full of dirty dishes. The plates were crusted with food particles that had been left on so long they were practically concreted onto them. She could barely see the living room floors with all the paper and cans littering it. The bathroom stunk with urine and the toilet bowl was stained yellow. This would definitely take awhile to clean! That's guys for you Jeanie said to herself as she shook her head in disgust.

Bert and Jeanie spent several hours cleaning the filthy apartment. It was so clean when the two tornadoes tore through it, that it practically shined. After they had performed the near impossible feat, Bert went to Jimmy's apartment which was at the other end of the apartment complex. He told Jeanie that he wanted Jimmy to help him move a large wooden chest.

Bert arrived back at the apartment with his friend Jimmy. Jeanie followed the boys outside. Together they walked down a connecting path of the condos. Bert and Jimmy struggled to carry out the large wooden chest. Jeanie walked behind them and watched the struggle while she listened to their conversation.

Although Jeanie was trailing behind Jimmy and Bert, she could hear parts of their conversation. "I feel sorry for whoever gets this half because it's going to be heavy." For some reason Jeanie got the impression they were talking about her oversized derrière. She pictured the wooden chest as being a coffin…her coffin!

As Jeanie walked, she became increasingly aware of the bright moon as it peered over her shoulder. It was almost beckoning her to come to it. Then, as the girl walked past the pond, she felt a strange weakness come over her. Jeanie's body felt totally drained of energy. She felt all the life she had in her flow from her physical shell. Her legs buckled out from under her. For several minutes, the weakened but alert girl laid in the grass by the pond. She just couldn't move. The very earth around her seemed to be absorbing her energy. Jeanie was strong spirited. So, despite her weakened state, she once again summoned all the strength she could muster to push herself into a sitting position. Once again, the confused girl looked up at the moon. Silently she prayed for strength. Immediately it was given to her.

What a great relief it was when Jeanie finally arrived back at the apartment. She perched herself up on a chair and tried to put the pieces of that perplexing puzzle together. As usual, she would logically sweep away anything that happened. Her world did not make sense, but somehow she had to make sense of it to settle her bewildered mind.

"I was just weak from the diet," Jeanie told herself. Still, that explanation didn't satisfy the disturbed girl. Something strange was going on, not only within the apartment but also within herself. But what?

A very uneventful day followed the confused events of the previous evening. Jeanie spent the day walking in the sun. It's vibrant rays re-awakened her senses. She admired the picturesque countryside, while she breathed in the moist Louisiana air. Sometimes it seemed like she had all the time in the world. She wanted to spend every hour of that day singing and playing in the sunshine. She wanted to enjoy her life to the fullest while enjoying the company and love of her newfound friends.

In the evening of that same day, Jeanie walked into Jim Lee's bedroom to get something out of her purse. There, she saw Jim Lee laid out on the bed wrapped up like a mummy from his neck down. She could actually see the athletic type bandages wrapped over his entire body. The atmosphere in the room was filled with an unusual heaviness as well. The sensitive girl could perceive a thick sense of evil throughout the entire area. She could not blame this feeling on marijuana paranoia for she was totally straight! Jeanie was struck with the most alarming fear. She had to get out of there. Not knowing what else to do she ran. She didn't even take the purse. She was afraid if she didn't leave that second, she would lose her soul.

Except for the people who frequented that apartment, Jeanie knew no one else in town. She was so shook up, that she didn't know what to do. Her life had been filled with such strange events lately. Jeanie felt like a lost little child all alone there in the city. Tears poured from the trembling girl's face. "Oh God help me! What am I going to do?"

Jeanie didn't know what to do. However God had a way of answering prayers even for those who had forgotten how to pray. Before long, a car pulled up beside the troubled girl. A most handsome, fair man asked Jeanie if she was in trouble and offered his assistance. This sweet man was as beautiful on the inside as he was on the outside. He comforted the distraught girl and held her close. Jeanie could feel love in this young man's arms. She could see love in his sky blue eyes.

After riding a few minutes, Sam and Jeanie crossed the long bridge to Metarie, Sam's hometown. Jeanie became acutely aware of the way the moon's brilliance played against the water. The ethereal rays gave the lake a mystical effect. It looked as if a thousand glistening diamonds were being cast upon the water. As Jeanie gazed down at the sparkling springs, she felt like her soul was being purified by it. Her quivering heart felt…so light…so at peace. It was a feeling that the girl had never before experienced.

Sam seemed to drive 100 miles on that endless night. Finally his car pulled up into a driveway. "This is where I live," stated the fair, young man. Without hesitation, Sam and Jeanie stepped out from the car. They walked up the cobble stone path that led to his front door. He gave the girl a quick tour of the downstairs portion of the house, then proceeded to escort the sweet girl to his bedroom upstairs.

Surprisingly, Jeanie wasn't frisked as expected, but was treated like a lady. When one is treated like a lady, one usually acts like a lady. Obviously, Jeanie wasn't treated like anything but a whore since she danced in a grimy nightclub. No, she couldn't expect to be respected there. She didn't even respect herself working in a sleazy nightclub where one's morals were constantly jeopardized. Jeanie thought the dancing job was perfect for her at the time since she loved to dance, sing and listen to music. Now she realized how wrong that place was for her.

The atmosphere in Sam's room was completely different from that of the club. Sam serenaded Jeanie with his electric guitar. His long fingers glided across the strings with ease. The two sang together beautifully as if their hearts and voices belonged together.

A most unusual conversation came about as Jeanie gazed at the mobile hanging from Sam's ceiling. It was a model of our solar system. Although Jeanie studied astronomy in school years ago, she couldn't recall the order of the planets. She could pick out Saturn with its' tell tale rings and of course earth, but she couldn't name the others. When Sam asked Jeanie if she knew what planets were in the solar system, she was embarrassed because she couldn't name them all.

"Do you know what planet is past Jupiter?" Sam inquisitively asked. Jeanie couldn't say. He then asked the girl, "Which planet do you think your spirit comes from?"

Jeanie quickly responded, "Venus, because that's the planet of love." Sam looked at Jeanie and smiled, a most beautiful, serene smile. He looked like an angel and acted like one too!

After Sam and Jeanie were together for awhile, he suggested that he should take her home. Jeanie was afraid to return to the apartment where all the strange events took place. With much hesitation, she returned to Sam's car. The ride back to the apartment seemed so much shorter than the ride over to his house. Sam gave Jeanie a tender kiss at the door and slowly walked back to his car.

Jeanie definitely didn't return to Jim Lee's bedroom. She locked herself in the bathroom and spent the night on the rug next to the tub. She wasn't very comfortable, for she kept banging her head on the feet of the porcelain vanity. However, she felt safe... somewhat. Right now what Jeanie needed more than anything else, was to feel safe.

Gratefully morning finally arrived. Jeanie was somewhat sore and very confused about the events of the previous night. Still, she was filled with happiness and excitement about meeting such an honorable, handsome, young man.

Cheryl and an Indian girl named Rosalita were among the early risers of the day. Jeanie must've been beaming for Rosie said to Jeanie as she smiled, "Pretty is as pretty does."

Jeanie did feel beautiful inside, especially when she sang. She felt such love nestled in Sam's arms. The good feelings must have carried over into the next day for all to see.

Smiling, Jeanie told the girls about the Sam. They grinned back at the glowing girl and one of them said, "He's quite handsome isn't he?"

Perhaps they already knew him or maybe they saw his face illuminated in the moonlight when he brought her back the night before. Cheryl asked how old Sam was. Jeanie was almost embarrassed to admit that he was only 18 (Jeanie was 21).

"He's really smart isn't he?" stated Cheryl. Indeed he was. Sam had so much going for him. He was handsome, musical and intelligent, but he also had a fiancée. Unlike Jeanie he was probably pure of body and soul. That thought made Jeanie sad. She already carried deep feelings in her heart for Sam. She hesitated to call these feelings love, after all she just met him. She also questioned whether she knew what love was at all.

Rosalita must have noticed that Jeanie's mind was in a cloud of perplexity and confusion. She reached for her hand and placed something inside it. The object was a piece of teak wood with a small round notch carved into the middle of it. Upon receipt of that small piece of wood, Jeanie rubbed it. Soon her fears and nervousness vanished. Her nervous energy seemed to flow from her fingers into the wood. She felt an indescribable calmness inside her body. What was so special about that little piece of wood Jeanie wondered.

For the past few days Jeanie was aware of some strange sensations within her body. Something just didn't feel right inside. She hitchhiked down the road in search of a health clinic. Along the main highway, Jeanie found a doctor's office. She entered the doors to the clinic and made out the admittance form. Since the girl didn't have a job, money or insurance, the doctor refused to see her.

Jeanie was convinced that there was something horribly wrong inside her. Perhaps these strange experiences she had were preparing the poor thing for the afterlife. Jeanie cried. Although she had endured many unhappy events in this life, who's to say how happy she would be in the after life.

After leaving the clinic, Jeanie hitchhiked to Metarie to find Sam. She was intrigued by the angelic sweet man, and found him beautiful in every way. Sam seemed to know everything about Jeanie. It was a mystery how he knew as much about her as he did. He knew what was inside the confused girl's mind, and he also knew what was inside her enormous heart.

Jeanie waited at Sam's house for a few minutes. Shortly, a car pulled up and out stepped two rather robust figures. Jeanie assumed they were Sam's parents. His younger sister was also in the vehicle with them. Upon exiting the car, his sister became focused on the teakwood and feather talisman Jeanie held tightly in her hand. His sister saw how upset Jeanie was and blamed it on that foreign object. She thought the teakwood was some kind of supernatural, evil object. Sam's sister plucked the soothing piece of wood from the wide eyed girl's hand without uttering a word.

Sam's parents were wiser than his little sister. They explained to their daughter that it was just a piece of wood. If Jeanie wanted to calm herself by rubbing it, then let her. Being quite nervous, Jeanie was grateful to get the teakwood back.

Thoughts kept popping into Jeanie's mind while waiting for Sam. Sam lived on Athena Street. Isn't she the goddess of love in mythology? My friends lived across the bridge in Kenner. Can her? Can she? Can she what? Can she pass the test? Sam lived in Metarie. Met hurry or met Aries. Aires being the ram. Isn't the ram the symbol for Satan?

Jeanie's mind was caught in a whirlpool of thought. She was so happy when Sam finally walked into the living room. He appeared surprised to see Jeanie. Still he greeted the needy girl with a gentle embrace.

After Sam grabbed a quick meal, he once again escorted Jeanie upstairs to his bedroom. The girl left behind all her previous fears when she entered Sam's room. Jeanie felt so at ease. She felt like she belonged with Sam, in his room, enveloped in his loving arms. Jeanie wanted Sam to love her mentally, spiritually, and physically. He wouldn't make love to Jeanie though. He only said "fornication is breaking God's law." Keeping God's laws were very important to the spiritually attuned young man.

Sam was still an untouched virgin. That was probably why Jeanie could see a white aura around his head as he played his guitar. Sam was pure in both body and mind.

Shortly after dinner, Sam guided Jeanie into his bedroom. She was aware of the light, airy atmosphere in the room. It was unlike anything she had felt before. There in the blue walled room, Jeanie felt totally loved and accepted. She felt so much love radiating from Sam as well. The girl wanted to kiss, cuddle and make love all through the night. Although Sam cared about Jeanie, he refused her offer to go to bed with him. The love that Sam was after, was hid deep inside Jeanie's soul and not within her sensuous body.

Jeanie was content to rest her head on Sam's shoulder while engaged in light conversation. While she laid there beside him, she stroked his smooth, bare, chest. His skin was as fair and unblemished as his heart.

While laying besides Sam, Jeanie suddenly became very conscious of the loud roar the furnace was making. She felt a tugging inside her heart every time the furnace would come on. It felt like a giant vacuum was trying to suck up her soul. Jeanie cried. If Sam was pure of heart and body then perhaps through Sam's love she also became pure. Perhaps Sam had come to cleanse Jeanie's soul in preparation of the afterlife which she would be journeying into soon.

As Jeanie laid beside Sam all she could think about was if she was going to die that night. Only her strong will and fear of the unknown kept her from reaching the other side. Although Jeanie's life had been previously void of prayers, the frightened girl prayed fervently. She prayed to her father in heaven all through the night, "God of love, God of mercy, help me!"

Jeanie was glad to see the morning come after such a restless and frightening night. Upon awakening the girl followed the sound of some voices and wound up in the kitchen. Sam's mother and father were there sipping their favorite hot beverage. Sam's mother stood in the corner of the big room where as his father sat alone with his newspaper at the table.

When Sam's dad left the area, his mother talked to Jeanie about some very personal matters. She told the wayward girl how wrong it was to go to bed with all those different men.

"I just wanted to feel I was loved, if only for a minute or so," Jeanie told her sheepishly bowing her head in shame. Sam's mother looked at her with love and understanding. She did not judge the mislead girl, nor did she condemn her. For that Jeanie was thankful.

After Jeanie finished the brief conversation with Sam's mother, his dad walked back into the room. At first Jeanie was afraid of him. He appeared to be stern with a straight, rigid facial expression. However, he turned out to be just as compassionate as the mother. Sam's dad proceeded to talk to Jeanie along the same subject his mother had talked earlier. He told Jeanie that there was a venereal disease that originated in Germany in which there was no cure. Jeanie fought back the years. A few months ago she had unprotected sex with a man who had just gotten back from Germany. Perhaps, Jeanie thought, that she contracted this horrible disease and that she was now dying.

Oh God! Jeanie got upset thinking about how she would let her mother down. She thought of all the nasty things people would think of her for dying in such a manner. She didn't want them to think badly of her even though there was just cause for it.

Sam entered the room thus breaking off some of the tension. Jeanie tried to put things together in her mind. Jim Lee is the father, Jimmy the son, and Sam is the Holy Ghost.

Sam must have been reading Jeanie's mind for he smiled at the confused girl and said, "You almost got it." Perhaps Sam's father was "the Father". Who or what was Jim Lee the one who was wrapped up like a mummy?

Sam's dad again spoke to Jeanie. "Jehovah is more than just a God of love and mercy. You must realize that. You must acquaint yourself with the Bible to become more familiar with Jehovah and his laws."

After that short conversation, Sam reached for Jeanie's left hand and walked out of the kitchen with her. Only after the two of them were alone in the living room that Sam began to speak.

"I think you left home too soon," he said. Perhaps he was right. Jeanie probably should have made sure she was financially and emotionally secure before leaving the nest. She did however survive 12 years in the school despite the bullying, so she considered that an accomplishment.

Sam spoke softly to Jeannie, "I think it's time you go back to your own place in Bossier. Once you've straightened your life around, I'll come back for you."

Although Sam didn't say so in words, Jeanie knew what he meant. He meant that Jeanie should quit smoking pot, drinking and fooling around. She wondered if she could leave behind those worldly things she enjoyed so much. Sam also told Jeanie she should join the Jehovah witnesses and get to know God through the Bible. She had read parts of the Bible when she was involved in a Christian youth group years ago. The Bible confused her. So much of what she read just didn't make sense. Still, she would try to take time to read it.

Tomorrow," stated Sam, "I will take you home." Jeanie knew inside that she really should go back to the security of her little shack, but she didn't want to leave Sam's side. She didn't want to leave her group of friends there either, but leave she must.

Early the next morning, Jeanie and Sam started on the long journey to Bossier City. Surprisingly, Sam stopped along the way to pick up a friend. The young man Sam invited along for the ride was also quite blonde and handsome. Part way through the journey Sam's friend lit up a joint. Jeanie wanted to smoke some of it in the worst way…but she didn't. Sam gave her an approving smile. Yes, Jeanie passed the first test, the first trial of many yet to come. Finally, the long journey came to an end. The girl was glad to get out and stretch her legs. Her mood saddened quickly however with the realization she may never again see sweet Sam.

Jeanie tiny house was quite shabby and sparsely furnished. Nevertheless it was hers. It was home. Jeanie was ashamed to let Sam come in for it was far inferior to his large, beautiful brick home.

To add to her embarrassment, Jeanie could not find her key. In order to enter her little cubby, she had to climb in through the back window. Sam didn't say a word when she unlatched the front door to let him in. Just being polite Jeanie thought. Reluctantly, she gave Sam a quick tour of her shabby shack ending with her bedroom.

Upon entering the doorway, Sam lifted Jeanie up in his arms as though she were a bride being carried over the threshold. Her eyes were fixed on Sam's clear, blue eyes. While she gazed into his sparkling orbs, she felt absolutely no fear…just a great inner peace. With her eyes fixed on Sam's, the angelic man carried Jeanie over to her bed. He held her over the mattress and allowed her body to free fall on to it's cushioned surface. Jeanie fell without fear. She puts her total trust into this unearthly being.

Before leaving Sam looked deep within her eyes, "You do all the things I've told you and I'll come back to you."

Sam hugged Jeanie one last time before he turned away from her. She watched her saving prince twist the doorknob of the front door. She watched him as he walked away from her house and got into the car where his friend sat waiting. With tears in her eyes Jeanie watched the man she barely knew but deeply love walk out of her life forever.

Yes, Sam departed from Jeanie's life that day, yet the thought of that sweet mysterious man lingers on. Who exactly was this strange man who knew her every thought? Who was this beautiful being who mysteriously knew every detail of her life? The memory of that perplexing week haunts Jeanie still. After all these years…it haunts her still.

# CHAPTER 8

# Shadows

One might think that after that supernatural weekend Jeanie would've pulled her life together. She tried to get her life straight…at least for while. Jeanie thought that if she could stop her pot smoking and boozing, she would be able to tame her wild sexual escapades as well. Perhaps if she said goodbye to her seductive sex games and flushed her body of the poisons she routinely put it, she would get sweet Sam back.

The fact was, Sam was too good for Jeanie. His soul was as pure white as fresh bleached sheets. Jeanie's soul was severely stained with the repercussions of careless behavior brought on by warped thoughts and a distorted belief system. Her marred soul was deeply hid beneath a thick coat of dust. The grey gauze blanketed around her heart like a protective armor. One could barely see beyond what lay hidden beneath that cloak. Even if the girl did straighten her life around, it didn't change Jeanie's past. She had already been around the block of life a few times already. Could her soul ever be cleansed enough to deserve Sweet Sam's unconditional love? Would she ever be worthy of God's everlasting love? Was she good enough for love at all?

For awhile Jeanie attended church on a regular basis. She even tried reading the Bible, but didn't get much out of it. She just couldn't understand it. Although she desperately wanted to believe everything written in the holy book, many sections in it didn't make any sense. After all, how could a person be swallowed up by a whale and live in his stomach for all those days? How could Adam and Eve suddenly appear out of thin air? What about evolution? Jeanie was sure God made man but he did it through evolution. Yes, many things written in the good book made about as much sense as the fairy tales mother used to read to her as a child.

Although Jeanie was an artist, she had a fairly logical mind when she wasn't stoned. To her, the Bible just regurgitated a handful of stories misinterpreted by a superstitious group of men with caveman intelligence. Although she didn't believe in many of the far fetched stories, she believed in God. She lived through too many unexplainable things not to believe in some type of higher being. There had to be a great, divine entity watching out for her or the consequences of her careless escapades would have snuffed out her life years ago. Jeanie wanted to believe that God had put her on this earth for some purpose. She just didn't know at that time what that purpose was.

Jeanie had been slightly out of touch with reality but not so much where she could not distinguish fantasy from fact. There were times when her idealistic dreams reached beyond practicality. Still, Jeanie knew what was within her grasp and what was not.

For a month or two Jeanie tried to mold herself into the kind of person she thought Sam wanted her to be. Since she could not become such an angel, the disheartened girl gave up trying.

"I'll never be the kind of girl Sam wants or needs," Jeanie said to the Indian princess poster which hung up on her bedroom wall. Since she could not become a perfect angel, Jeanie went back to being the wild lonely girl she had previously been.

She soon became tired of working at the low paying job she currently held at the local seafood restaurant. The girl thought if she was going to be working nights anyway, she might as well work where she got some good money. So, once again Jeanie went back to work at the clubs. As usual, within a few weeks, she was good and sick of that dancing gig as well.

On one very tough night at the club, Jeanie met a nice man who understood her plight. Tom agreed to take the misplaced miss to Alexander, Louisiana. There she could start her life new. The kindly gentleman already had a girlfriend named Amber who worked at the same club as Jeanie. She would be joining them on their trip as well.

Jeanie and Tom would not be having a sexual relationship. That suit her fine. She wasn't physically attracted to Tom in the least. Besides. The bouncy brunette was sick to death of guys using her for a few days or weeks, and then tossing her aside like an old pair of shoes. Jeanie thought that if the two of them were just friends, then she would be able to stay with him and his girlfriend until she became financially stable. An easy, caring, platonic relationship started between Jeanie and her rescuer. This trip to Alexander led the ex-dancer on an interesting but disappointing journey.

Within days of moving to southern Louisiana with her friends, Jeanie found another job. Even though the waitress job didn't pay much, it was just down the street from where she lived. She could just walk to work. Jeanie relied solely on her own two legs to get to work. It seemed like a perfect situation.

After only two weeks of employment, Jeanie's host told her that she must find a place of her own. The young waitress hoped she could stay there for while. She thought she could pay a small amount of money for her board while she saved for a decent apartment. Now, that was out of the question. Jeanie's salary was low. Even with her tips she couldn't afford much for rent. She definitely didn't want to go back to living in a roach infested shack. She didn't want to keep living like an animal. She didn't want to keep working at low-wage jobs either. However, Jeanie didn't have any vocational training, or other job skills. How could she obtain a decent job without some added training somewhere? The girl appeared to be stuck with whatever job options were presented to her. That was when the discouraged girl met Skag.

Shortly after Jeanie's friends evicted her, was when she met Skag. The man was one sly dog. He sweet talked Jeanie into believing that he was everything that she could ever want in a man. The weasel also convinced her that the low funds he presently experienced was temporary. He spent a good part of the morning drinking from his endless cup of coffee, while feeding on Jeanie's sympathy.

"Yup, I've had a barrel of tough luck sweet Miss. Got jumped outside my hotel room last night and lost everything I had. The varmit even stole my car. I guess I'll have to hitchhike to New Mexico to see my brother. I lent him some money while back. Sure could use it now. Say, how about you going out there to New Mexico with me? After I get the bucks owed me by my conniving brother, I'll get us a real nice place together. Little darlin', you don't need to be working in a grease pit like this!"

Skag knew just what to say to send Jeanie packing. Unfortunately there wasn't a word of truth to anything that the scoundrel told the gullible girl, but she didn't find out until much later. That afternoon the two of them gathered their scant belongings and begun the arduous task of hitch hiking across several states. Since the guy didn't have a dime to his name, Jeanie bought the food which kept them both alive until they got to New Mexico.

Eventually the two weary travelers arrived at their destination. Skag did indeed have a brother in Albuquerque. However his brother wasn't the slippery snake Jeanie was told he was. No Scag was! With much embarrassment, Skag's brother told Jeanie how she'd been played a fool. The disillusioned dreamer choked back the tears and walked away with nothing more than a duffle bag full of clothes. She never saw Skag again after that day, nor did she want to. Jeanie's thumb brought her to the local truck stop. Once there, she hitched a ride out of the desert town that had brutally scorched her trusting heart.

Jeanie didn't know where she would go from there. She remembered visiting one of her dad's brothers several years earlier. Jeanie thought since she was fairly close to her Uncle Rodney in proximity, she'd hike up to see him. Maybe her uncle would take in the homeless, penniless girl until she got back on her feet.

Although her relatives were glad to see her initially, Jeanie soon outgrew her welcome. Besides experiencing intense, inner turmoil about her place in the world, Jeanie had the bad luck of getting into poison oak. The once beautiful girl had big, red, itchy patches all over her body including her pretty face.

During the two weeks it took the disillusioned lass to heal her blotchy body, she must eaten her weight in food. The old pattern Jeanie got into when she was younger had resurfaced. When growing up at home, both her mother and herself turned to food for solace in time of stress. When her intense emotions became so strong she felt her heart would burst, Jeanie stuffed food in her mouth. Eat. Eat. Eat. Eat away the hurt. Push down the pain. Push down the guilt. Swallow the loneliness. Swallow away the sadness. As long as a depressed girl ate, She felt better…at least momentarily. Through food she tried to deny the tremendous turmoil that churned within. Unfortunately, no matter how much food Jeanie pushed into her body, she still felt like crap.

It was obvious after two weeks that Jeanie was both an emotional and financial strain for her uncle's family. It was only a matter of time before she was asked to leave their once happy household.

The distraught girl accepted the bus ticket Uncle Rodney purchased for her. With much sadness, Jeanie boarded a bus and headed to Florida. Grandma and Grandpa loved me, Jeanie thought. She was Grandma's little Pipa Squeak. Surely her grandparents would take her in.

After nearly two days on the Greyhound bus, the saddened youth made it to the sunshine State. At first Grandma and Grandpa were happy to see her. But even her loving grandparents could not put up with Jeanie, not the way she was at the present time. She had plummeted into such a state of horrible depression, that there was no crawling out. Their granddaughter did nothing all day but watch TV, eat, and sit around the pool. Jeanie may have wanted to do something productive with her life, but she didn't know what she could do. She definitely didn't want to go back to being a waitress at a little café barely making enough money to live on. She didn't have the money to buy the fancy uniforms to work someplace classier. She probably wouldn't have fit into such an establishment anyway.

The depressed dreamer didn't want to go back to work in the sleazy nightclubs where she felt like a little whore just for being there. Besides Jeanie thought, she was too fat to go back to being a dancer. The more Jeanie thought about her life, the more she attempted to escape from it. TV, like food was her way of escaping the reality of life which so far had been one big disappointment for her.

Although Jeanie's grandparents loved her, they surely couldn't keep her there forever. So, once again Jeanie was pawned off on another relative...this time her mother and stepfather in Connecticut. Jeanie hadn't spoken to her mother or sister since she moved south over a year ago. Both her family members turned their back on her when they found out she was having an abortion. Just when the immature girl needed her family most, they turned their back on her. The bitterness of rejection was hard to swallow. Although the saddened girl didn't want to go back to the cold state, she didn't feel she had much of a choice. She surely couldn't take care of herself at the present time.

Despite the way Jeanie and her mom had ended their relationship the year earlier, the homeless, hopeless wanderer reluctantly boarded the bus. Her trip had a four hour wait period between buses in New York city. That's ok, Jeanie thought, she always wanted to go to New York. Years ago when her grandma lived in Hartford, she told her young granddaughter that upon high school graduation, she would take her to see the sights in New York city. Unfortunately, her grandma and grandpa moved to Florida way before Jeanie graduated. The disappointed teen surmised that grandma probably forgot about that promise, but she certainly didn't. Being there in New York for all those hours would be the closest thing she'd get to that promised trip. So, it was up to her to take advantage of the situation while she could.

Jeanie should have realized that the big city was no place for a gullible, naïve girl to be on her own. At first, she only wandered a few blocks away from the bus station. However, strictly gazing at tall buildings became old fast. The little wanderer wanted to experience more than what she could from the sidewalk's edge. So, she decided to extend her parameter. There was so much to see, so much to do there. However, Jeanie had very little money left, so how far could she go on that?

Grandma gave Jeanie a twenty dollar bill for food before sending her aboard the bus. She had spent over half of her allotted money already on snacks. If she was lucky, she may have enough greenbacks for a couple of drinks and a sandwich. After that… she'd go without. If only there was someplace else she could stay for awhile. Jeanie thought she got her wish when she met Doug.

Doug huffed his hefty load over to the local bus stop bench where Jeanie aimlessly sat. While he waited for the city transportation to take him home, he initiated a conversation with the husky but pretty girl besides him. Doug had recently moved to the city and knew very few people. Obviously the guy was lonely and in need of some company. When Jeanie told the friendly stranger that she was basically homeless and was in the process of crawling back to her mommy, he invited her to stay with him.

Doug lived alone in a little apartment just up the road. It wasn't very big, but big enough for him. The guy had health problems and could certainly use someone to assist him with some of the household duties for a little while. He assured her there were no strings attached. She would merely be required to cook, do some light house cleaning and run errands. Doug appeared sincere in his offer. Jeanie was certainly in no hurry to go live with another relative who didn't want her. After Jeanie pondered her options for a few minutes, she decided to take Doug up on his offer. After all, how bad could it be?

Doug's small apartment had only one bedroom and one bed. That fact alone should have clued the girl in about the guys intentions, but it didn't. Just prior to bedtime, Doug made himself a sleeping spot on his rugged red couch. The cordial man kindly allowed Jeanie to have the bed. The guy treated Jeanie so nicely, surely she could rest peacefully in his comfy, cozy bed. Jeanie definitely didn't expect Doug would make any inappropriate moves on her in the night. However what she didn't expect, never the less happened.

Jeanie awoke in the night with the sweating hog pulling at the buttons of her pants. He nearly ripped them off her trying to get to the hidden honey. Jeanie tried to push the massive man off of her, but it was to no avail. There was little she could do to stop the newly energized monster from forcibly raping her. After he spent every ounce of strength getting his sexual needs fulfilled, he rolled off her. There he laid besides her, enjoying the afterglow, feeling smug and powerful. He continued to lay in a big sweaty heap on the bed besides the angry girl for several minutes, before he fell asleep.

Jeanie didn't bother telling anyone about the rape. After all who would believe her? Even the police would think the sex was consensual. As usual, the gullible girl told herself that she set herself up for the ugly incident. Jeanie talked herself into believing, it was her fault the rape occurred. She might not have verbally asked for it. However she begged for something horrible to happen to her with her naïve thinking and her impulsive actions.

Jeanie definitely shouldn't have left the bus depot. She shouldn't have wandered from the safe sidewalk's edge and she definitely shouldn't have followed that strange man to his apartment. Doug seemed so nice though. Obviously, people aren't always how they seem. Jeanie berated herself for making another stupid mistake. Yes, she was stupid to think that Doug wanted her solely for light housework and companionship. How could she be so stupid? Maybe, Jeanie thought, she deserved everything rotten that had happened to her in life.

"Why do bad things happen to me? Because I'm a bad person. I'm a bad person who does bad things." Jeanie tried to shake off the terrible way she was feeling about herself and the world, but the anger she felt chewed cubby holes in her heart.

"Well, this bad thing isn't my fault!" the sobbing girl said. "I'll show that bastard that he can't do that to me and get away with it!"

While the rapist slept, Jeanie pulled the wallet out of his pants pocket. She slipped inside his billfold and took all the money that the pig had…a whopping $36 "That'll teach him," the bitter girl screamed silently to herself. Just before she walked out of his apartment, she stole the portable TV he kept in the kitchen as well. "I hope he always remembers this night that SOB!" Without so much as a flicker of feeling, Jeanie grabbed the handle of her stolen property and headed to the bus stop. There she waited at the depot for the first bus that would leave the area. Jeanie knew that she would be long gone before Doug awoke to discover his missing things. He should consider himself lucky Jeanie thought. She really wanted to cut off his balls!

Despite her reservations, Jeanie was almost glad to be going back to New England. In many ways she longed to return to her roots. She felt she had to make peace with the past despite what had recently happened to her. Jeanie called her mom along the way to tell her she missed her connecting bus, but would be arriving in Connecticut at ten o'clock the following morning. The girl bit her lip in anticipation and anxiety. She rode the remainder of the bus ride home saying little to anybody.

Along the way, the Greyhound bus stopped a few miles short of her destination for the scheduled breakfast break. The sleepy girl left the bus for a few minutes to use the bathroom and get a drink. While she sat on an outside bench drinking her cola, something strange happened. From out of nowhere a big black bird swooped down on her and came inches from her head. Jeanie didn't have any food with her, so the thing couldn't have wanted what she was eating. No, the dark entity from hell appeared to be trying to scoop out Jeanie's eyes with it's beak. Surely, Satan was trying to claim her soul for all the bad things she had done recently.

Jeanie raced back to the bus and waited inside the safe sausage like vehicle until it once again began to move. She was afraid to go outside. She didn't know what else would be after her. She felt her very soul was in the middle of a tug of war game…and she was on the losing side.

"Oh God, protect me. I'll try to do better…really!" Jeanie didn't know whether God heard her that day or not, but she felt better after she said that little prayer. Jeanie felt comforted. Soon, she would be back into her mom's safe and secure home…but for how long?

Jeanie's mom welcomed her daughter with open arms at the bus depot. She even helped Jeanie get another low wage job working at a pizza parlor making pepperoni pies. Unfortunately, there was much friction created in the household with Jeanie's arrival. Her mother and step father lived a quiet, predictable life before the return of their prodigal daughter. The girl didn't feel at home there. The two appeared to view the girl with suspicious eyes. The atmosphere in the household was so heavy at times that Jeanie just wanted to run, and eventually she did.

Jeanie left her mother's house after less than a month's time. She couldn't wait to get out of there. She had no freedom to do anything other than work. She felt smothered. She almost thought she would be better off in jail. Jeanie had gotten used to certain freedoms living on her own. Now, they were all taken away from her. After Jeanie's mother forbid her daughter to accompany her girlfriend on a rather tame evening out Jeanie knew she had to leave. She'd just assume take her chances in the outside world than live this slow death!

"That's it," Jeanie proclaimed. "I'm out of here!" So again, the wild child headed for the bus depot. This time, she mounted a bus to Arkansas. She had many friends there at one time. Back when Gina and her ran the streets, they had all sorts of friends. Things would undoubtedly be different now though. Jeanie was no longer the raving, tanned beauty of the yesteryears. How receptive would her friends be to her now?

Although Jeanie had put on 20 pounds, she was still an attractive girl. She was also a dynamite lay. For the first month or so in Arkansas, Jeanie fluttered from one man to another. She loved everybody but she loved no one. She would stay a week or two here and a few days there. Life was full of fun and adventure. As long as the wild girl put out, she would always have a place to stay and usually a little something to smoke and eat. Yes, for awhile Jeanie considered that a good life. Unfortunately, that kind of life got old fast.

Once again Carmalita Jean became weary of life's little games. She grew tired of the mutually appealing trade offs. She'd used guys for a place to stay, eat and smoke and they'd use her for sex. At least, Jeanie felt she had some control over the situation. After all both parties knew what the rules were. Still, after awhile, Jeanie wanted more than she felt she could ever have with her buddies. She grew weary of the type of life she had previously settled for. She didn't want to continue to shack up with who ever would have her at the moment. She wanted someone to want to be with her because he truly cared for her. She wanted someone who would stay with her for more than a few fleeting days. Jeanie grew tired of wasting her love on screwball guys that only wanted her for sex.

Since Jeanie knew her job options in the small, familiar town were limited, she hitched hiked to the big city of Little Rock. She wanted to start a new life there. It was in that particular city where she met a guy who she liked and who liked her. He willingly allowed the girl's to stay at his place for more than a few fleeting days. Jeanie even found a waitress job within walking distance from their little love shack. Things started looking up for her...or so she thought.

Jeanie's new man, Picket was a fairly likable person even though he didn't have much ambition. That was okay, for the only thing the carefree girl wanted out of her life at the time was the bare essentials. As long as she had a roof over her head, pot to smoke, something to eat and someone to cuddle with her, she was alright. Unfortunately, after a few months together, Picket started becoming physically abusive to her.

At first the short, small framed man would only give Jeanie an occasional push when he became agitated at the mouthy girl. Before long, the guy's hand would irately slap her because she wouldn't agree with him or do his bidding. Jeanie wasn't about to stay in a relationship like that again!

The same abusive pattern the free bird had with Slugger started all over again with this little runt. Jeanie's hope for a life together with this scrawny man was coming to an abrupt end. The weary waitress made plans to find a small apartment with the money she had saved. She knew she had to get out of Pickets domain. The abuse escalated with every argument. She had to get out of there before she ended up with broken bones.

Jeanie didn't have a car so getting around would be rough. She knew that without transportation, she wouldn't be able to get to her night job. Even if she obtained an apartment in the vicinity, it was unsafe for a single woman to parade the streets alone at night in the big city. The girl certainly didn't make enough money to pay for a taxi every night. It was at that point in her life Jeanie decided she would answer the AD in the paper for someone looking for a live-in housekeeper and cook. The positions specified that she would be working for a couple, so surely she would be free from sexual harassment. It seemed like a good deal. She could live in fairly nice accommodations and not worry about paying rent or how she would get to work. As long as she did her daily duties, she would be ensured of a home.

The house Jeanie lived in was nicely furnished and was located in a fairly safe location in Little Rock. She had an ample sized room nicely decorated with table runners and drapes. The lady of the house left a matching pair of butterfly pictures hanging on the wall as well. Jeanie liked it there. She felt really fortunate to have obtained that position.

The housework itself wasn't strenuous or too time consuming either. In between the daily chores, the housekeeper could do her writing or drawing. When alone, she could play her music loudly and dance with no one bothering her…no one trying to pinch her butt. Since both Candace and Ralph worked during the day, she did not have an employer under her feet. She was basically her own boss. She liked that!

Jeanie thought that she had the ideal situation. However, Candace was extremely jealous of the tanned, young girl. For some reason she thought Jeanie was after her man. Ralph was twice her age and balding with a gut to boot. Why on earth did Candace think she wanted him?

Jeanie didn't want to be with him, but Ralph sure did want to be with her. The girl really didn't want to move again, however she was tired of putting up with the horn dog's propositions every time the misses turned around. So, Jeanie once again searched for another job. Despite the little homemaker's continued bad luck with the various live-in jobs she obtained, she continued to work them.

The fact was, Jeanie liked being a surrogate housewife. She didn't mind the chores and she actually liked cooking. However, what she didn't like was the man of the house propositioning her. Jeanie always had to keep her guard up. Her carefree ways and her natural beautiful were a turn on. Still at times she wished she could turn it off!

Jeanie didn't realize that the seductive way she moved, her colorful style and her long, straight hair, never mind the fact that she went braless, gave everyone the impression she was easy. The very reputation that Jeanie tried to get away from, followed her wherever she went. The poor girl wasn't perceptive enough at the time to understand why that was so.

Jeanie's residency and jobs frequently changed during the following years. Still, the girl felt she had some control over her life. The insecure youth no longer had to live on the streets. Nor did Jeanie have to put out to someone just to have a place to stay. She didn't have to live in a roach infested dump either. Food was always available for her as well. She didn't have to concern herself over what she would have to eat that day. She wouldn't have to worry about starving.

Despite Jeanie's psychological problems dealing with her insecurities and self-esteem, she appeared to be getting better emotionally. Now that her basic needs were being met, Jeanie could perhaps work through improving her life in other ways. Even though her life was not all roses, at least she wasn't as depressed as she had been. She even managed to save some money and lose weight.

It was about that time when Jeanie's wants and desires started changing. At the time she was living with an elderly man who was old enough to be her grandpa. After working at the man's home for several months, Jeanie began to feel real lonely. She hadn't had a date for over two months, since she's moved in with the elderly man. One day, she reluctantly asked her employer if it would be alright to go out some evening with a young man she recently met. Even though the elderly man rarely needed her at night, he told her "No". He insisted he wanted her to be there just in case he did need her. Jeanie decided that she had to get some male companionship somewhere or she was going to go crazy. She was too young and beautiful to become a hermit. So the attention starved girl gave the old cowboy a week's notice to find someone else. She no longer wanted to be there!

The following morning, Jeanie awoke at 6 a.m. to the horny grandpa's hand over her breast. She planned on moving out anyway, but that certainly speeded up the process! Her new boyfriend helped Jeanie move into a small but cute furnished apartment in the city. Jeanie thought once she lived in her own domain, the couple would continue to date frequently. She was wrong.

That relationship fizzled out within two weeks time. Outside of the mad sex they shared, the two had little in common. Jeanie once again felt rejected. She felt herself spiral back into her pit of depression. Wanting to once again feel desirable as well as make good money, she resorted back to her previous career as a dancer. It was there in the nightclub that Jeanie met the dark haired Donald.

Donald was a goodhearted man with a body of steel. He was a construction worker with rippling muscles bulging out everywhere! Jeanie always seemed to have a good time when they went out together. Donald was real kind to Jeanie too. They would go out to eat or go to the local pub to play pool. He was as carefree and happy go lucky as she was. Don didn't have a lot of money, but what he did have, he was happy to share with her. What really attracted Jeanie to this man was the fact that he was so affectionate. He loved to cuddle and kiss about as much she did. They were both young and virile. They routinely spent hours kissing and making love. They were both fit and naturally energetic. It didn't take pharmaceutical drugs to enhance their sexual prowess. Except for a little weed, the couple were as natural as Adam and Eve.

Jeanie continued working at the club for awhile after her and Donald began seriously dating. After a few months of nightly co-habitation, their growing love and lust for one another deepened. Their fast paced relationship speeded up with an unfortunate run in with the law.

Since the sexy dancer worked two in the afternoon to eight at night, she had the early part of the day to herself. Sometimes out of sheer boredom, the spirited lass would hop on a bus downtown and go shopping. On this one particular day, Jeanie walked through the Metro Center in Little Rock. She enjoyed looking in the store windows at all the newest fashions and such. Occasionally, she would go into one of the multitude of stores to try on something that caught her eye, but rarely would she buy. While walking along the sidewalk, she bumped into her ex-boyfriend, Picket. They had broken up on pretty bad terms. The inner pain Jeanie felt about their last day together led the girl to say something to him she would always regret. Still feeling anger towards the slap happy elf, Jeanie said something to the little punk that ignited his explosive temper.

"You know that old violin you left me? Well it turned out it was an antique. I got $50 off that piece of shit," Jeanie snidely told Picket.

When Pickett heard that he actually left Jeanie something of value, he became a raging beast. He's started pushing and shoving the frightened filly right there on the street. The girl tried to flag down cars on the road for assistance, but no one would stop to help. No one wanted to get involved.

While fighting off this savage runt, Jeanie saw something out of the corner of her eye. There were flashing blue lights just up the next block. What luck Jeanie said to herself. Yes, what luck indeed!

Jeanie decided if she made enough noise and commotion, she would get the attention of the policeman up the street. Well, Jeanie did indeed get the cops attention. Rather than listen to what Jeanie had to say, the black militant pushed her against the police car and slapped a pair of handcuffs on her. Jeanie was outraged. Pickett was arrested also and brought into the police station in a separate car.

"That creep deserves to be arrested!" Jeanie cried, "What did I do?"

The arresting policeman looked at Jeanie. His eyes held no compassion and gleamed with disdain. "Just tell it to the judge," was all he said.

The disheveled dancer spent the next 26 hours in jail. She tried to bail herself out, but she couldn't get a bondsman to respond to her request. Guess there wasn't enough money involved to make it worth his while. At any rate, the poor girl was forced to spend a night in jail. She shared the jail cell with a drug pusher, a prostitute and a big bad lesbian (who later on that night got mad as Jeanie and threatened to kick her butt). The agitated, misunderstood girl was treated like a criminal for trying to get the help she needed. This was the second time the judicial system let her down.

"People get away with murder and innocent people like me get sent to jail!" Jeanie's faith in a just world got crushed a little more that night. Who could blame her.

Jeanie got to see the judge at 11 the next morning. At first she pleaded not guilty to the charge of disturbing the peace. However, her public defender told the girl it would be better if she pleaded guilty and paid the $10 fine. If she forgot about the court date and didn't appear in front of the judge, he would have a warrant out for her arrest. Reluctantly, Jeanie changed her plea. She didn't ever want to go back to that stinking court if she could help it.

Since Jeanie wasn't allowed to pay her own fine, she contacted Donald, her date mate from the club. The sweet guy paid that fine for her and rescued her from the concrete confines. The two hugged and kissed each other for several minutes upon Jeanie's release from jail. Neither one cared who watched the incredible make out scene. Jeanie was so glad to be out of the cold, dingy jail cell. She really appreciated her freedom after being cooped up in that place.

It wasn't a month later when Jeanie quit the nightclub and moved in with Donald. Her boyfriend made good money with his construction job, so Jeanie knew they would get by fine if she found a different line of work. Also, Don didn't want to see his fiancée flash her body in front of all the boozing baboons. Since Jeanie lacked other options, she went back to working as a waitress in a local café.

Six months after Jeanie and Donald had been seeing each other exclusively, something awful happened to Jeanie that would change her life forever. She woke up one morning with an intense burning inside her vagina. It hurt so much that she could barely walk. It pained her even more when she went bathroom.

Don accompanied Jeanie to the emergency room. Although her ailment wasn't life threatening, it was earth shattering. Turned out her excruciating pain was caused by a venereal disease. Jeanie didn't know all the lifelong effects this disease would have on her body until several years later. The doctors didn't tell her. All Jeanie knew was that she was in so much pain she wanted to die.

Herpes was the terrible disease that Jeanie acquired. Besides being painful, there's no cure for it. This viral disease remains inside a person's body for life. Although most of the time, the disease is dormant, however, it remains in it's host. The virus settled inside the nerve endings where the blisters originally appeared. Under extreme stress on the body, the ulcers would reappear over and over again. Jeanie was devastated!

For the longest time, the faithful fiancé thought that she had contracted herpes from one of her previous boyfriends. However, the virus had a 4 to 8 week incubation period. Jeanie hadn't stepped out with anyone else since her and Donald started seriously dating six months ago. Perhaps her boyfriend had harbored the disease all that time and was afraid to tell her for fear she would leave him. Maybe he had cheated on her with somebody else who had the virus. However many people harbor that disease that have absolutely no symptoms and are totally clueless that they have it. Jeanie thought that may have been the case with Donald.

Jeanie apologized profusely to Donald about the virus she contracted. That was before she knew the incubation period. She really thought it was all her fault…that she was the filthy one. Don had been a wild child himself before he met Jeanie. He had been with many, many women in his past. He was the one who gave the disease to Jeanie although she wouldn't come to that conclusion until many years later.

The poor girl harbored a tremendous burden of guilt for years, a guilt that should never have been hers. Unfortunately, even though the guilt of how the girl contracted herpes had lessened, the disease itself left Jeanie shamed. The trusting girl was left with the kind of emotional pain and physical affliction that would follow her around forever. It was a black cloud that could never be lifted from her life.

## CHAPTER 9

# Lost Child In The City

Jeanie and Donald lived happily together for over six months. Sure they had their problems. Who doesn't. Still, the two of them were like two peas in a pod. They were young, foolish, 22-year-old kids. Together they had a grand time smoking and joking. kissing and loving. For awhile they were both content living with the barest necessities. As long as they had a roof over their heads, food to eat, pot to smoke and each other...they were fine.

After living together for several months, Jeanie and Donald decided to go to the Justice of the Peace to get married. Carmalita Jean wanted someone who would always be there for her. She wanted stability and love in the worst way. Don was not perfect, but he was perfect for her (or so she thought). He didn't have much money, but he had a good heart and he loved her tremendously. Jeanie was a very emotionally needy person. In order to feel good about herself she required affirmation and affection from another person. So, the lovable girl latched onto a man whom she thought would provide her with all she ever needed. However, the things she really needed was self-love and that was something she could not get from an outside source.

Jeanie loved Donald, but he wasn't as practical and responsible as she would have liked him to be. He didn't have the financial means to start his own business nor the intelligence to operate one. Still, every year, Don would get the notion that he wanted to start his own construction business. They really couldn't afford to take unnecessary chances with their hard earned money. Still, Jeanie wanted to be supportive of her husband's dream. She knew he got tired of busting his butt working for someone else.

All during the previous year both parties worked hard at their jobs. Their object was to save as much of their earned income as possible. They ate bologna sandwiches nearly everyday and shopped thrift stores regularly. They needed to get a decent running car in the worst way. They didn't have any transportation of their own at that time! Jeanie was tired of standing out in the rain and cold to catch the city bus to work. Luckily Don worked with his brother, so he had a steady, almost free ride to his place of employment. The two didn't have the money to gamble away on a dream. Still every year for three years that's just what Don did.

Jeanie wasn't thrilled in the least with her husband's decision the first time he chose to leave his good paying, stable job to start his own construction company…but he did it anyway. She definitely didn't like the idea of him blowing all their car money the following year on something that may or may not pan out. However, since he convinced her that he knew what he was doing this time, she reluctantly stood beside him.

In two months, the guy spent every dime they had. The young couple had to humble themselves and beg his mother for grocery money. That was not the life Jeanie envisioned for herself! Even though he failed at his dream of starting his own company two times already, he still didn't abandon his dream. When he repeated the same behavior pattern for the third year in a row…that was it! The guy just didn't learn from his mistakes! Jeanie wasn't about to be poor forever. She needed stability! The little waitress was more than little angry! It was obvious she wanted more than she would ever have if she stayed with Don.

Every spring for as long as Jeanie knew Donald he would quit the construction job to chase his dream of starting a business. After a month or two trying to become successful in construction, his business would fail. Donald would once again be hopeless and penniless. When he became broke and desolate after trying to make it on his own, he crawled back to his previous employer and begged him for his previous job. Since he was a good worker, the construction firm always hired him back (with a large pay decrease of course).

Even though Donald may have wanted to start up a business of his own, he just didn't have the common sense, intelligence, or the training to do so. He wasn't a total dumb ass. No, he was just stupid for trying to repeatedly do something that was beyond his capacity.

For while Jeanie didn't say too much about Donald's impulsive schemes. However that instability really took its toll on their marriage. Jeanie even talked to her man about getting a divorce. She needed to feel financially secure enough so she could be a stay at home mom eventually. But she didn't ever see that happening. They wouldn't have any offspring the way their life was going. Marrying Donald was supposed to give Jeanie emotional and financial security. Unfortunately, it gave her neither of those things. The angry girl hated Donald for not living up to the unsaid agreement they entered into when they became hitched.

"Donald, I just can't believe in you anymore," Jeanie barked at her husband. "I've lost so much respect for you it's ridiculous. I want a divorce!"

Donald pleaded with the lady not to leave him. He wanted Jeanie to stay with him so badly that he even agreed to go along with an open marriage arrangement when his wife stated she wanted to start seeing other men. Donald would have let her do anything so long as it made her happy. "I'll let you go out with other men honey, if that's what you want. I just don't want you to leave me."

Jeanie might have stayed Don's legal wife, but emotionally and mentally she left him a long time ago.

The idea of an open marriage was quite a nifty thing at first. Jeanie could still have a husband to take care of most of her physical needs, but she would still be able to do things with other guys. Jeanie thought that this type of relationship would be perfect for her. Like any new idea, it was quite exciting…at first.

For several months Jeanie would go off with one of her girlfriends and have fun with another fella one or two nights a week. After a while though, the novelty of going with different guys as well as the open marriage concept got old. Jeanie wanted to be with only one man, but she wanted someone who could provide her with all she needed. She desired to have someone who would protect her, provide for her and most of all love her with all his heart. She in turn had to be able to respect the man as well as have an intense, beautiful love for the man she was with. It was important for Jeanie to love the whole man and not just certain parts of his body. As much as the girl tried, she could not love Donald entirely for she couldn't respect his mind.

Although she had several short flings, Jeanie never did become seriously attached to anyone. After all, it was pretty stupid to get serious with someone since she was still officially married to Donald. Although an occasional lover set off a spark within the sexy girls quivering body, they did little for her emotionally. Jeanie needed more…much more than Donald and the stupid open marriage arrangement could give her.

In the final months of their marriage, Jeanie started feeling guilty about having sex with anyone. She didn't even want to have sex with her husband any more even though Donald was a good lover.

During those last six months together, Jeanie harbored so much anger towards her man that she could barely stand to look at him. She no longer had that intense hatred she felt for her husband though. The emotional attachment Carmalita Jean once felt towards Donald chipped away a little more each time he let her down. Eventually what little love she had for the man sizzled away until there was nothing left. Eventually the disillusioned girl's heart felt totally void of any positive emotions she held earlier towards her husband. Now all she felt was emptiness inside for the man she once loved.

Despite Donald giving Jeanie more freedom within the marriage through the open marriage concept, Jeanie felt trapped. She felt as long as she remained married to Donald, her life would continue to be one big disappointment after another. Three months following Donald's latest failed dream chasing, Jeanie left him for good.

Immediately after she left her husband, Jeanie applied for a dancing job at a local bar. The bar there was relatively tame compared to where she was used to working in Bossier. The girl was employed to dance and waitress the afternoon/ early evening shift. She thought that was great. She wouldn't have as many drunken slime balls to deal with, and she could still have a social life. Since it was a small bar with a lady manager, she didn't put up with guys pinching and pawing her girls. The ones who did were given a warning. If they continued to break the rules….they were given the boot!

While employed there Jeanie was able to live in a small but nice apartment. She could easily take care of the bills out of the money she made working there. She definitely wouldn't be able to live nearly that nice if she held onto her part time waitress job she previously had. Also, she thought it was a good way to meet guys. Unfortunately, most of the guys who went in there were only after a girl for one thing. That was ok though…at least for awhile. Considering what she had just gone through with Donald, she didn't want to get emotionally involved with anyone.

Naturally, many of her casual dates turned into wild nights of passion. Even though she met a guy or two Jeanie thought she might like as a steady boyfriend, she didn't get serious with anyone for several months. After all, she was still married. Eventually, she would settle down and be with somebody for more than a few fleeting moments. Even though she was far from perfect, Jeanie wondered if there was any man available who could meet up to her expectations.

Jeanie worked at the bar for several weeks before she saved enough money to pay for a divorce lawyer. Since she was the one who wanted the divorce, Donald told her it was up to her to pay for it. How ironic is it that a couple could get married for $10. However it cost big bucks to get a divorce. That's probably why so many people stay together. Surely the economics played a big factor. A lot of people stayed together for the kids too. Jeanie counted her lucky stars that she never had any children by that loser or she may have felt trapped too!

Shortly after her divorce, Jeanie met a handsome, country boy in the club. They dated just a few weeks before Jake asked her to move in with him. Jeanie had already gotten sick of the nightclub scene and all the dirty old men who frequently patronized it. She thought if she lived with Jake, she wouldn't have to work for a while. She saved up nearly a grand and thought that big chunk of money should last her awhile. At least that was what the poor naïve girl thought when she moved in with Jake. He would take care of the basic bills where as she would only have to use her money to buy clothes and personal items. Wrong! Moving in with Jake was one more impulsively stupid mistake she made in her life.

The former dancer thought the guy would provide her with security and love but all he did was screw her eyes out. Which was ok for while. What Jeanie didn't like though, was the way Jake used her in other ways. Since all of Jakes money had gone towards fixing up his place in the sticks, Jeanie bought all the food for him and his other two friends who lived there. She also paid the utility bills and the mortgage. Within two months time, Jeanie was practically broke. When she became financially impoverished…Jake told Jeanie that she had to move out.

Since living with Jake, Jeanie gained a few pounds. She could no longer be a dancer (not that she wanted to be a dancer anymore). Also, all of Jeanie's so-called friends turned their backs on her. When the going got tough, she found out who her friends were. The people pleasing, social numb skull could count her friends on one finger. Sometimes even then, she didn't think that she was much of a friend to herself. Still, she was all she had at the time. Knowing this sad fact, Jeanie knew it was up to her to rescue herself. This was when she went looking through the newspapers once more for another live in position.

The first one Jeanie accepted was from a man in his 40s. Basically, she thought, he just wanted someone to cook and clean for him. In return for doing those monotonous household chores, he'd give her a place to stay and food to eat. Considering the girl had nowhere to go and no possessions except her clothes and stereo, she jumped at the man's offer.

The first night with PI turned out to be her last night. When the pig returned from his friends barbecue, he went right up to the extra bedroom where Jeanie was. Without an ounce of thought, PI jumped on to Jeanie waking up the frightened girl. The porky prick practically crushed the surprised girl beneath his massive weight. The pig pulled on her panties while Jeanie squirmed in an attempt to foil her fate. Jeanie cried, but there was nothing she could do to escape the inevitable. After the animal raped her, he crawled off the vulnerable girl and crept back into his cave like a big hairy bear to sleep. Jeanie didn't call the police for she felt she should've known better. Besides, he'd probably just lie about their sexual encounter and tell them it was consensual.

When the first rays of sunshine lightened the blue room, Jeanie grabbed her packed suitcase and snuck out the door. Once more she put out her thumb out to hitch hike. She didn't know where she was going, but she knew she didn't want to stay there.

God must have been with Jeanie that day for a kind, young man stopped to give the little runaway a ride. When Jeanie disclosed her sad story, the man offered her a place to stay with him and his grandmother. Having nowhere else to go, the girl accepted his offer.

For a short while things, were rather serene in Jeanie's new residence. Both Tommy and his grandma treated Jeanie quite nice…almost like family. However, Tommy and his grandma lived on a very tight budget. Jeanie knew it wouldn't be right to stay with them long considering their financial circumstances. Within a couple of days, Jeanie landed another live-in job on the other side of town. Tommy and his grandma hugged their new friend, said their goodbyes and wished her luck. They didn't know at the time how much luck she needed.

The new position Jeanie accepted was with a well to do man in his 80s. Not only did Jeanie get to live in his large mansion like house, but she got $125 a week salary as well. That was perfect Jeanie thought to herself. Unfortunately if something seems too perfect…it usually is. This job was no exception.

Within two weeks time, Mr. Black made it clear that he wanted sexual flavors from Jeanie. For awhile she put up with grandpa's advances. After all, he was old. How much sex can a guy that age have before he died of a heart attack? Besides, the guy treated her really nice. He regularly took her out to dinner. He bought her things at the store. He even paid for her doctor when she was sick. Yes, if Jeanie could have closed off her conscious for a longer period of time, she may accumulated enough money to get a jumpstart towards having the kind of life she wanted…but she couldn't.

Once a week the old geezer invaded her private chambers and got his jollies. For the rest of the night, the sickened girl couldn't sleep. She felt so dirty inside. She wanted to have sex with a man she loved. She didn't want to keep having sex with someone so she could have a nice, secure place to live. For days after their sexual encounter, Jeanie would avoid Mr. Black as much she could. Just by the time she began to get rid of some of the self-hate she felt towards herself, grandpa once again approached Jeanie for sex. Despite her uncomfortable home life, the kept girl managed to stay with Mr. Black for two months…enough time to save up a little bit of money. She wanted nothing better than to leave her living hell, but the thought of making it out in the world alone again didn't appeal to her in the least. With a little luck and perseverance, she wouldn't have to.

Since Jeanie did have Saturday nights off, she would frequently go dancing at the local disco. It was during one of those boogie nights she met Burl. Burl was a year older than Jeanie and was rather handsome. They were immediately drawn to each other. They both had dark hair and dark eyes with high cheekbones. They looked like a little Indian couple dancing together.

After seeing each other twice, they decided they would find a small house together and share expenses. Burl wanted to move out of his sister's house and Jeanie definitely wanted to move out of Mr. Black's house. She had about all she could take with Mr. Black. She thought she found an affordable way to escape her self-made hell. The girl also knew that since she had some money saved, she would be financially secure for awhile.

Jeanie and Burl were lovers, but mostly they were friends. Still sometimes Jeanie wondered just what kind of a friend Burl was. True the girl was a little stocky but she was still pretty. She couldn't hide good genes. However whenever Burl took the insecure girl out to eat, he would order her a salad with light dressing and nothing more. It was something he did automatically, without even asking her what she wanted.

The man didn't have an ounce of sensitivity when it came to Jeanie's intense feelings. He always made mean little comments about her weight. That really damaged the girls self-esteem. A little bit of kindness and consideration would have done more for Jeanie mentally and physically than Burl's little digs about her weight. All those cutting remarks did was make the slightly overweight girl feel even worse about herself. When Burl went out somewhere on his own, she would go to the local fast food restaurant and eat all the things she was otherwise denied. After she ate all those yummy, fattening things, Jeanie felt bad about herself for losing control with her eating again. Often after her quick, tasteless gorging, she would make herself puke up whatever she ate. Jeanie was physically and psychologically ill and drastically needed some professional help. Even if she wasn't in such a state of denial, she didn't have the big bucks to pay for a therapist, so Jeanie's emotional state continued it's downhill spiral.

After a month's time, Burl moved out of house the two shared. The troubled girl really didn't like staying there alone. Still, she didn't miss Burl when he moved out. It was good to have a room mate to share expenses with, but he really wasn't much of a friend. He wasn't even much of a lover. He may have had the right equipment to satisfy the nymphomaniac in bed, but he didn't have the desire to do so. On many occasions, Burl would climb off the girl immediately after he was satisfied, leaving her flustered and frustrated. The love starved girl would leave her bedmate's side after he fell asleep and would finish the job herself. With toy in hand, Jeanie would please herself like no man ever could. Afterwards, she would stow her rubber appliance beneath her socks without any further thought. Who needs a man, the under loved girl told herself. She did and she knew it.

It was during that time in her life when Jeanie started to get involved with some foreigners. It was a challenge just to understand what her tanned, middle Eastern men tried to say to Jeanie. Still, the language of lust was universal. No one needed to talk much when in the throes of passion.

What really attracted Jeanie to those guys was all their vast differences. Everything about them was new and exciting... their customs, their clothing, their cologne. The very things that attracted the sex depraved girl to these men were the things that would utterly destroy any chance of her relationship with any of them. Although her men wanted and loved sex, none of them respected Jeanie for the spirited, free loving girl that she was. Those kind of guys loved to have sex with a particular type of girl but usually married a sweet, innocent, submissive girl from their own country. Although Jeanie had fun with her foreign friends, she knew that she would never be able to build a permanent relationship with any of them.

After a few months of living it up, Jeanie was nearly broke again. She wanted to have one more fun adventure before she settled down to another live in job. So the day before her rent was due, she packed her suitcase and hitched hiked down to New Orleans. One of the things she always wanted to do, was visit the city during the Mardi Gras. This was going to be the year she did it.

Good fortune must have smiled on Jeanie throughout her trip. She made it down there without any problems at all. When the sweet hitch hiker arrived at the bordering city of Reserve, she met a friendly, kind man who invited her to spend a week at his place. Carl was a gentleman the whole time Jeanie stayed in his home. He slept on the couch and gave up his bed for the girl. Jeanie couldn't believe that the giving man didn't want anything from her. She was almost beginning to think that all guys were pigs. Carl changed her mind about that. The guy even brought Jeanie to the Mardi Gras parades. He stood there on the streets with her as they watched the floats. Together they caught the dabloons and party favors that were thrown from the colorful displays. The man was so nice to Jeanie. However, she didn't feel anything inside for him for if she did, she would have invited herself into his home and his life for more than a week.

After the Mardi Gras festivities were over, Carl reluctantly brought the little wanderer back to the local truck stop. From there Jeanie hitched a ride back to her abandoned apartment. Soon after arriving at her home in Little Rock, she called Tommy and his grandmother. Jeanie was about to be evicted and didn't have the money for rent. Reluctantly, Tommy came by Jeanie's house to help her with her few remaining material things. Shortly after Jeanie moved back in with Tommy, she put in an AD in the local paper looking for a live-in job.

Within days, the girl acquired another job as a live in housekeeper, cook and nanny. This time the lass would be working for a young couple in the country. It sounded like Jeanie would have the peace of mind and serenity from life that she needed. Perhaps this live-in job would last longer than a few weeks or months.

During that time Jeanie had gotten a painful urinary tract infection and had to have her IUD removed. That was okay Jeanie thought she wouldn't need the protection anyway. Living far out in the country might have an advantage. As much and she loved having a man in her life, she hadn't had a very good relationship with any of them.

"Maybe it's best that I stay by myself for while," Jeanie told herself. However, I might as well take advantage of these last few days of freedom.

Since she just had her monthly, Jeanie thought she would be free from pregnancy for a week or so. The wild girl had 10 whole days of rough riding before she put her libido into hibernation. Within those short 10 days, Jeanie had a short fling with two different men. What she didn't know was that one of those men provided her with a gift, one that would change her life forever.

# CHAPTER 10

# A Sweet Rose Blooms

Jeanie adapted to life with the Smith's fairly quickly. Life in the country was far less complicated than the hectic city life. Her new employers were so kind to Jeanie too. They made her feel right at home. Jewel Smith wasn't much older than Jeanie, so they quickly became friends. She didn't see much of George, Jewel's husband for he owned and operated a big farm, and there was always a lot to do on the farm. When Jewel wasn't busy helping her husband feed the farm animals or canning her raised vegetables, she was back at the main house with her two girls. When all the household chores were done and Jewel didn't need Jeanie to watch Sarah and Samantha, she could pretty well do whatever she wanted to do.

Jeanie spent a great deal of time in her room listening to her music. Her cozy corner of the house was like a haven to the former dancer who used to shake it down in front of the horny, drooling pigs in the nightclubs. She danced alone in her room now without an audience. That suited her just fine. Sometimes at night before the girls went to sleep, Jeanie would light a candle and do some shadow dancing. She didn't feel quite so alone on the dance floor when her shadow accompanied her.

In some ways Jeanie missed this city. There was always something to do there if she had the transportation and the money. Still, the country was nice and quiet. Perhaps right at that time in Jeanie's life, she needed the serenity of the country more than the hustle and bustle of the city. Still, there were times when the girl felt she would die if she didn't get out of the house. It was on those occasions she walked alone on the country roads.

The curvy country roads with purplish mountains greeted Jeanie as she walked behind the Smith's rustic farmhouse. Often she scanned the surrounding fields looking for wildflowers to pick. Plucking a bouquet of fragrant flowers always seemed to cheer her up. They brought much sunshine to her room and to her spirits.

Often while walking Jeanie would sing along with the meadow larks. Many feathered foul frequented the rich farmland. That day was no exception. Snowy egrits appeared like angels in the sky in multitude that afternoon. Occasionally one would swoop down from the sky to pluck a horsefly off one of the cows. They served the hoofed animal well while taking care of their own basic need to nourish themselves.

Jeanie loved gazing up at the sky. In between admiring earth's feathered friends, she'd look at the fluffy, white puffs in amazement. She envisioned God and all the angels smiling down on her while on her journey. He was leading her along the life's path she was meant to take now. There was no doubt in that. She needed this time in the country to rejuvenate her soul. She needed this time to get in touch with herself and find peace within her heart.

It took the peace and serenity of the beautiful country setting to send the wild child's heart and mind in the direction of God. When Jeanie grew weary of walking, she'd sit on one of the fallen trees in the field. Often she would plop herself down on the earthy surface and write poems. She always had paper and pen handy in case she had the inclination to write. Much inspiration graced her on that particular day.

Jeanie's words flowed out of her heart like water. After she laid her pen down, Jeanie felt a fountain of tears stream from her heated forehead. Bleary eyed, the girl placed her wanton arms around the oak tree that had shaded her face from the sun's rays.

"Oh God, send me someone to love. I need love so badly. Please send me someone special to love!"

What Jeanie didn't know, was that God intended to give the needy girl someone to love. However, this particular gift wasn't exactly what the lass had in mind. Still, this person which would become a part of Jeanie's life was someone very special indeed.

Lately, Jeanie had lead the life of a recluse. She hadn't thought anything about her exceptionally light first monthly after her arrival in the country setting. She thought even less about her two missed periods after that. She couldn't get pregnant through immaculate conception. She certainly wasn't the Virgin Mary.

One time when Jeanie's menstrual cycle was to start, she was fasting. The husky girl's body had conserved it's red blood cells due to iron deficiency she thought. The following month, Jeanie became very ill due to the erratic eating patterns of her unhealthy diet. She was so sick the week her "friend" was supposed to arrive, that she cared not that it didn't.

Jeanie never thought in a million years that her monthly cycles were erratic or absent for a reason. It never occurred to her that she was pregnant. The other times she was pregnant, Jeanie felt sick all the time. Except for that lousy flu she caught from the semi-starving diet, she felt great. It wasn't until Jeanie noticed something leaking from her darkened breast that she began to wonder about the possibility she was pregnant.

The promiscuous girl was shamed that she didn't know which of the two men she slept with prior to her relocation, was her baby's father. Still, she was thrilled to death of the prospect of having a baby. Jeanie loved Sarah and Samantha. She truly enjoyed bringing them on their nature walks, playing kick ball or merely just reading to them. She knew that she would make a good mother to her little boy or girl. Jeanie wished she had already married the man of her dreams before she brought a child into the world. However, life's circumstances never did go according to her dreams. Why would her little unplanned papoose be any different.

A month after Jeanie recognized she was pregnant, she lost her job with the Smiths. Jewel hurt her foot and could no longer assist her husband with the farm chores. They hired someone to help with the farming chores while Jewel stayed home and watched their children. They could no longer afford to pay Jeanie for her services because of their added expense.

Maybe it was best that the little mother headed in another direction. After all, she had to worry about setting up a stable home environment for herself and her unborn child. Maybe, Jeanie thought, she should go back north to be near her family. Despite the problems of the past, Jeanie felt certain that her mom and sister would stand behind her and her developing child.

Jeanie phoned her family and told them about her unplanned pregnancy. Rather than being angry at her, they were thrilled. Jeanie was 26 years old. Although she wasn't married, her kin folks thought it was about time she settled down. Having a baby would surely force the wild, spontaneous girl to start living a more responsible, respectable life.

Jeanie wanted a more stable life long before she became pregnant. However, she had trouble finding a sweet, considerate, loving, financially secure man she could make her own. Although Jeanie may have wanted to fall madly in love and get married, she was unable to give of herself totally to anyone. There was always a cloud of mistrust and suspicion around the injured girl's heart. Those shadows got in the way of any relationship she became involved in. Jeanie did not know when she made the sincere request to God to she was incapable of that type of emotional attachment at that time, but He knew. Our heavenly Father also knew Jeanie desperately needed someone special in her life to love. That was undoubtedly why He honored the wanton girl's request.

God deliberately planned this pregnancy for Jeanie. Although life for Jeanie and her child would without doubt be difficult at first, she felt certain that she was meant to carry and care for the embryo growing inside her. In the beginning things were going to be so unstable and rough for both of them. She definitely wasn't bringing her baby into the world under the most ideal circumstances. However, she already loved it and wanted it in the worst way. Still, the girl wondered if she was being selfish for wanting to keep her baby. After all what kind of life could she give it?

Within a week, Jeanie was once again seated inside a Greyhound bus. The journey this time promised to be most pleasant. The girl knew where she was going. She knew that at the end of the trail, family would be there to greet her with open arms.

Many times in the past, when the melancholy girl needed the love and support of her family…there was none. It was during those desperate times when she needed love and acceptance the most, it was unavailable to her. Her family couldn't accept and love Jeanie when she fell short of their expectations. Is it any wonder why the distraught girl had such a tough time loving and accepting herself.

Jeanie's mom and stepfather greeted the tired girl at the bus stop. That week was the first time Jeanie had spent any length of time with her mother in years. During that time with her mom, Jeanie tried to rebuild whatever relationship they once possessed. Despite the way her sister and her mother had turned their backs on her in the past, Jeanie desperately needed to feel she belonged.

So often in her young life, the wandering waif didn't feel like she belonged anywhere. She always felt like she was the families misfit. All through the young lady's life it was clear that she was different. She didn't just march to a different drummer. No, she danced to a whole different beat. Her uniqueness wasn't a curse though, it was a blessing…only Jeanie didn't know it at the time.

That week Jeanie spent with her mom was so wonderful. That was the first time in years that the misunderstood girl received the life affirming nurturing from her mother that she craved. It almost made her wish she became pregnant years earlier. She wasn't mature enough to handle a baby's needs back all those years ago. In many ways, Jeanie herself was just a babe. She needed special care then and she needed an abundance of loving care now.

The twenty six year old girl wasn't even sure she was ready for motherhood now. Still, Jeanie was thrilled at the prospect of being a mom. Jeanie's future life with her baby appeared uncertain at the present time. However, she was confident that everything would work out fine. Hopefully, the deep amount of love in her heart would act as a counterweight against the financial security that the girl lacked at the present time.

The next weekend Jeanie's mom drove her daughter to Windsock to stay with her sister, Deana. Even though the house was crowded and unkempt, Jeanie was thankful she had a place to stay for while. In exchange for room and board, she babysat the tribe of children her sister had. Even though Jeanie loved kids, there were times when the little darlings would get on her nerves.

In many ways Jeanie missed the serenity experienced in the Smith's country home. How she longed for a peaceful, environment that she could call home. Although the girl had a little money saved, she vowed she wouldn't waste it. She was afraid of renting a place of her own at the time. She knew that small amount of money she saved would dwindle in no time. Then, what would the desolate girl do?

When the soon-to-be mom got to be six months pregnant, she went on aid to families with dependent children (AFDC). She wasn't proud of receiving government assistance, but she didn't know what else to do. She had to survive somehow until she was able to return to work. Maybe, Jeanie thought, she could get job training. That way she would be able to take care of her little baby properly. Jeanie's family barely had enough resources to take care of themselves. They couldn't help her much, not that she would ask. Jeanie kept that small amount of money she saved hid from all. She would soon need to buy all the little household things necessary for when she did get her own place. At the time though she couldn't fathom how she'd possibly afford something like that on her own. Obviously the girl couldn't get any financial help from her baby's daddy for she wasn't even sure who he was.

Shortly after Jeanie started getting the assistance she needed, she found a nice apartment down the street from her sister. It was in the process of being refurbished and the landlord told the pregnant girl that it would soon be approved for subsidized rent. That would mean that Jeanie wouldn't have to spend all her monthly aid on rent. No, she would just have to personally pay one third of the gross income on housing. She was elated.

Just six weeks before her due date, Jeanie moved into her own little apartment. At first she didn't have much to put in it, but that problem was easily remedied. The girl located some decent furniture at a reasonable price in the local paper. She also received a free crib from one of her mother's friends. God was certainly helping her take care of her and her baby even now!

Jeanie heard that some unfortunate souls had to lay their babies in drawers because they were too poor to afford a proper crib. Jeanie would have slept on the floor if she had to instead of letting her little papoose go without. She was determined to give her child whatever she needed to be comfortable and safe.

Many of the household things that made life easier for her were purchased at the local thrift store. It was rather funny how she obtained the material items she desired. Jeanie would just think about how grand it would be to own a toaster or a crock pot and within a few days she would see it on the thrift store's shelf apparently waiting for her.

Jeanie began to feel a tad anxious a week prior to giving birth. She no longer had a financial cushion. However, since she had all her necessities and a few of the nonessentials she desired, she felt a bit more at ease. She was about as ready for her baby as she could be. Even though Jeanie's relocation north started out with much uncertainty, things had steadily gotten better. It was more than a miracle that the girl managed to smooth out her rocky world just prior to the delivery of her Rose.

Jeanie was still unhappy that she didn't have a man in her life. However, she did make a couple of friends since moving back to Windsock. That made Jeanie's life a little less lonely. One thing was for sure, her life would be neither lonely or boring when her child would be born. The little mother could hardly wait for her little bundle of joy to make her presence in the world.

All through Jeanie's pregnancy the baby which snugly slept inside her womb was breech. The doctor hoped that child would turn prior to being born, but she didn't. The babe continued to sit like a frog on Jeanie's tail end. The baby enjoyed that position so much that the stubborn little thing didn't move head first into the birth canal like most babies did. That made the new mom's labor painfully long.

Jeanie didn't have a ride to the hospital when the contractions started, so the ambulance brought her. The frightened girl arrived in the unfamiliar hospital setting all alone. She continued to be all alone with her contractions and her pain. X-rays confirmed that her child remained in the breach position. However, her doctor didn't want to perform a cesarean delivery…not unless he had to. Although Jeanie was in excruciating pain for hours, the nurses administered nothing stronger than a mild sedative. The angels of mercy explained to Jeanie since she chose general anesthetic for her C-section, they couldn't give the pained girl anything stronger. Jeanie knew a girlfriend who had trouble with the spinal tap she received during labor. She chose to be put to sleep because of what her friend Alice experienced. So, despite the pain she endured, Jeanie couldn't take any more chances…not with her and not with her baby. Her life had already been plagued by complications created through uncalculated risks. She didn't want to take any more chances…especially now.

For the next five hours Jeanie laid in a gurney in the hall. Every body heard her screaming in pain. Once in a while an unfamiliar doctor or nurse would peek in on her, but they did nothing to alleviate the emotional distress and the physical pain Jeanie experienced. Finally at 10 p.m. her water broke. Things were terribly rough for her hours before that event. However, after that point the poor girl didn't get any time off from her torturous contractions. At 11:45 p.m. the doctors were in the process of wheeling the frightened, whimpering girl into the operating room. Unfortunately, the team had to do an emergency C-section on a woman whose baby was in distress. Poor Jeanie didn't know how much longer she could endure the intense, nonstop pain. She hurts so much that she wanted to die. In between screaming in agony, Jeanie cried to God above for help.

Maybe she deserved the incredible amount of suffering she was enduring now. Maybe that was God's way of making her pay for the multitude of mistakes she had made in the past. "Oh God, please have mercy! Help me God! Help me! It hurts so, so much. Oh God please take away this pain!" She pleaded with God continuously for hours. Eventually, she got her wish when the surgical team wheeled her into the operating room.

It was almost two hours before they brought Jeanie back into the awaiting surgical room. That last thirty minutes of her labor seemed like an eternity. Once in the sterile surroundings, the nurses prepped the distressed girl in preparation for the surgery. Jeanie was happy to finally get some relief from the pain that tortured her body for almost ten hours. She didn't even mind the sting of the big needle as it penetrated the vein in her left hand. She didn't like the big bulky plastic mask that was placed over her face, but she didn't fight the gloved fingers that put it there. Soon, Jeanie would be delivered from the physical agony that her poor body endured. Soon, she would be gazing into the eyes of her beloved baby.

Jeanie was barely awake when the voices around her asked if she wanted to hold her baby girl. The fatigued mom was still so groggy from the sedation that she refused. She was afraid to hold the child for fear she would drop the infant on her head. A green, cloaked nurse held the sleeping angel in the direction of Jeanie's face. The fatigued mom briefly looked up at the tiny pink face of her newborn daughter before she dozed back to sleep. Finally, all the hell Jeanie went through was over. The girl smiled as she thought about the new life she had brought into the world.

Jeanie's baby was beautiful. A large amount of dark hair covered her well rounded head. Her legs were incredibly long and skinny. Most babies legs weren't usually that long. Yup, she's got the legs of a dancer and her face is as beautiful as a rose.

"That's her name," Jeanie said to no one's listening ears. "Rosa. That is what your name will be." The new mother looked at the beautiful Rose God had blessed her with and smiled. "I promise to be the best mother in the world to you my little angel." After she made that heartfelt promise to her sleeping baby, she thanked God for the new love He blessed her with. Totally fatigued, the new mother laid back in her bed not fully awake but definitely not asleep. She basked in the restful yet alert state she was momentarily in. The persistent throbbing she now experienced was barely noticeable. After the many hours of hell she endured waiting for her deliverance, the pain she felt now was nothing.

Although Jeanie was mentally alert, her body was entirely tuckered out. While she laid there in the quiet darkness, a strange feeling came over her. It was a feeling the girl experienced before, on that first trip to New Orleans. Jeanie's soul felt so incredibly light…almost like it could float away. She could feel it trying to escape from the top of her head. Once she realized what was happening, fear gripped the girl's heart. Once the fear settled inside her, she felt her soul plummet back into her exhausted body. "What is happening"? Jeanie said to herself as she felt her moist forehead.

Jeanie was pretty certain she wasn't meant to die, yet this feeling that came over her today, of all days reminded her of that weekend. Having that feeling now, just didn't make sense. That was just it. Jeanie always tried to make sense of the world, even when there was no logical reason for such perplexing things to occur. However, much of Jeanie's life was an array of unexpected happenings. Why would this day be any different? Without thinking about the near out of body experience any longer, the tired girl drifted into a deep sleep. After what she had just endured alone, Jeanie felt that she could sleep for a hundred years. Unfortunately, she wasn't given the privilege.

Rosa, Jeanie's little gift from God, hungered for her mother's breast milk often. She got the fatigued girl up every 2 ½ hours to feed. Jeanie no longer had the privilege of sleep, not as long as she nursed that child. The girl would no sooner fall asleep before another nurse brought her crying daughter in to suckle her two hours later. Jeanie wondered what she got herself into. Little did the frustrated mom know that this was just beginning of the troubles the two of them would share.

Jeanie began feeling the loneliness and stress of raising her daughter alone in just two days. Her hospital roommate had a very large and involved family. Joy always seemed to be having people visiting her and her newborn. Jeanie felt envious of her well loved roommate. The isolated girl hurt inside her body and soul. She was saddened to the fact that she didn't have anyone there to visit her. Although Jeanie's sister knew she had her baby, she had not yet made it up to see her and her precious daughter.

After a couple of days, Jeanie's roommate went home. She had a natural delivery, so her hospital stay was shorter. Although Joy appeared nice enough, Jeanie didn't have many chances to talk to her. After all, she was always so busy with all her visitors. When Jeanie's popular roommate left, the saddened girl couldn't help but cry. Even though she tried to muffle her sobs, one of the nurses making her rounds heard her.

"What's wrong dear?" the kindly nurse asked Carmalita Jean.

Jeanie reluctantly told the nurse, "I'm going to be all alone raising this child. I'm scared! I don't know if I'm strong enough to do it."

This sweet nurse didn't say a lot to Jeanie in words, she just held on to her hand and gently rubbed it. The lonely girl needed to feel the warm tenderness of another human being that night. She needed to know that somebody cared for her. There were times she wondered if God himself cared.

"God, if you care about me at all, then why has my life been so bad…so rough?"

Jeanie wondered if Rosa's life would be as tough as hers had been. She prayed it would not, yet inside the girl felt her daughter may also have a life filled with pain and disappointment…just like hers.

## CHAPTER 11

# Baby Love

Two days after Rosa was born, Jeanie had a visit from an unfamiliar doctor. She could tell by the expression on the man's face that something was wrong. Little Rosa was born with hip dysphasia. One of Rosa's hip bones weren't formed right due to the way she positioned herself in Jeanie's womb. Upon hearing the news about her daughter's physical condition, the distressed girl cried. Jeanie remembered having her legs in braces as a young girl and the tears that accompanied the ordeal. It was a miracle she could walk at all now. Already her daughter was following in her footprints. Jeanie didn't want her daughter to have the many bad experiences she had lived through. Unfortunately it looked like her girl might be repeating many of the same hardships that crippled her.

"My poor baby," cried Jeanie. "What exactly does that mean doctor? Is my little lamb going to be okay?"

The kind, young physician smiled at Jeanie as he told her of a recently released medical device. He reassured the troubled mother that Rosa would be all right if she went to a specialist and followed the recommended course of action. Jeanie choked back the tears.

"Already my child is paying the price of my mistakes. Why is God punishing Rosa the way he was? It isn't her fault that she was born out of wedlock."

The troubled mother felt that her little girl was being penalized for mistakes she had made. Jeanie was willing to accept whatever punishment that God felt she deserved. She wasn't however ready to accept whatever difficulties her precious daughter would endure. The fiercely protective mother would battle Satan himself if she could shield her daughter from a moment of pain.

"My poor little lamb. I'll see to it that you get all the help you need. You'll grow up big and strong. You'll be able to climb stairs and run like a rabbit…I just know it!" Jeanie smiled lovingly at her darling baby. She had only been in the world for two short days, yet Jeanie loved her more than life itself. Her unplanned gift would teach the affection starved girl how to love…truly love. Perhaps in learning how to truly love others, she could finally learn how to love herself.

Jeanie had a long five day hospital stay due to her C-section. It was bad enough going through all those hours of labor without having to be carved up like a turkey besides. Still, despite the poking and prodding Jeanie got regularly from the nurses, she was glad she was in the hospital longer than a couple of days. Rosa was always waking the sleepy mom every 2 ½ hours around the clock for feeding. Jeanie was thankful that she didn't have to go home earlier then she did. At least in the hospital she managed to catch a little shut eye. Besides, there was no one there at her little apartment in Windsock to be with her or help her. As fatigued and tender as Jeanie was, she didn't know how she would have handled the job of taking care of her baby. She didn't even feel strong enough to take care of herself at the time.

During the first four days of the Jeanie's hospital stay, she had no visitors at all. Finally, the day before Jeanie and Rosa were discharged her sister Deana, came by to see them. That made the girl feel a little better. The next day, her mom came from Connecticut to see Jeanie and her little ward. It was mom's intention to bring her daughter and granddaughter back to Windsock as well. Jeanie was thankful that her first night home from the maternity ward she wouldn't be all alone with her baby.

Originally, the little mother would have brought her baby girl home in boy's clothes. That was all Jeanie purchased for her child. However, her mother brought over a red laced dress so Rosa could look like the little girl that she was.

Jeanie felt certain that she was going to be blessed with a boy child that everything she bought was blue. The ultra sound she had months before couldn't determine the sex because of the position Rosa was in while in her stomach. Jeanie wanted a boy for she thought that would mean that her father had come back to her. She really believed that he would be with her in this new reincarnated form. Although it had been more than eight years since her dad's death. Jeanie still missed her dad terribly. She thought that his love would never leave her. Jeanie remembered what the Indian girl told her on that strange week in New Orleans. Love is Eternal.

Despite her dad's flaws, Jeanie loved him with no end. She was sure his love for her was equally strong. She believed that he would find a way to be with his precious daughter and that way was through Rosa. She devotedly believed in reincarnation, despite what her previous religious instructors had taught her. Still, that didn't mean that she disbelieved that Jesus was God's son. Nor did her differing religious views negate the belief of the numerous miracles Jesus performed while on this earth.

Helping this confused woman child get her life together was one more miracle that the Lord would perform. No problem existed that was too small or too large that God and His Son couldn't solve. If a person asks the Almighty with a sincere, open heart and believed without doubt that He would intervene to dissolve those obstacles, then it would be so. Human love, Godly faith and a pure heart despite a shadowed past would lift the girl's broken existence out of the bottomless pit that once devoured her troubled life.

It was important for Jeanie to be the best mom that she could be. She loved this wonderful gift from God with all her heart. She had to do everything perfectly right for her Rose even if it meant she had to put her own needs on hold. Whatever needs Jeanie did have she believed weren't important. Many of the experiences she lived through thus far in life only proved it to be so.

Often Carmalita Jean felt unwanted, unappreciated and unloved while growing up. Her father was so busy working two jobs that eventually the close emotional ties father and daughter once had were severed. Although Jeanie loved her mother, they were so different. She couldn't talk to her about what really mattered. She didn't know about the molestation on the hill nor about the years of bullying until much later in her adult life. Her mother couldn't cater to her daughter's emotional needs for she never knew what they were. Besides Jeanie's mom had her emotions stuck in a black hole since her dad walked out on the family. Her heart struggled through a dark state of depression for years. Jeanie's mom couldn't give her what she needed then. The poor woman couldn't even help herself at the time!

Jeanie's negative thinking intensified when she endured the taunting bullying from her uncaring, cruel classmates for all those years. The emotionally and physically abusive years she endured while being with Slugger certainly didn't help the girl's self esteem either. Even when she moved 1800 miles away, the destructive inner voices followed her. The multitude of men she spent time with for the next six years only reinforced her belief of how unimportant a thing she actually was. Those men would satisfy their own selfish, physical needs and then toss Jeanie to the dirt when they were through draining from her whatever they could extract. Is it any wonder why she felt so unimportant and unwanted. She didn't deserve to be shoved in the quicksand struggling just to live...but she was. Since most of her male acquaintances didn't acknowledge her emotional needs, she didn't feel that they were important. She didn't feel like she was important. Still she tried to fill her emancipated heart with what it needed the best she could. However it would take more than a few minutes of tenderness, acceptance and love to even partially fill Jeanie's emotional cup. Even if her needs did get consciously recognized…she believed that they didn't matter. She didn't feel like she mattered…not really.

The young mother couldn't seem to do enough for her daughter. If she thought she hungry, she was fed. Right after the feeding, Rosa would be burped, changed and held. If her daughter even whimpered, Jeanie would jump. There were times when the attentive mother would lie awake in her bed for hours just listening to her baby breathe. It was on one of those long sleepless nights, she reached for her faithful notebook and wrote this poem.

Guardian of the night

Night after night
I lie awake for hours
just listening to her breathe.

She's so small, so fragile,
so beautiful
and I love her so.

But I'm afraid I'll lose her
like all the other things
I've ever loved.

And so I keep watch
over my tiny infant
night after night.

It was frightening to think that something so beautiful, and so helpless depended on Jeanie for its very survival. It was important to Jeanie that her daughter got all the tenderness and love she needed while growing up. Maybe if she got those essentials met, she wouldn't be, the needy person she was. Jeanie wasn't about to starve her child emotionally like she had been starved earlier on in her formative years. No, things were going to be different for her child…so different.

Jeanie's still felt a little sad when she thought back on her childhood years. Although her mother loved her, she often didn't feel loved. Mom was critical. Mom was always in a hurry. Once the love hungry girl grew too big for her mother's warm lap… that was the end of physical affection. Jeanie did get regular hugs her father, but they were far and few between. Dad always seem to be working. Young Jeanie would often wake up at 5 a.m. just so she could visit her daddy before he left for work. Since he worked two jobs, she rarely saw him. Things changed for awhile when he had his ceramic studio though. Jeanie enjoyed spending time with her dad, Leif while they painted their clay wonders. She wished those days never ended, but end they did. Her parents marriage ended shortly afterwards as well. After that, she didn't hardly see her dad at all until that trip to Arkansas. The time she moved in with her dad was supposed to turn out so differently. That was supposed to be when father and daughter became really close again. Well that didn't happen!

Jeanie always thought that if she was smarter or prettier when she was in grade school, her father would have loved her more. If she was only more like the person he wanted her to be…then he may not have left her. Of course it wasn't up to her to keep the family intact. It never was up to the young girl to be the savior of her little world. However, it was a role she took on as a child. It was a role she worked diligently at. Unfortunately, it was also the role she failed miserably at. She couldn't keep her parents together anymore than she could have prevented the Korean war. Still, Jeanie felt like she let them down. She couldn't save her world from disintegration. She couldn't even save herself from the array of tortures life had thrown at her. The girl felt as powerless in her world then as she did now.

As a child Jeanie took on enormous roles in her life in order to feel she had some control in her world. However, the vulnerable thirteen year old girl found out how little control she did have. Even now Jeanie longed for a sense of control, for she felt powerless all too often. She couldn't change how others saw her nor how they treated her. She couldn't control her eating, nor could she will away her emotions. Too often she still felt like a victim. She hated feeling that way. To feel so powerless, so worthless, so unwanted, so unloved…was awful!

"Well, those days of feeling unloved are over now. I have my beautiful Rose. I know you love your mama don't you sweetie" Jeanie softly cooed to her attentive baby. "I'll do everything I can to raise you right. You'll be proud of your old mom! I'll be strong for you my angel." Jeanie knew that she had to become strong for herself too! She was tired of feeling like she was just a helpless little worm stuck on the end of a big hook. She would no longer play the role of victim. She would have to make smarter, more responsible decisions in her life. After all, the health and well being of her child depended on it!

Yes, if Jeanie had just a smidgen of the kind of love for herself that she felt for her child, maybe her life would have been so much different. Past mournful memories continued to tear at Jeanie's soul. Still the remorseful girl liked to believe they occurred for a reason. Although these past recollections still hurt her heart, Jeanie was sure that God orchestrated these occurrences for a reason. These not so random experiences were meant to teach Jeanie specific lessons in life, things that she was required to know. With all the errors she made so far in her adult in life, she must have needed to learn a great deal. Finally it appeared that Jeanie was starting to learn her life lessons. After repeating similar mistakes for years and years, it was about time. It was also about time Jeanie settled down. It was definitely time for the girl to get her act together too. She still couldn't financially take care of herself, but she was going to learn how and the time was now.

Even when Jeanie was still pregnant for Rosa, she asked her social worker about college. The young woman was perceptive enough to realize that without some additional training, she would be back to working minimum-wage jobs with no future. When she was alone in the world, she could have squeaked by with a low-wage job with no future. Now that she had her baby to support, it was important that she would earn a decent living. She didn't want her child growing up impoverished like she had.

The emotionally stunted mother had come from a poor family. She still felt ashamed when she thought back on fifth grade. That was the year her dad left the family and moved halfway across the United States. Money was terribly scarce back then. Her mother barely scraped by on what little the government graciously gave her while she raised her daughters alone. Jeanie had only three dresses that fit her that year. They were all the same style but in different colors and they all had happened to be 70% off at the time.

It was during that year Jeanie found out what it was like to be real poor. The other kids at school had even more reasons to pick on the chubby, shy girl that year. Jeanie's self-esteem plummeted. If one looked at the youth, you could see the shame and hopelessness in her eyes. Often when the girl walked, her head was bent forward. It was easier for the shy girl to look at the ground than it was to look into her classmate's faces and see their ridiculing smiles. The following year, her tormenting peers had another reason to verbally torture Jeanie, for that was the year she got molested. That was the year she became "Sex pot"!

Jeanie's identity was all wrapped up in her little pink bundle from heaven now. When she held her baby, she didn't feel so alone. The damaged girl felt loved and needed when she embraced her squirming infant. Although Jeanie didn't have any experience with the care of such a small baby, she did the best she could. She was so nervous when she tended to her babies needs though. The baby quickly sensed Jeanie's nervousness and reacted to it by crying. Only after the visiting nurse showed the inexperienced mother the proper way to hold her baby, did Rosa's screaming subside. Jeanie was tenderly taught the correct way to hold her baby so she would feel secure in her arms. After her daughter quit crying every time Jeanie held her, things became somewhat peaceful. The anxious girl definitely felt a little bit better about the parenting job she was doing.

Those first few weeks after giving birth slowly slid by. All Jeanie seemed to do was eat, sleep, nurse her baby and change her. Even though Jeanie was lonely, she was glad that she didn't have a man to cater to. Right now she had all she could do to take care of herself and her demanding little child.

After six weeks passed, Jeanie brought Rosa to the specialist. She didn't have the transportation to bring her out there though. In order to get Rosa the help she needed, the girl took the 9 a.m. bus to the city of Harden. Despite the trouble to get there, Jeanie was glad that she brought her tiny bundle to the doctor. The white cloaked man carefully examined Rosa and took some x-rays of her legs. After going over the results, he put the little baby in a special harness to separate her legs. This allowed the hip bones to properly form. The doctor ensured Jeanie that the device would heal the socket in which the head of the hip bone fit into. He also told the uneasy mother that if Rosa didn't get the help she needed now, she probably would have had crippling arthritis when she was a teenager.

With a sigh of relief, Jeanie left the doctors office. Her baby looked a little funny with those straps hanging on her like that. Still, it was a small price to pay for the ability to walk. Since the bus out of Harden didn't depart for another four hours, Jeanie pushed her baby all across town in her stained, wobbly carriage. Sometimes, she would splurge and buy a small meal at the fast food restaurant. Mostly though she spent her time and her money at a nearby thrift store. It was important that Jeanie didn't waste any of her money. No, she had to make every dollar count living on federal assistance.

For the first few weeks Rosa didn't seem to mind being in the Pavlik harness. After the baby turned three months old, it was nearly impossible to put her back in it after her bath. Rosa would cry and cry. Although Jeanie tried to comfort her unhappy baby, nothing made her happy. The squirming infant wanted to kick her legs but was not allowed to because the device restricted her movements. Jeanie couldn't hold her baby girl close to her chest as she wanted to either. That made both of them sad.

During the first months following birth the bonding process was so critical. Through no fault of their own, that all important step was tampered with. Jeanie couldn't cuddle her baby close enough to fill the maternal need within. That's probably one of the reasons she smothered her with the wrong kind of love later on in her developmental years. Through no fault of their own, neither mother or child got their emotional needs met during those important months. Life never seemed fair for Jeanie and they sure didn't seem fair for her sweet little girl either.

It was a chore going to the out-of-town doctor, still Jeanie religiously mounted the bus to Harden no matter what kind of weather slowed her journey. Despite the obstacles the doting mom had to endure, her daughter was worth it. Her little girl was worth any kind of hell she had to go through. She was just thankful that Rosa's legs were taken out on that contraption two weeks before her first Christmas.

Wintry air started holding the New England town hostage several weeks earlier. The last two times Jeanie took the bus to Harden it was very cold. To make her travels worst was trying to maneuver the rickety carriage along the icy sidewalks. How the girl wished she had a reliable ride to Rosa's specialist besides the city bus. Well, she didn't. For now, all she had was herself and her own wits. Soon those long necessary trips to Harden would be over. How wonderful.

The holiday was so much brighter since Rosa was no longer in the uncomfortable harness that made her cry. Jeanie's mother and stepfather drove up to Massachusetts Christmas eve and stayed until the following afternoon. Yes, that holiday was filled with much hope, love and thankfulness. Unfortunately, the furnace in Jeanie's small apartment broke down late Christmas day, and they had to rely on an electric blanket to keep from freezing. Still it was a good day. Both mother and daughter got to cuddle together and enjoy each other's closeness and shared love.

Shortly after the first of the year, Jeanie decided she really needed transportation of her own. It was then that she decided to go to driving school. Even though she was 27, Jeanie had never learned to drive. Several past boyfriends had attempted to teach her but none had succeeded. The girl felt fearful behind the wheel. She lost all desire to learn to drive after that accident she had in her boyfriends car eight years ago. Her boyfriend thought he could teach someone with very little driving experience to drive a standard on a curvy road in the dark. Jeanie thought she was doing okay until she went around the sinuous mountain road and forgot to turn the wheel back after the turn. When she realized the car was going out of control she pressed what she thought was the brake…only it was the clutch. Obviously the car didn't stop. No, it speeded down the sloping hill barely missing a tree. It was a wonder that neither one of them got killed. Needless to say, Jeanie and her boyfriend broke up shortly after the wreck. He couldn't even look at the girl without thinking about what she did to his fancy sports car. Since Jeanie didn't even have a learner's permit, her boyfriend took the fall for her. He cared enough about her to shield her from the prospective trouble with the law. However he didn't care enough about Jeanie to stay with her.

After that driving experience, Jeanie lost all desire to learn to drive. She didn't trust herself behind the wheel of a car. Actually the girl didn't trust herself to do much of anything. Despite her reservations, Jeanie signed up for a few driving lessons. She spent more money than she really could spare but she learned how to drive by a patient professional. She even obtained her driver's license the first time she went for her road test.

Jeanie was proud of herself for conquering her fear of driving. She felt like she could do almost anything. The first thing she had to do was to get a cheap but somewhat reliable car. Unfortunately, there was no such thing as a car being both cheap and reliable. The car Jeanie bought from that small amount of money she saved turned out to be a dud. Although she drove it only occasionally, within six months time the transmission went out on it. Her little bug was squashed and unable to return from the dead. It was a good thing God gave Jeanie strong legs for she was going to need them with all the walking she would be doing!

For those few months Jeanie did have her own working vehicle life was great. She felt independent and strong. She felt empowered...like she could do anything. Up until then she managed to get by without having a car because she went with guys who had their own vehicle. Cars were an expense and a headache though. Jeanie liked the idea of not having to rely on anybody to bring her shopping or to the doctors. Living in the cold country there were many days where the temperature was too frigid to safely walk. Jeanie had done her share of walking in the past, but she wasn't about to subject her daughter to the freezing cold temperatures of the new England winters. Not if she could help it! Luckily Jeanie's blue bomb managed to keep ticking until an early spring graced the countryside with fair weather. Walking would be a necessity she could deal with now that the intolerable cold winter was over.

Despite the many bleak days the both of them shared the first year, it was as much a growing experience for Jeanie as it was for her daughter. All went fairly well for the first ten months or so in their lives. Both mother and daughter seemed to be getting just the right amount of love and nurturing they desperately needed. Still, the little mother felt wanton inside.

Even though Jeanie was blessed with her daughter's love, she felt that she was missing out on something. All those months Jeanie tried to deny the need for a man. Still the idea of spending time with a sweet, caring man was becoming an obsession with her. Jeanie didn't know how she would find compatible dates until she saw an AD in the paper about a dating service.

Although Jeanie was an attractive girl, she wasn't close to many people. Even now there seemed to be a giant cloud around Jeanie that kept her at arms length from people. Even though the veil of mistrust loomed heavily inside Jeanie's heart, she knew that she did not want to spend her life alone. She craved the love and companionship of a good man. She didn't think she could find a man to her suiting by sheer luck alone. She couldn't meet anybody at church for the one time she attended the Catholic church, she was asked to leave due to her noisy baby. That's pretty bad, to be kicked out of God's house! Still, after all Jeanie had done in the past, maybe she didn't deserve to step into the holy place. She wasn't good enough for church. Perhaps she wasn't good enough for God either. She may not have been deserving of a man's love either, but she wanted it anyway. So, she decided to pursue that idea. Maybe with the aid of the dating service, she could find someone whom she could build a relationship with. Yes…maybe.

The first few dates she got from the dating service weren't such a great match. Every single time Jeanie had a date with someone new, her hopes would soar so high that it felt like her feet floated off the ground. With much exuberance and energy, the elated young lady would dance and dance. The exercise made her feel happy. It made her feel sexy. Sometimes Jeanie would watch herself in the mirror as she danced. Physically, she was perfect or nearly so. Her weight was down and her face had a creamy, rosy complexion. Still, she couldn't help but wonder, what was wrong with her as a person. Surely there must be a reason why she didn't have anybody in her life. Maybe she was just not pretty enough. Maybe she was not sexy enough. Maybe she was not smart enough. All those self doubts which plagued Jeanie when she was younger still haunted her.

Just when the girl was about to tell Brent what he could do with his dating service, she met someone she liked very much. Will was a tall, handsome man in his late 20s. He had a good job and a giving heart. He was also very accepting and kind to Jeanie's baby. There had been times when the new mom dated guys and they were turned off by the fact she had a baby. Having a child to cater to seemed to get in the way of any impulsive plans a confirmed bachelor might have. Obviously, not everyone wanted a ready-made family. Still, if someone wanted Jeanie, he would have to accept her daughter too.

Jeanie and Will spent an incredibly romantic Saturday evening together. After that weekend, the two of them fell madly in love (or lust). That was the start of what would be a long term relationship with Jeanie…the first one she had since her divorce four years ago. Perhaps, the former wild child had a shot at obtaining the type of love that she had desired. She could only hope so.

## CHAPTER 12

# Say You Will

During the first few months together, Jeanie and Will spent almost every waking moment with each other. The physical attraction between the two was strong. Will was tall and slender with thick straight hair which touched the collar of the casual shirts he regularly wore. The blue jeans he daily wore fit snugly against his well formed derrière. Beneath the left cheek bone on his otherwise smooth face was a distinctive mole which added to the man's beauty. What made Will even more beautiful in Jeanie's eyes was the way he treated her and Rosa. His gentle kindness made him even more desirable to Jeanie.

Jeanie loved looking at Will but mostly she just loved being near him. He made her feel good inside. He made her feel loved. He always asked her what she wanted or where she wanted to go. Jeanie wasn't used to a man being so considerate of her. This trait wasn't something she had seen a lot of…especially lately.

For a long while, the two love birds went out together with the baby on board. They rode around in the car and waited for Rosa to fall asleep. When she did, they made a mad dash to engage in their planned romantic escapade before Rosa woke up. They would drive off to a deserted road in the country, find a nice spot to park and then get real natural.

There's something magical about making love in the outdoors. The nature lovers really got turned on sexually and sensuously when out in the glorious splendor of nature's canopy. The melody of the birds combined with the sweet scent of the nearby wildflowers heightened their senses. Once in a while Jeanie and Will timed things just right and expressed their passions to each other in the rain. When they engaged in their love making during those ideal times, Jeanie's whole body came alive. The tiny droplets of water that fell from the sky made her body tingle as it touched her exposed skin. The shivering and quivering they both experienced brought the two lovebirds to paradise. Still, the couple needed more than good sex to keep their romance going. That was something the two lovers had yet to discover.

For the first few months together the pair got along pretty well. In between idle talk, they played board games to pass away the hours. During much of their spare time they kissed and cuddled like a couple of giddy school kids. Besides Will's good looks, he possessed a passionate soul. Jeanie loved how affectionate her boyfriend was. That was the thing Jeannie liked the most about Will, that and the good job he had. He was an extremely, good mechanic. Being a talented auto technician, he earned an above average salary. The man could fix practically anything. He sure knew what to do with Jeanie's neglected broken down parts. He also knew what to do to fix her jaded, disillusioned heart.

Within three months time, Jeanie and Will were engaged. They really believed that this was the start of a long, happy life together. It may actually have been a real nice union for the both of them. However, neither one of them was mature enough to handle marriage with all its myriad of difficulties and trials that went along with it.

In some ways, Will and Jeanie were both like little children. Neither one wanted to wait for what it was they desired. Neither of them believed in delayed gratification. Jeanie craved attention and affection. Will was obsessed with purchasing an array of new mechanic tools. The costs of all the shiny items he bought slowly ate a big hole in his pocket. His need to continue buying those expensive tools took over his life and robbed him of all logic. Naturally he was stressed when the accumulating bills ate away the majority of his pay check every week. Under extreme duress people act differently than they normally would. Will was no exception. His demeanor changed for the worst the more debt he sunk into. Jeanie wondered if the two of them had any future together anymore. This fear turned the carefree, lovable lass into an uptight worry wart. They may still had been together if Will hadn't dug himself so far into debt.

Jeanie's frivolous fella spent most of his money within a week of earning it. Although he spent some of it on her and Rosa, mostly he spent it on his fancy, work tools or the parts needed to fix up his own used vehicle. Even though the guy made good money, he always seemed to be broke. Since Jeanie was financially insecure, it did not settle well with her. She definitely needed to feel secure…more so now that she had her child.

The stress of being in debt along with Rosa's growing bad temperament, slowly drove Will away from Jeanie. Jeanie tried to talk to Will about his debt problems, but he just turned a deaf ear and kept on charging the world on his gold master card.

Things between the both of them became even more stressful when Will accepted a job in another part of the state. He was so far in debt that he needed to take the higher paying job offered to him, or else remain in a financial money pit forever. Although it took an hour and a half drive to visit Jeanie, Will continued to travel to her apartment every weekend to see her…at least for awhile.

Those first few months apart from her boyfriend was hard for Jeanie to handle. She was used to seeing him every day and cuddling next to him every night. For a year, the frazzled girl had someone taking care of her emotional needs and helping with her terribly tempermental toddler. Now she was basically alone to cope with things the best she could. Since Jeanie was not close to her family and did not have many friends, the pressures of life very rapidly placed a tight grip on the sensitive, distraught girl.

It was the middle of winter. The days were long and gloomy on that cold and miserable day. Jeanie tried comforting her whining, temper throwing child the best she could. That day Rosa drove Jeanie positively berserk. The overwhelmed mother was in the process of cutting the carrots for her stew when Rosa wandered into the kitchen. She was balling her eyes out over God knows what. The intense screaming along with Rosa's tugging drove Jeanie off the edge. She was so stressed and depressed that for a moment, for one second, she thought about taking the knife she was holding and stabbing the horrible, little monster to death. Jeanie was horrified that she could even think about doing something so vicious to her baby that she took the knife she held and pressed it against her wrist. Jeanie felt that she deserved to die. Anyone that could think of doing something so terrible to her child deserved to be put to death. Almost trancelike, Jeanie began to cut through the skin of her left wrist. When she started to feel a little pain, and saw the blood trickle down her arm, she stopped.

"Oh God, what am I doing!"

Reluctantly, Jeanie called her neighbor upstairs and told her what happened. Darlene came down immediately and stayed there with the two of them until her boyfriend arrived at her home. After her lover arrived, Rosa was brought to her aunt's house. Jeanie was brought to the hospital and then to the mental health center for evaluation. The staff there wanted the suicide risked girl to stay that night, but the now calmed Jeanie insisted on going home to get her clothes. She also had to find someone to take care of her birds and cat.

Although Jeanie was ashamed of going to the psychiatric ward in the hospital, she knew she needed help. Her sister Deana wasn't close to Jeanie nevertheless she was nice enough to take care of Rosa while she got the help she desperately needed. Jeanie and Will cuddled together in bed until 7 am. He tried to comfort the distressed mom, but all she could do was cry. The next morning, Jeanie bit her lip as she mounted the steep cement stairs of the mental health hospital.

The doctors evaluating Jeanie talked about her family history. It was at that point they told her that she undoubtedly was manic depressive. Her father was extremely moody at times. Her mother definitely was, especially after her dad left her. Jeanie herself had periods of extreme hyperactivity along with periods of deep depression. The hyper active, manic phases she went through were wonderful…at least for her. During one of those phases, Jeanie had the energy to do most anything. However, when she was in the down side of that cycle…she couldn't do hardly anything. On those days she had all she could do to roll out of bed in the morning and get dressed. Her emotions were so intense that she felt that her insides would explode if she did not find some way to release them. However when Jeanie became real depressed, it was usually for a reason. No one could've expected Jeanie to be joyous over the rapes, the physical abuse or about her father's murder. Since she was an extremely sensitive girl with deep feelings, she experienced heightened emotions during those life shattering events.

Jeanie had been like that most of her life. She thought what she was feeling was natural. True, people had different aspects of their personality, but to experience such extreme emotions was frightening. These feeling weren't natural or wonderful…they were just plain scary.

Actually, Jeanie had been frightened of many of her emotions lately. They were so strong. They were so unpredictable. The distraught lass was glad that she was in the hospital. There, she could feel safe. There, she could perhaps gain control over her emotions as well as her life. So far Jeanie's life had been one big roller coaster ride after another. Often the girl would get so wrapped up in her emotions that she couldn't think. All she could do was to feel.

During the short ten days in the hospital Jeanie was put on lithium. She also received daily sessions with a therapist as well as group therapy. One time, her entire family joined her in a therapy session. The psychologist dug into the family dynamics while at the same time wrote notes in his ledger. As usual, the mute girl sat in a corner and did little as the group individually and collectively carved her up for dinner. Everyone who attended the family help session, all seemed to have a different outlook on Jeanie's condition. Everyone blamed everyone else as to the reason their overly sensitive relative went off the deep end. Jeanie was glad that awkward hour finally came to an end. Now, Jeanie thought, she knew what a fish felt like staring out of it's bowl into the eyes of a hungry cat!

While in the hospital Jeanie definitely felt better. The staff just assumed it was the medicine keeping the emotionally charged young woman sane. The therapy was definitely helping. The effects the medicine would have on Jeanie when she once again entered her insanely stressed world, was yet to be seen.

Yes, when the girl pulled away from all of life's stresses, everything was calm and serene. Jeanie's world became so peaceful while she resided in the hospital. While there Jeanie had no worries, no stresses, and no screaming child to look after. Being there felt like summer camp to the sensitive girl. She spent most of her spare time doing the artwork she loved. The mental health unit had all sorts of art projects available to her. Jeanie was only too happy to be making them all. She didn't have the money or time to invest in those nifty little projects at home. She thought that basically, the whole experience in the psych ward had been great.

Since Jeanie had Rosa, her whole life revolved around her. The previously irresponsible girl no longer had any time just for herself. While in the hospital, she had all sorts of time. Everyone needed a few minutes out of the day where they could unwind. Except for those few hours of nightly sleep, Jeanie didn't have the privilege of uninterrupted time for herself. Things became a lot worst for her when she didn't have Will there to help with her teething tyrant. Carmalita Jean desperately needed the emotional pampering she had grown dependent on as well. Now that her boyfriend had moved so far away, those needed moments were scarce on the weekend and nonexistent during the week.

Despite the stigma of being in the loony bin, Jeanie learned much about herself and her feelings. She obviously had a fun time in between therapy doing the art she loved. Despite all the honest conversations she had with her counselor, she never told him about what happened on the hill. Even then, she felt that it was her fault. She definitely didn't tell her counselor about the cruel, hurtful names her peers called her especially after Mr. Martin accosted her that day on the hill. Jeanie never told her counselor about any of the other times she was raped either. She felt that since she had willingly gone somewhere with the perpetrators, then she got what she deserved. It was her fault. She allowed it to happen. Jeanie never told her therapist about her bulimia either, because that was just plain sick. Besides, she had just about eliminated that self bullying behavior herself, without any type of professional intervention.

After ten days, Jeanie's lithium level had stabilized in her bloodstream so the doctors discharged her from the unit. She was sent home with the understanding that a family counselor would visit her at home once a week. Jeanie left the facility relaxed and ready to start a new life with Rosa and her part-time boyfriend.

Jeanie wasn't home more than three hours when her daughter started throwing one hell of a kicking, screaming, head banging fit. The former mental patient could feel the emotions within soaring.

"Those damn pills worked fine when all was calm and serene, but out in the real world, they're not worth a shit!" Jeanie cried.

When put to the test in the real world, the pills failed miserably. Since Jeanie felt herself losing control, she quickly placed her girl in the playpen where she could safely continue her fit. She further distanced herself from her screaming child by retreating into the nearby bathroom and covering up her ears with her hands in an attempt to muffle out Rosa's loud screaming. With disappointment and anger Jeanie reached for the vial of pills which were supposed to make her life so blissful. With the bottle in her hand, she walked over to the toilet and lifted the lid. With one loud swoosh, the prescribed miracle drugs were all flushed down the commode.

"That's about all those suckers are good for!" Shouted Jeanie. After checking on her daughter, the discouraged girl raced to her bed and dived into a pillow. Tears poured from Jeanie's eyes leaving stains on her pillow, further marring her troubled heart.

"Oh damn! Why did I think all my problems would be solved by a couple of pills? I should know by now nothing is easy. No, nothing in my life has ever been that easy!"

The pills Jeanie obtained from the doctors at the mental health clinic didn't do much good outside the hospital. However the ongoing therapy the girl received after her dismissal helped her a lot! For the next year or so Jeanie had a nice lady counselor making house calls once a week to check on her and Rosa. Together they talked about whatever problems the mother and daughter recently encountered. Angela was a real sweet lady and never pushed Jeanie to divulge anything more than what the reluctant girl was willing to tell. Angela was never judgmental nor demanding. Jeanie felt lucky to have such a good wonderful person to visit with her. She felt she could tell the even tempered, kind lady anything.

Although Will and Jeanie had their share of problems, they remained a couple. It was hard keeping up their relationship at times though. Will wanted more time and affection than the young mother could give him. She tried to tell him how small children needed a lot of mommy time as well as lots of attention. That fact may have been known, but Will still needed as much emotional nurturance from Jeanie as before. However, he kept receiving much less of the physical affection he desired.

Will had become discontented in waiting for his turn at Jeanie's devotions. He no longer wanted to wait for Rosa to go to sleep before Jeanie and him made love. Lately the little girl just didn't want to sleep at all. Her boyfriend became increasingly resentful when the couple had to forfeit their days outing because Rosa was sick or overtired and crabby. Many little things worked towards pulling their relationship apart. Although there was much feeling between the both of them, there was also much friction.

Jeanie didn't know what to do to smooth things over with her honey. He was obviously unhappy with the path their relationship had taken. She also was unsatisfied with their love affair and very unhappy with his attitude he had concerning her little girl. She tried to talk to Will, but he saw things one way while Jeanie saw things another way. Neither one of them could deny the intensity of their problems for as the weeks went by, they became more and more apparent. Neither one of them readily accepted the fact, that they both needed to change in order to make things work between them. Despite their difficulties, Jeanie and Will continued to see each other every weekend. They received little tidbits of affection and time with each other whenever they possibly could. That would have to be enough until Jeanie's not so sweet little girl toddled out of her terrible twos.

Jeanie and her daughter lived in a multi-floored apartment building in a fairly safe section of Windsock. When Rosa learned to stay out of the road and to stay around the house, Jeanie would let the girl go outside to play. Jeanie had a swing set assembled right outside her living room window. Since she lived on the first floor, the trusting mom would allow her little one to play outside the house without her. After all, there was hardly any traffic and most of the time the little boy upstairs was outside playing on the swing set too, so what's the harm? Besides Jeanie needed time to do her English composition homework.

Yes, Jeanie had recently started college. She loved art and had talked to Will several times about furthering her education. Actually, if it wasn't for her boyfriend, Jeanie never would have signed up for college. She didn't consider herself smart enough. The girl fooled every body who doubted her…including herself. Jeanie liked school and she was doing quite well in it. It was hard work though. Attending college was probably one of the smartest things Jeanie ever did for herself. The girl would learn a trade so she could one day take proper care of her and her daughter. Jeanie focused on her art interest. She approached her lessons with such gusto. She definitely built up her self esteem through her course work. Jeanie started to think her life was coming together. She could permanently tuck away all those horrible things that happened to her in the past, or so she thought.

Jeanie had only been attending college for six months before she got a call from Mary, her child's daycare provider. Rosa had been acting inappropriately with her dolls. She thought the child was acting out some type of sexual abuse issues. Jeanie was mortified. She tried to protect her little lamb from all the evils in the world and now this.

Rosa didn't want to tell her concerned mom why she was doing what she did with the doll. The little girl thought she was in trouble, so she either would stop talking to her mom or else begin talking about something else. Jeanie was so happy when her counselor came to her house the following day.

Angela talked and played dolls with little Rosa for quite awhile before they began talking about the serious issue. When the kindly counselor began asking Rosa if anyone had touched her here or there…the young innocent child hesitantly told her someone had touched her in those private parts. Turned out the six year old boy upstairs, the same one who played with Rosa on a regular basis got her behind the building and touched her genitals. He didn't do anything else. He was just curious about the difference between boys and girls. Since there wasn't much of an age difference between the two kids, nothing legally would be done to the boy. He would however have a counselor talk to him about inappropriate touches.

Jeanie probably would have been content to brush the whole improper touching thing under the carpet, especially after it was discovered who exactly touched her daughter. Nothing really happened. It was just child experimentation and nothing more. Angela was mystified over Jeanie's laisser-faire reaction to her daughter's molestation. The week following Angela's talk to Rosa, her counselor asked Jeanie questions no other therapist had previously asked.

"Have you ever been sexually molested?" Angela asked.

"Yes, but it was so long ago. It doesn't matter any more," Jeanie answered without a flinch of emotion.

However what happened in the past really did matter. It mattered a great deal. For the next several years, Jeanie began unraveling the feelings that had been hid away concerning the many times she had been sexually abused. Everything had happened so long ago, Surely it wouldn't matter anymore. No one had a clue as to what the secretive girl went through in the past. She never told anyone at the mental health clinic for she thought that something she did provoked the attacks. It took Angela's sensitive, perceptive spirit to unlock the mysteries in Jeanie's mind.

It was at that point that Jeanie told the kindly counselor about how her uncle would feel up her breast while he embraced her in front of the other family members. The girl never told her mother or father for she didn't think she would have been believed that at the time. Maybe it was just an accident that he had grabbed her breast. One time, may have been an accident. However every single time Jeanie and her family would visit her Uncle Vance, he would fondle her breast. The girl felt ashamed and helpless and so dirty. She felt obligated to hug him at the family get-togethers but she didn't want to. Still to keep peace. To keep from making waves in her already rocky family group, Jeanie would do what was expected from her…reach around her Uncle Vance and gave him a big hug. While hugging him she could expect her uncle to sneakily cup her tender breast within a just a few feet from where her clueless parents were standing. Jeanie knew that what her uncle did wasn't right, but she was afraid to say anything…so she didn't.

Jeanie told Angela about Mr. Martin on the hill. She told how the big man intimidated her and made her feel so frightened. She let him feel on her body. She just stood there and let him do those things to her. Surely, she wanted what the man had done to her or she would've run sooner. Yes, why hadn't she run sooner? She believed all those years that she was a bad person. She was a bad person because she did bad things.

That ugly circle of shame and self hate kept getting bigger and bigger throughout the years. Eventually, poor Jeanie was utterly surrounded by the thickened black cloud life's circumstances created. She could not see around it anymore. Never did she think she would be able to get through it. She thought that feeling of powerlessness and shame would be with her for the rest of her life…keeping her from ever feeling at peace, keeping her from a normal life, keeping her from self acceptance and self love. She felt she didn't deserved to have a good life or feel good about herself…because she was a bad person, who deserved bad things.

Those rumors that followed the molestation about finished off whatever self esteem Jeanie had inside. She was chewed to pieces by the cruel comments which poured into her heart daily by her uncaring classmates. How could people be so cruel Jeanie asked herself. The girl actually believed that she deserved all the punishment and torment she received from her peers…after all she did let Mr. Martin touch her there.

Just because Jeanie didn't run from the tall, overpowering man, didn't mean that she wanted him to touch her. She was still a child at thirteen. And she was scared, so scared she couldn't move, she couldn't think, she couldn't feel. One of the involuntary defensive mechanisms Jeanie had was the power of disassociation. Whenever things got so unbearable, Jeanie would separate herself from her feelings, and sometimes her memories. For a few minutes…they didn't exist. The experiences she had almost felt like they had happened to someone else. She did not allow herself to be fully conscious of what was happening to her at the time they were occuring. She continued this disassociate behavior all through her junior high years. She had to the day on the hill and all those endless days of taunting and bullying. She had to in order to survive…emotionally.

For years Jeanie denied the overwhelming pent-up feelings that she had hid from herself. The poor girl actually had talked herself into believing that not only didn't the abuse exist but that it did not matter if it did occur. Angela realized that no one could continue to disassociate from their inner core without playing havoc on their psyche. All the times Jeanie had been physically and sexually abused took it's toll on her mind and her heart. Only now did Jeanie's mind allow her to acknowledge and feel all that her damaged heart should have felt a long time ago. Only in the company of her trusting companion and counselor did Jeanie allow her mind to go back into another place and relive all the trials she had suffered so far in her life.

The journey into Jeanie's past was difficult as well as painful. Still, the determined brave girl kept on opening up the doors to the almost forgotten pain. In reliving the abuses, she allowed them to be acknowledged. This was a major factor in Jeanie's healing process.

After fourteen months of intense therapy Jeanie was now mentally healthier than she had been years. Still, there were parts of her personality that would continue to attract the type of person who would hurt her. Even though the girl had gone through hours of self discovery and healing, it was not enough to keep her from repeating some of the past mistakes all over again at a future time.

For now anyway, Jeanie felt emotionally strong and physically powerful. She had been attending college all through her painful therapy sessions. She still had her share of troubles with Rosa, but since she took a parenting class, Jeanie was able to understand many of the developmental stages in her child's life. She understood herself better and she was making every effort to understand her daughter better.

It was also during those college years that Jeanie once again became very interested in writing. She wrote poetry ever since she could remember. She still recalled some of her writings from grade school. However, lately Jeanie was writing short stories. She had also gone back to journaling. Through those journal entries Jeanie delved deep inside the inner most regions of her heart. They helped her to understand herself better. These writings helped her heal her severely damaged heart.

Jeanie studied psychology in college as well. It was fascinating for the schoolgirl to understand the reasons behind her intense sometimes out-of-control feelings. Understanding why she experienced the emotions that she felt, helped make Jeanie's world a little more predictable. It also put her more in control of her life. There were so many times in the past when Jeanie felt she was a victim of circumstance. She just now was coming to realize that she had more control over her life than she had previously imagined. Still, that didn't mean that she had control over people or events in her life. No one can gain control over that. Still, that was what Jeanie tried to do with Will.

The artistic girl had good intentions when she talked to Will about his spending habits. Her boyfriend had become too far in debt. He was drowning in bills. Jeanie could see what that added stress was doing to his personality. She may have gotten too preachy to him, only because he wouldn't listen to her words of wisdom. He resented the truthful words his girlfriend told him, almost as much as he resented the time Rosa took away from him.

Jeanie wanted someone who was responsible and reliable as well as a loving and intelligent. She couldn't accept Will's impulsive, immature way of handling his finances. The man was getting more and more demanding of Jeanie's time as well. He didn't like competing with Rosa for attention and was quick to tell her that.

The arguments between Jeanie and Will kept getting worse and worse. The cold war between them stayed icy cold for weeks following the couple's most recent argument. Although the girl loved the type of affection Will provided her with, that obviously wasn't enough to keep them together. Jeanie even painfully remembered the proposition Will gave her one evening. Her boyfriend told Jeanie that he would marry her in a heartbeat if she gave her daughter to someone else to raise. Although Jeanie loved Will, she wasn't about to give away her own flesh and blood. Rosa certainly wasn't some kind of stray cat to pawn off on who ever would take her!

One spring morning, the couple sat down at the kitchen table and talked about their grievances over tea. It was then, that the two of them decided it was best to say goodbye. With tears in her eyes, Jeanie let go of Will. They had been together for 2 ½ years. The last six months however seemed like an eternity. The couple had been having more bad times than good times lately. Things weren't getting any better for them…so what could either of them to? There was nothing to do but say goodbye and let time slowly dry the tears.

# CHAPTER 13

# Designated Lover

For a few months following the breakup Jeanie was an emotional mess. She spent many days wondering if that romance with Will was her last chance at love and happiness. She wondered whether she would ever find anyone who could love both her and her child. Although her girl could be a handful at times, Jeanie loved Rosa dearly. Anyone she went with would have to understand that since Rosa was her child, her needs would have to come before either of theirs. That's just the way it was. If the guy she's with couldn't accept those terms…then he didn't need to be with her.

Jeanie tried her best to act happy. Her daughter didn't need to see her mother so broken up she couldn't function. Jeanie said affirmations regularly in an attempt to crawl out of her defunct mood. Maybe she could talk herself into being happy. She said a group of affirmations everyday while she was getting dressed, driving to school or in between classes. "I am a worthwhile person who is worthy of love. I am a a beautiful, intelligent woman with much to offer. I am a child of God and I am loved and guided by Him". Maybe if she told those things to herself enough, she would truly believe them. She certainly didn't enjoy feeling like a misunderstood misfit. Still just because she felt like one, it didn't make it so. No!

Jeanie also directed much of her time towards her artistic interest. These distractions certainly helped pass the time, but they couldn't completely fill the emptiness she felt inside. Jeanie still mourned her lost love, though she didn't know why. They were both unhappy. She knew Will would never grow up and be the responsible man she needed. He wasn't as emotionally needy at she was, but he was close.

"Come on Carmalita Jean! Snap out of it!"

What Jeanie needed now was someone to take her mind off her disappointing relationship she had with Will. Somehow, she had to get over her recent heart wrenching romance.

The fact was, Jeanie was miserable without a man in her life. She required the physical closeness of another human being. She loved kissing and cuddling more then the actual sex, although that was nice too. Yes, she needed a man in her life…someone who she could do fun things with. The girl wanted love but for the time being, she would settle for a nice guy who would take her dancing.

The bruised girl's self-esteem still wasn't completely healed from her past abuses, nor would she probably ever completely be. Although many men had hurt her in her life, Jeanie decided it was time to actively seek out a nice, caring, honest, affectionate man who she could spend time with. She had already moped around for a month,. It was about time for the studious, yet fun loving Jeanie to get back into the dating scene.

She decided it was time to once again contact her dating service. Her membership was put on hold when she was with Will. Now it was time to reactivate it. It was now time to take Jeanie's heart out the deep freeze and to start living again.

Jeanie began to meet the selected men from her dating service within a weeks time. Although she met a variety of guys she didn't take to someone right off like she had Will. Still, the sentimental dreamer continued dating hoping that one day she'd hit the jack pot. Eventually she would find someone through her stockpile of responses. So, Jeanie sorted through the pile of letters she received from potential boyfriends after Rosa finally went to sleep. She hoped that her search wouldn't all be in vain.

The insecure girl became more and more anxious as each day passed away. Sometimes, after a particularly tough day with a temperamental toddler, Jeanie wondered if she did indeed make the right choice in keeping Rosa and rejecting Will. Things weren't perfect with her most recent boyfriend, why would she think the communication problems and financial difficulties would change just because Rosa was out of their lives. They would probably have difficulties even if they lived alone on their own little island somewhere. Besides how could she live with herself knowing that she gave away her own little baby?

Jeanie made it through the lonely months following the breakup by exerting as much time as possible in her art classes at school. While Jeanie created something, she felt her life had a purpose after all. She felt even more empowered when she expressed herself through her various writings. Jeanie was thankful for her college's curriculum. Not everything the scholar studied in school came easy for her. Still, she wasn't about to give up on her dream to make something of herself. Jeanie didn't quite know what she would do with her knowledge and degree at the time. She had a couple of years to burden herself over that detail. She knew that all the coursework she struggled through now would pay off in a couple of years. Her life would be a whole lot better off in the future because of what she was doing for herself now.

Jeanie smiled at her reflection in the mirror as she hurriedly brushed her hair. She was actually beginning to like the person she was. Now, at least she can look at herself and feel pride and not shame. Although Jeanie had a long way to go before she attained her scholastic goals, she persevered on. That in itself was an accomplishment for the ex-hippy girl who at one time didn't have enough motivation in her past life to accomplish anything worthwhile. She hardly seemed like the same person from those wild yesteryears.

Just a few weeks before her semester in school ended, Jeanie met someone she really liked. Barry was very charismatic and funny. The man was okay to look at, but no one Jeanie would have looked at twice previously in her life. How ever the man's personality shined past any physical imperfections that may have clouded the girls vision. Jeanie was quite impressed by the mustached man with the Santa Claus laughter.

The first time the two of them met, was at a local café. Usually Jeanie chose to meet her new date mate in a public place just in case he turned out to be a mass murderer or just plain creepy. After meeting with Barry and talking for a few skin minutes, he suggested they go for a ride to visit a local state park. Normally, the now cautious girl would have said No, and made a giant leap to her car. However, this time she felt pretty certain that the man before her would be a gentleman. The more she looked at his impish face, the less sure she felt of her own self-control over her sexual impulsivity.

Barry led the two man caravan up the wooded area near where the state park was located. After parking her car behind his, Jeanie carefully stepped out of her vehicle and locked the door. There wasn't a soul around, but still one never knew when someone would drive up to the parking area and break into the car. Jeanie felt pretty certain no one would steal her car. Still, they could steal her treasured music tapes or worst yet her car stereo.

The couple looked at the trail map that hung behind a pane of dirty glass attached to the welcome sign. There were several trails clearly marked on the map. They decided to follow the one with the red triangle. Barry commented that it should be a nice, scenic walk. Jeanie shook her head in agreement.

Barry and Jeanie leisurely hiked the flowery trail, stopping occasionally to admire the variety of birds nestled in the shrubbery. Barry reached towards Jeanie's fingers, but hesitated for a moment. He searched her brown orbs for permission to hold her soft, smooth hand. Jeanie's eyes told him yes, After gazing into each other's irises for a brief moment, Jeanie held her hand out for him to hold. The two of them strolled down the grassy path which led to the heart of the Rhododendron forest.

The couple walked a few hundred feet down the secluded path until they came across a tiny trickling waterfall. The two nature lovers stopped their walk for a few minutes to appreciate the serene beauty which lay before them. Before continuing their magical hike through the forest, Barry turned to Jeanie and held her close to his chest for a few moments. With his right hand he gently turned her face towards his. Barry gently leaned his face towards her and planted the sweetest kiss on her moist lips. The romantic young girl became starry eyed as he lifted his full lips from hers.

Jeanie could feel her heart beating furiously inside her chest. Despite her inner distractions, she continued walking along with the charming man beside her. After making a loop through the wooded area, they wound up at the trailhead. After a few minutes of small talk, the two said their goodbyes. One more brief hug was exchanged between them before they stepped into their own individual cars. Barry promised to call Jeanie. The question of when he would call her was on the tip of her tongue. Jeanie wanted to know, but she dared not ask. If she appeared too anxious, that might scare the man away she thought. Jeanie left the flowery park all smiles. She had finally found someone she wanted to be with for more than a few days. She had to pursue this relationship slowly. She surely didn't want him to think she was desperate.

The next few days passed slowly. Just when Jeanie thought that Barry wasn't going to call her back, he did. Their second date together would be a dinner date. How wonderful Jeanie thought. How wonderful indeed!

The nervous schoolgirl didn't care for the restaurant Barry picked out, but that was not important. What mattered to her now was that she shared company with someone she wanted to be with. Barry was the first man she dated whom she really liked since her breakup with Will. The way Barry looked at her while trying to impress the giggling girl with his silly jokes was comical. It was obvious in his actions that Barry really liked her.

After a most enjoyable evening together, Barry brought Jeanie to his little apartment in the small city of Hummer. It was but a stone's throw from Windsock. Jeanie thought that the two of them would spend only a few minutes at his place kissing and cuddling. That may have been only what the two of them planned. However, their hormones were flying high that evening. One thing eventually led to another. Before Jeanie knew it, she was in Barry's bedroom sharing sweet love with the desirable man before her.

That one romantic evening set the pace for the many, hot steamy nights ahead. There was so much Jeanie liked about Barry. He was kinda cute, slim, clean shaven and rather impish. He was definitely fun to be around. He made the serious, but fun seeking girl laugh. She couldn't help but become light hearted and joyous while in his company. The guy had a good job besides. Jeanie thought that Barry was just what she was looking for. Still, there was something he told her when they first started dating that kept Carmalita Jean from getting too close to the passionate man.

Barry made it clear that he wanted to move back to Indiana. He made out a multitude of job applications. He was sure that it would only be a matter of time before one of the employers called him in for an interview. It would only be a matter of time before he would be hired for one of those jobs. Of course when that happened, he would move.

Jeanie had a year to finish her coursework at the community college She obviously wasn't going anywhere for a while. Besides, she had already been accepted at the local state college the following year. If things between them did get beyond the physical point, she decided she would continue her college education no matter what. The ambitious girl was determined to make something of her life or die trying.

Jeanie really did like being with Barry though. He was so fun to be with. The two routinely went out to dinner together, often bringing Rosa along. Every weekend they went dancing as well. He drank a bit more than Jeanie, but she didn't mind. She appointed herself the designated driver when they went clubbing. At first Barry's drinking didn't bother her in the least. When Barry got drunk, he was funny and silly. He wasn't abusive and foul mouthed like Slugger.

Barry greeted Jeanie with a small bouquet of flowers he bought at the local supermarket every Friday night. They weren't costly, but they sure were a nice gesture. The pretty flowers made Jeanie feel special. The girl graciously received them and carefully arranged them in her favorite green vase. The bouquet would last 5 to 7 days if they were carnations or mums. So all week long Jeanie would look at the beautiful flowers before her and be reminded of her boyfriend.

Since Barry lived only 20 minutes from Jeanie, they saw each other quite often the first few months they went together. After three months, Barry acquired a better paying job in Worcester. Obviously, the visitations were cut way down. Usually he would come over to Jeanie's apartments on the weekends. Even though Jeanie didn't like driving in the big city, occasionally she cruised over to Barry's apartment during the week. They liked each other but neither one of them were real serious about the other. For practical reasons it was agreed that they would date other people. They also agreed that they would sleep only with each other. For awhile this arrangement worked out quite well. Actually, the whole thing made perfect sense. It was better to give your physical love to a friend, someone who cared about you and knows your likes rather than to give in to your sexual urges with one night stands. That arrangement was easier on the ego and eliminated the potential hazard of catching diseases.

Although neither one of the two wanted to get serious about each other, they couldn't help falling madly in like with each other after nine months. Sometimes Barry would tell Jeanie what a special girl she was. He really liked her, but he had his mind set to father kids someday. Jeanie had a tubal ligation years ago so she made it clear to Barry that her baby making machine was permanently closed. If she could have children, their relationship may have gotten further along emotionally than Barry wanted at the time. Since Jeanie was crazy about Barry, it wouldn't have taken much for her to fall in love with him if she let herself. Yes, it was Barry's aloofness that kept Jeanie's feelings at bay. But maybe that was for the best, especially after that horrible hiking trip to Mount Monadnock.

Jeanie's life changed forever the day her and Barry went mountain hiking. Halfway down the mountain, Jeanie and her boyfriend stopped to rest among some huge boulders close to the trail. While she sat there enjoying the cool breeze brushing against her face, Jeanie suddenly felt an intense sting in her genital area. The rock she rested against had a deep crevice in it. Inside that crevice was a slew of ants. The loose shorts she wore that day provided access for the red devils to climb up her leg and bite the hell out of her. Jeanie managed to brush off the pesky insects. Still the vicious bites left some awful welts. Since the swelling caused by the bites didn't go down after a couple of days, Jeanie swallowed her modesty and sought the services of her family physician. He gave her some ointment, took some tests and sent her along her way. Jeanie thought that would be the end of things…but no.

Much to Jeanie's surprise, she received a call from her doctor informing her that the blisters on her Vulva was herpes. The girl had almost forgotten that she even had the disease. Actually she had hoped that doctors misdiagnosed her, for she never had any other outbreaks until then. After that incident with the ants, Jeanie broke out with those painful lesions quite frequently… at least once a month. Needless to say her herpes played havoc on her sexual relationship with Barry. Even though it definitely set the relationship back a spell, the two continued seeing each other. Eventually, the girl was put on suppressive therapy to prevent her breakouts. As long as Jeanie and her mate didn't have relationships when she had open sores, the two of them did all right. Jeanie could control her lust over Barry for a few days if she had to. Barry on the other hand could if he had to. However he really didn't want to!

The lust the two of them had for each other was strong. The growing love they had for each other was becoming stronger. Despite the self imposed shackles around their hearts, Barry and Jeanie were obviously falling for each other. At one time when Jeanie was waltzing with Barry, she felt a strong pulling in her heart. Fear encircled her being. She tried to pull back from the man, but he held her close. It was at that point, that Jeanie knew that Barry knew she loved him. Still, Jeanie had to keep guessing how he felt about her.

One Friday night not long after their fiery dance, Jeanie got a call from Barry. Although she could tell that he had been drinking, she was happy to hear from him. After a few minutes into their conversation Barry said, "You know how much I love you Jeanie! I love you so much. I wish you could come over here to my house tonight. How I long to see your sweet face. How I long to feel your sexy taunt skin. Oh baby, please say you'll come over here tonight!"

Jeanie wondered whether Barry said all those things because he was drunk or if he really felt all those things. Sometimes people would only let their guard down while under the influence of alcohol. Perhaps her boyfriend did feel the love for her he proclaimed. Although she didn't want to make the long drive into the big city, Jeanie wanted to feel the love that Barry had denied her for so long. After being thoroughly convinced that what her honey said was indeed being said with a truthful heart, Jeanie packed a few things for the road. After bundling up her sleeping tot, she climbed into her car and headed off to the distant city where her love waited for her.

Jeanie didn't arrive at Barry's house until after 10 that evening. She was tired before the long trip. Her poor little girl must be pooped too! She was quite surprised to discover that the large iron door at the bottom of the entrance way to Barry's apartment was still locked. Barry said that he would leave it unlocked for her. Oh well, Jeanie thought, he probably fell asleep and forgot to unlock it. Jeanie didn't have a way to get her man's attention without waking up everyone in a three block radius, so she decided she could just climb over the door. Since Jeanie was athletic and agile, she was able to climb over the protective door without too much trouble. After she reached the other side of the barricade, she opened the door for Rosa. Both of them quietly walked up the stairs towards Barry's apartment.

When Jeanie and Rosa reached the top of the stairs, the door was left unlocked. Only after Jeanie turned on the kitchen light did she see Barry. He had passed out on the floor with his head still partially in his own vomit. If it wasn't such a long drive back to Windsock, Jeanie would have went home immediately. Since both mother and daughter were totally fatigued, the two of them remained at Barry's house that night. All evening long they've listened to Barry puking up the alcohol he drank earlier. Jeanie was disgusted with Barry and his childish behavior. The whole ugly episode didn't settle well at all in her stomach and it undoubtedly left quite an impression on little Rosa. Jeanie was so angry at Barry that she never thought she would be able to forgive him, but of course she did…at least that time.

Despite what happened that night, Jeanie continued to see Barry. Although she really liked him as a person, there were several things about him that drove her crazy. The main one of course was his drinking habit. Another thing about Barry that bothered her was that due to his careless spending, he too started to get in debt. Barry certainly wasn't like Will. He didn't charge up the world. No, the man just lived from paycheck to paycheck. Jeanie knew that many people do that, but she wasn't one of them. The girl became quite fearful of being materially impoverished. Who could blame her after all the times she had gone without even her basic needs. That wasn't going to happen to her anymore and it's never going to happen to her little girl! Although Jeanie received far less money than Barry did with her government check and her work study job, she usually had more cash than he did. Jeanie had learned years ago that in order to keep her world from falling into financial chaos, she had to set up a budget and stick with it. That was one thing that Barry never did. That bugged the devil out of the girl almost as much as his drinking did!

Little by little the girl started losing respect for the silly, irresponsible man child. Not long after the drunken episode which Rosa and Jeanie observed, Barry got into a minor car accident. It wasn't anything major, still it made her think about the man's character. The fool actually bragged about how drunk he was when he crashed into the utility pole. His car was still drivable, it just looked like hell. The pole he hit was scraped but was still standing. Naturally, the guy didn't call the police to report the accident in his drunken state. He would be a fool to do that. Jeanie was beginning to think she also was a fool for putting up with her repulsive, drunken buddy. Her disappointment in him was getting bigger and bigger. There was no denying that. Jeanie's positive regard for her lover was going down the tubes as well. She no longer knew if she wanted to be with Barry. She didn't think she would be able to build a relationship with someone she had no respect for. So with much contemplation, Jeanie broke all ties with her good timing friend.

Their relationship ended the first semester Jeanie entered the state college. Although the breakup was Jeanie idea, she still felt a little sad. Despite her lonely nights, she really thought the breakup was for the best. The girl rarely drank and only occasionally smoked. Usually nondrinkers don't hang around with drinkers. Jeanie enjoyed Barry's company when they went out dancing. She didn't mind if he drank a little then. However, she couldn't stand to be with somebody who regularly guzzled down the stuff. Besides, the school year had gotten off to a rocky start academically. It was obvious that in order for Jeanie to succeed in that higher institution of learning, she would have to put her all into her studies. She definitely had the time to do that now. Actually, she had a lot of time to do many things now.

## CHAPTER 14

# Oh Perfect Love

With everything going on in Jeanie's life she didn't have much time to be lonely except on Saturday night. That was usually the one evening when she was all caught up in her schoolwork. That was the time when she had a few minutes alone in the house without anything there to occupy her mind. Usually Jeanie sat alone in front of the TV hugging her pillow, hoping beyond hope that she wouldn't be alone forever. Rosa was asleep at that hour of the night. Except for the crickets outside, everything was quiet…perhaps a bit too quiet. Sometimes the lack of noise around Jeanie scared her back into the dark reality of life. Jeanie's reality had about all the darkness it could handle.

On those long lonely night's Jeanie would think about how wonderful it would be to have a man in her life. One night the idealistic girl took out a piece of lined paper and wrote a list describing all the fine qualities that she wanted in a man.

"Wow, a person would almost have to be a God to have all those qualities," Jeanie proclaimed to her invisible friends hiding in the wall. "Well, I know for sure that my new beau must not be a smoker or a boozer. That would cut out about half of the male population. He should also be close to my age. It would be nice if he was somewhat creative. Oh yes, he must have a good job, and like children. And of course, he must be fairly attractive. He doesn't have to be model handsome, but fairly good looking." Although Jeanie didn't consider herself to be too superficial, she did not want someone who she thought was butt ugly!

After looking over all the qualities she desired in a man, Jeanie shook her head in disgust. There's probably not a single man registered in her entire dating service that would fit her specifications. Hmmm, Jeanie thought, maybe she should put in a personal AD. It's not very romantic but it is practical. Rather than keep wasting her time with a variety of different men who she considered all wrong for her, perhaps she could find just the right man out there in a personal advertisement. What the heck. The small $20 investment might just help the idealistic lady find the love of her life! Before putting in a personal AD, she decided for safety sake to get a P.O. Box. She didn't want every creep in the area to know who she was and where she lived.

The following day Jeanie decided to put the AD in the paper. Within a weeks time, it was in print. Jeanie giggled with excitement, "Boy that looks good," she told herself as she read the AD over and over again. Anticipation swelled inside the lonely girl as she wondered when she would start getting responses. She checked her post office box twice a day for the first few days. Slowly the letters started coming in. Several letters were quickly discarded after the first reading though. Jeanie was lonely but she wasn't desperate.

"This guy can't even spell," Jeanie said with disdain. He obviously wasn't very smart. She decided long ago that she wanted someone who was intelligent. She wanted someone she could communicate with on her own level. There were many times in her past, where she did not use the brain God gave her. Still, she knew she was a smart girl. Besides, intelligence usually meant college educated. College educated usually meant he had a good job with a decent salary. She had to be practical in choosing the right mate. She wasn't merely looking to have a good time with someone, although that was important. She was looking for a long term relationship. She was looking for love, hopefully accompanied with marriage.

"No, I don't want to meet with him. He's 13 years older than me," Jeanie said as she shook her head. Although she had been told in the past she was looking for a father figure, she was sure that her friend didn't have that in mind. The guy probably had arthritis, a balding head and a pot belly. No, she could definitely be choosier that that! Although, it certainly would be nice to have someone take care of her financially and emotionally. Still the idea of going to bed every night with a man who was older than the age her father would be, made her cringe. Besides the guy wouldn't be able to keep up with Jeanie. The girl had a lot of physical and sexual energy. She wanted someone who also possessed a similar degree of stamina.

Yes, Jeanie definitely had energy to burn. Her body hummed with a lot of nervous energy and it was just waiting for an outlet. Luckily the girl was able to channel most of that bottled energy into her dancing and her aerobics. That kind of exercise may have been good for Jeanie's body but it didn't do anything to alleviate her strong sexual desires. No, bouncing on the dance floor certainly didn't take care of the growing lust she felt inside her loins. Maybe soon, she would have somebody with whom she could build a relationship with. Perhaps real soon she would find someone she could love mentally, physically and emotionally. When that happened, she would then be able to express her feelings towards him in a sexual way. Just thinking about the passionate kisses, the bountiful hugs and the intense nights of love making they would share created an involuntary shiver.

Jeanie met six of the men who responded to her AD within two weeks time. Although she had met a nice man with a son close to Rosa's age, things just weren't right. There were two things about

John that didn't settle well with Jeanie. She could probably get used to the idea of dating a man slightly shorter. However the thing about John that she could not ignore was the fact that he was as poor as a church mouse.

Jeanie had been through some really tough times in her past, so she was still very insecure money wise. She remembered how her husband and her struggled financially for the two and a half years they were married. They argued about money all the time. She didn't want to get involved with a man that was financially depleted like Donald. Jeanie was tired of going without. She had learned to ignore her basic sexual needs but how could anyone ignore their need for shelter and food? Although Jeanie agreed to see John for their second date, it was mostly so Rosa and his son could go to a carnival together. The two single parents enjoyed a pleasant evening together watching their youngsters ride the various attractions. However when the night was over, John didn't ask the girl out again. She was actually glad he didn't. She didn't want to lead him on but, she knew their time together would not lead to anything else other than friendship. This time around she wanted so much more!

In the meantime Jeanie made several dates over the next week. She had to go through the list of her potential mates carefully. She had talked to a young computer wiz several times on the phone for the past few days. The guy seemed really nice, but he didn't send her a picture. Actually, the guy was pretty vague as to what he looked like. That made Jeanie curious. She just hoped that he wasn't a total dog!

That Saturday night they had made arrangements to go to the classiest restaurant in Windsock. Jeanie was so excited she could burst. Originally she was going to meet Norman at a local pizza pub but he insisted on bringing her someplace much nicer. Obviously money wasn't a problem. It had been a long time since Jeanie had been to a really nice restaurant. She nervously searched her closet wondering what she was going to wear on that special night.

Jeanie decided to wear a nice, knee length dress with a delicate flower pattern. Although it was old, it was still quite pretty. It's soft pastel colors brought out the pink in her cheeks. It gathered at the waist and highlighted her tiny midriff. After dressing, Jeanie spent several minutes curling her straight hair with the antique curling iron she hid in the bathroom drawer. It was a wonder she didn't burn herself that night on that monstrosity. It didn't have any safety features like a protective coating over the red hot rod. Jeanie had burned herself using that thing previously. It was important that she would be extra careful that night. Even though the rod was a potential scar maker, she held onto it. She just couldn't justify spending the $10 it would cost her to purchase another one. She only used a curling iron occasionally, so why waste the money. Hopefully, the magical wand would turn Jeanie's limp hair into a bountiful head of curls. She wanted so much to impress the young man who she was to meet that night.

Jeanie met Norman at the parking lot behind the police station. She didn't plan that location because she suspected him of being a mass murderer, although the thought did cross her mind. Wasn't Bundy the serial killer, intelligent and charismatic? Jeanie chose that location because she lived real close to it. The lighted building with the high flying flag would be an easily seen landmark for an out-of-towner.

Jeanie couldn't help but think that the guy she had conversed with seemed too good to be true. Why would a sweet, fairly young man with money be scanning the personal ads for mates? Norman did say that he worked a lot and that he was a bit withdrawn. That's okay Jeanie thought, she was a little withdrawn at times to. Although the girl liked people, she was very leery of them. She had been burned so many times in her past that she approached each person she now met with extreme caution. Once in a while she would let her guard down long enough to let someone into her life. Unfortunately, when that happened she was usually sorry afterwards for the person she trusted would inevitably deceive her. Yes, Jeanie was determined to be real cautious the next time around for her sake as well as for her daughter's.

Finally the time came for the curly haired lass to meet the man she had been conversing with on and off for days. She was anxious and very nervous. She was a little scared too. She fought the impulse to bite her lip.

"What if I really like that guy and he doesn't care about me," Jeanie thought. That's basically how her life had gone so far. Jeanie would meet someone that she really felt for but he wouldn't care anything about her. Or, the guy would be married, or a creepy con artist thief, or a druggie. That would be just her luck. Here she was getting all excited about meeting someone she had talked to on the phone, and he might be just another lying creep out to use her and abuse her. However, Jeanie was impressed with the things Norman told her about himself. Still, for all she knew, he could be feeding her a pack of lies.

True Jeanie had become disillusioned with life and love, but she wasn't about to give up on either of those fine things. She truly believed that somewhere out there was a wonderful, sweet man just for her. She would find him somehow, someway. No matter how much time it took her or how great the cost, she would find her true love. Maybe Norman was meant to be her lifetime love…maybe not. Either way she wasn't going to find out a thing unless she walked out her living room door and got into her car.

Norman was right on time for their rendezvous. They both got out of their vehicles briefly to introduce themselves and to check each other out. Hmm Jeanie thought, he certainly was a good-looking man and look at that cute caboose. Norman must have found Jeanie equally fair to look at for the clean-shaven man smiled warmly at the girl as she approached his car.

"It's good to finally meet you," Norman said.

Jeanie flashed a full smile towards her date and nodded in agreement.

"Would you like to follow me to the restaurant?"

Norman politely answered, "Certainly."

The three mile drive down Central Avenue seemed to take forever. So far so good Jeanie thought. He's handsome, charming, sweet, and if he's loaded too…wow! Maybe Jeanie was being too superficial to place so much emphasis on financial security. She had her reasons for being that way though. She was still on the welfare roles while she attended college. If it wasn't for her Pell Grant, she didn't think she would have the money to keep that old junk heap of hers on the road. Jeanie worked hard at school so she could obtain a degree. Once completed, her education should open up the doors to a good career. Still, she didn't have enough faith in herself to succeed. The gentle girl was scared to death of failing and winding up even more broken and miserable than she had ever been in her past.

In the not so distant past she had done some pretty horrible things just to keep alive. It's terrible to have to sleep in a vacant house for she had nowhere else to go, or steal from a grocery store to get something to eat. She didn't ever want situations to get that bad again. As much as she loved Rosa Jeanie would give her away before she dragged her down in the gutters where she had previously crawled.

Jeanie needed security in the worst way. Since she didn't think she could get that on our own, she constantly sought to get it from a man. Even now, she was looking for a daddy to fulfill her financial needs. Subconsciously she searched for the father who turned his back on her when she was eleven. She was still looking for the man who traveled 1800 miles away from the girl he supposedly loved so he could escape the consequences of not paying child support. Her poor mother so desperately needed that money to support Jeanie and her sister. Although the girl deeply loved her dad, she still felt angry about the way he left the family. She could forgive him for being a selfish human being who deprived his family of the time and money they deserved.

She could even forgive him for all those unfair beatings where both daughters would get swatted because he didn't know who did the dastardly deed. What Jeanie had a hard time dealing with the most, was the way he left this earth. Her dad left without saying good bye.

Death was the ultimate abandonment. It was so final. There wasn't a way now to bridge the chasm opened during all those years of separation Jeanie thought. There was no way to heal all the past pain unknowingly created by her absent, artistic father. Jeanie still felt sad when she recalled how he bragged about her to all his friends before she went to Arkansas to live with him. She felt a twinge of pain when she thought about how she let him down. She could not be the Virgin Mary that he wanted her to be and so she felt flawed.

Jeanie couldn't be what anyone wanted her to be. She could try and try but the only thing Jeanie could be, was herself. Since she was a human being, she had faults. She wasn't perfect. Jeanie's father expected everything to be perfect and since Jeanie could not be flawless in his eyes, she saw herself as being unacceptable. Yes, she was an imperfect being with too many flaws. Since the girl spent so much time focusing on those flaws, she could not see the inner beauty which lay beyond her imperfect mortal traits.

Since much of Jeanie's attention focused on her downfalls, she really didn't believe that she deserved anyone good and decent in her life. Within her subconscious mind she thought she deserved the scoundrels she had encountered in her past. Although Jeanie may have thought she deserved all the garbage the universe threw her, she knew her precious little daughter did not. No, her sweet Rose deserved so much more than that. Jeanie was determined to give her daughter all the advantages that she lacked in her life.

Norman and Jeanie had a splendid first night together. Between bites, they shared in light conversation. Norman's eyes sparkled in the candlelight. There was a gentle honesty about the man that was seated before her. Although Jeanie enjoyed dinner, she was happy when the meal was over. Everything was so formal that her back ached with anxiety. Even though the sweet lass didn't make it a practice to invite strange men to her small apartment, she decided that she would make an exception that night. So, while they waited to collect their coats, Jeanie invited her dinner date to her place to get better acquainted. Naturally Norman accepted the invitation to be with the charming, pretty lady who stood before him.

Norman followed Jeanie to the apartment building where she lived. The outside light shined a path to her clean but small apartment. Once inside Jeanie went to the kitchen to get them both something to drink. The two sat together on the living room sofa while they conversed over their nonalcoholic beverages. After an hour into their conversation, Jeanie felt so comfortable with Norman that she wanted to share something special with him. She knew that the fine man before her would appreciate the rhythm of her heart's song. She could tell during that short time together that he was intelligent and refined. Jeanie felt certain that he would be appreciative of what she would share with him. The sensitive artist opened up the hidden compartment inside the end table and withdrew from it a large loose leaf binder. Inside it was some of her poetry and prose pieces. Hiding behind a smile, Jeanie gazed over the titles of her favorite pieces of literary work. She had to be choosey concerning which ones to share with the reserved man before her.

Norman sat quietly besides Jeanie and intently listened to her as she recited a few of her prose pieces. She could tell he was captivated by her poetry. That made Jeanie smile even more. A man that appreciated the finer things in life didn't come along every day, she thought. The ideas and perspectives that she shared with Norman opened up the doors to their relationship. The man was so turned on by the talented, beautiful lady sitting beside him that it wasn't long before the exchange of kisses began.

It had been such a long time since a man turned Jeanie on as much and as fast as Norman did that night. The soft-cheeked gentleman before her had so much to offer. She couldn't rush into things like she had in the past. Jeanie really wanted to know this wonderful man before her inside and out.

She wanted to be able to touch his mind and heart as no one else had ever before. She wanted to feel his chest pounding hard against hers. However, she wanted him to feel something deep inside his heart for her besides physical sensations.

She felt his throbbing penis as it lightly brushed against her leg. She wondered what it would be like to finger his love machine She wondered what kind of a lover he was. If he was as caring, loving and gentle in bed as he was with her now, then she knew that romantic interlude would be dynamite. The way Norman stroked her cresses of hair with his long fingers made her almost breathless. The way he kissed her warm, moist lips almost made her want to strip out of her panties. Still, the girl contained her libido. She was no longer the out of control sex addict of years ago. She did not want a one night stand. Jeanie wanted the sweet man before her for a lot longer than a few reckless hours.

The girl squirmed out of his encompassed arms. While separated from their passionate embrace, they looked into each other's eyes.

Norman gazed at the dazed dreamer and said, "Wow things are going a little too fast aren't they?"

Jeanie agreed, "I guess we're like a couple of school kids. It's just that it's been so long since I felt this way about anybody. I don't want just a one night stand."

Norman sincerely smiled at Jeanie, "I don't either. I guess I really should be going now."

With that Norman stood up and retrieved his coat that was draped across the arm of the dining room chair. "I'll call you tomorrow," Norman said. Before he left, he bent over and placed one more sweet kiss across Jeanie's lips. Jeanie just smiled at the handsome gent as he opened up the door.

Jeanie was so excited over that promising date with Norman! She felt like doing a somersault across the living room rug. Things were so dynamite with this man. He was passionate, sensitive, intelligent and so handsome. Maybe, just maybe he's the one God sent for her. He seemed to be everything that Jeanie had longed for in a man. Perhaps it was too much to hope that this beautiful person would fall in love with her, but how she prayed that he would.

## CHAPTER 15

# Trouble In Paradise

The following evening Norman called Jeanie on the telephone. He said that he had just wanted to talk to her to see how she was doing. Jeanie could feel her face flush as she spoke with her sweet date mate from the night before. The two of them engaged in a long conversation. Norman was interested in finding out all he could about the beautiful brunette who had caught his attention. Just as they ended their conversation, the charming man asked the blushing girl for another date. Jeanie spontaneously said "Yes."

When Norman arrived at her house the following Saturday afternoon, he had a camera in his hand. He spent several minutes taking picture after picture of Jeanie. She was like a beautiful dream for the shy, socially awkward man. Jeanie smiled radiantly every time he pointed the camera her way. She couldn't help but smile. It was apparent that the young man she fancied was crazy about her as well. She was ecstatic!

After the camera was put away, the two of them went out to eat at a more casual restaurant. In between bites the two lovingly looked in each other's brown eyes. Already there was an uncanny attraction between them. Already there was love blooming in the hearts of both Jeanie and Norman.

After dinner, the couple talked with one another for hours. Neither one of them wanted the evening to end, but end it must. Before Norman walked out the door he gave the passionate, poet one more long embrace.

Norman whispered in Jeanie's ear, "You are such a special girl. I can't believe I found!"

Jeanie looked at Norman lovingly with her brown orbs. She didn't have to say a word. Her eyes spoke for her. Yes, I really feel for you too, far more than I dare say.

Although Jeanie's schedule was very hectic the following week, she thought about Norman all the time. That Thursday night he surprised her with a visit. He appeared really shook up, so the girl naturally became quite worried herself. Something was wrong, Jeanie told herself. Maybe he got transferred to Siberia or something. Norman greeted Jeanie with several long passionate kisses.

Finally the man stopped kissing Jeanie long enough to say, "I've been trying to call you for days. When no one answered the phone I thought that something had happened to you. I couldn't bear to lose you now."

Jeanie couldn't believe that Norman cared about her so much already. Although he never outright said he loved her, she could see love in his eyes. She could feel it in his touch. After several hours of kissing and cuddling, Norman pulled away. The two of them were so close to sharing their physical love that night, and he just wouldn't allow himself to do so.

"I want to make sure that we really love each other. If two people don't truly love each other than sex isn't anything special at all. I don't want our sexual relationship to be nothing but dick in a hole. I want something better for me. I want something better for us."

Although Jeanie's loins ached for Norman's physical love, she readily agreed to postpone the sexual relationship. He cared about her enough to wait. She cared enough about him to let the emotional side of their fast blooming love fully mature before starting a physical relationship. By waiting until the time was right, they would surely not confuse sex with love as they both had in the past.

Time passed very quickly for the next several weeks. Their emotionally charged desire for one another continued to grow stronger every day. During one Saturday visit, Jeanie asked more than a few questions concerning Norman's residence. Rather than go into details with the location, how many rooms it had, what it looked like, etc Norman decided to bring both her and Rosa over there instead.

During the 45 minute drive out in the country Jeanie and Norman carried on an intense conversation about psychology. She thoroughly enjoyed their shared conversations. Not only was the guy a great kisser, but he had such an intriguing, complex mind. That turned Jeanie on as much as his sexy, swank body. Yes, everything about the handsome man beside her turned her on.

The fact that he was a little mysterious about where he lived had Jeanie puzzled. Surely he must be hiding something Jeanie thought on more than one occasion. Now though the mystery concerning his habitat was about to be solved. Jeanie grinned ear to ear trying to imagine what kind of a house Norman lived in.

Finally, the car turned into a long blacktop driveway. Jeanie couldn't see the outside of the house too well for the evening sky darkened the surroundings. Norman pulled into the driveway, opened the garage door and parked the car. The gentleman held Jeanie's hand while Jeanie held Rosa's hand. They carefully maneuvered through the obstacles on both sides of the outer stairs. When Norman reached for the light switch, Jeanie could see how roomy the garage was. Another vehicle was parked in it as well. Jeanie wondered if her boyfriend had a roommate he didn't tell her about. The big surprise came when Norman turned on the lights in the kitchen. It was so beautiful that Jeanie just looked around stunned.

"Wow! This is beautiful. Do you live here alone?" Jeanie asked.

"Not exactly" Norman replied. "I have my two dogs in the basement. After we get settled I'll bring you and Rosa down to meet them."

When Rosa heard the word dogs, she got all excited, "Mommy, I want to see the dogs!"

Norman could see how excited Rosa was and smiled down on the little girl. After they peeled off their light spring jackets, he slowly opened the basement door to allow his two fuzzy friends to come into the kitchen. "The black dog is Comet and a brown dog is Peabody. They don't get much company, so they're real excited."

The dogs nervously jumped all over Rosa. Even though the girl had been thrilled about seeing the dogs, she backed away from the furry critters and whimpered.

"Mommy, that big one scratched me," Rosa whimpered as she showed her mommy her newest boo-boo.

"That's enough guys!" Norman shouted as he pushed the two rowdy dogs back into the basement. "Maybe we'll try this again after they calm down."

"OK," Jeanie said in agreement.

Since it was getting late, Norman decided it might be best for all of them to spend the night at his house. None of them had eaten dinner yet so Norman suggested they could cook the hamburgers that were left in the refrigerator. There weren't any restaurants of any kind close to where he lived. He definitely liked his privacy.

After dinner, they all made idle talk while they watched some TV. Before long, it was time for Rosa to go to bed. Norman went upstairs to put clean sheets on the guest bed. He came back down the stairs a few minutes later.

"Everything is all set," the man said as he smiled at mother and daughter. "I've even found a night light for her."

"I've got to warn you," Jeanie said, "Rosa is not used to sleeping in strange houses. I don't know how she'll do this evening. I just hope that she doesn't cry all night."

As much as Jeanie wanted to spend all those glorious hours with Norman, she was nervous that her five year daughter would scare him away. Even if her youngster didn't scare him away, he might get scared away when she told him about her wild past and her health problems. Jeanie was afraid to tell him and she was also ashamed. What if he couldn't handle her wild, reckless past and her unfortunate disease? Those details about her weren't something she should hide from him. She had to tell him. It was the right thing to do! If he cared about her enough, he'll accept her despite everything. If not, she would have to accept it. It would hurt…but she would have to accept his rejection.

After Jeanie put Rosa to bed, her and Norman went downstairs to get another cola. While they were alone in the dining room having their drink, Jeanie decided she would use that time to tell her boyfriend everything about herself. She just had to find the right words.

"Norman, I think our relationship has gone past the friendship level…don't you?"

"I think you should know by now that I care very deeply for you. Is there something bothering you?"

"I have something to tell you, but I don't know how to tell you," Jeanie sheepishly said. She couldn't even look at him, but she knew she had to tell him.

"Well tell me. It can't be that bad."

"You know, I'm not a little Virgin Mary. I've been with a lot of guys in my past. I got a disease. I take three blue capsules a day to keep the disease from becoming active. Most of the time these pills work, but not always. Then I'm contagious. I've got Herpes. I hate that I have it, but there's really nothing I can do about that now. Also, in the not so distant past, I had a nervous breakdown and was in the mental health ward for ten days."

Jeanie kept talking without barely taking a breath. She was so afraid if she stopped talking, she would never be able to finish telling the honorable, kind man the important things about her that he needed to know. "I really like you. I wouldn't be telling you any of this stuff if I didn't really like you. If we're ever to have a future together then we have to be totally honest with each other. After all those things I've done in my past, maybe I don't deserve love. I don't know..."

"No, you don't deserve love," Norman said almost seriously to the remorseful girl.

Jeanie walked over to the window in the corner of the dining room and gazed out. She told herself she wouldn't get overly emotional when she told Norman what he had to know. She told herself that she wouldn't cry...but she couldn't help it. She tried to muffle back the tears but they came gushing from her eyes like a waterfall. There was no stopping them. She couldn't help but cry. She wanted a love, a true beautiful love, but because of everything she had done, she would probably never have it. She wanted a good man in her life, but she didn't think she deserved one. She may have wanted the fine man she had been dating, but she wasn't good enough for him she feared. Tears poured down her face. "Tears of sorrow, tears of pain, erase all of my hurt and shame," Jeanie recited poetry spontaneously to herself in helping her deal with her intense emotions. She had to sooth her soul somehow.

"Hey, I was just trying to lighten things up. I wasn't mocking you and I'm certainly am not rejecting you," Norman told the girl with compassion and love. "Your physical health problem bothers me a little, but your past breakdown concerns me a lot. Either way, we'll deal with your health problems. I'm crazy about you Carmalita Jean. I don't think there is anything you could do or say that would scare me away now. That is what you were doing right? I'm not running. I'm still right here!"

Just hearing Norman say that made her start crying again. This time, she was not crying because she felt rejected. She was crying because she felt accepted…and loved!

Norman stood behind Jeanie and wrapped his warm arms around her shoulders. Gently he turned his weepy woman towards him. He brought his arms around Jeanie and enveloped her with a full embrace. He pulled back from his sensitive lady for a minute to look into her eyes. Jeanie tried to bend her head forward for she didn't want him to see her with red, swollen eyes, but he tilted her head forward with his right hand never the less. With the tips of his fingers, he dried away the tears that dripped down her cheeks.

"Are you alright now?"

Jeanie didn't say a word, she just nodded her head.

"It's getting rather late. Let's say we go lay down."

With his arm still around Jeanie's shoulders, Norman guided the girl upstairs where their bedroom awaited. Much to their surprise, Rosa was in the hallway waiting for her mother. By then Jeanie's eyes were no longer teary, though they were probably still swollen. Rosa thankfully wasn't aware that anything was wrong.

"Rosa, it's time to go to bed honey," Jeanie said as she guided her young child back into her room.

"I don't want to sleep in there. I want to be with you mommy," the little girl insisted.

"Mommy and Norman are going to be right over there. If you need us, we'll be right over there," Jeanie calmly told Rosa while she pointed at the other bedroom. Jeanie once again tucked her sleepy eyed girl into bed.

Jeanie didn't even make it into the other room before she heard Rosa's bedroom door open again.

"Mommy, I don't want to sleep there. I want to stay with you."

"You're going to stay in that room and mommy will be right over in the next room. You have Mr. Bear to keep you company, and the nightlight is next to the bed. Just close your eyes and let the sleep come."

Rosa looked at her mother with betrayal in her eyes, "No mommy!"

Jeanie tried to walk away but she could feel her daughter's arms tugging on her leg.

"Now Rosa stop it," Jeanie firmly told her. "I said I'd be right over there. Now you be a good girl!" Oh please be a good girl, Jeanie prayed silently to herself.

The guilt ridden mom retreated into the next room where Norman patiently waited for her. She wasn't in the room five minutes, when she heard her daughter crying outside the door. Jeanie didn't know what to do. In some ways, she thought she should try to console her daughter, even though Jeanie herself was still a little emotional after her heartfelt discussion with Norman. She needed some consoling of her own. Norman could accept Jeanie and her health problems. Could he accept her whiney, spoiled daughter as well?

Norman looked at Jeanie. "Come lay beside me. Try to ignore her cries. She'll be all right. She'll just have to learn that you're not going to come running every time she cries. Besides, right now I think you need some TLC!"

After what seemed an eternity, Rosa stopped crying. Good, now maybe we can get some sleep Jeanie thought. However, Jeanie found it next to impossible to sleep besides the sexy, dark haired man who she had fallen in love with.

All during the night Norman held Jeanie. All through the night he kissed her and whispered. "God I love you so much. I can't believe I have found you!"

Jeanie felt a few teardrops fall down her cheek. "I love you too," she proclaimed. "I love you too!"

Norman and Jeanie held each other and kissed each other most of that long loving night. Even though they both felt so, so much for each other, they decided to postpone their desired love making a little bit longer. Since Norman knew about Jeanie's wild past, he wanted to be sure that she didn't have that dreaded disease everyone was scared of getting…AIDS.

Jeanie couldn't blame Norman for being afraid of having relations with her. Considering she had been with a variety of men in our lifetime, he was only being practical to wait. In many ways the former wild child felt she deserved AIDS. After all the different guys she had been with, maybe she deserved to get that awful disease.

With dread and fear in her heart, Jeanie made an appointment the next day to get that all important blood test. The two weeks it took to get the test results back seemed like an eternity. When they finally came back, Jeanie held her breath anticipating the worst. The test results were negative. Thank you, God. Jeanie was afraid if they were positive, that would mean she would be a lonely lady forever. Now that the test indicated she wasn't infected with AIDS, it meant the couple could consummate their love. At last they could engage in what was sure to be a very passionate and tender sexual relationship.

The first night that the two released their passions was incredible. It was almost as if their bodies were meant for each other. Norman was gentle and considerate and so patient with Jeanie. Their time together was magic. Their relationship had become even more intense now that they've overcome the physical barriers that had previously put a wedge between them. The two had indeed become one.

The next year Jeanie and Norman spent as much time together as possible. Naturally, Rosa came with Jeanie on the weekends but that was all right. Even though Norman didn't have much experience with children, he was quite a good father figure for Rosa. Norman was patient and kind to the little girl. Jeanie was thrilled that Rosa and Norman got along so well together. Sometimes all three of them would go to the local elementary school and played basketball together. Sometimes they ventured to a nearby pond to go ice skating. At least once a week, Norman would load up his dogs Comet and Peabody in his recreational vehicle to go trailblazing. Jeanie and Rosa were fast becoming a big part of Norman's life. Norman was no doubt a big part of Jeanie and Rosa's life.

A year after Norman and Jeanie started going together, they became engaged. One afternoon Norman brought Jeanie to a wholesale jewelry store. Norman wanted Jeanie to pick out the engagement ring she wanted.

"Jeanie, look around the store and pick out any ring you would like up to $5000. Take your time. I'll help keep an eye on Rosa."

Jeanie looked and looked. There were so many pretty rings to choose from. She didn't mean to take so long making up her mind, but she had to choose just the right one. Norman was being very generous. Still, Jeanie thought it was quite frivolous to spend so much money on a piece of jewelry. Besides those big stones looked gaudy on the girl's delicate fingers. After looking through the store for almost an hour, Jeanie decided on a small ruby and diamond ring with the stones arranged in the shape of a flower.

"I want this ring Norman," Jeanie proclaimed.

"Are you sure?" Norman asked. "It only cost $239. Out of all the rings here, this is the one you want?"

Jeanie nodded her head in agreement. The chosen ring was a size 8 and had to be sized down to fit Jeanie's tiny finger. The following week, Norman picked up the ring at the jewelry store. While there in the store, Jeanie's boyfriend carefully took it out of the box and gently placed it on her finger. Jeanie proudly wore the ruby flower on her finger for all to see. She loved the ring. She loved Norman so much more!

Everyone was happy that she had found such a good man. He was successful and he had his own house. The guy was crazy about Jeanie. Most important, he readily accepted Rosa as his own. Jeanie thought that their life together would be long and wonderful. However nothing is perfect in Paradise.

Even though Jeanie and Norman loved each other and wanted to marry one another, they had cold feet about making things legally binding. No one could really blame Norman, after all, he did have a lot to lose financially if he and Jeanie got married but later divorced. His house was valued at $125,000 and was almost paid for. It wasn't just the money Norman was afraid of losing, it was his home. Norman's home was his castle. He had his house all fixed up just the way he liked it. He even had a huge fenced-in yard for his dogs in the back along with their own cast iron bathtub.

Jeanie wanted to sign a premarital agreement, but Norman said that wouldn't be necessary if he knew for sure they could make it as husband and wife. The only way to do that was if they lived together for awhile. After seeing how each other was on a daily basis, they could see how compatible they were. If all was still right between them, after a year, he wouldn't think twice about making things legal. So it was agreed that they would move in together to see how they would function as a family.

Norman wanted to make some changes to his two bedroom house. He thought that although his home was fairly large, he still didn't think that his residence would be big enough to comfortably accommodate everyone. So, Jeanie's beau decided that he should get a few rooms added onto his house. He wanted Rosa to have a playroom, someplace out of the way where she could get rowdy, make a mess without getting in trouble and merrily hang out with her friends. He also knew Jeanie would be happier living there if she had a place of her own to indulge in her various artistic endeavors. Norman possessed a modest of money and he didn't mind spending it on whatever was needed to make the little additions to his family happy.

Jeanie knew her girlfriend's husband did construction work so it was mutually decided that the job of remodeling would be given to him. Even though Fred did a great job on the addition, it took him a lot longer to complete the building project than was anticipated. The two month construction job quickly turned into a six month monster.

Coping with the noise and the dust the building project created wasn't easy. The hassle of having to continue digging into the packed boxes which held Rosa and Jeanie's personal property became more and more of an inconvenience with each passing day. Of course the two had some of their frequently used items easily assessable. However trying to find the things that they only occasionally needed was a nightmare!

Within two months time everyone who lived at the house became edgy and grouchy. Norman found it difficult to perform the various projects on his home computer that his boss required him to do while the hammering and drilling was going on. Jeanie couldn't concentrate at all on the multitude of reading she was required to do for her psychology classes. Trying to focus her mind to complete the accompanying homework was nearly impossible as long as she was in that house during the hours the loud construction work was going on.

Often Jeanie would drive to the nearby lake and sit by the water to get away from the noise. While seated on her portable folding chair, she would do her various school projects. Most of the time she did not feel too ill at ease being all alone at the secluded lake, but sometimes she did. When a stranger parked his car and journeyed in the direction of the cautious lady, she would quickly pack up her things and leave. Not wanting to go home to the disrupting noise and commotion, she would drive her car to the super market parking lot to complete her necessary homework assignments there. Her life together with Norman had definitely gotten off to a rocky start.

Despite their current inconveniences, Jeanie and her fiancé both thought that the idea of a trial marriage sounded good. In theory it appeared logical. Although Jeanie was an artist, she prided herself on being practical. She had made so many dumb mistakes in her past. She vowed that the next time she got married it would be forever. How can you really get to know someone? By living with them of course.

Yes living together appeared to be a good idea. However, in a trial marriage there was no legality involved and so no real commitment. When things would start to go awry, it was much easier to part company. After all, there were no legal papers binding the couple together. They had to be strongly bound together with their hearts and minds. If each of the partners weren't equally committed to the union, then it was so much easier to say goodbye than to try to work out their differences. That's exactly what happened to Jeanie and Norman nine months after they ventured into their trial marriage.

There were a lot of little things about each other that aggravated the young couple. Jeanie was particular about her food but Norman was even more so. He didn't like the idea of opening up his margarine dish and finding crumbs in it. So, he had his own margarine and Jeanie and Rosa had their own. He saw Rosa lick the top of the catsup one day so, he had his own catsup. The same with salad dressing. It seemed like everything in the house was his or hers or Rosa's.

Norman owned a nice hand carved dining room set, but Rosa wasn't allowed to eat on it for fear she would wreck it. It didn't hurt Jeanie's feelings at all when Norman bought a cheap dining set for the kitchen. Most meals were conducted on that table except on the rare occasion when Jeanie and Norman ate by themselves. Even then Jeanie was so paranoid about accidentally putting a scratch on his beloved cherry dining table, that she rarely ate on it. She didn't want to be around anything that made her that tense.

Jeanie and Rosa had a small living room of their own separate from Norman's too. There, mother and daughter relaxed, watched movies and ate popcorn while they enjoyed family entertainment. Many of the tv shows and movies Jeanie and Rosa liked, Norman couldn't stand. So, Rosa and Jeanie watched them without Norman.

Jeanie's boyfriend was more than a sport's fanatic. He was a sport's lunatic. He spent most of his spare time watching sport games on tv. He would watch one after another every chance he got. In the master bedroom he had four televisions set up. That way he could watch four different sporting events at the same time, (this was way before the multi- picture televisions that are available now) He was so obsessive about his shows that he insisted he watch them live. No way was he going to record any of them to watch later. The family based their entire weekend around what games were on tv. It got so bad that Jeanie had to serve Norman his dinner upstairs in front of his tv during halftime.

Many times when Jeanie and Rosa watched movies downstairs, Jeanie would make popcorn to munch on. Norman however, couldn't stand the smell of popcorn cooking. So, Jeanie had to put her popcorn maker outside in the garage to cook her favorite snack out there…even in the winter when it was below thirty degrees. After it was made, she would hurry to put it in a bowl and then scurry into her living room. Without hesitating a moment she shut the door behind her to eliminate those unpleasant smells for Norman. Once in a while her boyfriend would just be coming down the stairs when she made her mad dash. When that happened, Jeanie would hear about it later.

Norman was basically a social isolate. Jeanie knew the man didn't enjoy going out in crowded places, but she didn't know how fanatical he was about it. When they first dated, he would routinely go out to semi-crowded restaurants and said nothing about it. Now that the guy had her number, he was quite verbal about what he wanted and what he didn't want. Now he rarely went out with Jeanie to any public place.

Norman would say, "Most people are noisy, inconsiderate and rude. Can't we just order Chinese takeout food and eat it here?"

Rather than fight and argue about such frivolous things, Jeanie would back down from their disagreement. It just wasn't worth the fight. Once in a while Norman and Jeanie would go out alone to a restaurant to eat. However, they would go at off-peak times to minimize the number of people they might encounter. That was fine. Jeanie didn't mind eating her nighttime meal at four in the afternoon. It was probably healthier eating a big meal earlier in the evening anyway.

Norman started to do less and less with Jeanie and Rosa. He still watched Rosa when Jeanie attended night classes or when she needed a break from her daughter. However when all three of them got together, tensions would arise.

Rosa was used to pulling her mom in this direction or that direction and Norman didn't like it at all. Jeanie just thought that she was being kind to her daughter. Norman thought that Jeanie was being controlled by a manipulative child. He was probably right. Jeanie spent so many years catering to the number one priority in her life that now certain behaviors were just expected from her. Rosa didn't like Norman being crowned the king and taking her mom's attention and time away from her. So the demanding child quickly asserted her control over her people pleasing mother. Although Jeanie saw Norman as her king, her daughter would always be her little princess. The little lady had enough time and love for the both of them!

Parental issues with Rosa caused much friction with Jeanie and Norman. In many ways what Norman said to Jeanie made sense. How ever putting into practice what the man lectured her on was something else entirely.

"You can't raise kids like you raise dogs," Jeanie often told Norman.

"When I tell my dogs to do something, they do it or else pay the consequences," Norman would logically say.

It would be difficult making changes even when you want to make them. However, it's even more difficult to make changes when someone else thinks that you need make them. Jeanie respected Norman's intelligence. Now, however she started seeing the man as an unemotional, logical robot. Just what she needed, a relationship with Mr. Spock.

Jeanie wanted to make things work between her and Norman. Both her and Rosa needed emotional and financial security more than anything. The stressed mother was definitely tired of jumping from one relationship to another. She could see the lines of communication breaking down between her and Norman. For months, both Jeanie and Norman could see that things weren't right, but they ignored the signs. Jeanie hoped things would get better all on their own…they didn't. When Norman started pulling his affections away from Jeanie, she knew that something had to be said.

Early one evening Jeanie got the nerve to approach Norman about her unsatisfied emotional needs.

"When we started going out together, you were so affectionate, so loving. I just haven't been getting the attention and affection I need. What's wrong?"

"Nothing is wrong," Norman insisted. "I've pretty well caught up on my affection. I don't need that much anymore".

"I need more cuddling and kissing then that," Jeanie insisted.

Much to her surprise Norman replied, "Well I'm sorry baby. That's just how I am. Take it or leave it."

"I'm just not happy," Jeanie again stated. "I think we should go to marriage counseling."

"Hell no! I'm not going to have some stranger tell me how I should live my life!" Norman loudly proclaimed.

Jeanie looked at Norman with tears in her eyes, "Well, if you're not willing to work on our issues or give me the affection I need, then there's no reason for us to stay together. I'm not going to stay some place where I'm unhappy. The fact is I can't afford to move out. You know I lost my subsidized rent when I moved in here. You told me when I first moved in, that if we broke up you would let me stay here until I completed my college education. Are you going to honor your word if we break up?"

"Yes," Norma replied. "I do want you to be happy. I'm sorry that I can't make you happy. That's just the way I am. I'll move the extra bed into my office and you can continue sleeping in the master bedroom." With those words Norman stood up and walked to the door. Not once did he look back. Not once did he show any emotion about the end of his dream love.

## CHAPTER 16

# Helpful Friend

A t first life was real tense around Norman's mansion like house. A week after their friendly breakup, situations began to lighten up some. Norman and Jeanie started talking to one another on a friendship level. At first conversation was stressed, but it became increasingly easier. Sometimes they would even hug and kiss each other when the timing felt right. Jeanie hoped their encounters would turn back into the beautiful, romantic love of yesterday, but that was too much to hope for. That didn't happen. However, Jeanie was happy to get whatever affection she could from the man she once thought she would marry. Despite their distancing relationship, she still loved him. He was a good person, with a good heart. She hadn't been with anyone quite like him and probably never would.

During the first couple of months following their breakup, the two of them would occasionally engage in a physical relationship. After all the time they were together, Jeanie figured that it was better to give her affections to a friend than a stranger. It was rather funny how Norman actually became more affectionate after they broke up. Maybe it was because neither one of them had to live up to each other's expectations.

Jeanie and her former fiancé still held a great deal of feeling for each other. There was no denying that. They would undoubtedly always care about the other, but it was clear that Norman could not give Jeanie the intense degree of emotional or physical closeness she required from him. That realization hurt more than being stung by a hive full of bees. However, she was limited to as what to do considering her current living conditions. It would be awkward to start a relationship with anyone while living with her ex-boyfriend. That certainly was one reason Jeanie held onto the physical aspects of their emotionally dead relationship. However they were placing their hearts in limbo by trying to maintain a sexual relationship with one another. What felt nice at the moment would only cause their hurting hearts further agony in the long run. That arrangement wasn't really fair for either one of them. Their hearts needed to heal but they probably wouldn't while engaged in the pseudo type of love they were now practicing. There was too much confusion about the boundaries in their friendship. There was too much confusion in how they should maintain their own individual lives while they lived in such close proximity to each other.

Their great love affair was definitely over. There was no doubt about that. Still for a couple of weeks following their breakup Jeanie was happy with the arrangement that her and Norman fell into. She should be happy that she had a sensitive man to give her the physical affection she craved. Jeanie didn't get exactly what she wanted but she thought that it would have to do until God knows when. Jeanie was indeed free as a bird now. She was now free to meet other guys and spend time with them without guilt. She should feel happy about that, but she wasn't.

Since the girl felt confused and depressed, she went back to seeing a therapist. Jeanie's counselor was quick to point out what seemed real nice now would cause a great deal of emotional pain later. It was decided that it would be best for both their sakes to either work together to mend the relationship or else call the whole thing off. Since Norman was still adamant about going to marriage counseling, Jeanie pulled away whatever physical and emotional ties she had with Norman. The disenchanted girl fought the loneliness inside and finally came to terms with her and Norman's disintegrated relationship.

During the following months, Jeanie devoted all her time to her school work and her daughter. Jeanie enjoyed her college years especially her various art classes. She was thankful to have the opportunity to develop her talents. Lately however Jeanie spent most of her time with her nose in one of her psychology books. She was totally engrossed with that subject and signed up for many more psych classes than her course of study required her to take.

Originally, Jeanie took those mind boggling classes in an attempt to understand herself and her world. After a few classes, she changed her English major to Human Services. She wanted to use her bad past experiences to help others going through similar experiences. Surely there was a reason she went through those years of hellish turmoil. She was certain that she went through purgatory for a reason and that was so that she could develop the empathy to help those individuals who were going through what she had. Those very experiences that nearly killed her spirit could now be used to heal others.

Jeanie exercised her brain with the psychology classes but she nurtured her heart through her art. It was her painting that helped the girl's psyche heal after the emotional withdrawal of her former lover. Even though she was the one who initiated the break-up, it didn't mean that it didn't hurt. It would take a long time to mend her scarred disillusioned heart. It would take a long time to get over losing the great love that she once had.

Jeanie still had three semesters to go before she earned her bachelor's degree. She didn't know how she could survive all that time without affection. She shouldn't have to slither off somewhere on the sly to meet someone for a date. Still, she was currently living in his house under his grace. Although the girl didn't want to become a nun, she certainly didn't want to tick her cordial friend off to the point that their remaining time together would be total hell.

Jeanie gathered up the nerve one evening to have a talk with Norman about the uncomfortable subject of dating while still living with him. It was agreed that since they were no longer a couple, she could indeed date other men. Her date could come over to the house to pick her up, but that was it. It would be too uncomfortable to bring anybody into the house as well as an invasion of Norman's privacy. Jeanie's former fiancé even offered to watch Rosa for her when she went out if he wasn't doing anything.

"Thank you Norman. That's very sweet of you."

"You know I still care about you," he said. "I'll probably always care about you."

"I'll always have feelings in my heart for you as well."

That statement was true, the two would probably always care for each other. However, their relationship had dramatically changed. Norman went from being a lover to a brother. Jeanie always wanted to have a brother. Norman would be the closest thing she would ever get to having one.

Jeanie went on an occasional date with different men she met for the next eighteen months. However the girl never saw the same guy more than two times. She didn't want to became emotionally involved with anyone else for awhile. Still it was fun just getting out of the house and back into circulation. She definitely wasn't the wild girl of the past. She didn't let herself get sexually involved with any of her date mates. The fact was, Jeanie secretly hoped that Norman and her would work things out. If that happened, she didn't want any past fling to get in the way of their reunion.

Jeanie made up her mind that if her and Norman didn't get back together, she would move out of the state. Maybe she would move to Florida. She visited her grandmother there before and the countryside was really quite lovely. Of course it's hot as hell in the summer. That was ok for she didn't mind the heat nearly as much as the cold. Jeanie loved the palm trees, the orange trees and the big ferns. There was a whole different type of terrain out there. It was almost like living in a different country only she didn't have to learn a foreign language.

Jeanie wanted to start over someplace where no one knew her. She also wanted to live in a warm climate. How she hated the long, cold winters of Massachusetts. They seemed to last forever. Often the temperature didn't get above 20° for weeks at a time. It was even more of a bummer living in a cold country if you had to go out in the freezing temperatures any length of time. She hated shoveling snow off the walkway or scraping ice off the car windshield. Yes Jeanie thought, she certainly wouldn't miss those long, miserable winter days. Just thinking of winter sent chills all through Jeanie's body.

Suddenly she remembered a night that occurred nearly ten years ago. That was the evening she thought she would literally freeze to death. Jeanie couldn't believe she lived through that night. She shook her head in disbelief while remembering the details.

Jeanie and Donald (her ex husband) broke up briefly during their courting days. For a month or so during December and January, she went up north to live with her sister while she thought about what she wanted to do with her life as well as with her boyfriend. While living at her sister's house, Jeanie worked as a cocktail waitress at a local pub. It was on one of those nights, Jeanie almost froze to death on the streets.

Earlier that evening, the little bar-maid accepted a date with a cordial, young man she met there. She didn't know until closing time that the guy didn't have a car.

"I only live a couple blocks up the street. It won't take us long to walk over there," the young man explained.

Jeanie had not dressed for walking. She wore a short dress, pantyhose, and black leather shoes. Still, everybody else had gone for the night and there was no way she was going to call her sister's husband to come to Harden to pick her up from work at 2 am. She surely wasn't going to call a cab to drive twenty miles either. She worked too hard for her money!

"All right," Jeanie agreed. "It had better not be too far. I hate the cold and all I have to wear is this short jacket."

So Jeanie and her friend trekked up the street to where his little apartment was located. It was early January and extremely cold. Jeanie's breath left white clouds in the air every time she exhaled. As she walked, she felt her to toes becoming more and more numb. Her ears stung so much she thought they would get frost bit and break right off her head. Just about the time she was about to tell the guy to take a flying leap, they arrived at his apartment. The two of them stood at the doorstep with chattering teeth. The guy couldn't open the door fast enough for her. How ever when the apartment door opened, Jeanie discovered that it wasn't much warmer in there than it was outside.

"Why is it so damned cold in here?" Jeanie asked.

"Oh, the gas had been turned off," the young man told her in a unapologetic tone. "We won't be here but a few minutes. I just need to grab joint. After that we'll walk to my friends house down the street."

"I'm not going anywhere else with you on this cold, miserable night," Jeanie angrily told the young man as she raced out the door. The girl felt that she would die of hypothermia if she didn't get someplace warm fast.

The human snowman thought that if she ran, she might just escape death. She felt her knees lose sensation. Her body kept getting weaker and weaker.

"I can't stop now," Jeanie said to herself. "Oh God, don't let me freeze to death in the snow!" As the girl ran down the deadened streets of Harden, a car stopped to offer assistance. The frozen girl didn't hesitate for a moment. If she didn't get out of the cold, she would surely turn into a Carmalita popsicle.

She considered herself lucky that the two guys who stopped to help her were honorable. They weren't rapist or on the FBI's most wanted list. They definitely weren't the common creeps that you would expect to encounter at that time in the morning. One of the guys even offered the red faced girl his coat.

"Here put this on your cold legs. That will warm you up."

Those two gents probably didn't know it that night, but they probably saved Jeanie's life. It wasn't long after that incident that Jeanie packed up her suit cases and her pride and went back to Arkansas to be with Donald.

"No wonder I hate it here so much," Jeanie sighed to herself. "I can't feel my feet half of the time. If it wasn't for me sipping on this hot tea all day, I probably wouldn't feel my fingers either!" Jeanie shook her head as she recollected the reasons why she left the state she loved and moved back to Massachusetts. All for Rosa.

Jeanie thought that if she went up north, she could build the type of relationship she always wanted with her family. She thought that her kin folks would open up their heart to her and they'd be just like the Walton's. However, she had to face facts. Her dysfunctional family would never be like that fictional tv family. It's hard to rebuild that type of relationship if you never had it in the first place. She thought that the strained relationship she had with her family would somehow all magically disappear upon her arrival. Some things would never change, like Jeanie's unrealistic expectations.

Why was it that Jeanie kept playing the same song over and over again in her head but expected the lyrics to be different each time? Why was it she kept returning time and time again to an unfriendly family environment? She still expected her mom and sister to treat her differently, more open, more giving, and more loving. Jeanie desired to be treated the way she wanted to be treated as a child, but that expectation never become a reality. She had to accept the fact she was powerless in controlling other people's thoughts, actions and feelings. Hell, half the time she couldn't even control her own.

Jeanie grew up a people pleaser. It was hard to alter that personality pattern now after all those years. Even to this day if someone didn't like her or she didn't live up to someone else's expectations, she felt it was because of her. She had failed them. Jeanie thought that she wasn't good enough, wasn't smart enough, pretty enough or whatever enough. The poor girl always internalized how others thought of her as being her problem. The girl never saw their rejection of her as their problem. Jeanie thought if she tried hard enough, then she could win over the person who had rejected her or abandoned her earlier…if only she would try harder. The girl could try as hard as humanly possible to be the most loving, sweetest, caring person in the world, but she was not God.

No matter what Jeanie did, she was still imperfect. Therefore, she shouldn't expect a perfect love, even though she wanted it. She couldn't force anybody to give her the time and love she needed. She couldn't force Norman to open up to her and love her the way she wanted to be loved. What made her think she could force those loving feelings from other people? She had to accept the fact that she did not have control over someone's feelings, thoughts or actions. At times, she didn't even have control over her own heart and mind activities. However thinking that she did, made her feel more in control of her private world.

Thinking about that whole night sent Jeanie racing to the kitchen to get another cup of hot tea. With her mug in hand she headed back to her art room. These days, she spent more time there than anywhere. How she would miss the spacious room she used solely for her art pursuits. Yes, even though Jeanie wasn't getting her emotional needs met, she certainly was getting her basic needs met. She lived like a queen in Norman's mansion. Too bad she didn't feel like a queen. Although she had all the beautiful material things around her, she felt like a pauper for she was empty inside.

After an extremely tough fall semester, Jeanie made arrangements to go to Florida for ten days. Originally, Rosa was to accompany her on this trip. However, she acted up so badly the previous week, Jeanie cringed at the idea of taking her demanding child anywhere with her.

Once or twice a year the airlines offered one heck of a special rate to sunny Florida. A person could fly round trip for $218. Jeanie took advantage of that deal a few years ago and brought her daughter to Disney World. Although her two-year-old daughter became tired and whiny, Jeanie was glad she got to go to the Magic Kingdom. Every child should go someplace where all their storybook characters came to life. It thrilled Jeanie to see Rosa get so excited over meeting Mickey Mouse and his friends.

The doting mom did everything in her power to see that her daughter didn't grow up deprived of anything. She didn't want her experiencing what she had endured growing up. Jeanie often went without the very things she needed so she could give her child what she thought would make her happy. Often Jeanie went overboard getting Rosa things. She was just trying to nurture her own inner child by giving everything she could to her daughter. Jeanie purchased all sorts of things at the local flea market that she once had as a child or else always wanted. Although Jeanie could play with her daughter's toys, it still didn't stop the angry, hurt little girl inside from feeling deprived.

Little Jeanie always seemed to get other than what she wanted out of life. As a child, she didn't get the toys she wanted. She settled for a cheap substitute for her parents couldn't afford the real thing. As an adult, she rarely got the people she cared about to return her affections. She thought she had broken that pattern when she captured Norman's attention years ago. However what good was it to love a man who could not or would not love her the way she needed to be loved? For a short while the man had opened up to Jeanie, but the inner door to his heart closed as fast as it had opened. The girl was left wanton, discouraged and very, very hurt.

It had been almost a year since Jeanie and Norman officially broke up. Except for Rosa's chicken pecks, she had not gotten anything more than a tiny kiss from anyone. Besides enduring the cold temperatures, Jeanie was currently putting up with the frozen atmosphere of the household as well. She definitely needed to get away for a while!

Jeanie had planned to take the Florida vacation with her daughter several months ago. However, since Rosa had been so disagreeable lately, the girl decided it would be better for her mental health to embark on that trip alone. Jeanie readily jumped at the opportunity to put her selfish thoughts into action when Norman volunteered to watch Rosa for her the week of her planned Florida vacation.

Norman could be so nice to Jeanie. Although the guy didn't have to make the forty minute drive to the airport, he volunteered to do so. During the last year, he had allowed Jeanie to drive his second vehicle to school after her car became broken beyond repair. Yes, her former boyfriend made good money and was very generous with his possessions. Too bad he couldn't be equally generous with sharing his emotions or his affections.

Oh well, Jeanie thought. No one can have every quality that she admired and desired. But she hoped she could meet someone who came close to that ideal vision she had in the back of her mind.

Jeanie's grandmother had a friend pick up the lone traveler at the Tampa airport. The girl was happy that her grandmother had such nice, caring neighbors. Boy, if people were that friendly in the little town which she temporarily called home, maybe she wouldn't be so emotionally needy Jeanie thought.

People in Norman's small town were so spread out, that it was difficult to maintain a close friendship with anyone. Jeanie wasn't at home much either, so that didn't help the social isolation she felt with the community. Jeanie felt uncomfortable in Norman's domain lately. He was becoming increasingly stringent about the house rules. He was very verbal with Jeanie about his likes and dislikes. When she broke his rules…she heard about it!

So, the diligent student worked hard at school and put as much time and effort into her studies while still giving her growing daughter her mommy time. Jeanie and Rosa spent the weekends traveling around the surrounding area looking for fun things to entertain themselves. Rosa was a bit restless at times. She was an emotional, high strung little entity much like her mom. Often Jeanie would take her daughter to the lake or to the amusement park. They both looked forward to their weekly outings and Norman looked forward to his weekend of peace.

Since Jeanie's schedule was so hectic, she barely had time to develop any kind of a relationship with anyone except her next-door neighbor Barbie. Sometimes during the week, Jeanie and Rosa would go next door with a plate full of cookies to visit her next-door neighbor. Yes, Barbie was the closest thing she had to a friend out there. Of course, Despite their break-up, Jeanie still considered Norman a friend.

Carmalita Jean was glad that even if things between her and Norman didn't work out as a couple, at least they stayed friends. Hopefully, she would have him as a friend for a long, long time. She could talk to the man on an intellectual level about almost anything. Jeanie considered their conversations to be perceptive and enlightening. Talking to Norman would have been much like talking to Mr. Spock on Star Trek. Although she liked Mr. Spock, Jeanie couldn't imagine being married to him. Even though she liked Norman as a person, she couldn't see being married to him right now either.

After a restless first night in Florida with her grandmother, Jeanie took a bus to one of the many museums in the downtown area. As the lone girl walked along a green strip park, she met a young bicyclist named Pete. Pete was 13 years her junior, but the two of them really hit it off. It bothered her that he was so young though. However he was over 18…just barely. After their brief conversation in the park, Pete wrote down his phone number and asked Jeanie to call him later that night. Even though the girl felt a little like Mrs. Robinson, she decided to give the young man a call.

Upon arriving back at grandma's house, Jeanie told her about the sweet, young man she met in the park. Grandma was happy that she found someone she liked and encouraged her to go with him. The young man could show her some of the sites her grandmother told her. So shortly after dinner, Jeanie dialed Pete's number and gave him her Florida address.

"I think I know where that Street is. Are you near a mall?" Pete inquired.

"Yes, I can see it from the front porch," replied Jeanie.

"I'll be there in half an hour. How would you like to go to Clearwater Beach tonight?" Pete asked

"That would be fun," Jeanie told him through smiling lips.

The next few days passed so quickly that Jeanie didn't remember much of her shared conversations with Pete. She did however distinctly remember sweet sensations he left in her heart. She still tingled inside thinking about the warm, moist kisses he planted on her lips. It had been a long time since Jeanie had gotten so much affection. She was sure that God planned that wonderful week so that her poor, empty heart could heal. Those seven days were meant to revitalize the love starved girl, she was sure of it. The starry eyed romantic caught up on her affection during that time. It made it possible for the disillusioned girl to go back to her life of emotional deprivation with Norman. The sweet memories of the gentle affection she received from Pete that week was truly just what Jeanie needed to keep her spirit alive another year while she finished college

In between spending time with Pete, Jeanie spent time getting to know her grandmother. It amazed her to know that her grandmother also had a dream of compiling and publishing her life story. Until that visit, Jeanie didn't have any idea that her grandmother had such dreams. Her grandma wanted to write her story so she could feel she left something behind when she died. Leaving behind the next generation of children to populate and pollute the earth wasn't enough for her granny. It also wasn't enough for her either!

Like many elderly, Jeanie's grandmother had a variety of health problems. She knew it wouldn't be much longer until she joined God in his paradise. It hurt Jeanie to see her grandma tired and partially disabled. Surely no one deserved to live in poverty and pain like her sweet, dear grandma did, Jeanie thought. Little did Carmalita Jean know that within a short year, God would come to claim her beloved grandmother.

During Jeanie's trip to Tampa, she also found out a bit of family history. It turned out that her grandmother was descended from royal blood. That meant that she had some royal blood in her as well.

"Yes, my dear if the dictatorship wasn't overthrown and you lived in Poland, you would be a countess."

Just knowing those little tidbits of information made Jeanie's cheeks flush. Her ancestry didn't mean squat here though. However it meant that Jeanie was worth something after all and not just $1.78 in minerals found in her body.

After everything Jeanie had been through in her life, she still didn't think she had been worth much as a person. Although she was living in nice accommodations with her ex-boyfriend, Jeanie still received government help. The way she was often treated at the department of human services made her feel totally worthless. The last time she was there, she had to miss several hours of school to listen to an impersonal lecture (which involved a room full of people) about how important it was to get motivated in life and learn how to take care of herself. That degraded Jeanie for she had worked her butt off for years trying to get her college degree so that she could do just that!

Up until the past few months, Jeanie had planned on moving to Florida partially so she could be with her grandmother, partially to escape the cold. Now, however she wondered if she should move to Arkansas instead. Perhaps, when she established residency, she could get some assistance in locating her daughter's father. Jeanie could surely use the support money she would get if she located Rosa's dad. Even though Jeanie was close to graduating, she didn't feel real confident in her ability to find a good paying job. She had reason to be worried about her job prospects.

The job situation had been really bad during the past year. It seemed every company was making cutbacks in an effort to stay afloat. The economy was the worst it had been in years. This frightened Jeanie. Although she was happy to be graduating from college soon, it made her anxious about employment possibilities. Except for her work-study jobs and her job as a counter person at a local bake shop, Jeanie hadn't worked in years. Just where she would fit into the world was anybody's guess…including hers.

The last year in college was really tough. Jeanie didn't think that she was going to be allowed to graduate due to the personal problems she encountered along life's thoroughfare. The ambitious student made a mistake in talking to the wrong person about the many abuses she endured earlier in her years. It was important for Jeanie to understand how her life became as screwed up as it was. The knowledge Jeanie absorbed from her chosen courses unfortunately, opened up many past wounds. Although these wounds had crippled Jeanie in the past, it was time now to face those demons in a different light. While studying one of her psychology courses, she divulged a little too much information to one of her professors in her journal. Initially the person Jeanie confided in helped her. Her professor wrote insightful, comments in her submitted paperwork. However, later on, that same professor tried to blackball the hardworking, distraught girl from going any further into the human services field. Jeanie was shocked. Since she only had another two semesters to go before she was finished with school, she wasn't about to drop out of her chosen major.

Jeanie had to fight tooth and nail to keep in her chosen career path. She was required to go in front of the entire human service board and answer a slew of questions while they decided her fate. They all agreed that although Jeanie was a smart girl, she had many problems with which she hadn't resolved on an emotional level only on an intellectual level. The jury decided that although Jeanie was allowed to continue on in her fieldwork, she would be not be permitted to work directly with people. Even though Jeanie had a burning desire to help people, she was denied admission to such a fieldwork job. The proper field work experience would have made obtaining a job working directly with people much easier for Jeanie after she graduated. However, she was denied that option.

During Jeanie's internship she didn't learn much. She was basically an errand girl for a non profit group. The girl felt like she did nothing but waste her time there. Jeanie couldn't help but feel angry. Still, she went along with what the board decided on for she was afraid to make any waves. She didn't want to drown any efforts she previously made to keep her floundering degree afloat.

Jeanie did indeed graduate that year. Norman, Rosa and four of her nieces attended the elaborate graduation ceremony. Jeanie radiantly smiled as she wore her black gown. Despite the many obstacles the girl had encountered, she stuck it out in school. She was proud of herself. Rosa was equally proud of her mom. An important chapter of Jeanie's life ended, while another was beginning. Jeanie shuddered with excitement. She shook with fear. Many changes would be occurring in the next three weeks. Although she wanted these changes and planned for them the best she could, Jeanie was still frightened. The day before her long bus ride south, she could barely sleep. Even though Jeanie carefully planned her trip to Arkansas, there were still so many unknowns. Jeanie knew where she was headed and what she wanted. Now she had to turn those plans into action. Now she had to make those dreams a reality.

Norman agreed to keep Rosa as Jeanie embarked on her journey to the natural state. The fanciful lady did not know where she would be going to go once her bus arrived in Hot Springs. She didn't have a job waiting for her, nor did she have a place to stay. Jeanie did have a little bit of money saved to help her get settled. That would have to do for now…that and her small station wagon which Norman had agreed to drive down for her once she got an apartment.

Before boarding the bus to Arkansas, Jeanie took one more look around. It was another snowy, miserable, winter day. She couldn't wait to get away. After giving her daughter many long hugs and kisses, she looked at Norman. With tears in her eyes Jeanie hugged the man she almost married. Norman was a lover turned brother. Despite their differences and their previous problems, Jeanie was happy that she still had him in her life.

"Thank you my friend," Jeanie whispered to Norman as he embraced her. "I'll call you when I arrive in Arkansas."

Jeanie gave her daughter, Rosa a great big hug. As she looked in her girl's eyes she could see tears forming. Jeanie almost cried too.

"I love you my little Rose. You'll join me in Arkansas real soon."

Shortly after Jeanie's suitcases were loaded under the bus, she went inside to claim a seat. As she looked out the window, she saw her little girl waving at her. Rosa had the most solemn, frightened eyes. That must have been how Jeanie looked the day her dad walked away. Unlike her dad, Jeanie would be reunited with her child in just a few weeks.

A mixture of sadness and gladness crept inside Jeanie's heart. The future awaited her. The past was behind her. The frozen tundra that had encompassed much of her life would soon be melted away by the wonderful Arkansas sun. The pain which flooded her spirit was numbing. Although it was cool on the bus, the temperature inside her heart was colder still.

# CHAPTER 17

# Starting Over Again

The long thirty six hour bus ride to Little Rock Arkansas seemed to take forever. Although Hot Springs was Jeanie's final destination, there wasn't a bus going there until the next day. She didn't want to spend a night in a hotel room, but she didn't have a choice. At least, she wouldn't be quite as fatigued after a long night's rest.

Despite the array of problems Jeanie encountered in the past, she started to feel good about herself. For the first time in Jeanie's life she had a purpose. She felt she was brought on this earth to help people, but first she had to help herself. Since the courageous girl didn't have friends or family down there in Arkansas any more, she knew she had no other option but to rely on herself. That was a frightening thought.

Jeanie didn't like the idea of living on her own, but she knew that was what she had to do. At least in her home she wouldn't have to follow anyone's rules except her own. Jeanie knew that she had to get herself together. The wandering waif had to find a decent place to stay and get Rosa down here as soon as possible. Her poor little girl must be feeling the same abandonment issues she felt twenty-five years earlier when her dad left. Her nine-year-old daughter may also be questioning her mother's whereabouts and whether or not she was coming back for her. Jeanie couldn't keep her daughter waiting in the shadows much longer. No, she just couldn't do that to her beloved Rosa.

Jeanie had absolutely nowhere to go when she arrived in Hot Springs. She asked the person manning the bus station if she could possibly leave her six suitcases there at the station while she looked around for an apartment. The kindly man agreed to do that for Jeanie. From the bus stop she walked the streets searching for a suitable place she could call home.

Jeanie found several listings for apartments and duplexes in the local newspaper the day before. Unfortunately, most of the apartments were already rented by the time she called about them that day. Finally after Jeanie made about twenty phone calls, and walked miles in her flat soled shoes, she found a nice apartment on the bus route. Immediately after signing the lease, the tired girl went back to the bus station to claim her baggage. After Jeanie tucked her luggage safely away in her apartment, she called Norman and Rosa. She told them that she made it safely to Arkansas and found an apartment. She also excitedly told Norman about the job that was listed in the paper concerning a career as an activities director for classy resort down the street.

After Jeanie conversed with Norman for a few minutes, he put her little girl on the phone.

"Mommy, I want to go down to Arkansas with you. I miss you. It's boring here," Rosa exclaimed.

"You'll have to stay there only for a week or so honey," Jeanie assured her.

Although Jeanie missed her child, she knew it was for the best that she stay up there until she got more settled. Besides, Norman was still trying to find someone to watch Rosa while he drove Jeanie's car down. It was packed full of stuff she didn't want to part with.

"Norman, why don't you just bring Rosa along with you on your trip to Arkansas?" Jeanie inquired.

"I don't want to put up with a whiny fidgety kid," Norman proclaimed. "I'd just assume pay for the plane fare rather than do that."

"Well ok, if you feel that way. then fine," Jeanie replied to her ex- lover turned friend.

After that long fatiguing day, Jeanie couldn't wait to get back to her small apartment. Although the duplex had little furniture in it and no sheets on the bed, Jeanie was glad she had a place to rest her head that night. Unfortunately, the apartment was on a very busy side street. Jeanie didn't know when she rented it that many locals used that street to escape the Hot Springs racing traffic. For several nights Jeanie tried to sleep, but found it difficult even with her earplugs in. She was used to sleeping in the country. The only sounds she heard on a nightly basis there was the crickets and the birds and an occasional dog. Even though she signed a year's lease with her new landlord, she decided it was best to try to find a different apartment.

Her landlord didn't like the idea that Jeanie wanted to move out so soon. After explaining the situation to her, the woman was a little more understanding.

"I'm giving you three weeks notice," Jeanie stated. "I will be getting my deposit back…right?"

"Yes, of course as long as you pay for another advertisement in the paper. We would like that apartment rented before you leave."

That sounded fair enough Jeanie thought. "Sure."

Within a weeks time Norman drove Jeanie's car down from Massachusetts. It was packed to the hilt with all the little expensive gadgets and electronics that collectively would have been too expensive to buy new such as her blender, deep fryer and microwave. Carefully packed among the boxes of course was her stereo, tv and her word processor. Norman agreed to box up and mail several of the unbreakable items such as the remainder of her clothes and some of Rosa toys.

Jeanie looked at Norman with deep affectionate eyes.

"Thank you my friend," the girl said as she reached up to hug him. After making up the bed with some of her favorite quilts, Jeanie and Norman sat on it briefly just holding each other. They obviously still felt a great deal towards each other so it was very easy to get into a nice long make out session.

"This will probably be the last time I see you," Jeanie told her ex-boyfriend in between kisses.

"You'll come back sometime to see me. Just because we're not going together anymore doesn't mean we can't be friends," Norman stated.

"I just wish things could have been different. Even though Arkansas's beautiful I'm scared to be out here all alone," Jeanie whimpered.

"Oh, you'll do just fine," Norman said as he looked down into Jeanie's eyes. "You're a survivor. Don't you forget that!"

"Yes, I mustn't ever forget that!" Jeanie agreed.

Norman took a short nap on Jeanie's bed. He was obviously tired after that long drive. While Norman caught up on his rest, Jeanie caught up on her hugs. She snuggled by him the whole duration of his nap, taking in his warmth, smelling his hair, touching his skin. After just a few scant hours, he got off the bed and announced that he wanted to walk around to see the sights. After strolling along the immediate streets, the two of them went driving around town.

"I can't believe it's this warm in February," Norman shook his head in an unbelievable fashion. "It's almost balmy."

"Nice isn't it," Jeanie agreed. "Now you know why I chose to come back here to Arkansas. It's about the prettiest place I've ever been to." Jeanie smiled while she looked around at the green lawns that lushly grew around her.

After a short sightseeing trip around Hot Springs, Jeanie headed towards the Little Rock airport. Norman had a flight out later that evening and he surely didn't want to miss his plane.

"When do you want me to send Rosa home to you?" Norman inquired before going to the airport lobby.

"How about Valentine's Day," Jeanie answered.

"Sounds like a plan," Norman said as he gave his friend one more embrace.

"I'll call you from a pay phone in a few days," Jeanie told him as he opened the glass doors to the airport terminal. "Are you sure you don't mind me calling collect?"

"Not at all," her friendly ex said smiling.

Jeanie watched Norman as he walked away. He could be so, so nice sometimes. He certainly did have a kind heart. Too bad they couldn't have worked things out as a couple. Even though he really didn't have to help her with her child or with her vehicle, he volunteered to do it. Norman knew how stressed Jeanie got on long drives. He also knew that the girl didn't have a place to stay when she moved to Hot Springs. That was why he volunteered to keep Rosa that first month. Originally, Jeanie was going to leave Rosa with her sister Deana, but she just couldn't do that after what happened just five weeks earlier. Jeanie could not believe that her only sister could have done such a cruel thing to the daughter she loved so much.

Rosa was to spend her last Christmas vacation in Windsock with her aunt and family. Jeanie was thankful for the little break for she was becoming increasingly stressed about her upcoming move. Rosa wanted to spend several of her last days in Massachusetts with her beloved cousins. She would miss them terribly. Jeanie would miss them too. Nearly every weekend Rosa had one or more of her cousins over at her house. Four of Jeanie's nieces almost seemed like they were her own children! Everybody thought that the little vacation would have been great for all. That would probably be the last time the family would see each other for awhile. However, the wonderful visit they planned ended quite abruptly. Jeanie got a call from Rosa only two days after her vacation started.

"Mom, I want to come home," the weeping girl told her mother.

"What's wrong Rosa?" Jeanie inquired.

"I can't tell you right now. Come out here and get me please!" Rosa said in between sobs.

"Of course I will honey. I'll be there in an hour."

As soon as Jeanie got off the phone she made the long forty five minute drive to her sister's house. Rosa and several of her cousins were all alone in the house without parental supervision. That didn't surprise Jeanie. Usually the older kids took care of the younger ones in the household, so she didn't think anything of it.

"Shouldn't we wait to talk to Auntie?" Jeanie asked.

"No mom, I want to go now!" Rosa said with tears in her eyes. As soon as Jeanie gathered Rosa's clothes and toys, the two of them headed back home.

"Mom, Auntie told me all sorts of bad stuff about you. Are they true?"

It seemed that Jeanie sister told Rosa about all the wild times she had in her rebellious years. This included her experimentation with pot and alcohol, her shoplifting days, even the truth about Rosa's absent father. Jeanie couldn't believe that her sister could be so damned cruel to her nine-year-old daughter. Why on earth would that woman do such a thing to an innocent girl? The two of them were going to start a life far away from everybody and everything they knew. It was important to believe and trust in each other more than any time before. The only reason Jeanie could fathom why her sister would do anything that vicious was because she had just completed college. She had her whole life ahead of her. For once in Jeanie's life, she shined like a star… and Deana didn't like it. Rosa as well as Deana's own kids looked up to Jeanie. Deana couldn't compete with Jeanie's moment of success. That made her look bad. Her sister just barely completed high school and hadn't done anything extraordinary with her life.

Deana's low self-esteem forced her to take vengeance on Jeanie's poor, sweet innocent child. She was furious.

"Well darling, that's probably going to be the last time you see any of them!" Jeanie proclaimed shaking her head. She couldn't believe her own family could do anything so malicious. Even though Jeanie felt like calling her sister and giving her a piece of her mind, she decided not to. Jeanie talked to Norman about the series of events centering around Rosa's Windsock trip. Naturally, the man used logic and intelligence to explain away all the mean things that had been said and done that weekend. Jeanie could understand why the woman did the things that she did, still it didn't make it right. Knowing the possible reasons of Deana's cruelty didn't change anything. Jeanie felt like someone seared her heart with a hot iron. And her poor Rosa…only God knew the extent of the pain her little girl felt.

Along the way home, Jeanie and Rosa spent nearly an hour talking. It broke Jeanie's heart to tell her young daughter about her not so perfect past.

"Those events and behaviors are in the past honey. You do understand?" Jeanie asked her little girl. Rosa nodded her head in agreement. "Mommy was all mixed up inside her head. I got help from a professional and things are much better now. I'm sorry you had to find out about my wild days when I did a bunch of stupid stuff. I'm real sorry that you had to find out about your dad like you did. Although you were conceived in the way you were, I never thought of you as a mistake. No my honey, you were God's little unplanned blessing and I love you so much!" Jeanie reached down and hugged her hurting child. "I'm going to do everything I can to find out which man is your father. You deserve to know who your dad is. You should get to know him as a person," Jeanie added. Rosa looked up at her mother and forced a smiled. "Everything is going to work out for the best my little darling. Just you wait and see!"

After that rough day, there was no way in hell Jeanie would've left Rosa with her sister. If Jeanie didn't have a babysitter for her trip south, she would've dragged her reluctant child with her on the bus and went apartment hunting with her. Thank God for Normans intervention. If it wasn't for him, Jeanie knew that those first few weeks in Arkansas would have been even more stressful than they were.

After Jeanie got her car back, she sought out the local housing authority. She was shocked to hear that she would have to be on a waiting list for years before she could get section 8 rent subsidy. Jeanie was offered a place in the projects but she quickly declined. That wasn't an option. Before leaving the office, the kindly worker told Jeanie about a group of apartments down the street. They had eight apartments there that were government-subsidized.

Upon learning about the apartments, Jeanie quickly drove down to them and put in her application. Although all the subsidized apartments were taken, if she lived there she would he on an in-house waiting list. With any luck at all, she could possibly get in one of those apartments within a year's time if she needed one. Hopefully she wouldn't need a rent subsidy. However, since Jeanie had little job experience in her field she didn't know when she would be able to get a decent job. Although she had high hopes for her future she also had much doubt in her abilities to support herself and her daughter without any outside help.

After talking to the apartment manager about her lack of funds, the lady showed Jeanie an apartment which was in need of minor repairs.

"The rug is a bit dirty and the countertop is stained and the walls need painting, but if you want this one as it is, I'll take $75 off the rent each month."

Jeanie shook her head in agreement. Rosa would like this place a lot better than the other one she thought. Her daughter will have her own bedroom and there was a girl downstairs around her age. There was a swimming pool outside too. Yes, Rosa would like it here so much more. Jeanie smiled as she signed the rental contract to her new residence.

Even though Jeanie's moving day wasn't for another two weeks, the kindly landlord gave her the keys to the apartment that day. Good deal, the newcomer thought. She could take her time and fix up the apartment at her leisure. Since the place wasn't furnished, she would have to scout around and purchase some cheap furniture as well.

For the next two weeks Jeanie busily got her apartment in order. Once or twice a week, she would get several packages from Norman too. Within ten days time the place started to come to life. Jeanie was fatigued in her pursuit to find work. In between job hunting, she spent a great deal of time trying to get her new home in order. Besides furniture, she had to get all the little things necessary to make the house a home such as dishes and toiletries, curtains and towels. The cost of all those little things needed in a home sure added up to a lot of money. Jeanie was quick to discover that. Good thing she knew how to shop for bargains. The little dollar store down the street quickly became her best friend.

In the meantime Jeanie had started dating a nice man she met at a local convenience store. Jerry was sweet and kind with a daughter not much older than hers. The two started going out together a week or so before Rosa was to join her mom in Arkansas. Although Jeanie liked Jerry, the man smoked cigarettes. Jeanie didn't. The smoking thing became quite an issue several weeks later but for a while, the girl enjoyed the man's company and tried overlooking his bad habit.

Jerry liked being around Jeanie and showing her around. Due to Jerry's sightseeing drives, Jeanie started learning about the city's layout. Being with Jerry also made Jeanie forget how lonely she was inside. The displaced mom even liked being with Jerry's daughter. Jeanie knew that her daughter would like Lacey just as much as she did. When it was time to pick Rosa up at the airport, Lacey naturally came along for the ride. Jerry would have accompanied them as well, except he had to work. Jeanie should be working too. Unfortunately, she did not get any of the jobs she applied for since moving to town. That worried the girl somewhat. Still it had only been a month since her relocation south.

On the way to pick up Rosa that Valentine's Day, Jeanie's car died along the side of the road. Lacey and Jeanie were stranded there on the highway with no phone, no man and no hope. Finally, an elderly couple stopped to pick up the two desperate comrades. Jeanie was practically in tears.

"We are on the way to pick up my nine-year-old daughter at the airport and my stupid car broke down. I just have to get to the airport in time. I don't want my little girl wandering around that big place by herself wondering where her mom is!" Jeanie told the elderly couple crying.

The kindly elders could see Jeanie's plight and offered to take a little side trip to the airport so she could be there when Rosa's plane landed.

"Thank you so much for everything," Jeanie enthusiastically said. "You have been a God send!" Indeed they were. The elderly couple who helped her and Lacey get to the airport was indeed sent by God. There was no doubt in Jeanie's mind that it was so. It made her smile knowing that despite the way many individuals kicked her around previously in life, there were still good hearted, kind people in the world. God did indeed plant roses among the thorns.

Jeanie and Lacey weren't at the airport five minutes before Rosa's plane landed. Jeanie stood at the end of the runway waiting for her daughter to join her. Upon seeing her mother's face, the little girl excitedly ran towards her.

"I missed you mom! I missed you so much!" Rosa blurted out as tears streamed down her crimson cheeks.

"I missed you too honey!" Jeanie quickly told her daughter. "We had a little trouble getting out here due to car problems. We might be in the airport lobby for awhile. Ok?"

After getting reunited with one another, Jeanie introduced Rosa to Lacey. "This is my boyfriend's daughter," explained Jeanie. Rosa smiled.

"Let's go look at the planes," Rosa insisted.

"First let's make a phone call to see if Jerry can pick us up since he'll be off for work soon," informed Jeanie.

"Ok," the two girls shouted in unison.

The next two hours seemed to hang on forever. Jeanie was so happy to see Jerry that she put her arms around him and gave him a great big kiss. "Thank you for coming," Jeanie graciously told the man. "Thank you for being here for me today!"

Despite the previous transportation problems, both mother and daughter slept well that first night. Rosa was quick to make friends with the nearby neighbor kids. Yes, it was the right choice to move out here Jeanie thought. Now to get a job that she liked.

Jeanie had her life all planned out before she moved out to Arkansas. She would get her apartment all settled, then find a good paying job she liked within a month's time. She would work with the Child Enforcement Agency and find Rosa's dad within six months. After a year she would meet and marry a sweet, Southern gentleman. All of them would live happily ever after in a perfect world where nobody ever got mad at each other and there were never any mosquitoes. That was Jeanie's plan. That was what she really believed would happen. Unfortunately not everything in life went according to plan.

It was definitely a good thing Jeanie moved into that apartment complex which had a few subsidized apartments. It was also a good thing she was on the in house waiting list for receiving one of those units. For although the girl had a college degree, she had a difficult time obtaining the type of job which she sought. Since

Jeanie was so inexperienced, she never got hired for the many jobs she applied for.

In an attempt to balance the federal and state budgets, social services were hit hard financially. Many programs which would benefit displaced women and their children as well as many others took a beating. There just weren't many entry level jobs available. The positions that were available to her weren't the ones the agencies were able to pay for. In that particular area, the active retirees worked many the very jobs that she qualified for. Jeanie's heart sunk. Just what did she get herself into? She couldn't afford to merely volunteer at those human service jobs. She had her daughter to support! They couldn't live on the street and live on dandelion greens!

After several months of being out of work, Jeanie's little nest egg nearly dwindled away. Finally, in early May she was hired as a summer camp counselor. The position would start right after Memorial Day. It was only temporary of course, still Jeanie was thankful that she found some type of employment. It was a minimum-wage job but at least Rosa could attend summer camp for free. That was one nice perk, for Jeanie couldn't afford to pay a babysitter and the rest of her bills on the puny check she brought home.

Luckily by the end of that first summer, Jeanie was able to get on subsidized rent. She was so thankful for that. The despondent girl had nearly spent all that she saved moving to Arkansas. She was scared sick. She wondered what she would do if she didn't find more employment after her summer job ended. As long as Jeanie wasn't working, she'd didn't have to pay any rent. Thank God for that! That little bit of money she had in the bank would cover her paper goods and car expenses for a little while yet. Just knowing that made Jeanie breathe a little easier. Her and her daughter weren't going to be homeless and living on the streets after all!

Jeanie was so discouraged. She never thought that after she busted her tail in college, she would end up like this. She felt that she was no better off financially than before. It broke her heart to go to the Department of Human Services for help. Jeanie wasn't proud to go back on food stamps, but they had to eat. Even though Jeanie was out of work with no money coming in, she was denied any type of monetary help.

The social worker at the local office looked Jeanie in the eye and snottily told the heart sunk girl, "We can't give you any kind of monetary assistance. You're job ready."

The fact was that although Jeanie had her college education, she still was not job ready due to her inexperience in the field. Her professors at the state college didn't do her a favor by refusing to allow her to work directly helping people. The only thing she learned in her fieldwork job was how to play errand girl. Without the much-needed experience or professional license, Jeanie was doomed to work minimum wage jobs for a long, long time.

Since Jeanie couldn't find a job in her field of study, she even considered going back to being a waitress. The jobs she inquired about all required night and weekend work. Jeanie was raising a young girl alone. She had nobody down there to help with the babysitting and she surely wasn't going to leave her young child alone at night. She had to find a job that she could work during Rosa's school hours and she definitely couldn't work weekends. Those type of jobs were very scarce out there in Hot Springs!

Jeanie didn't realize how poor her job options were until she had been living in Arkansas for several months. Earlier that year Jeanie inquired at the social work licensing board about getting licensed as a social worker. Unfortunately they took forever to answer Jeanie's letter of inquiry. When her letter was finally answered, they told her that they could not even allow Jeanie to take the test to be licensed. They told her that there were 11 three credit courses in their curriculum that were similar but not exactly what Jeanie had taken up north. If Jeanie wanted to become licensed, she would have to take all those courses at a distant University. Since Jeanie already had a bachelors degree, she didn't qualify for any type of grant either. The only way she could pay for those courses was to get a student loan. The thought of going in debt for thousands of dollars didn't appeal to Jeanie at all, so the disheartened girl didn't even consider that option.

If only Jeanie knew what she was up against when she moved to Arkansas, she would have done things differently. She would have made sure she got her social work license while in Massachusetts. She would have made sure it was transferable to Arkansas, if not she would have decided upon another destination. It would be unfair to move to another place now though. Rosa was just starting to become settled after their move. It wouldn't be fair to uproot her child again, and Jeanie knew it. She had to put Rosa's needs ahead of her own. She didn't want her girl to grow up angry and alone as she had. No, she wanted something better for her angel.

The main reason Jeanie decided to move to Arkansas instead of Florida was so she could find Rosa's daddy. Trying to find her dad was an ordeal though. Jeanie knew the address of one of the two men who could be Rosa's father. When one of her daughter's potential fathers didn't go to court concerning the paternity case, Jeanie could have sworn a statement in front of the judge claiming he was the father. His name would have been automatically slapped onto her daughter's birth certificate. The guy would also be obligated to pay a certain amount of back child support as well as continue to pay monthly for Rosa's upkeep until she was eighteen.

Jeanie couldn't send an innocent man to the gallows. Much to the judge's surprise and her lawyers amazement, Jeanie insisted on a blood test to determine if he was indeed Rosa's father. The blood tests did not match him, so it was obvious who Rosa's father was. Finally the mystery around who fathered Jeanie's child was put to rest. For the first time, Jeanie knew without a doubt who her daughter's daddy really was.

Unfortunately, trying to find Rosa's father was an impossible task. Jeanie was only with the guy for a few fleeting hours. Except for knowing his name, the type of work he did and what his favorite color was, Jeanie knew very little about him. She did know that he used to live in North Little Rock. She also knew that he used to be married and had a son three or four years older than her daughter.

Since Rosa's father had such a common name, it was impossible for the child enforcement officers to find him. They needed a Social Security number or birth date and birthplace to aid in the search. Jeanie couldn't supply them with any of that relevant data. After several months, the agency determined that they were wasting their time and gave up the search. Jeanie was so upset that she cried. Her little girl would never get to meet and know her daddy. What's more due to the financial predicament Jeanie found herself in, she felt her and her child were bound to live in poverty and deprivation forever.

## CHAPTER 18

# A Time To Forget
# A Time To Heal

After the series of events that had come about so far, Jeanie was so depressed that she had all she could do to think. There were times when she would barricade herself in her apartment for days and do nothing but eat and cry. She knew she had to do something to make her family's life better. She could accept her fate of doom and gloom. However she wanted so much better for her child.

Jeanie decided to once again put in a personal AD in the paper. She wanted to meet someone sweet who would love her and take care of her both financially and emotionally. Jeanie carefully worded the AD and submitted it to the Little Rock paper. Even though she was financially impoverished, the girl felt she still had a lot to offer. Jeanie was pretty and smart. She knew how to cook and sew. She didn't have any bad habits like drinking and smoking or gambling. Jeanie was also quite affectionate and loved giving love as well as receiving it.

Jeanie thought for sure she would find the perfect man for her in the AD. She met with several men she liked, but never developed a personal relationship with any of them. The fact was, she still held a candle in her heart for Norman. Until she got over him entirely, she would never be ready to love someone else.

At the end of the first summer in Arkansas, Jeanie started dating a really nice guy named Donny. He had a son named Johnny who he had custody of. Although Donny lived far from Jeanie, he came up to Hot Springs every weekend to see her. Jeanie, Donny and their young ones would eat a good breakfast somewhere then go to the local amusement park for the day. Donny was so sweet to Jeanie. However since they both had their little wards, they really didn't have any time to get to know each other on a more personal level.

Even though Jeanie really liked Donny, she didn't consider him as serious husband potential. When both of their kids got together, it was so chaotic. Their rough housing and silly loud interactions with each other about drove Jeanie crazy. She was nervous enough with her own child. All the noise and commotion created when those two pre-teens got together, made Jeanie flinch with anxiety. Still they were kids, so she would have to learn to be tolerant with their loud antics as long as she continued dating Donny.

Since Jeanie had lived in Norman's mausoleum in the country all those years, the girl wasn't used to all the noise and excitement on a daily basis. She had all she could do to stand the noisy, rowdy children at the summer camp. On weekends, she wanted peace and quiet as well as time to think. She certainly didn't get that on the weekends when Donny and Johnny visited. Still, Donny was so nice to her. Jeanie really didn't want to let him go but she didn't know how much she would allow herself to get involved with him. Things just weren't right. But then again, what in life is ever just right?

At the end of the summer, Jeanie decided to use her two free American Express travel certificates to go back to Massachusetts for a visit. Those left over student certificates permitted her and a guest to fly round-trip anywhere for $129. They would only be good for a few more weeks and she didn't want to waste them. Besides, Jeanie had a burning desire to see Norman once more as well as try to make peace with her sister Deana.

Donny was kind enough to watch Jeanie's hamster and cat while she was away. He even brought Jeanie and Rosa to the airport so they could embark on their journey without unnecessary hassles or worries. Even though the man knew that she would be sleeping in Norman's master bedroom, he never said a word about it. He knew about her past relationship with Norman and the sleeping arrangements she had prior to moving south. The ex-lovers slept separately in different bedrooms for eighteen months prior to moving out of his home. Besides, Jeanie didn't owe Donny an explanation about anything. After all, they weren't seriously involved with each other. Still, the guy obviously cared about her, so it was probably calloused of Jeanie to accept the man's offer of assistance. If she had another person who she could depend on to bring her to the airport and watch her cat, she certainly would've asked them. However, she had no one else she could rely on, so she relied on him.

So with a hug and a kiss, Donny said farewell to Jeanie. Although mother and daughter both were excited about going north, they were also anxious about the trip too. Just what would this trip to Massachusetts accomplish Jeanie thought. It had only been eight months since she moved away but it seemed like eight years. These past few months had certainly been rough on both of them, a lot rougher than she had ever imagined

Norman met Jeanie and Rosa at Bradley Airport in Hartford Connecticut. She could tell by looking at him that life had been tough for her ex-boyfriend as well. He had recently broken up with a woman he went with for seven months. He unfortunately fell head over heels in love with a woman who couldn't make up her mind how she felt about him. After having his poor heart dragged into a dumpster and left for dead, the guy finally got the professional help he needed. He was now getting in touch with his inner feelings through weekly therapy sessions.

"How ironic he should be seeking professional help now," Jeanie mumbled to herself. She begged Norman for months to see a marriage counselor to heal their rocky relationship but he wouldn't do it. Now, he readily sought the help of a counselor without any coercing from anyone.

"Norman, why couldn't you have gotten in touch with your emotions back when I was going with you?" Jeanie inquired.

"I guess I just didn't hit rock bottom yet," Norman tried to explain.

"Why couldn't you hit rock bottom with me?" Jeanie questioned the solemn man.

"I don't know. I guess I just wasn't ready to get in touch with my feelings," Norman told his ex-girlfriend.

Jeanie felt sad for Norman but she also felt angry at him as well.

"Why couldn't he have made those much-needed changes for me?" Jeanie whimpered. "Didn't he think that I was worth the time and trouble? Didn't he think that our love was worth fighting for? Now he's getting all sensitive and in touch with himself and where am I?" Jeanie wondered, where was she?

Jeanie was in emotional limbo and financial hell. Although she tried not to be angry at Norman, she couldn't help but feel inklings of that emotion seep out of her skin. While she was there in Norman's house, the two talked, cuddled and even kissed. They spent several hours crying on each other's shoulders. They talked about what went wrong with their love as well as what each one of them wanted out of a relationship.

When Jeanie and Norman first started to get cuddly, Jeanie thought that there might be a possibility of them getting back together. The two had gone through so much. He was there when Jeanie had to have her hysterectomy. He waited on her hand and foot when she was released from the hospital that winter. He lovingly took care of her needs as well as took care of her six-year-old daughter. Norman had such a good heart. Jeanie could see that kindness in his being, yet at the same time she could also see the terrible hurt that still lingered inside his heart for his lost love.

The more Jeanie and Norman talked, the more she realized how wrong they were for each other. Jeanie still remembered being physically and emotionally neglected by Norman when she was going with him. Norman bluntly told Jeanie several months after going out together, that he didn't need affection as much as she did. He told her then, that he wasn't much of a kisser. He'd much rather hugged. Jeanie wanted and needed many hugs and kisses in order to feel loved. If she went back to him, her physical needs would never be satisfied and she knew it.

The enormous amount of love Jeanie desired couldn't be satisfied with tidbits of affection. Even if Norman finally made an effort to open himself up to her again, that aspect of their life would never change. That was just the way Norman was. Jeanie had to either accept him or forget him. Although it hurt her, she knew it was best to forget about Norman ever being such an important part of her life. She was glad that the two of them were still friends though. Jeanie knew that if the going ever got rough, Norman would help her out any way he could. Yes, they couldn't make it as a couple, but they were doing just fine as friends. How many people could remain good friends with their ex-lover? Not too many!

While Jeanie was up in Massachusetts, she borrowed Norman's extra car and drove to Windsock to see her sister Deana. Rosa was undoubtedly still hurt by what happened at her aunt's house the December before. That day, Rosa chose to visit her old school and all the classmates she left behind while Jeanie visited her sister.

At first the vibrations that were felt between the two sisters were so heavy that everyone around them was uneasy. Within a few minutes the atmosphere lightened up somewhat. After visiting an hour or so, most of Deana's children went outside to play. Jeanie took the opportunity to talk to her sister about what was said to Rosa during the Christmas break the year before.

Deana said something about how a certain friend used to do this or that. Jeanie listened on and waited for a chance to make a few choice comments.

"Surely you can't hold something like that over the girl's head," Jeanie blurted out. "After all, were all human. We all make mistakes. As long as we eventually learn from our mistakes, then I think it's wrong that someone should keep bringing up the past. Don't you agree?"

Deana couldn't comprehend what Jeanie was trying to tell her. She didn't link what Jeanie was then saying to the careless, cruel words she vehemently spewed at her daughter the last time she saw her. She couldn't acknowledge the importance of the event nor the consequences that followed. Of course Deana quickly changed the subject. Jeanie readily let the conversation shift to something else.

Deana obviously felt uncomfortable with the subject and wanted out of that awkward scene as quickly as possible. In Jeanie's meeker days, she would not have said anything to her sister about what was tearing at her heart. Although Jeanie hated confrontations, she felt she had to say something to her sister about what happened that past December. The girl actually hoped that her sister felt remorse over the calloused things she told her daughter. If Deana did feel remorse over what she had said, she didn't show it. The only thing Jeanie felt was Deana's reluctance to continue on in the conversation. Jeanie quickly let go of the subject she tried to engage her sister in, Despite the unresolved issue between the two siblings, Jeanie didn't push things. The friction between Jeanie and Deana definitely was not settled. Jeanie left her sister's home within an hour, feeling very unsatisfied with the visit.

"Well this was a waste of time," Jeanie said to herself.

Jeanie's sister couldn't even acknowledge that she did anything wrong. Deana didn't even approach the subject concerning the mean things she said about her to Rosa a few months back. She could not either consciously or subconsciously own up to that rotten thing she did that day to her little girl. Deana tried to put a wedge between them by telling her young daughter the many stupid things Jeanie had done in the past. As if Deana's an angel? Deana had screwed up in her life too! Some of her screw ups weren't so obvious as Jeanie's were. Some...were just that much more hidden. Since her sister didn't admit to any wrongdoing, she of course didn't apologize for all the pain she caused.

That was the only time the dismayed girl went to Windsock that week in Massachusetts. Jeanie had other people to see while she was up north, primarily her mother.

Jeanie and Rosa ventured the two hour drive to visit her mother and step father during one of their vacation days. Although Jeanie and her mother were never close, the young lady gave her mom a big body hug. They had a nice visit that early fall day. Her stepfather loved to barbecue and obviously Jeanie still loved to eat. Both her and Rosa readily wolfed down the cooked patties with their yummy condiments of choice.

Rosa played with the little girl next door while Jeanie and her parents talked. They never did talk about anything personal, just light chitchat. Jeanie never could open up to her mother, but oh how she wanted to.

Jeanie wanted to tell her mom about the anxiety she felt living so far away from everything familiar. She couldn't tell her parent of the amount of fear she harbored inside her heart. Although she had a college education, Jeanie felt that she may not be able to get the type of job she trained for. She definitely didn't tell her mother how very, very afraid she was that she would fail...again. She didn't confess to her how fearful she was that she might once more fall in a total financial shit hole if situations didn't improve for her soon. Mom never knew about the times Jeanie was totally desolate in her teen years and early twenties. She didn't know that her daughter had on more than one occasion been homeless and hungry.

Mom never knew about any of that. Most of all she never knew about what happened on that hill. She never knew about the relentless teasing, name-calling and prodding she obtained from her peers all those years. She didn't acknowledge the type of physical and mental abuse she endured from Slugger or the reason why she had to leave Norman. She definitely didn't know about the times she was raped or how she often prayed for death to come and take her away from this cold, uncaring world.

Carmalita Jean didn't go into details as to why she left Norman, the man who could fulfill her intellectual needs, but left her physically wanton. She couldn't live with a man who could not quench the thirst her body craved. She wasn't talking about just the sex act. Sex without feeling just wasn't worth the effort anymore. It wasn't just good sex Jeanie wanted and needed. No, it was the rising of desire, the whirlwind of untamed emotions that the body expressed through making love. At one time she loved Norman with such an abundance, her heart burned with desire just thinking about him. Before Norman came into her life, she had never experienced such a love. Still, she couldn't force someone to love her as she wanted to be loved. It really hurt her that Norman was so quick to seek counseling after only being with his lady friend for a few months. He was willing to do so much for his fickle short term love and he wasn't willing to do it for Jeanie. The nostalgic lady shook her head and tried to shake loose the remnants of a love gone bad. She rolled her eyes towards her temple and allowed the sun to dry up the clear salty drops that threatened to fall from her eyes. She had wasted too many tears on that unfulfilled relationship. Physically, she had moved on, but spiritually she remained still.

Jeanie and Rosa stayed over at her mom's house until nearly dark. She hated driving after sunset. Besides, she wanted to return to Norman's rooming house and prepare for bed. It had been a challenging day.

Rosa fell asleep in the car along the way to Norman's. It was way past her bedtime and her youngster was completely tuckered out. After Norman helped get the sleepy girl to her bedroom, he went to the kitchen where Jeanie was preparing some decaffeinated tea. They carried on a thought provoking conversation about the details of her trip. She was quick to tell him about the disappointing conversation she had with her sister. Jeanie listened to Norman speak to her about his thoughts concerning the reasons some people seem to deliberately hurt others as well as her reactions to the whole perplexing mess. As usual, the conversation was engaging and totally enlightening. Just when had Jeanie become more interested in what was between a man's ears than what was between his legs?

Norman penetrated her mind with his intelligence that was the fact. Norman challenged Jeanie's mind like no other lover she had been with. The conversations the two shared around psychology and philosophy were intense. Outside of college, Jeanie couldn't remember the last time she so thoroughly enjoyed a stimulating conversation with anyone. Yes, Jeanie thought if she wanted to marry Mr. Spock...Norman would be perfect. However she would never be satisfied with sharing her life with a brainy guy if her emotional needs weren't met and she knew it.

Jeanie and Rosa returned to Arkansas with mixed feelings at the end of the week. Massachusetts wasn't home but Arkansas didn't feel like home either.

Jeanie and Donny resumed dating after she returned to Arkansas. He was there to greet her and her daughter at the airport. He was there the following weekend to bring her and Rosa out to eat and to the miniature golf course. However the hours spent with her and Donny became strained. Three short weeks after Jeanie's return trip home, the relationship ended. The girl just didn't feel like she wanted to go further into their relationship. Her thoughts were still on Norman. Part of her heart was too. Jeanie knew that when she told Donny that she didn't want to be anything more than friends at the time, it hurt him. She was sorry that her words hurt him, but she couldn't lie or lead him on. Jeanie didn't like to be strung along by a man and she surely did want to do that to someone else. Donny wasn't willing to make the long trip to see Jeanie if there wasn't a chance of something developing between the two…so they said goodbye.

"Goodbye my friend," Jeanie said. "Maybe our paths will cross again in the future." When Jeanie told Donny that, she didn't have any idea that in the future their paths would indeed cross again.

After Donny and Jeanie broke up, the confused girl once again crawled into her safe little cocoon. In the confines of her small apartment Jeanie collected her thoughts and re-evaluated her life. She was content for a while to sit alone in her cozy apartment and listen to music while reminiscing about her past relationships. Finally, it got to the point where daydreams alone could not keep the girl content. It was then, she rummaged through the stack of old AD letters and selected a few prime ones from the pile.

"Maybe some the guys who wrote these letters were still available," Jeanie said convincingly to herself as she pulled out her purple stationery.

Jeanie wrote several letters, and waited a week or so for a response. Much to the dreamer's dismay, she discovered that most of the men who had written to her earlier had found girlfriends and were presently unavailable. There was still one man in her letter stack who she had written several letters to her that she knew was still unattached. She had written several letters to him previously, but quit writing to him when she discovered that he was in jail.

Much to Jeanie's disappointment, Tex was in jail for fraud. He tried to cheat on a business deal and got caught. Jeanie wasn't too keen on getting involved with a guy in prison, but he wasn't a rapist or murderer. Besides, it was getting harder and harder to find someone who could put up with her and her sweet, sometimes bratty daughter.

Jeanie also wanted someone who could give her a comfortable, secure life without worry. If the girl had her way she would sing, dance, write poetry and paint all day long. The nights were of course reserved for something more exciting and romantic. What Jeanie wouldn't give for a nice long lovemaking session with someone she cared deeply about. Right now she'd settle for pure lust with someone she could stomach for more than a few fleeting hours.

Although Jeanie's body craved for someone to put out the hot flame within, she was extremely choosy of who she now went with. For a while, Jeanie went with someone she had met from a church social. Although she really liked him, he liked someone else. After wasting her time and attention on the man for two months, Jeanie decided it was best not to throw herself at Bill. He knew where to find her if he wanted to…unfortunately he just didn't want to.

Bill's rejection, hurt Jeanie's feelings, but she had to get over it. After all, what choice did she have. None. She couldn't make someone love her. Bill was not a robot. He was free to do whatever he chose to do. He was free to be with whoever he wanted to be with. She had a choice to either get over the guy or continually pine over him. Jeanie decided that she had already wasted too much love and on the affections of that particular guy. So, it was definitely time to say goodbye to him too! Maybe eventually she would find someone who cared about her as much as she cared about him. Oh, how she hoped and prayed that her search would not last forever!

At the end of her first year at Arkansas, Jeanie was working at a low wage job as a home health aide for a local company. That was quite a kick in the pants since the smart girl was a college graduate. There were people working for the agency with a tenth grade education who earned the same amount of money she made. That was discouraging for Jeanie. What was worse than the puny wages she received, was the type of work she did. Day in and day out, all Jeanie did was bathe dirty old men and women, cleaned the toilets and basically acted like a personal handmaid.

Jeanie got little pay and even less respect for the type of work she did. Sometimes her clients were outright mean to the sensitive girl. There were many times when Jeanie went home crying. It was during that time in her life when she started writing to Tex again.

Tex would be getting out of prison soon and wanted a sweet lady in his life when he was released. Jeanie was all for giving the guy a second chance at life after all she had made her share of mistakes. Tex knew of Jeanie's jaded past for she told him bits and pieces of her insecure, unstable life. She also confided in the man about how she and her daughter, Rosa both needed to feel financially secure for at the time they certainly were not. Of course Tex quickly reassured Jeanie how lucrative his former businesses were and how the both of them would want for nothing if she was to be his woman when he got released from prison.

Jeanie eventually drove the long journey to meet Tex in the prison several hundred miles away. He even got his sister to mail her some gas money so she couldn't use restricted finances for the reason to decline his requested visit. Although it was a long trip, Jeanie and Rosa made it up there before visiting hours were over.

Tex certainly wasn't a bad looking guy, Jeanie thought after she met him. He was real polite to her when they met and was kind to her daughter as well. After that one visit to see him in northern Arkansas, Jeanie and Tex continued to write letters to one another for the next several weeks.

Jeanie's letter writing came to an abrupt end when Tex suggested that she leave her subsidized rent when he got out to live with him on the lake. That didn't sound like such a bad deal. Still, Jeanie hated to lose the security of her own apartment. Still, the girl gave it much thought. However what Tex told Jeanie after his enticing offer totally turned her off. He wanted Jeanie to do something that she felt very uncomfortably with. Tex wanted her to have sex with a variety of different men while he stood in the corner and watched. He said he didn't want her to do that all the time…just once or twice a week. In return, the guy would give her and Rosa the financial security they both needed. Materially they would want for nothing.

Although Jeanie was afraid of her future, there was no way in hell she was going to go along with Tex's proposal. She no longer viewed the cowboy as a disgraced businessman who got his hands caught in the cookie jar, but as a total pervert! A life of luxury wasn't worth a damn if she couldn't look herself in the eye every morning and like who she saw. Although Jeanie's financial security was quickly slipping away, she just couldn't bring herself to accept Tex's proposal.

It was better to be working at a low-wage job barely scraping by then to live a life that tears on the heart and mind. Tex had accomplished one thing through all the degrading talks he gave her about receiving food stamps and subsidized rent. He convinced her that she wasn't going to make squat in the human service field even if her degree was accepted. That was when she attended school full time with a dream of being a graphic designer.

Jeanie obtained a student loan from a local bank and attended one semester at a nearby college. She would have gone further into her studies, but she became acquainted with someone at church who had earned an associate's degree in that field. He now worked as a desk clerk at a local hotel. It appeared that unless you had at least a bachelor's degree in graphic design, it was very difficult to get a job in that field. Jeanie wasn't about to go in debt over her head to attend school another two and half years. If she decided to go to school that long, it wouldn't be to get another bachelor's degree. If she was going to go to college for that amount of time, she would get a masters degree in something. Still, without any kind of monetary assistance from the state or grant funds to cover tuition, Jeanie wasn't about to go to school that long. So, after one semester of community college studying graphic design, Jeanie dropped out of school.

Jeanie hated making bills. She was very conservative with her money and so she had more to show for what little money she made. Jeanie had learned at a young age how to scrimp and scrime to make ends meet. Stretching the old dollar was almost like a game to Jeanie. She enjoyed going to yard sales and thrift shops. She hated paying full price for anything. Sometimes though, she would buy her daughter the brand name clothes she liked. Jeanie wanted Rosa to feel she fit in with the other kids. Of course the clothes were all drastically marked down and all she could get her were just a few of the high priced, brand name outfits. That had to suffice! Jeanie stuck to her allotted budget and allowed her daughter to pick out whatever she wanted from that money only. Her daughter had to learn to make responsible choices. Jeanie was only too happy to teach her how.

Jeanie remembered how important it was to feel you belonged…especially when you were young. Jeanie didn't want her daughter to grow up feeling bad about herself because people made fun of what she wore. She remembered how badly she felt about herself while growing up poor. Her peers viciously teased the girl frequently without any concern for her feelings. Their name-calling left holes in the sensitive girl's spirit even now. How cruel children could be Jeanie thought. How cruel life could be too.

With a heavy heart, Jeanie went back to the place she had worked for previously before she attended college. Since she was such a dependable, good worker, the agency happily hired her back. What made her job much easier this time, was the clients she had.

Jeanie was very fortunate to get clients that were much more easy-going and kind to her. One particular elderly woman she worked for was extremely religious. Every day the lady asked Jeanie to read passages of the Bible to her. Every day before lunch, Granny Blackstone would say a blessing. Although this lady was crippled and blind, she still found much to be thankful for. It was this sweet lady who made the greatest impression of all. It was this remarkable woman who brought the despondent girl back into God's hands.

After taking careful inventory of her life, Jeanie once again felt she was in good graces with the Lord. Although her prayers were not verbal, they were forever in her heart. Jeanie had to believe in something. The girl once thought that as long as she followed her calling, and was kind to others along her way, then everything would turn out great in her life. She hadn't counted on the many obstacles she encountered while living in Arkansas. Maybe if Jeanie had become close to God years ago, she wouldn't be so spiritually impoverished now. Maybe she wouldn't be monetarily impoverished either. For a minute her mind flashed back to a couple years ago when she was living with Norman. It was when the Jehovah's witnesses came to the door.

Jeanie was home that day so she was the one who greeted the trio of visitors. Two ladies and a child approached Jeanie at the front steps with Bibles in their hand. Jeanie was about to let them in the door when Norman came down from his home office. When he saw the group of God's witnesses, he shouted at them to get off his property while chasing them down his driveway. Jeanie didn't know what to do, so she just stood by helplessly looking at them. All she could say was I'm sorry before she went back inside Norman's impenetrable fortress.

Jeanie saw Norman in a completely different light that day. The couple certainly had differences to be sure. She knew prior to that day that Norman's views on religion were different than hers. He may have believed in God, but he definitely didn't support organized religion. Still it was difficult for Jeanie to fathom how a man could be so kind to her, Rosa and his dogs yet be so rude to the Jehovah witnesses. Although Norman was mostly a good caring man, he didn't have God in his heart. Being a logical, scientific type of guy, it was hard to believe something he could not see with his eyes or hear with his own ears. He thought religion was for the weak minded. It was for those who had to believe in something outside of themselves. He felt those religious fanatics didn't or couldn't believe in themselves and their abilities, so they put their faith in an unseen, often uncaring God. Now that Jeanie thought about it, she felt quite sad for Norman. The man had the whole world at his fingertips, yet he did not have God. All the earth's treasures could not fill what the soul needed.

Jeanie soul was in need of something much greater than she had now. Still it was her fervent belief that something better in the job field would come along. This optimism was what made the girl continue on in the steadfast manner that she did. Jeanie kept checking the papers for other employment. She continued to go to the Department of Human Services to get the statewide job listings. Several times a month she made out applications for the jobs posted. Although Jeanie went on job interview after job interview, she didn't get hired for any of them. She kept getting one rejection letter after another mailed to her. One day she got three "I'm sorry but I hired someone else" letters in the mail. Jeanie climbed into her bed and cried all night long. For many, many months she had controlled her eating binges and her bulimic purges, but she didn't on that day.

Jeanie's spirit was broken. She didn't have the inclination to even try to get better employment at that point.

"Doesn't anybody want me?" Jeanie cried to the sky above. "Doesn't anybody think I'm worth taking a chance on?"

## CHAPTER 19

# Betrayal

After thinking over her options, Jeanie once again decided to pursue her search for her husband. She was tired of being alone. She was equally tired of pinching pennies so that Rosa and her could have a decent life. Since, Jeanie worked one on one with her elderly clients, she knew she wouldn't meet any prospective mates from her work place. The little church Jeanie frequently visited didn't have many younger people there neither. She knew that she wasn't about to find a potential partner there. So, once again Jeanie decided to put out a personal AD in the paper. Maybe, if she kept at it long enough, she would find just the right man for her. She couldn't give up her quest for love…she just couldn't

The people Jeanie confided in thought that the girl was being ridiculous trying to find love in the personals. Jeanie just thought she was just being practical. The young woman knew the type of person that she was. She also knew the type of person she hoped to share her life with. The star gazed girl figured she might be successful in her quest if she was honest and sincere in her AD. If she stated the type of person she was and the qualities she was looking for in a man, she just might find the one. She had to believe the right person would see her AD and respond.

Jeanie desired someone who would not only be a good provider but would be kind and loving to her and her daughter. Even though looks were somewhat important, the girl decided not to put any great emphasis on them (as she had in the past). After all, in a few years everybody's face will be weathered with age.

Beauty does indeed fade. Jeanie could see hers begin to fade as well and it scared her. For so long, the young woman thought that the only thing she had going for her was her beauty. Jeanie no longer felt that way now. She could finally see beyond the outer mask and recognize the inner beauty she had in her heart, spirit and mind. At last, she was beginning to feel a little love for herself. Yes, even though she was mortally flawed, she was still a worthwhile human being with a lot to offer the right person.

Jeanie could remember back when all she had to do was make eyes at a man and he would follow her around like a puppy dog. A pretty girl had a certain advantage in life Jeanie said smiling to herself. However it was terribly hard on women emotionally when their beauty began to fade. Unless the woman developed her mind and spirit, she would be left with nothing but an empty shell…an ugly empty shell at that.

At one time Jeanie thought all she had to do to offer anybody was her pretty face and her sexy body. That was when she danced in the clubs. That was when the insecure girl wandered from man to man trying to find happiness and fulfillment from them. Jeanie searched for something even back then, but she never could figure out exactly what it was she was looking for. The fact was…Jeanie was searching for herself.

After all those rough years of life, the young woman had just now started to discover who she really was inside. There were still many mysteries to unravel in her life though. There was much left to discover behind the cloaked veil inside her mind. This shield protected her from the harshness of the world but it also kept her from becoming who it was she was meant to be inside.

The fragile girl's mind hid away a multitude of pain from her almost forgotten past. Little by little she began to remember the details of the lost years. Slowly the picture puzzle of her existence was becoming assembled. The girlish woman had found most of the missing parts to the mysterious days of long ago. She could now understand why she acted nervous and anxious the way she did. She knew why she had a tough time maintaining a stable relationship with a man. It's true that many of the guys Jeanie went with in the past were a bad choice as far as boyfriends go. It seemed for awhile, she was automatically attracted to the kind of seedy character that would use her or abuse her. Jeanie now sympathized with the frightened child within. This included the trust issues that crippled her as a youngster and as an adult.

At one time, Jeanie trusted mostly every body and yet she trusted no one. It seems a contradiction in terms didn't it? After thinking about what her mind had told her, the girl scratched her head in amazement. That made her reflect back to her hitchhiking days of yesteryear.

Jeanie hitched hiked sporadically before her father's death yet, the unsafe habit increased dramatically after her father's murder. A person with any kind of common sense would have given up such unsafe practices especially after a beloved family member was murdered by someone he picked up hitchhiking. However, her hitchhiking increased ten fold.

Just months following the murder of her father, Jeanie hitchhiked almost every day. At first the girl told herself that she only resumed that unsafe behavior because she needed transportation to get someplace. Except for the small towns Jeanie lived in, most of the time there was public transportation available. The girl could easily catch a city bus to get her to the destination of choice. Riding a bus wasn't particularly the best way to go, but it was safe, reliable and cheap transportation.

Jeanie acted out a death wish through her dangerous behavior. She almost dared someone to pick her up and do to her what was done to her father. Jeanie was so discouraged in life and so down on herself, that she didn't want to live. She may not have wanted to live but she obviously didn't have the guts to kill herself either.

Jeanie didn't know what her purpose in life was or if she had one at all. She knew she was lonely and miserable. She also knew that no matter how hard she tried to fit into the world, she always felt like a misunderstood misfit. No matter who the girl was with or what she ever did, she always felt like an outsider looking in.

There were several instances where Jeanie's life was put on the line. Between the ages of 19 and 26, she took many unnecessary risks. How she made it through life beyond that point was a mystery in itself. Jeanie's memory lapsed back in time to when she lived in Tampa, Florida briefly. This was right after her grandmother told her she must find another place to live.

Jeanie didn't travel to her mother's house right away after being kicked out of granny's domain. No, she wanted to have a little bit of fun first. She hooked up with some sweet talking vagabond who lived in a van. He was a free spirit like Jeanie so they got along great for awhile. It was late springtime in Florida. The days were warm and the night's temperature was moderate. The two wouldn't need much to survive. They had a roof over their heads at night, a little money for food, and each other. Life was good…at least for the first few days they were together. They bummed around at the local beach soaking up the sun. They smoked weed, ate snack cakes and screwed like the energizer bunny on Viagra. They didn't have much money, but they didn't need much. However they needed something better to eat than sugar-coated, shortening cakes.

Within a couple of days, Vinny's dope was smoked up and the rest of his resources were all exhausted too. They tried pan handling on an interstate ramp, but didn't receive much money. The motorist were quick to turn their backs on the lazy, doped up, overgrown kids. At the end of the day, they didn't even have enough money to pay for a cheap meal at the local fast food joint. Jeanie definitely didn't enjoy that last day with her wild man. The exciting, carefree life she thought she wanted, wasn't all she thought it would be. She left the thieving scoundrel early one evening after an argument broke out over who was going to steal that night's dinner. Jeanie wanted excitement not jail time. So, the carefree hippy packed her two suitcases and headed out on her own one more time.

With baggage in hand Jeanie proceeded down the road with her thumb in the air. The person who picked up the lonely hitchhiker took the girl on the scenic route along Tampa Bay. Jeanie asked the man where he was going, but he didn't answer her. He kept driving along the deserted beach not saying a word. The creep pulled up along a sandy, secluded shoreline and stopped the car. Jeanie surmised what the guy had in mind and knew she had to get out of there fast. As she reached for the inner door handle, she discovered that it was missing. The hairy brute leaned over to her side of the car and tried to rip her shorts off. Jeanie screamed as loud as she could while she kicked her legs. Fortunately, that night the vulnerable girl's cries for help were heard by an unmarked police car. The timely officer pulled along side her would-be rapist and rescued her from the inevitable. The kind policeman even drove Jeanie to the bus stop so she could be safely off the street. There the girl waited until her designated bus came to carry her away to mom's house.

Jeanie could also remember being picked up by a real maniac when she was hitchhiking to her uncle's house in redwood country. The unkempt character who picked her up asked Jeanie a question in a very, serious monotone.

"What would you do if someone picked up a knife and tried to slice your throat?" The scraggly toothed dog smiled cunningly at Jeanie. That was a serious question to him. She could sense it was so.

The disheartened girl looked at the potential murderer and told him, "I wish to hell someone would take my life! I'm sick of living here on this miserable earth!"

Jeanie's response wasn't what the murderous hound thought he would hear. He probably didn't want to do the girl any favors by putting her lights out permanently. What fun would it be to cut that little thing up if she wasn't going to struggle, scream and try to get away. The entire demeanor of the demented man totally changed. Jeanie really thought she spoiled the sicko's fun that night. What a bummer for him. Despite the moment of terror, Jeanie made it through the night and lived to tell about it. Shortly after that strange conversation, she was dumped off at a local café to continue her journey with someone else.

"Now why am I thinking about all those things now?" Jeanie said to herself. "If I cared about myself at all back then, I would've given up those hitchhiking days years ago."

There were so many things Jeanie subconsciously blocked out of her mind. If she could've acknowledged them earlier, maybe she would have straightened out her life much sooner than she did…maybe not. Jeanie wasn't ready for the much needed changes. Until recently Jeanie thought she was one of God's mistakes. It took many years for her to realize that no one is put on this earth by mistake!

Jeanie sealed the envelope which held the personal AD she wrote and mailed it to the newspaper office. Within a few days following its publication, she got a flood of responses. How thrilled the girl was.

"There are so many guys out there that want me," Jeanie squealed.

It had been so long since she felt wanted by anyone or anything. The huge response Jeanie received, put her ego soaring with the eagles.

"Now which of the letters should I open first?" Jeanie said as she sorted through the pile of envelopes before her.

The grinning girl slowly read one letter after another. As usual there were some men that responded who weren't at all what she was looking for. She didn't smoke or drink, so if anyone mentioned in a letter that they did, they letter got trashed. If the guy was more than 10 years her senior, those letters got chucked away as well. If they were an unemployed bum or convict, the responses got tossed out too. After going through the twenty two people who responded to Jeanie's AD, she was left with only three envelopes. It was only those few guys she decided to write to. If after exchanging information they still wanted to meet, then she would be thrilled to do so.

The first man Jeanie contacted, she met at a local café downtown. She hardly recognized the guy for he looked nothing like the picture he had sent her. The photo which was given to Jeanie was about 10 years old but she didn't know it at the time. The man who sat before her in a café although quite nice, was also quite fat. Jeanie tried to be polite to him but he could probably sense her disappointment.

Jeanie took good care of her body, so she liked the man she was with to also take care of himself. The energetic young adult liked to do active things in her past time. She enjoyed keeping fit by walking, swimming and dancing. Her potential mate had to be fit enough to do at least some of those things with her. Although appearances weren't everything, she couldn't be with someone who's looks totally repulsed her. She definitely couldn't imagine going to bed with someone as huge as a whale either. So, after enjoying dinner and light conversation, they said their goodbyes. It was obvious that Jeanie didn't want to see the gentleman again by her body language. She was grateful that she didn't have to make up a lame excuse if he asked her out again. She didn't enjoy being mean to others. She knew how much the sting of rejection hurt through past experiences.

Jeanie made arrangements to meet another person the following night. Although she was excited about meeting the guy she was writing to, she was a bit reluctant to go. What if he turned out like the last guy she met? What if he totally misrepresented himself too? Well that was the chance she had to take or else stay alone in her small, cocoon like apartment forever.

Jeanie arranged to meet Roger at a different café. She certainly didn't want the hired help to think she was a hooker. The girl spent a few minutes getting primped before leaving for her date. After waiting at the designated location with a white carnation pinned on her left shoulder, a dark man approached her.

"Are your Jeanie?" The man inquired.

"Yes I am," the lady responded. "Shall we have a seat?"

The next ninety minutes was a mixture of delight and boredom. The man was sweet and kind to Jeanie, although a little too quiet at first. When she finally got him to talk, all he wanted to talk about was work. The man jabbered on and on without taking a breath in between sentences. For thirty minutes, all he did was talk about his trucks. Although the evening didn't go as wonderfully as she had hoped, Jeanie accepted another date with Roger. When people were nervous, they sometimes talked excessively, Jeanie told herself. Besides, she can't keep crossing all her potential suitors off her list. Everyone had flaws, even herself. She could never be perfect, so why did she expect someone else to be perfect? No one could measure up with such unattainable standards!

The next Saturday Jeanie decided to bring Rosa with her to the inexpensive restaurant. Much to her surprise, Roger had also brought his teenage son along. In between bites, the four of them engaged in light conversation. After she felt relaxed with Roger and Junior, Jeanie and Rosa followed them to one of the local recreation areas. While the kids threw around the Frisbee, the adults talked more on a personal level. Jeanie decided that although Roger wasn't her ideal man, he might be worth taking a chance on. Still, there was something about him that made her so nervous. She just couldn't put her finger on it, at least not at that time.

Jeanie had been seeing a therapist in town for the past eight months prior to meeting Roger. It wasn't until her counselor prodded Jeanie's mind that she figured out why she had lingering feelings of discomfort with Roger.

Roger was a tall, man with a slender build. He was also exceptionally hairy. His rugged face highlighted his many years of work and worry in raising his son alone. Suddenly, things began to click in Jeanie's mind. The body structure, the height, the hair, the lines of worry strategically placed along his cheeks. It all began to make sense. Roger, the man she had been dating, had a strong resemblance to someone Jeanie wanted to forget about in the worst way. Roger reminded the girl of Mr. Martin, the man who molested young Jeanie on the hill in Windsock over twenty years ago.

Even though it pained Jeanie at first to look at Roger's face, she continued to date him. He was so sweet to her and Rosa. It just didn't make sense to dump the guy because his face reminded Jeanie of the creep who took advantage of the young, vulnerable girl so long ago.

Jeanie spoke frankly with her therapist on a weekly basis. She started to come to terms with the uncanny resemblance of Roger and Mr. Martin. Jeanie knew that the two were totally different people. It would take awhile for the girl to look beyond Roger's appearance and concentrate on his inner qualities.

It took months for Jeanie to become comfortable with Roger, but she did finally reach that point. The woman could finally look into his face and strictly see him and not the monster who stole away her youth years ago. After Jeanie reached that point in her healing, things between the two steadily increased in intensity. By Valentine's Day, Roger and Jeanie were engaged. Although they still had little battles to overcome, the two excitedly made plans for their marriage and their life together.

It was customary that Jeanie and Rosa cleaned up the bachelor's house on the weekends when they visited Roger. It was such a mess that neither one of them wanted to spend any time there until they did. Every time mother and daughter visited Roger, he would have a dozen or so cola cans cluttering the floors and tables. Scattered among the cans were food wrappers, half eaten sandwiches, gum wrappers, dirty clothes, newspapers and all the mail that was delivered previously that week.

One morning while Junior had left the house to visit a friend and Roger was in town doing chores, Jeanie accidentally discovered something distressing about her man. Stashed among the stacks of papers on the floor, was a letter from a lawyer. The letter addressed the multitude of credit card bills he hadn't paid in months. The creditors threatened legal action against the man unless he paid so much per month towards his debts.

Roger was obviously in debt big time. Jeanie wasn't happy about what she discovered, but she couldn't bring herself to question her boyfriend about the letter she accidentally found. She did ask him about the house he claimed was his though. Jeanie knew that her fiancé was making rent payments to his father. The deed to his residence was indeed in his dad's name, but supposedly would be put in his name when he completely paid for it. Considering what Jeanie unearthed, she didn't quite know if she could fully trust him anymore.

Jeanie discovered many things about Roger that she didn't know. The guy obviously wasn't being entirely truthful with her on many important issues. He had financial problems, that was for sure. However Jeanie wasn't going to get rid of someone when the chips were down. If nothing else, the girl was loyal. Besides, her conservative approach to spending as well as the extra income she would bring into the household, would straighten out Rogers array of bills.

The thing Jeanie couldn't take, was Rogers lying. She caught the man in several lies already. He obviously hid the amount of debt he was in. However, Jeanie was certain that her man didn't tell her the truth, for he was afraid it would scare her way. If she knew about all those bills earlier, she may have been scared away…but not now.

Unlike many of the men in Jeanie's past, Roger accepted her as she was. He treated her like a princess and treated Rosa equally nice. They always went out together. His light, easy going character made Jeanie more relaxed about life. Roger even accepted her herpes her body harbored without making her feel she was undesirable or blemished. He accepted the few times when it was unsafe for them to engage in sexual relations without making her feel bad inside. Jeanie needed someone to love her unconditionally. Roger seemed to do that!

Even though Jeanie knew her and Roger would be starting out their life together in debt, she decided to continue with the marriage plans anyway. Everything changed that one fateful day her and Rosa were traveling back from Little Rock with him.

Jeanie, Rosa and Roger had traveled to the nearby city to see a play. The young lady wanted to celebrate her 40th birthday doing something she liked with the people she loved. So far it had been a splendid day. The play was funny and the performers were terrific. The food served at the theatre were equally wonderful. The drive back to Jeanie's house was sunny and bright. The birthday girl was thoroughly enjoying her day.

Along the way home, Roger stopped at the rest stop to use the facilities. Rosa decided to use that opportunity to take care of her business as well. For once, Jeanie didn't have to use the bathroom. She was content to remain in the truck and listen to music while she waited for the two to return to the vehicle.

Roger often put chewing gum in his glove box, so Jeanie opened it up to find some. Instead of gum, she found a blue envelope. As the lady picked up the envelope to move it aside, she saw a woman's name on the return address. Curiosity burned inside her, so she carefully opened it up. When Jeanie read the short letter to her fiancé, she quickly put it back into the envelope before Roger came out of the restroom.

The distraught girl pretended that nothing was wrong when Roger and Rosa came back to the car smiling. After everybody got into the truck, they took off down the road towards Jeanie's house. All the while, the betrayed woman looked out the window and tried to keep a straight face. She silenced her inner cries and wiped away the occasional tear. She didn't want Roger to know what she found in the glove box, at least not yet. The letter which Jeanie read minutes ago was that of another woman...one that Roger had written to and planned to see later that week.

The stone faced woman was thankful to get that day over with. She was grateful also that Roger left almost immediately after he escorted her and Rosa back to her apartment. He had to get up early for his job and he claimed to still have things to do at his place. Yeah, like call the woman he was cheating on her with!

Jeanie was never the less happy when Roger started delivering his good night repertoire. She forced herself to give the snake a tiny kiss. She wanted to kiss him off permanently that night. She wanted to put an end to their relationship right then and there, but she had to do some things first. She wanted to collect all her movie tapes, clothes and personal items left at his house and of course have Rosa collect all her things as well. The minute Roger left Jeanie's apartment, the heartbroken woman couldn't keep a straight face anymore. The tears came pouring down, flooding Jeanie's face.

"What's wrong mom?" Rose inquired.

"I don't want to talk about it now honey. Just leave me alone for a while," Jeanie told her daughter in between sobs.

Jeanie spent the rest of the afternoon under the covers in her warm, comforting bed. She couldn't believe she almost married that cheating, lying, no good country hillbilly. How could she have such terrible judgment when it came to guys? Jeanie had accidentally discovered the truth about the man's personal finances and now she discovered even worse things about the laid back, compulsive liar. The needy woman probably should have backed out of the marriage when she discovered Roger's multitude of lies about his house and finances, but she didn't think it was fair to do so. Why did she think that her man was being truthful to her in all the other aspects of the relationship? He lied up a storm on those other important issues. so why would he be honest with her with other things.

Jeanie definitely didn't want to continue raising Rosa alone on a minimum wage job going nowhere. She needed someone to assist her with providing her the type of life she wanted and felt she deserved. Most of all she wanted someone to light up the inner chambers of her heart Although the girl was lonely and discouraged, she still felt that she had much to offer the right man. Although Jeanie had yet to get that important job break, she still felt she had much to offer the right employer. As discouraged as Jeanie was, she could see beyond the clouds. She knew that she had to break up with Roger and soon

Jeanie didn't think she would ever be able to trust Roger again. With pen in hand she wrote a short letter to the man she was to marry. She would leave it on the kitchen table when they went to his house next week while he worked. The broken hearted woman didn't want to see his cheating, lying face again. After all, if she couldn't trust the person that she was with, what good was their relationship? She had already made excuses for his lying about his finances. She certainly wasn't going to make excuses for his cheating too.

After Jeanie calmed down, she approached her daughter.

"Roger and I am not going to see each other anymore," Jeanie told her Rosa.

"Why mom?"

Other than making up lies to cover up lies, Jeanie told her young daughter the truth. The empathetic child placed her arms around her mother's neck. A much needed embrace was exchanged between the two.

"I'll miss Roger and Junior," Rosa softly told her mother.

"In many ways I'll miss them too," Jeanie agreed.

## CHAPTER 20

# Hurt Children Play Rough

The next several months Jeanie kept pretty much to herself. The girl had just about decided that guys in general couldn't be trusted. The two men Jeanie cared about since she'd been down in Arkansas, turned out to be total losers. Jeanie shook her head as she remembered the brief relationship she had with Decker.

Jeanie met Decker through a personal advertisement she placed. Yeah, she'd gone that route before but eventually she thought she would find a great guy she could build a long lasting relationship with. Besides, she no longer went drinking and dancing, so she couldn't meet anyone in the clubs. Besides, the guys she had met there in the past wouldn't make the best husband material. She was sick and tired of the games people played. She couldn't meet anyone suitable at the workplace for Jeanie still worked exclusively with the elderly. The church she attended were limited on younger congregation members and very few outsiders visited it. There were indeed many fish in the sea, but she didn't hang out where all the good fish swam, so she had to make the fish swim to her.

Decker was one of the multitude of men who responded to her AD, however, he was one of the few that lived in her town. Jeanie called Decker the day after receiving his letter. After talking several minutes on the telephone, they decided to meet the next day at a local café. The girl wasn't the least impressed with him when she first met him. He wasn't at all handsome to look at, but he was such a gentleman. That trait really turned Jeanie's head. Decker made it known to her that he had some medical problems that she should be aware of. The guy was a bad diabetic and had a tough time stabilizing his blood sugar. He gave himself insulin injections three to five times daily. The man's diabetes had played havoc on his body for years. What made his condition worse, was that he hadn't taken care of his health in the past. The diabetes had affected his vision already. His eyesight was horrible and it was slowly getting worse. Doctor's predicted that he would be totally blind in five years. Jeanie was as concerned as she was frightened about Decker's health problems. However, it wasn't his health problems that drove her away from him.

Jeanie didn't know that Decker had other problems beside his diabetes and the complications caused by the many years of neglecting his health. It wasn't until she had gone with the guy for two months that she realized that Decker had a drinking problem. Jeanie knew he drank a few beers on occasion, but she didn't hold that against him. What she didn't know was that although Decker only had a few beers when he was with her, he had several before he visited her and even more after he went home.

After the couple's time together was over for the evening, Decker's solitary drinking party continued. The girl found out first-hand what a lush he was when he stumbled up to her apartment late one night. While clinging to the rails outside her upstairs apartment, he staggered his way to Jeanie's door and woke the sleeping girl up. The disoriented jerk claimed that she was a reason he drank so much.

"If only you weren't so pretty and sweet, I wouldn't be drinking like this," the drunk slurred out.

The guy definitely had problems. She felt sorry for him but not so sorry that she would put up with him and his nasty habit. It was fortunate that she found out about his true character before she got anymore involved with him.

Decker had more issues than Jeanie could handle at the time. The girl struggled to accept his health problems, that was true. She kept her emotions at bay because of his medical issues. However, she didn't need this added bonus. No, all this drama was too much for the sympathetic girl to endure. It was easy to kiss off the drunkard as the embarrassed Jeanie stood in front of her downstairs neighbor's door. He staggered up the stairs and stupidly shouted for all the world to hear at one in the morning. After Jeanie ran Decker off, he came back later in the night and toilet papered her bicycle. A gaudy painted poster hung along the handlebars of her three speed bicycle. In big paint smeared letters Decker asked Jeanie to marry him. Jeanie didn't want to see Decker again after that night, never mind marry him!

Despite what Decker did to upset Jeanie the night before, he was there at seven o'clock the following evening to pick her up for their prearranged date. Jeanie wasn't about to go anywhere with the man. She wondered if he was so smashed the night before that he couldn't remember what he did. Surely if he had, he wouldn't have come up to her apartment expecting her to go with him.

After the breakup, Decker made Jeanie out to be a villain. That didn't surprise the girl. Often when people screw up they try to push the blame onto others. If that was what made him happy, then fine. Rosa and her both knew the truth. Knowing the truth didn't make the break up any easier though. It didn't make those weekends and nights any less lonely.

Jeanie was alone for months after the brief affair with Decker. It took over four months for her distrustful heart to allow herself to care about anybody else. Jeanie had been feeling so terribly hollow inside lately. She had all she could do to force herself out of bed in the morning. Ever since Decker and her broke up, she hadn't had the initiative or desire to do anything. Jeanie just marked off the foul mood as a bad case of the blues. She was already lonely as hell. She couldn't help but wonder how much longer she would be alone this time. There were times when the girl wondered if she was cursed to be alone forever. There were many times when it seemed her life was destined to be that way

Jeanie kept her composure during the work week but those weekends were hell. Saturday nights were the loneliest nights of the week for her. That was the time she usually cuddled in bed with her loved one. Saturday was the one day of the week that Jeanie looked forward to. Now Jeanie didn't have anything to look forward to except going to sleep.

In Jeanie's dreams everything was so perfect. Every night as Jeanie slept her imaginary lover would climb into her bed and gently kiss her lips then work his way downward across her shoulders. Afterwards he spent several minutes at her breast suckling her like a baby. While he hugged her he'd whisper in her ear how wonderful Jeanie was, how special she was and how much he loved her. Her beautiful, blonde Adonis would cuddle and kiss the sensitive, love starved girl all night long. Her sweet angel never pushed the girl for more than she was willing to give to him, but she always wanted to give her all to him for she loved him that much. Her special angel…looked a lot like Sam.

In her dreams Sam catered to Jeanie's every wish and whim, thinking only of her, how she felt, how she wanted to be stroked, how she wanted to be loved. After their passionate love making, he would sit on the edge of the bed and serenade her with his guitar. She would watch his long fingers slide across the strings the same way they slid over her soft, sensuous skin. Wearing only a smile, she would join her beautiful prince in a long duet. Their voices would carry far and long. Their eyes never left their partner's adoring eyes. Their heart sang together as one. They felt the heavens open the doors to them for their love was so perfect, so intense, so beautiful. Jeanie sighed. Too bad her angel was only in her imaginative dream. Oh, how she longed to make her dream a reality.

Jeanie hated waking up after such a sensuous dream for she knew she would once again be alone. How miserable the girl was when she was alone. There were days when the lonely lass wished she was still with the drunken idiot or the cheating liar…just to be close to someone. She wanted to feel she was loved for a moment or two. Right now she didn't feel very loved. She just felt used.

If it wasn't for the limited social interaction Jeanie received from her job and church, she would've slipped even further into her lonely, isolated world. Jeanie decided that her judgments were not to be trusted when it came to men. To keep from getting involved with someone who would later hurt her, Jeanie temporarily swore off those cheating, no good lowlifes commonly referred to as men.

For several months Jeanie put a great deal of energy and time into developing her spirituality through her church. She also devoted more time to her creative endeavors. Jeanie's emotions were no longer erratic like an out of control roller coaster ride. She was no longer swooning over the latest lover or bawling uncontrollably because her perfect Prince let her down or dumped her. How the girl currently felt about herself no longer depended on how her and her mate were currently doing in their relationship. The girl was lonely as she could be, but her demeanor showed her to be more relaxed and easy-going.

Jeanie was able to be more nurturing and accommodating to her daughter during those months following the recent breakup of Decker as well…that is when she was home. It saddened Jeanie that her and Rosa weren't as close as they once were. The teenager seemed more interested in hanging out with her friends than dear old mom. Of course she didn't have all sorts of money to blow on entertainment. No, she spent her money frivolously on things like food, rent and car expenses. Rosa chose to hang around with her school chum down the street. Her family owned a boat and often took their brood on day trips. Often they invited Rosa along on their excursions. She wished that they invited her too. That's just it, couples rarely invite a lone wolf to their dinner engagements or anything else unless they plan on paring her up with someone. The wives saw Jeanie as a seductress. They didn't want to temp their husband with a pretty, athletic young woman. So, Jeanie was excluded from Rosa's fun with Mandy and her family.

Jeanie didn't blame Rosa if she didn't want to stay home with her to watch tv, read or cook. That even sounded boring to her. Rosa used to do painting and crafts with her mom years ago. Unfortunately, her daughter no longer had the art interests she pursued in the past. Jeanie thought that their love for art was always going to be something they shared, like her and her dad. Oh well, maybe she'll redevelop her interests again in the future someday.

Jeanie decided that she had to make her own excitement. She had to live her own life. Soon, she would be living totally alone anyway. Rosa would probably fly the coop the day after she graduated from high school. She hoped she wouldn't though. Jeanie wanted her daughter to be more prepared to deal with the outside world then she was. However she already began to see Rosa's head strong temperament and her rebellious attitude permeating through her entire essence. She feared her daughter would be just like a chip off the old withered willow. God help her!

Jeanie wasn't going to let the disastrous relationships with Decker or Roger keep her down too long. She decided to try to coax out of her heart and mind a positive attitude. If she looked hard enough, she could find something good in every situation, even one that left her disappointed, disillusioned and depressed. Supposedly people learned the most through the various hardships that they endured in their lifetime. If that was the case Jeanie thought, she should be a genius by now! Still, she did learn something on that short relationship she had with Decker… don't take everything anybody says at face value, for often times people have hidden agendas. Decker's hidden agenda was to find someone to take care of him when he became stupidly drunk or comatose with his diabetes. Jeanie thought that an involved couple should take care of each other. Still, she didn't want to be used. Unfortunately people do have a tendency to use each other. She was so sick of those games though. When she was young, she was content playing those kid games…but not anymore.

In the past Jeanie used guys for good times, pot and of course affection. She would give up the booty as long as she got what she needed. Guys often gave girls the hugging and kissing they like in order to get sex. Girls often gave the guys sex so they could get the cuddling and kissing they desired. At the time, Jeanie thought it was a fair trade…it wasn't! Acceptance and love was something Jeanie may have desired, but didn't expect. She may have wanted it, but she didn't think she was worthy of it, so she didn't actively pursue it. She didn't feel she had much to give so she didn't ask for much. Now, she knows she had much to give so, she expected much, not just wanted much…expected much. Could God himself live up to Jeanie's expectations?

Shortly after Jeanie's break up with Roger, Jeanie had much more time to visit her girlfriend Paulette. Paulette lived only a few miles from Jeanie, so some evenings the emotionally distant girl would go out to visit her. The two had many things in common including a love for art. It was Jeanie's relationship with her girlfriend that kept her sane following the recent breakup with Roger. Unfortunately her dear friend moved to a distant city when she acquired a better paying job. Although Jeanie was happy that her friend found decent employment elsewhere, she severely missed their friendship. Through Paulette, Jeanie could fill some of her social needs. Even though it was wonderful to do things with a girlfriend, it didn't take the place of having a current relationship with a man she liked. Jeanie didn't realize how severely she missed being in a relationship with someone until her friend moved.

It had been five months since Roger and Jeanie parted ways. The scars that were left after the breakup had started to heal. Although Jeanie was still leery of people (men in particular) she was starting to evaluate her thoughts concerning getting involved with another guy.

"Surely there must be one decent man out there whom I could really love?" Jeanie said aloud to no one in particular.

Although Jeanie's expectations concerning a possible mate were high, she decided that maybe, just maybe if she lowered them a little bit, she wouldn't be doomed to a life of loneliness.

A week after Thanksgiving Jeanie silent prayers were answered, or so she thought. The girl met a talented, passionate young man during a social gathering. Although Jeanie wasn't exactly impressed by the man's physical appearance, he seemed quite cordial and funny. Jeanie had a tendency to take things a little too serious. Maybe this young man was just what she needed to bring out the carefree, laughing child that was hiding somewhere deep within Jeanie's jaded heart. She almost didn't accept James's invitation to go out for some coffee when she noticed a pack of cigarettes sticking out from his T-shirt pocket. Even though Jeanie knew immediately that he had a nasty smoking habit, she agreed to meet him the following day at a local restaurant when she found out he played the guitar.

James was blessed with many gifts besides the gift of gab. He was a talented musician. He composed and performed his own music. The first time Jeanie heard James played the guitar, she swooned. It didn't take much effort for the emotional, passionate girl to fall in love with him. James was quick to return Jeanie's affections. Within two weeks time, they had developed an emotionally binding relationship. It was during that time the couple declared their love for each other and united their bodies as they had united their hearts.

James lived just a couple miles from Jeanie, so they saw each other nearly every day. Right after work Jeanie would either go over to James's apartment or else he would go to hers. The two were practically inseparable. Even though Rosa, Jeanie's teenage daughter had an active social life, there were times when she needed her mother's attention and guidance. Since becoming involved with James, Jeanie seemed to forget about her daughter's needs. She was too busy getting her physical needs and self-esteem needs met through James.

It seemed like the two love birds had known each other forever. Jeanie felt so comfortable revealing her all to the sweet man who had quickly captured her heart. He was as accepting of her health problems as much as she was accepting of his health problems. James was relaxed in telling his partner all he could about himself as well. Although Jeanie liked the idea that her man was sensitive, she felt uncomfortable when he started crying over what she saw as nothing. When making out a simple sheet of inquiry at a doctor's office, James started weeping.

"Why are they asking me about my mother. She's been dead for years. What do they want to know my mother's maiden name and whether she had this or that ailment?"

It was obvious that James was still emotionally distraught over his mother's death. Jeanie still wasn't completely over the death of her beloved father and it had been years since he died. That was different, she thought. Her father had been taken from the earth by the hand of another where as James's mother died from natural causes. Still her death must have been hard for James because she suffered for years with her cancer. The poor guy took care of his beloved mother during the last stages of her death too. It was no doubt a traumatic experience for him, so Jeanie quickly offered a sympathetic ear to the teary eyed man.

Jeanie seemed to always be emotionally nurturing James and neglecting her own emotions. There were times when she felt angry at the man for being so needy. However, she quickly dismissed those thoughts and reprimanded herself for being so insensitive.

James and Jeanie did indeed have much in common including many unresolved issues to be worked through. Although Jeanie tried to help James work through his troubles, there wasn't anyone to help Jeanie work through hers. The girl always felt that she had to be there for James. However, was he ever there for her?

Once in a while Jeanie's angry inner child would act out and she would feel like such a fool afterwards. When she accidentally popped out the headlight of her car, she ranted and raved and hollered and cussed. James saw his angel as a foul mouthed banshee no doubt. Jeanie wasn't mad at James, for it was totally her fault she wrecked the light. He may have thought that Jeanie was trying to blame him for the untimely incident. In reality the girl was mad as a hornet at herself.

Once again, Jeanie screwed up. One more stupid mistake to go along with all the other times she's a messed up in her life. There were times when Jeanie saw herself as one total screw up. During those times it was easy for her to give herself a tongue lashing… just like her parents used to do. Just like what Slugger used to do. Little Jeannie was never allowed to make mistakes when she was younger without being made to feel bad about them. It wasn't acceptable for the girl to make mistakes then and it surely was acceptable for her to make mistakes now.

Every time Jeanie screwed up, she would feel like someone or something should punish her. The girl was a bad, imperfect little SOB. She must hide her face in a corner from everybody and everything, Jeanie was shamed into believing that if she was a good little girl, she wouldn't make mistakes…ever. If she did make mistakes, they were unacceptable. Her mistakes were unacceptable so she must also be unacceptable. She felt unworthy and undeserving of love much of the time. The things that little Jeanie wanted so badly, she felt unworthy of receiving.

Still the emotionally torn child inside this grown woman wasn't going to accept her punishment of emotional isolation without a fight. That's when Jeanie was diverted back to that screaming child of yesterday. That was when little Jeanie totally lost control of her emotions. For that moment in time, she was still a five-year-old child screaming for acceptance and love. Unfortunately, the more she screamed for those things the further away they became.

James almost broke up with Jeanie when he got a good view of her little child within. Rather than try to understand her as Jeanie tried to understand him, James criticized and scolded her. Jeanie's little child got the scolding she needed, and yet at the same time kept the love she needed even more. Although that was a rough night for both of them, something good did come out of it. The girl felt partially healed after that unplanned confrontation. Once in a while Jeanie's inner child still came barreling out, but mostly the innermost part of Jeanie was comfortably hid within the recesses of her mind.

The real trouble with Jeanie and James relationship started when James got fired. The job loss came at a bad time for her boyfriend was going into surgery the following week. He didn't know if he would have his job-related health insurance to foot the bill. Since his company assured him it would take a month for his insurance to be canceled, he proceeded with the operation.

What should have been a routine, uncomplicated operation turned into a nightmare. Initially, the surgery was to be performed in an outpatient clinic. Since James was paranoid about going under the knife, he was extremely agitated and anxious. Since the anesthesiologist viewed him as being anxiously disturbed, he refused to put him to sleep while in the ear, nose and throat unit's surgical unit. The only way James would be able to get the surgery he needed was if he was admitted into the local hospital. So, there the operation was arranged. Hopefully, her boyfriend's insurance would cover most of the bill!

Obviously James had never had an type of operation before. He was scared out of his mind. Jeanie knew that James had a right to be little frightened, but he acted like a 3-year-old that day in the clinic. Jeanie couldn't remember acting that badly when she had her tonsils taken out when she was eleven years old.

Although Jeanie tried to comfort James, she was more than a bit disturbed by her man and his unreasonable behavior. She was embarrassed also. Jeanie had a similar operation with his surgeon in the past. She was the one who recommended that James saw Dr. Salk in the first place. Now, she was sorry that she opened up her mouth at all. It was her idea that James should get his medical condition taking care of while he still had insurance. Now, she wondered if she had done the right thing. She realized she hadn't when it was too late.

James' operation was postponed until the following week. The doctor had to prepare for complications due to elevated blood pressure and unrest after the surgery. It was a good thing the operation was performed there, because the guy had such a horrible time. He was a bleeder. Nose packs alone couldn't stop the bleeding. The doctor had to perform another operation just to cauterize the veins that surrounded the extracted tissue. What should have been a one-day surgery turned into a three-day hospital stay.

Jeanie tried to be a comfort and help to the man she loved but it was hard being next to someone who was constantly cussing her. Finally, she had about all she could handle and walked out of his room. James followed her into the hall with his cheeks half hanging out of his hospital gown and called her every name he could think of. Jeanie was determined to break up with James right then and there, but she couldn't bring herself to do it. What kind of person would she be if she turned her back on her man when he needed her the most?

Although Jeanie was embarrassed over James' tantrum, she stepped into the hospital elevator the following day. The girl sheepishly hung her head so that she wouldn't make eye contact with the same staff members who viewed the ugly scene the night before. Much to Jeanie's surprise, James was awake and alert. Rather than acting happy to see her, he bombarded the girl with accusations of abandoning him and continued on with the cussing spree of the previous night. Once again Jeanie walked out of the door

"If you're going to be that way, I don't ever want to see you again!" Jeanie shouted at the irate man.

James screamed back, "That's it. Just leave me in the hospital to die. What kind of person would turn their back on someone in the hospital?"

James struck a chord with Jeanie. Although she left that night, she was there the following day to bring him home. If her boyfriend had a home of his own, Jeanie would have brought him there and left him on his own. If he was lucky, she would have gone over to his house once a day for twenty minutes, just long enough to make sure he was ok and hadn't collapsed on the floor or bled to death. Unfortunately, just prior to going into the hospital, James brought most of his things to a storage unit for he had no way to pay his rent that month due to his recent job loss. His clothes and personal items unfortunately were conveniently stashed inside Jeanie's apartment waiting for him. She had agreed to take care of him while he recuperated from his surgery and she wasn't about to go back on her word. Now that the worst part was over, things should get back to normal. At least that was what the little caretaker hoped for.

Jeanie took on a nurse's role while James recuperated from his operation. Most of the time the guy was pretty nice to Jeanie, but there were those other times. Jeanie's boyfriend obviously felt insecure and frightened about his future. He had lost his job because he tested positive for marijuana use in a surprise drug test. Now he was laid up for God knows how long due to the recent operation he had. No one knew how long it would take his body to heal enough for him to return to the job market, or how long it would take him to find a job.

Jeanie tried to take care of James's needs as best she could. Since James was living in her household, she naturally spent more time home. Rosa wasn't happy about that. However Jeanie was so tied up with trying to cater to James' every whim in between her work schedule that she had very little time left for her daughter. Jeanie obviously had no time for herself.

Rosa didn't like James and was quick to tell her mother so in no uncertain terms. Jeanie thought that her daughter was just saying those hurtful things about James because she was jealous of him. Jeanie didn't want to admit it at the time, but her girl's perception of him was right on the mark. It wasn't until two weeks later that Jeanie cognitively recognized that James was an emotional parasite. As long as she was with him, she would forever be a slave to his needy nature.

James's emotions were getting more and more out of control with each passing day. He handled his emotions by getting high every few hours all day long. In the end days of their relationship, James was high more than he was straight. This bothered Jeanie, for she rarely smoked weed anymore. At one time James used to be funny when he was high. Now however, he was just plain mean. When the man was high, he would fly off the handle without any warning. It seemed that everything bothered James. Jeanie couldn't even go downstairs to check the mail without James getting suspicious and angry.

One afternoon, two weeks after his surgery, James followed Jeanie down to the mailbox and screamed obscenities at her while shaking his finger in her face. Jeanie tried to ignore the man for she knew that in his frame of mind he was liable to do anything. Shortly after she walked into her apartment, she got a call from her landlord. Apparently she had gotten a complaint from one of the other residents about a disturbance involving Jeanie and her friend. Jeanie thought all of them were going to get evicted because of James. After Jeanie regained her composure, the peacemaker went over to the landlord's office to explain to them how James had just had an operation and had become agitated because of the pain medication the doctor prescribed. Well, it wasn't a total lie. Jeanie was left off with a warning not to let that happen again or she would be looking for another place to live.

The stressed girl knew that things with her and James had to quickly get better or else their relationship was through. Whatever happened to the sweet, passionate man Jeanie fell in love with? Lately the guy was so full of anger and rage that it was hard to recognize any of the good qualities she first saw in him. Not long ago, James was like a beautiful vision to Jeanie. Now, he was more like a demon sent from hell to torture her. Little did she know that the torture had just begun.

One night not long after the mailbox scene, James became involved in a heated argument with Jeanie and slapped her. She looked at the little pipsqueak with hate in her eyes.

"If you ever hit me or threaten me again, we're through. I don't care if you have no place to go. Do you understand?

After a brief apology and a gentle kiss, the storm passed. What would have produced a big hurricane of the mind slowly blew over. Their fierce inner conflict became downgraded to a tropical storm…one that soon dissipated.

The next day Jeanie, James and Rosa all went to the park to have a picnic. While eating their sandwiches, Jeanie and her daughter listened to James play his guitar. They had a lot to celebrate that day. James got a job working under a local contractor in town. Now, that the money situation wouldn't be so tight, maybe the atmosphere in the house wouldn't be so tense either.

Jeanie hated using her resources taking care of James. He hated digging into Jeanie's resources, but he always had the money for his pot and cigarettes. So much had happened between them that altered Jeanie's perception of James. Jeanie saw the emotional, out of control angry child that her boyfriend truly was. Still, she wondered if they could resurrect their dying relationship. At one time, Jeanie saw so much potential in their romance. Was it possible to regain the loving feelings that were lost during the past few weeks. Jeanie knew not anymore.

Jeanie and James both had problems from the past that had to be resolved in order to resurrect their romance. Even though they obviously cared a great deal about one another, there was much friction between them that had to be healed. Unfortunately mending their tattered relationship would be such a tremendous task. Now, both participants housed a broken spirit. This created havoc in the distressed heart and the diseased mind. Tears of disappointment stung the corner of Jeanie's eyes. However, the tears themselves didn't do the girl any good. Tears can't erase past pain. They can't heal the hidden scars within.

The day of singing in the park ended for Rosa but not for the couple. Jeanie and James took off alone for an afternoon of fun. They drove to Little Rock to see a cultural event. After carefully parking, the couples stepped into the darkened building to claim their reserved seats. Although the two of them had been arguing all during the trip over there, James still insisted on holding Jeanie's hand. Fine she thought, let him take my hand. It wasn't worth fighting about. During the 45 minute break, James thought that they were going to just kiss away the bad feelings that the former conflict created.

"James, I just don't feel like kissing," Jeanie proclaimed.

James looked at his girlfriend with angry, hurt eyes and said, "What do you think you're doing? You said you would never do kid shit like holding your affections from me!"

Since they started to get loud in the theater, Jeanie decided it would be best to finish the argument outside. James screamed accusatory remarks at Jeanie for several minutes. He insisted that she did not care about how he felt. Jeanie obviously cared about the guy or she would have dumped him in the hospital when he yelled and cussed at her then. Still, the angry, hurt feeling lingered in her heart. Jeanie wasn't about to give the man false feelings of love just to shut him up. That was what she probably should have done, just to keep peace.

James acted like an overly, emotional schoolboy. He tried to convince his girlfriend to forget about the tense scene they had earlier in the afternoon (as well as the one they were currently engaged in). He wanted Jeanie to cuddle up and kiss him and forget everything that had previously happened earlier that day, but Jeanie refused.

"I want to feel like I'm with a man, not some loud mouthed boy," Jeanie told her boyfriend.

James briskly turned Jeanie around and started spitting cruel remarks just inches from her face. Jeanie felt under attack so she slapped him. She wasn't going to allow anyone to verbally attack her like those unfeeling peers of yesteryears. After she slapped him, the angry, immature man left her alone. Slowly Jeanie walked back to the theater and sat down in her previous seat.

The battling couple sat in silence and watched the rest of the performance. When it was over, they quickly got up and walked towards the car. How Jeanie wished she drove her own car to Little Rock that day but she didn't. If she had, then she would've made up the rules concerning the trip back. If she drove her car and James continued to verbally assault her the way he did, she would've left him there alone on the highway to thumb home!

The minute James and Jeanie got into the car, an argument started. James began yelling and screaming at Jeanie with such ferocity that she was in tears.

"You're nothing but a f-cking pig! A f-cking pig! You got that." The out-of-control man kept screaming those words louder and louder at Jeanie until she felt she would go insane.

"How dare you say those things to me!. How dare you treat me like that!" Jeanie screamed at the monster beside her.

With one sweep from his muscled arm, he bopped his girlfriend across her jaw. Jeanie could tell that there was much power behind the punch for her whole mouth hurt. All the way home, she had her back towards James and looked out the window and cried. Jeanie knew that they had to break up and soon. Unfortunately she knew she had to put up with him for another two weeks at least. How was she going to do that? When he did get his first two weeks paycheck, he would have to move out of her home! She couldn't take his abuse any more!

Jeanie had put up with a lot of crap from James in the past. However that day, he crossed the line. There was no way Jeanie was going to stay with another guy who beat the hell out of her and treated her like dirt! When she was young, she put up with Slugger and his unpredictable beatings and his verbal abuse. She wasn't about to stay in another relationship like that. Although Jeanie's life was far from perfect, she knew she deserved so much more than an abusive little pipsqueak for a boyfriend. She didn't need to be someone's scapegoat…not any more! Someday, somewhere Jeanie would find the sweet man of her dreams. In the mean time, Hasta La Vista Baby!

## CHAPTER 21

# Healing From Within

Jeanie spent her 41st birthday alone, but she was happy to do so. She was now free of the man who physically and psychologically abused her. She was free of the emotionally needy boy who regularly pushed her spirits in the dirt and left bruises on her body. Rosa was glad that the man was out of their home and out of their lives as well. Now that Jeanie no longer had a man in her life, Rosa had her mom all to herself and she liked it that way.

For several months Jeanie hid in her apartment nursing her wounds. She still couldn't believe that she had put up with so much from James. It was almost a replay of her days with Slugger. Slugger would hit the young girl all the time, but she always forgave him. Jeanie was no longer that passive lady of yesterday. She wasn't about to resort to a relationship like the one she had with her first real boyfriend. The poor fool stayed with Slugger all that time because she really thought that if he loved her enough, he would change. Jeanie gave James a couple of chances to straighten out. When it didn't look like the necessary changes would be made, she bailed out of the relationship. She wasn't going to become someone's punching bag again.

Jeanie smiled as she came to the realization that she must be thinking better of herself than she had in the past. Even though the young woman still had difficulties accepting her flaws and limitations, she must like herself enough to want good things in her life now. At least that was an improvement!

After work, Jeanie spent most of her spare time alone or with her daughter. It wasn't until several months later that Jeanie seriously thought about dating again. The young woman occasional went out to eat with a guy, who was strictly a friend. However, she hadn't gone out with anyone she liked for more than a friend for quite some time. She just hadn't met someone she wanted to build a relationship with…until she became reacquainted with Charles.

Jeanie met Charles at the church she attended years ago when she first came to Hot Springs. He had just broken up with his wife, so his wounds were still quite recent. Jeanie didn't want to get involved with him then for she didn't think he was ready for another long term relationship. The guy was also flat broke then and had to sleep in his office. He wasn't good boyfriend material at the time never mind good husband material. Jeanie wanted love and marriage. He definitely wasn't interested in heading down that road any time soon.

One morning while Jeanie sat in the pew waiting for the service to begin, he just wandered in. That in itself was a surprise for the small church rarely had visitors and when it did, usually someone much older would enter through its heavy, stained glassed doors. Charles was young, somewhat handsome and was now, fairly well-off financially. Charles had it all including an impressive office a short distance from Jeanie's apartment.

Charles sat next to her during the church service. Occasionally, Jeanie would glimpse at the dark haired guy who sat beside her. She was aware that he looked at her more then once. It was obvious that he still found her attractive, so it didn't surprise the young lady when Charles asked her out after church was over.

All was going well between the two for the first few dates. The couple shared dinner and conversation. After feeding their bodies they would feed their inner passions by escaping to a quiet corner in his house to snuggle and kiss. When it looked like things were going to develop into something more serious than a casual affair, Jeanie decided to tell Charles about the herpes she contracted years ago. After all, it was only right that her potential partner should know about such things. Although most of the time, she was healthy and not contagious, she still felt it was something he had a right to know. She just wished she had that knowledge prior to getting involved with her ex-husband. She wasn't thrilled she had the disease, but she did everything she could from passing it on to her partner. The thoughtful girl hesitated before telling Charles. Surely he would understand and accept what it was she had to tell him.

Jeanie was real careful with monitoring her symptoms. If she even thought that she was on the verge of breaking out, she refrained from relations with her current mate. Due to Jeanie's acute awareness of her own body and her concern over her mate's health, she had managed to keep her herpes solely to herself. She just wished the guy who gave it to her had done the same thing.

When Jeanie told Charles about her health problem, he stopped kissing Jeanie. He abruptly got off the couch they were laying on and pushed the girl aside. Then he made some lame excuse about having to bring her home because he forgot he had to go somewhere early in the morning. Jeanie knew why their date ended so suddenly. She pretended not to be hurt over what just happened. Only when the girl got home did she let the tears pour down from her eyes.

"That guy's in the health field. Surely he must know that I'm not always contagious," Jeanie cried out between sobs. "He treated me like I was just some no good whore…like I was poison ivy or something!"

The way Charles treated Jeanie that night tore the young lady's heart out. It wouldn't have made such an impact on her if she hadn't really liked him The two had dated briefly years ago, so she knew he had a good heart with pure intentions. There was a physical attraction between them as well as a mutual respect for each others' well-trained, intellectual minds. Now, Jeanie didn't have any respect at all for his mind as she saw him as an insensitive jerk. Although the girl didn't tell him that in words, she called him up the following week and told him what she thought of the way he handled the whole situation.

The confrontation with Charles may have felt good momentarily, but it certainly didn't help Jeanie feel any better about herself. For awhile she was beginning to like herself as a person. All the progress she had made with elevating her self-esteem was destroyed in those few short minutes. What Charles did to the sensitive girl's spirit that night can be described as nothing short of emotional murder.

Before Jeanie started dating Charles, several of her teeth had started hurting her. Money was tight, so she postponed going to a dentist. She finally saw one when she broke off a corner of her tooth on a caramel apple. The dentist tried to repair her tooth, but it just crumbled in his hand. Several of Jeanie's teeth, though white and pretty on the outside, where slowly turning into dust. She rarely drank milk and stopped taking her estrogen pills a few years after her hysterectomy ten years ago. Her body now stole the calcium from her teeth to nourish her bones. Jeanie wasn't the least bit happy with what she learned. She could begin taking her estrogen again and the concentrated calcium pills until the day she died. Still, it wouldn't reverse the damage already done to her teeth.

The woman already lost most of her back teeth to the battle over tooth decay. Years ago she neglected her oral health for she didn't have the resources to take care of those needs. Chewing certain foods had already become a difficult challenge due to the missing molars. Jeanie decided that if she was going to have her teeth out pretty soon anyway, then she might as well do it now. After all, she had no one to impress anymore. What she looked like really didn't matter at all now. So, without thinking much about it, Jeanie made an appointment at the local dental clinic later in the week to have the remaining teeth extracted. She called ahead of time to see how much the entire procedure would cost. She was shocked at the expense.

The cost of having teeth removed was terribly high, for the dentist charged so much per tooth with no discounted rate for taking out a whole mouthful. Jeanie knew that she would have to dig long and hard to come up with that kind of money. Still, she wanted to have this procedure done. The girl had absolutely no intentions of getting involved with anyone for a long, long time. Charles's insensitive rejection sent Jeanie packing her heart in cold storage for an indefinite amount of time. She couldn't imagine getting involved with anyone for year or two.

Jeanie contemplated a life without two of the three things she loved most, men and food. She would still have God in her life though. She was going to need him now more then ever. She already had her hurting heart to heal. Soon, she would have her bleeding mouth to heal as well. It would be tough going without both food and affection for six months or longer, but that was ok. She needed to suffer for her mistakes. Jeanie felt so badly about herself that she wanted to have pain inflicted on her. Maybe if her body felt enough pain, it would ease the pain that relentlessly ripped at her heart. Maybe it was good that she suffered as much physically as she did psychologically.

Jeanie felt like she was a pretty but poisonous reptile. Maybe there was a reason why she contracted the horrible disease. Maybe it was to keep her from finding and keeping the special love that she so long desired. Maybe the disease was a punishment for all the wrong deeds the girl did when she was younger. Either way, there was no turning back the hands of the clock. Although Jeanie occasionally took medicine to suppress her herpes, the disease would forever be with her. She could cry and cuss about having it, but nothing she could do would change the fact that it's in her. It's part of her and there's nothing she can do about it. Nothing!

Money was scant, and the cost of having her teeth out was so expensive. Jeanie decided that she would take care of some of the extractions herself. The girl took five extra strength pain relievers and waited for an hour to pass. The distraught lady then brought out a bottle of liquid tooth ache medicine from the bathroom cabinet to help deaden the nerves in her gums. She also sterilized a pair of pliers by boiling them in hot water for ten minutes. As Rosa slept soundly in the next room, Jeanie started inflicting her self mutilation.

Jeanie sat on the bathroom sink and gazed in the mirror with her mouth frozen open. One by one she pulled out the nine teeth that lined the middle and side portions of her lower jaw. Occasionally, the unnerved the girl would place some clean gauze pads to soak up the oozing blood which flowed from one of her created crevices before she continued on. Jeanie hurt so much emotionally that she barely felt the throbbing pain that her digging and prodding had caused. As pathetic as it sounded, the poor girl wanted to feel pain. She wanted to feel just as bad physically as she did mentally.

After two hours, the desperate, desolate woman had her bottom gumline emptied of teeth. Jeanie decided to keep the dental appointment she made earlier in the week. She thought that it was best to let the professionals take out the teeth in her upper jaw. They were much bigger and had large roots. Besides, she had tortured herself enough for one night.

Despite having her teeth brutally yanked out just hours before, Jeanie went to work. She did however call in late that day so she could have her upper teeth taken out as well. Her employer found it difficult to believe that she went to work at all that day. Although Jeanie was bleeding and in pain, she did her job with little complaining and even less talking. As long as she kept her mouth closed, and put pressure on her bleeding gums, she would be ok. With her mouth clenched tightly on the gauze pads, she managed to keep the oozing blood contained. Jeanie went to work that day for she knew that she would need every penny she could get. She put her dental bill on her charge card with the intentions that she would pay it back within a months time before it accrued interest. After she paid for the tooth extractions, she would have to save money for a new set of choppers as well.

Except for the little infection she acquired, Jeanie's mouth healed up fairly well. After several months of healing, Jeanie saved enough money to buy a good pair of false teeth. Although it was a long drive, she made the trip to Little Rock to get her dentures made. The dentist Jeanie went to made the best quality dentures for the lowest price. Even though it was a hassle and expense to go the extra distance, Jeanie thought it was worth it… at least she did originally.

The dentist Jeanie went to acted like an insensitive, egotistical idiot. Even though Jeanie's teeth looked pretty, she couldn't eat anything with them. Her bottom plate would always rise up when she chewed her food. Jeanie made the long trip to Little Rock every week for a month in an attempt to get her teeth to fit right. Still they didn't operate the way they were supposed to.

Nothing the dentist did made her teeth work any better. When Jeanie voiced her displeasure about how poorly her teeth fit, the dentist got sarcastic and outright mean. He already had her lower plate in the other room, so she thought it odd that he asked for her upper teeth as well. After giving her upper plate to his assistant, he offered to the give Jeanie back her money. Even though she was very unhappy with her teeth, she wasn't about to face the world without them. She had recently started taking an art class at a local college and she wasn't about to face her peers at school without them. The only way the distraught girl could get her teeth back was by signing a statement agreeing she would not go back to Dr. Jerkinsein to get any kind of adjustments made, ever. From that day forward Jeanie was by herself in her misery and emotional pain that the ill fitted dentures helped create.

For the next several months Jeanie concentrated on her job, her relationship with God as well as her art projects. The sensitive artist was able to express her internal pain quite effectively in clay. She spent much of her spare time in the ceramics studio molding the clay on the wheel. The emotionally damaged potter was able to gradually get her heart mended through her art, her writing and through her various scriptural readings. As she kneaded the great mound of clay in front of her, more and more of her internal pain was released.

Despite a very difficult holiday season, Jeanie made it through all right. In spite of being deprived of the foods she craved and the love she needed, Jeanie managed to live through the next few months. Six months had passed since having her teeth out. She thought her gums had healed enough to consult another dentist for a relining. Jeanie had high ideals regarding a tight fitting lower plate. Her gum line must surely be stabilized by now. After the new dentist did her relining, her new false teeth were bound to fit like they were supposed to.

Much to Jeanie surprise and misfortune, even the new liners couldn't help her bottom plate stay in place. The girl was in tears. Jeanie thought that she would be doomed to a diet of soup and deprived of the deep passionate kisses she desired forever. Jeanie couldn't even imagine trying to resume dating again. The distraught young woman cried silently to herself. She thought for sure that part of her life was gone forever. If she had to live without the sweet affections that she craved, then she would rather be dead. She already felt dead inside.

The local dentist who did Jeanie's denture relining explained to her why her bottom plate wasn't staying down when she ate. He told her about a solution to her problem…implant surgery. The surgery would cost a lot of money, there was no denying that.

However in the end she would be able to get her smile and her life back. With much optimism, Jeanie called the Little Rock surgeon she was referred to and made an appointment to see him.

The kindly surgeon asked the nervous girl a variety of questions regarding when her natural teeth had been extracted. The problem lied in Jeanie's lower jawbone. When the girl was quite young, she had most of her back teeth taken out because they were so decayed. After nearly three decades, her body had absorbed much of the bone which had housed the roots of her massive molars. It was explained to her that the reason her bottom teeth didn't stay in place when she ate was because there was nothing for them to hold onto. Jeanie was about to cry while she listened to the wise surgeon. Even though the ridge to her lower jaw was scant, he believed that he could implant four posts in her bottom jaw. Once those were in place, a metal bar would be fitted across them. That fabricated piece of metal would help stabilize her denture and evenly distribute the pressure caused when she bit down on her food. After the implants were in place, Jeanie would need to have a new denture made to accommodate her new prosthesis. That new lower plate would have metal housings on each side of it. Each housing would hold a supportive cup. The cup inside the housings would snap into the metal bar, thus holding them tightly in place. After two operations and six to eight months recovery time, the girl could then be fitted for some new teeth.

Jeanie knew that she had to pursue a career that paid her far more than what she was currently earning. Doing all that, was going to cost a fortune Besides, she wanted to be able to take care of all her material needs and not have to rely on a man for it. Since she was already in the health field she thought about nursing school. She didn't want to take out a loan for it, but she knew she no longer qualified for a pell grant. She surely had help from above when she won a year's tuition at the local vocational school in town through a silent auction. She ended up paying less than $100 for over $1200 in education. That was indeed a blessing!

Obviously she wasn't going to be dating anyone for a long time. So, she might as well take advantage of the extra time she had. Jeanie was smart and saved some money while she worked as a home health aide. Since she was still on subsidized rent, she could continue living in her own small apartment while attending school full-time. She could live meagerly on the money she recently acquired until she was through with school.

Jeanie took all the preliminary tests necessary to attend LPN school. Intellectually, Jeanie had what was needed to do well in her studies. The nursing books were extremely expensive though. However she was able to get them loaned to her through a program for displaced homemakers. For that she was grateful. They even purchased for her a fairly good stethoscope for she had trouble hearing out of the one included in the student nurse kit.

Jeanie attended school every day. She diligently paid attention in class and did all her homework. Many nights she would be up until after eleven at night studying. Often, she woke up at five in the morning to study some more. She had to learn her lessons thoroughly, her life depended on it. Rosa's well being depended on it. Besides in that particular school, if you got below a C in anything, you would have failed and not be allowed to continue with the program.

Jeanie dutifully studied every day and earned all A's and B's in the first half of the LPN program. She tested extremely well in the actual book learning. Things changed however when she began her field work assignments. When she only had two patients to cater to, the student nurse did well. However when she had a multitude of patients who all needed her at once, she couldn't handle it. Jeanie would become so filled with anxiety, that she couldn't function. She could not draw on the needed information from her mind and act on that learned knowledge.

Jeanie had problems in the past with anxiety, but it was never like this. Although she went to her family doctor for medication, that particular medication was not the answer. The prescribed pills made the future nurse so lightheaded, forgetful and dingy. She was less than worthless while in her fieldwork assignments.

While in vocational school, Jeanie began the two surgical procedures to put the implants in her lower jaw. Although she hated charging things on her credit card she didn't feel she had much of a choice. With little hesitation, Jeanie made arrangements to start the long process of obtaining the much needed implants. Her mouth hurt like hell following the first operation. It was during that time the doctor drilled the holes inside her jawbone and screwed the metal rods in place. The poor girl cried to herself for days because the bone pain was so intense. She couldn't help but wonder what she got herself into. Despite the agony she endured while her mouth tried to heal, Jeanie continued going to school. Unfortunately the medicine the doctor gave Jeanie for her anxiety was taking it's toll on her. The girl became totally inefficient at school and more so in her fieldwork assignments at the local nursing home.

After wandering around like a zombie while taking the anti-anxiety medicine, Jeanie knew that she had to do something. She didn't want to endanger any of her patients and her patient load wasn't getting any easier. With much sadness, she came to the realization that she had to quit nursing school.

It broke Jeanie's heart to have to withdraw from something that she worked so hard at. Even though she diligently busted her tail in her studies, her anxiety disorder stopped her from doing what it was she sought to do with her life. Jeanie once again felt like a failure.

Feeling discouraged and disappointed in herself, Jeanie once again returned to her previous job as a home health aid. She couldn't afford to wait for a better job to come along with her credit card bills accumulating. Her implant surgeries had already cost her much money but the procedure was only half way done. She knew eventually all the money and pain she put into the mouth surgeries would be worth the expense. However, they were something she wished that she could have done without.

For her to have any kind of a normal life however, she knew they were necessary.

Except for the added expense, the second operation was a breeze. During that procedure, the doctor cut into the top layer of skin just covering her implanted rods and twisted the individual posts firmly into the implants. It wasn't completely pain free but it hurt a lot less than the first one did. After just a few days the gentle throbbing dissolved completely away.

Finally after six months, Jeanie was ready to have a new prosthesis made. After the connecting bar was manufactured, it was placed into Jeanie's mouth. From there a new set of dentures were made to accommodate the hagar bar that journeyed across much of her lower jaw.

Finally after almost 2 years, Jeanie had a stable set of teeth. She could finally eat something besides applesauce and banana bread once again. Her pearly whites were good for something else now besides smiling. Jeanie was elated. She had gone without many of the things she considered essential in life. Besides the chewy high protein foods her body craved, she went without the kissing and cuddling she so immensely desired. For the past two years the only type of physical contact she had gotten was an occasional hug from her minister and the reluctant hugs from her teenage daughter. Despite the social isolation and the physical pain, Jeanie had gotten through those solitary days of deprivation. Maybe her trials of life would be over…at least for a little while!

Within only a couple of weeks following the completion of her surgical miracle and the manufacture of her dentures, Jeanie placed another personal AD in the Little Rock paper. She decided that this time things would be different. She would give some of her perspective mates more of a chance then what she had given them in the past.

All too often the perfectionist had overlooked someone who may have been good for her because they did not possess a certain quality that she deemed important. Although Jeanie still desired to be with someone handsome, it was not a necessity anymore. Too many times the girl had been misled by a handsome face with a pearly smile and charming personality. This time around, Jeanie would look beyond what her eyes could see and what her five senses could detect.

Over the next few weeks, Jeanie received eighteen responses to her personal AD. Even though she surmised that some of the men who wrote to her were not the best match, she decided to meet with them anyway. First impressions do count, however they could be deceiving. Jeanie received an array of impressions from the men who wrote to her. However, even if someone wasn't the best letter writer in the world, she still responded to him. Just because the man couldn't express himself as fluently as she could didn't mean that he was illiterate or stupid.

Jeanie also decided not to unjustly judge someone by the material items they acquired. Just because someone wasn't driving a super nice car, it didn't mean that he was without ambition or motivation. Just because someone was wearing jeans and an unimpressive, plain shirt did not mean that he was not a creative and colorful character.

Although Jeanie liked it when a man opened doors for her, that action wasn't more important than his integrity. Pulling out the chair for her may have been sweet, but it didn't necessarily mean that the guy was a gentleman when it came to matters of the heart. Jeanie found out that some of the most charismatic, polite men could be total animals. There were many foxes which hid behind lambs clothing. She's had the wool pulled over her eyes too often. She had to be careful. She had to be discerning. She wasn't putting herself out there just to play the dating game. Jeanie wanted much more from a relationship...so much more.

Jeanie wanted much out of her life and her future love that was true. However, she felt that she had much to give. Her priorities had changed much since she was a flyaway filly. She readjusted her priorities in life and she was ready to move forward in it. She realized that she could make it on her own emotionally and financially without a significant other, she just didn't want to. Still, she couldn't let a stunning smile or a colorful personality blind her to the hidden qualities that she fervently desired in her man.

Jeanie tried to take all that into consideration when she went out with the different men who contacted her. Although the girl let her expectations way down, she nevertheless became easily disappointed with the men she had so far met.

It seemed that everyone except four guys Jeanie had met, had misrepresented themselves in one way or another. One smoked cigarettes. Now why would a smoker answer an AD of someone who specified that they were non-smoker? No way would Jeanie ever go with another person who smoked cigarettes. She only became serious once in her life with a smoker…and that was James. She wasn't going to be involved with another person who indulged in that nasty habit ever again! She detested the cancer sticks and hated the stench and bad breath that went along with that disgusting habit as well. Besides, her body craved fresh air and she knew she wouldn't get that living with a smoker.

One of the men that Jeanie conversed with on the phone started asking some very personal questions. He asked her such questions as, how she liked to make love, as well as what her bra size was during their second phone conversation. She obviously knew what he wanted. Physical expressions of love were beautiful with someone she cared about. Impersonal, uncaring acts of pure animalistic sex shared with an unknown being were no longer her thing! If all she wanted was a quick hop in the sack with a stranger, she would have merely gone to a local bar and picked up someone there. Obviously after that short second phone call, all communications with that creep ceased. He definitely got crossed off the potential boyfriend list!

Jeanie met briefly with someone from southwest Arkansas. Although the guy was quite nice to her, she just didn't take a liking to him. He had an unkempt appearance and was not on her intellectual level. It was important to the lady that she could carry on an intelligent conversation with the man who was in her life.

Jeanie met someone close to her age that she liked as a friend. Even though he wasn't very good looking and was missing his two front teeth, he was so sweet and kind to the girl that she couldn't help but like him. Even though Jeanie knew in her heart that she would not want him as a boyfriend, she accepted his offer to meet again for lunch the following week. After all missing teeth can be replaced. Having a problem child was something she would be stuck with forever.

Jeanie was having a terrible time lately with her troublesome teenager. Two of the months Jeanie was in nursing school, Rosa was in the behavioral treatment center in Little Rock. She began routinely running away and hanging out with small time gangsters, She experimented with certain street drugs besides. Jeanie tried controlling her unruly child herself, but she had difficulty doing so without intervention. Rosa was already taller than she was and was twenty three pounds heavier than her mom also. When Rosa tried exerting her demands over her mother with a fist Jeanie drew the line. That was when the over burdened mom sought the help of the professionals.

Rosa had been out of the behavioral treatment center for several months now. Although she was no longer violent towards her mother, Rosa definitely wasn't an angel. She was an angry, girl with a lot of inner turmoil. She often voiced her discontent in hurtful cruel words. Jeanie tried not to be too thinned skin when her daughter mouthed out her many verbal assaults at her, but those cruel words still stung. What they say about sticks and stones could break your bones but names could never hurt you… is all Bull. The many mean names Carmalita Jean was called earlier on in her life had damaged her tremendously. If it wasn't for God's help and the inner strength He had graced her with, she wouldn't have survived emotionally.

Besides her undesirable outer behavior, Rosa still associated with were the same kids she hung around with before going to the treatment facility. Their influence would without doubt be a problem in the future. Despite Rosa's choice of friends, she seemed to be making progress in controlling her temper and making better choices in her life. For that Jeanie was thankful. Her daughter had much growing up to do and much to learn along this weary road of life.

Jeanie dated a nice man named George for a couple of weeks. She met the man through her AD also. He seemed like a cordial enough guy, but he certainly kept his emotional distance with Jeanie. She understood why on the day she met his child. Her opinion of him and where their relationship was headed came to an abrupt halt when she met his eight year old daughter whom he had custody of. The child was the most disrespectful, ill mannered child she had ever seen. Jeanie thought her daughter was a hellion. Rosa was an angel compared to that girl! That date George brought his daughter along was the last date she made with him. She surely didn't want to become involved with someone who had an out of control eight-year-old. Jeanie's daughter was 15 years old and had already given her gray hairs. There was no way she would go with someone who had a problem child living with him. That would be pure torture to the sensitive, easily excitable woman. She probably would be in the wacky farm within a month's time if the two devils from darkness got together and collaborated their talents. God help the world. God help mom!

Within the letters Jeanie had gotten, a familiar name stood out. One of the men she had dated when she first came to town, had written her a letter. He even recognized Jeanie's AD as being her. The girl was impressed that Donny had recognized Jeanie's description, yet she chose not to answer his letter right away. The truth was she was hesitant of getting involved with someone else who had a teenager. Jeanie still remembered years ago when Johnny and Rosa would get together at the amusement park The two kids back then were loud and rowdy. Jeanie imagined how life together with two rambunctious, mischievous teenagers would be like. She didn't know if she was ready for that, so she chose not to answer Donny's letter...at least not for awhile.

After meeting her next prospective boyfriend, Jeanie was about to call her search off for a compatible mate for good. She was intelligent enough to realize that she would not find someone perfect. No one in this world was perfect except for God. Still, she just wanted someone perfect for her! The person Jeanie was searching for now should be someone she could relate with, someone she could do things with, someone whom she could share her love with and the intimate details of her life with. However the longer and harder Jeanie looked for her illusive love, the more he eluded her.

Even though Jeanie wasn't a raving beauty, she knew that she was somewhat attractive. Even though she would always have her herpes, the young woman saw herself as being desirable. She was honest and sincere, gentle and kind, considerate and perceptive and oh so loving. Despite Jeanie's flaws, the man who would win Jeanie's heart would get his share of affection and love. The girl wasn't afraid to show her beloved how she felt about him. If she could, she would move a mountain for the one who captured her heart.

It had been a long time since Jeanie had been with anybody that she really cared about. It had been two years since the girl had been with anyone she shared more than a hug with. Although Jeanie felt that she would wither away from lack of affection, she wasn't about to give her sweet love away to just anybody. Not anymore! Despite everything, she saw herself as someone special and she wanted to be with someone who was equally special.

Jeanie shook her head in disdain as she remembered the wild years of yesterday. Back then she would give her physical love to just about anybody. She found it hard to believe that she acted so casually about her sexual relationships. The girl knew now why she had jumped around from one man to another. In her desperate attempt to escape loneliness and find love, she about lost herself. Still knowing why the confused girl acted like she did, didn't make it right. It didn't make the past any easier to accept or to forgive.

Out of all the people that had done her wrong in the past, there were two individuals that she had trouble forgiving for their sins were so great. One of the two individuals who Jeanie couldn't forgive was the man who murdered and robbed her father. The other person who Jeanie had difficulty forgiving…was herself.

The task of self forgiveness had become a little easier these days since Jeanie's soul became one with God's. Jeanie cried when she felt for the first time that God dwelled inside her heart. She knew then, that she was not alone, nor was she unloved. The young woman found it hard to believe that despite everything she had done in the past, someone loved her to no end…and that was God. The Almighty had given Jeanie the gift of unconditional love, a love that the girl had heard of but had not yet experienced. She came to the realization that if God could love her, the flawed person that she was, then maybe she could learn to love herself. If God could forgive her for all her past wrongdoings, perhaps she could also learn to forgive herself.

Even though Jeanie had been in physical pain due to her recent automobile accident, something good did come out of it. Since she had been out of work, she had much more time on her hands. The extra time that Jeanie suddenly acquired brought her more in tune with herself and closer to the God that created her. Jeanie couldn't help but smile.

"I guess nothing ever comes about by pure chance after all," she told a friend.

No, nothing came to someone by mere chance. There was a reason why Jeanie experienced all the soul shattering tribulations she endured while growing up. There was a reason why all the horrible series of events happened to Jeanie when she was young. The molestation, the relentless bullying, the physical and emotional abuse she endured while still in her teens didn't seem right. So, young Jeanie rebelled against society and turned her back on God. God may have allowed such things to happen, but he did it to enhance her spiritual growth, not to torture her body and maim her heart. Jeanie was too young to see that. The sensitive girl acted out the barrel full of abuse she endured through angry, careless methods. Each action had it's consequence. Each consequence had it's own particular effect on her life.

Although many of the past experiences may have hurt Jeanie, in the long run they served a much needed purpose in her life. Through God's help and guidance Jeanie would rise above all the trials and be victorious in the end because of them.

Sometimes it was difficult for Jeanie to fathom that all the things that had happened in her life served any kind of useful purpose. She knew that it wasn't good to spread her love too thin, still she carried on with that reckless behavior. Consequently she got hurt by the men in her life in a multitude of ways. Jeanie knew what a person owned or how they looked or dressed didn't determine what kind of a person they were inside. Yet, she overlooked many prospective boyfriends in her past because she failed to look beyond what her eyes could see.

The fine qualities that Jeanie now saw in a man were those that were not readily recognized. She wanted someone who would be honest and truthful, gentle and kind, loving and ambitious. Jeanie desired to be involved with someone who loved her for the type of person that she was and not for what they wanted her to be. After all illusions fade. Jeanie did not want a mere illusion. She wanted a man of substance…a man of character. She wanted someone who could give love with the same extent that she was capable of giving. What was the sentimental dreamer describing, God or merely a godlike man? Even though her expectations were lowered, were they still too high? Was it too unrealistic of her to want and desire such qualities from a mortal man?

Sometimes Jeanie wondered if she ever would find someone who was capable of given her what she needed physically, emotionally and intellectually. Maybe she was being too demanding. Maybe she was too idealistic in wanting someone who would place her above all others except God. She didn't expect someone to bow down before her like some queen, but she did expect someone to think highly of her despite her jaded past. She wanted someone who would be willing to do anything humanly possible to win her love. Once her special man won her love, he must be willing to do anything possible to keep her love. Jeanie knew from experience that love like a flower would wilt and die unless it was attended to daily. The flower of Jeanie's heart was wide open. Who would walk into the girl's special garden and diligently tend to the rose blossoms that were housed within her soul?

## CHAPTER 22

# Donny

Jeanie decided that despite her reservations she would try to get in touch with Donny, the man she dated briefly five years ago. The girl couldn't remember a lot of details of their past dates together, but she did remember that the man was kind and considerate. Donny was also a gentleman who respected her wishes and boundaries. True he had custody of his teenage son, but that didn't mean he was a total hellion like her daughter.

One Saturday afternoon Jeanie decided to call Donny's house. The uncertain lass wanted to talk to the guy and let him know that his assumptions were right…she was the girl who he thought she was when he answered the AD.

Donny was glad and surprised to hear from Jeanie. He had about given up hope of receiving a response from the writer of the personal advertisement. Jeanie apologized for not answering his letter earlier. Then she explained the reason why she hesitated to contact him. The man was quite understanding and empathetic over the concerns of the overly stressed mom. She obviously had gone through a lot lately with her wayward daughter.

Donny and Jeanie made arrangements to get together later that same day. After giving her forgotten friend directions to her new residence, they ended their conversation.

"I'm looking forward to seeing you again," Donny stated.

"I'm looking forward to seeing you again too," Jeanie replied

Jeanie could hardly wait for seven o'clock to arrive. Unfortunately, her injured back hurt worse than it had in days. Jeanie took a couple more over the counter pain relievers. She would have taken the pills the doctor prescribed for her, but the young woman didn't want their first date together in years to be blurred by the use of narcotics. Those past few weeks had been tough on Jeanie's back and neck. She should heal from her physical pain shortly. She had already begun to heal from the emotional and spiritual pain that had plagued her a lifetime.

Donny arrived at Jeanie's house at seven that evening. It was their first date in five years. Things between them were kept pretty casual and low key at first. Since they spent all that time apart, neither one knew what to say to the another. After an hour into their date, Jeanie requested something of Donny...a back rub. The weak pain relievers she took earlier helped with some of the pain that still lingered from her recent car accident. However, those pills definitely didn't take care of her aches like the prescription medicine did. Jeanie's bruised body cried for attention. Her battered heart cried for love. The gentle massage Donny graciously gave her helped break the barriers that had become wedged between them during the five years apart.

Donny spent several minutes rubbing Jeanie's aching shoulders. After the massage was over, Jeanie propped herself off the floor and moved over to where he sat on the couch. She was now mere inches away from Donny. They were in touching distance, yet they were so far apart. Both parties wanted to reach out to the other but both were equally hesitant. It wouldn't be long though when the gap that separated them would be closed.

What made this date so nice was that Donny already knew much about Jeanie. He knew about some of her likes and dislikes. He knew about Rosa's behavior problems and her current stay in the mental health ward. Her teenage daughter took advantage of her mother's incapacitated state to run the streets and hang out with her hoodlum friends. When the rebellious girl began engaging in risky behavior, Jeanie knew she had to do something. Although Rosa did not want to take a nice, long vacation at the mental health hospital, that was where she was. Rosa could have been such a help to her injured mother, instead she used that time to pretty well do whatever she wanted. Although Jeanie didn't want her daughter to return to the facility, she knew that her daughter needed help and obviously the outpatient counseling wasn't as effective as she hoped it would be. The doting mother definitely did not want her precious daughter repeating her mistakes.

Donny was familiar with Jeanie's character also. He knew what she wanted out of life and some of the things she enjoyed doing. He also knew about Jeanie's herpes. Nothing Jeanie told Donny appeared to scare him away. He was always so accepting of her. It was easy to cuddle up to him when the sun faded and the quarter moon shone brightly through the living room windows.

Even though Jeanie and Donny dated in the past, things never got past the holding hands stage. There just wasn't a great deal of affection shared between them. Donny was just getting over his divorce and Jeanie was still trying to emotionally get over her busted relationship with Norman. The two were friends and companions but not lovers. All the times they went out together prior to this night, the children were with them also. That in itself made it difficult to spend personal time with one another.

There was one time only when Donny ever kissed Jeanie in the past. They shared one small kiss the night she stayed in the guest room of his house. Just before going to bed that evening, he bent over and gave Jeanie a peck on her lips. It wasn't a bad kiss, it was just a real small one. It almost felt like that kind of kiss

Jeanie's brother would give her if she had one. That night though everything was different including the way Donny kissed her. He definitely didn't kiss her like a sister that evening.

Donny left Jeanie's house later that night saying that he would make the long trip back the following night. She couldn't wait to see him again. He couldn't wait to see her again either. One more kiss for the road and Donny was on his way home.

"You've changed," Donny told Jeanie

"You've changed too."

Donny arrived at Jeanie's house shortly after four the following evening. The two of them exchanged small talk for an hour or so before going out to dinner. They enjoyed a buffet at one of the city's restaurants and later played a game of miniature golf. The evening was exceptionally warm and muggy. Still the two of them enjoyed their playful time at the nearby attraction. Neither one of the two were golfers. In between wild putts and extra steps to retrieve flying balls, they engaged in lighthearted conversation.

During most of the game Jeanie was ahead but Donny snuck up on her and aced the last hole. Both of them chuckled about the way they played the game afterwards. Jeanie felt good knowing that although she was ahead of him most of the game, Donny didn't feel intimidated by her. Some men were so insecure about their masculinity that they became threatened whenever a woman proved that she was better at something than they were. Donny wasn't like that. He was secure enough with himself that he could allow Jeanie to excel in certain areas of her life without compromising his ego. How nice!

The evening started to cool down little by little by the time the golfing buddies arrived at Jeanie's house. A nice cool breeze fanned their flushed faces. The two took advantage of the breezes strategic blowing and sat outside on the chaise lounges. After cooling off a few minutes under the trees, they went inside to escape the mosquitoes which were hungrily attacking them.

It had been two years since Jeanie had been with any man. She deliberately distanced herself from members of the opposite sex partially due to her formerly abusive relationship. However, Jeanie would have resumed dating months earlier if it wasn't for her denture problems. Even now that her implants snugly kept the lower denture in place, she didn't know whether her kisses would be natural or strained. Her mouth no longer felt like it was her own. And her heart…what was left of it, was in an extremely fragile state. Up until recently Jeanie didn't want to journey forth on the dangerous curvy highway of life. She wasn't ready to resume dating again, never mind try to pursue a meaningful relationship with anyone.

Although Jeanie began to feel some sexual desire stir inside her love starved body, she thought it best to put those feelings on hold. Surely another week or two of abstinence wouldn't kill her. Although Donny was getting worked up too, he did not try to wiggle his way into Jeanie's bedroom. He cared about her too much to unduly rush the lady. The timing just wasn't right either and they both knew it.

Jeanie and Donny both looked to start a relationship with someone special. Neither one of them wanted a casual fling. They had grown weary of sharing their physical love with somebody they didn't care about. Jeanie wanted to know that she wasn't merely a warm body. Donny also wanted to feel something significant for his mate besides her physical affections. Even though it was difficult, Donny and Jeanie parted company that night with their virtues still intact. Although the man didn't leave Jeanie's house until midnight, he promised to return the following morning to see her. He kept his promise.

Donny surprised Jeanie by arriving at her house at nine the next morning. Despite the hour long drive home and the equally long drive coming back, the guy was there to greet Jeanie just as she was having her morning coffee. Good thing she didn't hesitate to get dressed early that day. It was a tad early in their relationship for Donny see her in her granny night gown.

"I was just about to go for a walk before it got hot. Do you want to join me?" Jeanie inquired. Donny nodded his head. "Good. There is a little trail behind my house. We'll walk on that."

The couple walked hand-in-hand on the shadowed trail that led up the grassy hill. The gradual slope made climbing easy. It was breezy and cool on that morning climb. Tall trees shaded their every step. A variety of birds nestled in the evergreens which surrounded them. The sun shone rays of white light through the trees and burned off the dew which coated the grass and the various underbrush. It was indeed a great way to start anyone's day. Jeanie smiled to herself, for that morning…she felt kissed by God!

After climbing a good distance into the hillside, Jeanie led Donny to a little clearing in the woods. She sat down on the rock gravel that had bordered the trail. Donny joined his leader and sat down beside her. The two remained there on the moist soil and admired the scenic wonder before them. Jeanie leaned back into Donny's chest. His arms became snugly wrapped around her shoulders.

Both of them contently gazed at the beauty which was before them. They were comfortable enough with each other to enjoy the scenic paradise without feeling the necessity to speak. Neither Jeanie nor Donny were uncomfortable with the quiet stillness which had surrounded them. Serenity gently laid it sweet scent into Jeanie's heart. They stayed at the lovely location for several minutes admiring the view while they caught their breath.

"I don't just want a one night stand or short meaningless fling," Jeanie told Donny as she looked into his blue eyes.

."Neither do I," Donny assured her.

There was no doubt that the words spoken were true.

"We'll just have to take things easy and see what happens," Donny cautiously told Jeanie.

"Yes we must not rush into things like some immature school kids," Jeanie said in agreement. They both exchanged smiles.

Donny was such a gentleman. He may not have been the most handsome man Jeanie had been with, but he was surely one of the nicest. The more Jeanie knew about Donny, the more handsome he looked in her eyes. The time worn crevices that lined his face seemed to fade in time as well. Jeanie concentrated more on the inner beauty of the kind man before her and not so much on his outer appearance.

Despite the distance between Jeanie and Donny, he continued to drive to her house every weekend and sometimes once during the week. Things were definitely different for the two after becoming reunited the second time around.

One day Jeanie suggested that she go down to his country cottage to visit him in his domain. They had been involved now for over a month and she was curious as to what his new house looked like. Naturally, while there Jeanie could meet up with Donny's son again as well... and see first hand the wondrously smart dog he owned.

Jeanie seemed to have driven forever before she eventually found Donny's house. Luckily, she recognized his blue truck from the road or she may have driven by it for the third time. Up until that day Jeanie relied on the old tried and true map to find locations. She hadn't thought about getting a GPS for they were a new and expensive gadget for the frequent travelers. However, that day she vowed to buy herself one as soon as possible!

After Jeanie arrived at Donny's house, she carefully unhooked her seat belt. Her back wasn't hurting that much before she started on that long drive. That's ok, she said to herself as she pulled another pain pill from her purse. Jeanie thought that she may need something stronger than Tylenol that day. However, she refrained from taking anything stronger. She didn't take her prescriptions meds before, because she had to keep her mind sharp driving out there. Now she abstained from taking them, so she could have her wits about her. She wanted to remember every detail of that day. Happily, Jeanie stepped out of the bucket seat and walked towards the little wooden house. As she got out of her car a familiar face walked out to greet her.

"I see you made it," Donny said smiling.

"Yeah," Jeanie answered returning his smile.

Donny guided Jeanie into the massive living room.

"Well this is it. This house isn't as fancy as the other one, but we like it," Donny announced.

As Jeanie scanned the surroundings, she could easily tell that only men lived there. Deer heads were mounted high on the walls. Glassy, animal eyes gazed at her wherever she walked. Occasionally, she would see a different critter such as a stuffed raccoon with it's bandit masked face staring at her. Looking up at the lofts, she noticed two black squirrels frozen in place in animated play.

The windowpanes looked barren and bleak. Blinds hung unevenly down from the paint peeled frame. No flowery drapes decorated the sun filled window. The place definitely needed a woman's touch, Jeanie thought to herself as she looked past the living room to peer into the kitchen.

The old house was in dire need of fixing up, still it had potential. Donny and Johnny hadn't lived there long, but already they decorated their house as they liked. The two boys contently lived in their den with the souvenirs of their various hunts. They felt at home among the company of their critters. Personally, it gave Jeanie the creeps when she viewed all the murdered animals staring at her.

"If I knew that we'd be getting back together, I would have spent some time fixing this old house up," Donny told his girlfriend almost apologetically.

Jeanie graciously smiled. Once she overlooked the array of clutter on the wooden floors, and all those odd eyes staring at her, she decided the place wasn't that bad.

"Oh don't worry about the house," Jeanie reassured him. "It's fine. Besides, I came to see you not just the house."

After uttering those words Donny took Jeanie in his arms and gave her a strong embrace. It was good to be with him again, she thought. It had been a long time since she had been with someone who truly cared about her.

Donny definitely wasn't like Norman. Jeanie was glad of that. Her new boyfriend was lighthearted and playful. Those were the two qualities that Jeanie felt was desperately lacking in herself lately. There were occasions when the child like woman let her hair down and became playful, but those days didn't come often. On those rare occasions, she pranced around the dance floor like a carefree kid. She hadn't danced much lately for much of the time Jeanie was incredibly stressed with her troubled teen. Mother never told her that it would be this hard to raise a child. Yes, mother hadn't told her a lot of things. She had to find out for herself how cruel people could be and how unforgiving the world was all by herself.

In many ways Jeanie wanted to go back to being a little girl. Life in general stressed the hell out of her! Becoming a responsible, logical woman appeared to zap away much of her inner child. It was hard to believe that at one time Jeanie was so full of exuberance for life. However those carefree emotions felt like they happened to another person in different life.

The sunshiny days of her youth vanished way before her dad left and before the incident on the hill, but she couldn't remember exactly when. Too often now at the end of the day, Jeanie didn't feel much joy or enthusiasm for anything. She couldn't muster it for herself nor manufacture it for anyone else. She often felt like a worn out rag.

Too often Jeanie felt the burden of the whole world on her shoulders. The withered lady and her daughter were all alone in the south with no one to lean on. She hadn't formed any solid friendships while she lived in the city either. There was an occasion or two when she reached out her hand to make friends with one of her neighbors. The friends she made however, turned out to be users. They sucked the gullible lass of all she had to offer. Both the monetary goods and treasures of the heart were drained from the poor girl before her so-called friends parted company.

Jeanie's few attempts at forming meaningful relationships were about as unsuccessful as her previous attempts at finding her soul mate. Donny may not be the perfect man but he was sure nice to her. They had some common interest, but not as many as she would have liked. Still, she couldn't be too choosy these days, the pensive girl thought to herself. After all, she wasn't exactly a princess. No, but Donny treated her like one.

One of the qualities Jeanie liked most about Donny besides the way he treated her was that he could be depended on. The man had integrity. She realized after several dates, that the man was trustworthy and reliable. She already knew he was kind and considerate. Now she knew he was also loving and tender. No one could put a price tag on such admirable traits.

It was so difficult for Jeanie to build a strong relationship with anyone, for she tended to keep much to herself. True, she could effortlessly pour out the multitude of complicated thoughts and intensive feelings onto the paper in her journal. Never the less, she had difficulty trying to explain to others what it was she felt inside her heart. Even if she attempted to do so in the past, her thoughts and feelings were discounted…like they didn't matter, like she didn't matter. Oh, but she did!

Jeanie's unique characteristics was what made her so different from everyone else. The sensitive, young woman was blessed with the ability to feel, truly feel. She could experience a variety of emotions with such an intensity it was almost supernatural. She could feel heightened pleasure which sent her heart floating with the clouds. However, she could also become nearly drowned by the sorrowful pain of a love gone bad.

Jeanie knew the chance she would be taking if she chose to fully expose her heart once again. She may have wanted to become personally involved in a meaningful relationship, but she was afraid of giving her heart away and then have it trampled again. However, the lady needed love and affection so badly that she was willing to keep taking her chances. Still, she always kept a little bit of her heart tucked away inside her for safe keeping. She had to!

Jeanie and Donny continued to date for the next several months. Still how close could she get to someone she only sporadically saw? Once or twice a week for a few short hours weren't enough time to be with anyone to sustain an intimate relationship…at least not for her. Her boyfriend rarely stayed the night anymore, as he once had. He was afraid if he neglected his teenager, he may turn wayward like Jeanie's own daughter had. After the first month of dating, they were lucky to spend five hours a week together. That wasn't enough time for Jeanie. She wanted more time and she needed far more affection.

Since Donny severely cut back on the time he allotted Jeanie, she felt neglected. They barely got reacquainted before it was time for the guy to leave. Donny felt uneasy leaving his teenage son all alone at night even though his own father lived right next door. Jeanie could understand why Donny was so protective of his son. Although she admired him for that trait, she still felt pushed aside. Even when his boy made plans to spend the night elsewhere, her boyfriend chose not to remain there in her bed the entire evening.

It wasn't practical for Donny to spend the night at Jeanie's and both of them knew why. The guy snored so incredibly loud that Jeanie couldn't sleep. It didn't help matters that Jeanie herself was such a light sleeper. Even with ear plugs, she couldn't block out the distracting noise that kept her from her slumber. It hurt Jeanie not to cuddle next to Donnie in bed and peacefully fall asleep in his arms. Through no fault of their own that meaningful act was an impossibility.

Even though Jeanie cared about Donny as a person, she really didn't see any kind of future together. That realization made Jeanie quite sad. She wanted someone in the worst way who would be loyal and kind passionate and caring. Donny was all those things, but between his snoring problem and his lack of time with her, their love affair was doomed.

The couple at one time was optimistic with their relationship. That of course was when they first started dating. Naturally neither of them knew what the future had in store for them.

Jeanie desperately desired her heart to surrender itself to a sweet, passionate gentleman, whom she could build her life around. Although the compassionate man before her possessed many of desirable traits she sought in a man, he just wasn't the one. Jeanie knew that now with certainty. Still she continued to see Donny several months afterwards, partially out of loneliness and partially because he was just so nice to her.

The months that followed Jeanie's mental detachment from Donny was emotionally straining for both of them. Donny held back valuable time from Jeanie while she held back her heart. The sensitive girl didn't want to give anybody her all until she was certain of the outcome of the relationship. There were many obstacles in the way of her and Donny's courtship. Some of the boundaries were difficult to maintain. Other obstacles in their lives were totally out of their control.

Jeanie couldn't see a way of achieving the things she wanted from her romance with Donny. Slowly, she withdrew from her boyfriend's emotional bonds and physical closeness. Some things, she could endure, but she couldn't compromise what it was she felt she needed such as her desire for physical closeness. She couldn't alleviate her bodily need for sleep either. Since Donny was not wanting or just unwilling to seek someone to help him with watching his ward or muffling his snoring problem, Jeanie just couldn't see their relationship reaching beyond the level it already had obtained.

Jeanie knew before she got together with Donny for the second time that she wanted to pursue an intense emotional relationship. However, she wanted one where she already knew what the outcome would be…love preferably followed by marriage. How could she enthusiastically continue on in a romance when there wasn't any certainty that the relationship would go in the direction that she wanted? Still, how could anyone be certain of anything?

Jeanie couldn't continue wasting her time and love on an unpredictable, love affair. Each time she did, she felt a little more of herself dissolving away. She had to know for certain that the next time she became involved with someone that she would receive exactly what she needed, but how was that possible?

The idealist was looking for certainty in a world where there was none. The fact that nothing in the world was a sure thing bothered the dreamer. Except for checking out permanently, there was nothing that Jeanie or anyone else could do to stop the tides from turning. There was nothing the girl could do to ensure that things in her life went exactly as she had planned it in her head.

Although Carmalita Jean knew inside her mind that nothing in life came with a guarantee, her heart was still unwilling to let go of that concept. Jeanie held onto the believe that if she really wanted something, all she had to do was work hard at it and eventually things would come together. That concept was probably what kept the girl in a string of abusive relationships. She believed that if she tried harder to understand her man or if she did this or that, then things would change. Some things though, she just couldn't change…two of them being the behaviors and thoughts of others.

Yes, it was Jeanie's fervent push for love that often drove her man further from her instead of closer to her. That's why Norman became emotionally unavailable to her…she just pushed too hard. Donny started pulling away from Jeanie as well, early into their relationship. The man was kind enough to be honest when he told the distraught girl his concerns about his son and so their time together would be drastically cut down. Jeanie unwillingly accepted the boundaries Donny set between them although it weakened their romance and stunted it's growth.

After accommodating her boyfriend's needs, Jeanie was left feeling wanton. She gave her man what he needed, but she didn't get what she needed. She never fully adjusted to that. Unfortunately, there were so many other things that got in the way of their budding relationship. The differences in personality and interests combined with Donny's snoring problem continued to drive a wedge between the couple. Although they still cared about each other as people, they both knew that their relationship was far from ideal. However that was all they had at the time so they half heartedly held onto each other's heart until one or the other decided it was healthier for them to let go.

# CHAPTER 23

# Reflections

When Jeanie first started dating Donny, she was granted the luxury of unclaimed time. If she wasn't in so much pain from the automobile accident, she would have enjoyed the free time much better. During the first two months following the car crash her broken body hurt terribly. She didn't know until then how sore someone could get strictly from whiplash. Eventually her injuries would heal. She just had to get past the initial pain.

The next two months following the accident weren't great. Jeanie had good days and she had bad days. Just before she was released for work, she was having much more pain-free days. Jeanie spent those comfortable days going on nature hikes and getting into her poetry and art. Those serene days were what Jeanie needed to heal her troubled soul. Although she often felt lonesome during the weekdays, the tenderhearted girl knew that she had someone coming to see her on the weekend. At least that was something to look forward to. Yes, Donny was a wonderful distraction that entered Jeanie's life just when she needed him. He was also a great comforter to her when she drove that long journey to see her daughter in the psychiatric hospital every week.

During the first two months the couple went together Jeanie was not working. However that scenario soon changed. The day finally arrived when Jeanie's doctor signed her work release. With much optimism she made out several job applications in the immediate area. Much to Jeanie's surprise, the girl obtained a job almost immediately. Jeanie surmised she got hired so quickly for although her job experience had been scant, she was a good worker. She was dependable and trustworthy. She was smart and had a way with people. She enjoyed the elderly citizens she had recently worked with and it showed in her attitude and her dedication to them. Being hired so readily made Jeanie realize that some employers recognized her virtues. That made the previously discouraged worker feel better about herself.

Everyone needed to feel that they're wanted. Everyone needed to feel that they had importance and meaning. There were times when Jeanie wondered if her life had any meaning at all. The youthful woman felt like a misfit most of her life. There were times when she didn't feel she belonged anywhere.

Jeanie didn't have a strong sense of identity, nor a strong sense of self. The array of hard times the girl endured throughout her life almost stole away all Jeanie had of her precious soul. Still, God smoothed over the roughened edges of her life and purified her soul. Once she basked in the glow of his love, she felt at peace. Eventually much beauty would emerge from deep within the girls aching heart. A magnificent flower grew out of the garbage heap that once was her life.

The radiating warmth of God's love melted the protective icy shield that grew around Jeanie's heart. Through her faith in him, she was set free of the boundaries her injured spirit encased her in. Through the love she had for God, Jeanie developed an appreciation of the person she was inside. The understanding and forgiveness Jeanie learned to have for herself slowly developed into self-love. The type of love that the girl began to have for herself wasn't a selfish kind of love, nor was it a love that emanated from vanity. It was the kind of love that made her want to do good things for herself as well as for other people. That graced attitude opened it's doors to the compassionate compartment in Jeanie's heart.

Jeanie became more at ease with herself and the inner qualities she possessed. She started to become much more accepting of others as well due to this inner transformation. Now that Jeanie made that major breakthrough in her life, God was leading her to the career that she had been longing for…or at least she thought.

Although Jeanie liked working with the people at her job site, things were not right there. There was much more work and pressure associated with her job than she had imagined. Despite the tensions of her job, she was bound and determined to stay there. Surely once she thoroughly learned her position, things would get better.

When Jeanie's job placed her recuperative process in jeopardy, she knew it was time to quit. During the day she suffered with such relentless pain that it interfered with her concentration. She endured many sleepless nights as well because of the lingering tension. The stress from the job created massive muscle spasms in her shoulders. The longer she remained at her job, the more severe these pains became. One afternoon Jeanie left her workplace in tears. Things just didn't seem to be getting any better for her.

With a sincere and troubled heart, the stressed employee told her boss that she would have to leave due to health problems. Although her boss understood, he didn't want to see her go. Jeanie hated to lose the money she made too, but her health was her priority now. Besides, Rosa would be coming home from the psychiatric hospital soon. It was important that Jeanie gave her daughter all the time and attention she needed.

The anxious mom didn't want her teen to wander back into her previous behaviors that admitted her to the hospital. Jeanie made up her mind that she would do whatever was required to keep Rosa barreling ahead in the direction that was beneficial for her health and well-being. Jeanie knew that she had to do something drastic to keep Rosa away from the bad influences around her. When she came out of the hospital last time, all was fine for awhile. However, once she resumed her troublesome friendships, her out of control behavior returned. Jeanie wanted to shield Rosa from the world. She felt she had to do whatever she could to protect Rosa from herself and her thoughtless choices. However, she couldn't very well place her daughter in isolation. She didn't want to become a guard dog to Rosa even though she felt at times she had to be. Eventually, she would be required to return to work. When Rosa began to slide back into the same group of friends who had gotten her into trouble in the recent past, Jeanie knew she had to do something fast. There was only one way Jeanie could be sure her daughter wouldn't be associating with the juvenile delinquents in that town, and that was for them to move.

Shortly after Rosa got discharged in the hospital, Jeanie made arrangements for them to relocate to a different part of the state. With Rosa's happiness and well being in mind, the protective mother decided that the two of them would settle into a progressive little town a hundred miles away. The place Jeanie decided to move to, laid on the outskirts of a midsized city. They would have all the safety of living in a small, rural town and still be able to drive thirty miles to a bigger city for their weekend entertainment.

This small town should be a good place to start over, Jeanie thought. Even though she was ready for a change, she was shaking inside. There was something scary and unpredictable about starting over. Even though this move was in both of their best interests, Jeanie wondered if she would have the courage to yank Rosa away from everything she knew again. Her angry child often invoked her mother's guilt about their relocation to the sunny south.

Yes, they left their family and friends up north to start their lives over. Yes, it wasn't Rosa's decision but hers to move. Yes, things had not gone according to plan. Still, despite everything they've gone through so far, Jeanie was confident that things in the long run would work out fine. She had to believe that. She had to know that!

Even though Rosa was close to her cousins at one time, Jeanie herself wasn't real close to anyone up north except those four little girls who frequently visited Rosa and her at their home. Jeanie, however was never real close to her sister and even now still harbored ill feelings towards her for the cruel things she told Rosa prior to their move. She could never forget the impact that those truthful, but mean, untimely words had on her young daughter. Jeanie could forgive Deana, but she'll never forget what she had done.

Jeanie never was real close to her mother although she wanted to be. She couldn't talk to her mother about the important things in life, only idle chit chat. She felt sad about that. Of course, she could no longer converse with her father, the person who was most like herself. He entered the other realm and was no longer in this world. She missed him terribly. There were times when she still talked to him, but of course, he didn't answer back.

Jeanie's ex-lover turned brother, Norman discontinued all conversation with Jeanie after finding himself a long term love. That was too bad. His friendship would be truly missed. She respected his mind and truly liked him as a person. If she knew how bad off she would have been financially in Arkansas despite those college degrees, Jeanie would've continued living in the cold country that she hated and had stayed with Norman. Still, she wasn't happy there and she was tired of being cold. Jeanie felt that she had to move on.

Indeed, there was nothing up north worth sticking around for. Still, Jeanie visited her mother in Connecticut (in the summer) once every year or two. Her and her mom were now closer than they had even been before, but that wasn't saying much. Jeanie could initiate conversation on a few uncomfortable subjects, but she could never delve too deeply. In the days her mother grew up, no one spoke about the personal matters that Jeanie wanted to talk to her about. Such talk was just too uncomfortable for her mother. Jeanie would never be able to tell her mom even part of what was hidden in her mind and heart. She wanted her to know what she had gone through when she was an adolescent that caused her so much distress. Jeanie wanted her mom to know why her daughter was so mentally messed up growing up. However, her mother couldn't handle the painful truth, so Jeanie didn't tell her. Even though those uncomfortable subjects were never spoke about didn't mean the events creating them didn't happen or that the feelings that accompanying them didn't exist.

Jeanie had been living in the southern state of Arkansas for six years. She wasn't totally alone for she had her daughter living with her. However, Jeanie wanted more out of her life than what she currently had. She had the friendship and love of Donny. However, the pace of their relationship dramatically slowed down. As much as Jeanie liked the guy, she didn't see much hope of it developing into her great lifetime love. Still, if it wasn't for the help and encouragement Jeanie received from Donny, the concerned mom wasn't sure that she would have had the courage to do what she felt she had to do. Relocate! The sweet guy even helped her move her furniture and personal belongings. They would still continue to date too. Jeanie would now live thirty miles south of Donny whereas before she lived seventy miles north of him. That fact definitely encouraged her move to that particular town. She would need a friend!

Jeanie knew that she had made an unpopular decision with her daughter about their change of location. Still, the responsible woman had to do what she felt was right. Even if her decision didn't turn out to be perfect and without flaw, Jeanie prayed that Rosa wouldn't hold it over her head too long. If things didn't fall into place as they would like, then both mother and daughter would have to accept the facts without the temptation to push the blame on the other or worse yet blame God.

Although people usually do whatever can be done to secure their future life with happiness and success, there was no way to ensure it. Whatever plans were made along life's highway, the individual had to follow a certain path. The Master determined the ultimate destination of the chosen path. Although people including Jeanie, liked to think that they were in the driver's seat, in reality God was the driver. Humans were merely the backseat passengers in that beat up car of life.

There would always be little unexpected detours on that great thoroughfare which Jeanie drove on. Those diversions, though unexpected and unwanted, were when Jeanie learned the most. There were times when those arduous lessons she learned appeared to be near fatal crashes. Nevertheless, she survived, and grew stronger during those times. Those vital lessons had the greatest impact in her life.

Jeanie had learned much about herself and her life throughout the years. She learned that there was nothing stronger than the human will to survive. Although there were times in life when the girl wanted to say goodbye to her shattered existence, she forged the courage and determination to go on. Despite the many times Jeanie was kicked down in her life's pursuit, she always managed to lift herself up. She would brush away some of the pain and continued on in her life's journey. With fortitude and high hopes, the disillusioned girl trail blazed another path. When she determined that the road she was on wasn't leading her to where she wanted to go, she'd try another direction.

The strength and determination of character was what gave Jeanie the fortitude to forge her way through the thicket. Fortunately not everybody placed here on this earth had to cut away so many briars along their path. At times, she wished she didn't have to either.

Jeanie was a perceptive and intelligent person but she was also very headstrong. She had definite ideas concerning her inner beliefs. She also had unshakable thoughts about what she expected out of life, her potential mate and even out of herself. Even though the girl was proven time and time again that what she wanted was impractical or not feasible, she still stayed with her given beliefs…until they no longer served their intended purpose.

For too many years, Jeanie's defense mechanisms protected the girl from accepting the painful facts that were presented to her. Rather than acknowledge that the world was populated by people who thrive on innocent souls, Jeanie turned her thinking inside out. For eons, she convinced herself that she was molested because she had dressed provocatively or that she gave her attacker the wrong idea when she became too friendly to him.

Later on when Jeanie was beaten by her boyfriends, she justified their actions by believing that she somehow deserved their outflow of rage. If only she could make her man love her more, then he wouldn't beat her like he did. If only she could've been smarter, she could have warded off the attack. How irrational those thoughts appeared to Jeanie now. Yet at that time, those beliefs were so ingrained in her heart that she accepted them as the gospel truth.

Jeanie internalized all the bad things that happen to her throughout her life. It provided her with an uncanny sense of empowerment. She had to think that she had some control over her many abuses throughout the years. She had to feel safe in her world for she currently did not. This vulnerability led the girl to feel powerless and helpless. She had to think that she could have prevented those horrific things from bombarding her life the way they did. This vulnerability raised havoc with her developing inner self. The more things fell out of control, the more powerless she felt. These feelings left her more afraid than the actual physical and emotional attacks.

It was too painful for the child minded woman to accept the fact that she lived in an unpredictable world with hurting people. These damaged souls hurt other people either intentionally or unintentionally. In order to feel some type of comfort in the jungle like city, where the stronger animals hunt the weaker ones, she kept focused on her impractical beliefs. Jeanie had to feel safe in her mind despite the ferocity of the world.

The only way these unshakable ideas could have been defeated, was from the multitude of hard times that had rocked her life. Although the many painful experiences left deep scars on the woman's sensitive soul, they were not suffered by her without reason. Those abuses weren't experienced to torture her unforgiving heart or punish her for all her past mistakes. No, these actions had a purpose, they had a reason.

The various indignities were presented to Jeanie to further her along on her soul's path. She had many lessons to learn in her lifetime and God chose those particular experiences to fully teach Jeanie all that she had to learn. Even though the sensitive girl wished she could have absorbed those important lessons an easier way, it wasn't feasible to spend time wondering why they weren't given to her in an easily digested form.

Still in spite of everything, Jeanie's thankful that she was able to endure her life's hardships without buckling under it's tremendous weight. Despite the many occasions when she wanted to give up, the woman courageously continued on that rocky road of life. She tried to make the best of the situations which were presented to her. No matter how bad things got in her life, Jeanie always shook off her foul spirit and continued on the best she could.

Jeanie realized that one of the greatest lessons she had learned in her life was how to love others as well as herself. Jeanie was born into a critical, demanding home. She was taught at an early age it wasn't acceptable to have character flaws or to make mistakes. That particular lesson had been so difficult for her to learn. She couldn't love herself for having flaws, so she couldn't love others for being less than perfect either.

Jeanie also realized through years of trying to be a tough, hard, and immovable rock, that she could not pretend to be other than what she was. She played several parts in the great passion play of life but none of the parts she played were really her. Eventually it caused too much strain on Jeanie's inner being to continue with the role-playing. They were not her and she could no longer continue believing those characters she played were. Yet, after she shook herself loose of the many masks, she was left without a face at all. It took years of inner dissection to discover who Jeanie really was inside. Too often the girl would peel off one mask only to discover another one hid underneath it. She had been untrue to herself for so long that it was difficult for her to distinguish what was really her anymore.

Jeanie felt ever since she was rejected by her peers growing up, that in order to be liked, she had to be something other than what she was inside. The sensitive little poet who was shunned and misunderstood wasn't readily accepted by the brazen classmates around her. It was their rejection of her while growing up which helped to create that sense of self loathing that had been ingrained within her heart all those years. Even now, there were times when Jeanie struggled to shake loose similar feelings. She's not entirely rid of them yet, although they appear in her conscious mind much less often.

There were times when Jeanie felt bad about herself for not being the same petite size seven of years ago. When her weight fluctuated more than a couple of pounds, Jeanie would get in a panic. When that happened, the girl would once again begin to see herself as undesirable and ugly. The hideous female figure that stared back from the mirror was not worthy of the good things in life…not even love because her outer flaws were so obvious. During those times, a screaming voice inside criticized

Jeanie without mercy. The girl's own inner parent was far more malicious than her own parents ever thought about being.

There's so much emphasis on physical beauty in our society, especially with women. Unless a young lady had that certain look, she was usually unduly criticized and ostracized from her peers. This rejection had detrimental effects on the girls when they grew up to become a woman. Even now Jeanie had trouble with her body image. She had a terrible fear of being alone forever if she did not find someone to spend the rest of her life with before she lost her attractiveness. She feared that when her outer beauty faded, no man to her liking would find her desirable anymore. Jeanie often felt that once she lost her looks, she lost it all. She knew now, that wasn't true, for at last, she had opened up the inner pages to herself.

How cruel those school years could be, especially to someone as sensitive as Jeanie. It was important for her to be liked and accepted when she was growing up, yet too often she didn't feel either of those things. Is it any wonder she sought the attention and affection of men? Is it any wonder that she became the promiscuous rebel that she had become all those years ago?

Although Jeanie didn't talk much about those soul shattering times, they would always be a part of her life. Although the past has passed...those painful experiences still hurt. However, Jeanie had learned to accept what happened during those previous years without holding it over her head. She hoped that the person she chose to build a relationship with could accept her unconditionally and not turn his back on her for having experienced those hardships.

There were times Jeanie would love to erase those unpleasant memories that blackened her life and her numbed her heart. If it was possible, she wondered if it would be a wise decision to do so. Those endured soul purging times was when she learned the most. So, like it or not the many faded scars inside Jeanie's heart would always be there. They remained in her consciousness to act as small reminders of how those tough lessons of life were learned.

Some people do not have to go through the fires of hell to learn their life's lessons. Jeanie was not one of those lucky few. Still, she considered herself fortunate. Jeanie finally learned that most important life lesson and that was how to truly love. In many ways her life now was blessed, especially now since she found someone special to share her devotions with…her sweetheart Harry.

## CHAPTER 24

# Harry Honey

A couple months after Jeanie and Donny went their separate ways, Jeanie once again found herself alone and lonely. She wanted someone to love forever. Why was she having such difficulties finding that one special man whom she could spend her life with? Was there really such a thing as a soul mate? There seemed to be some people out there who had found theirs. She wanted to be one of those fortunate few. Despite her flaws, Jeanie thought that she would make her special man a good wife. If she were to find her one true love, she would be so good to him. She wouldn't cheat on him or blow all his money. She would cook and clean and make their house a home. Jeanie had so much to give, but she had no one to share her immense spiritual and emotional love with. She had no one to give her intense physical affections to. She could survive without a man in her life if she had to...but she just didn't want to. She needed to receive love as much as she needed to give love.

God, please help me find my everlasting love!

One thing was for sure, even though she desperately wanted someone to love, she wasn't going to settle for just anyone. The inner isolation chewed at her heart, still she wouldn't settle for just anybody. She knew exactly the kind of person she was looking for. However as picky as she was, she wondered if he existed outside her dreams. It would be a million to one shot to ever meet that special someone through a chance encounter.

So, the idealistic lady decided that she should place another personal AD in the local paper. Some people may think that only desperate individuals who were too ugly to look at or who were dumber than dirt would ever place a personal AD in the paper. Well, Jeanie wasn't any of those things...she was just picky. People like Jeanie who knew just what they were looking for and were tired of wasting their time and love on the wrong people, often put in personal ads. Meeting someone that way may not be the most romantic way of finding someone, but it was practical. She had considered computer dating also. However at the time, it was a new concept. That mode of finding a suitable mate then, was also much more expensive.

Jeanie carefully chose just the right words for her AD. She wanted to meet someone fairly intelligent, close in age, a non-drinker/smoker and of course have similar interests and loved affection. She wondered if a man like that even lived close by? If he did would he have read the paper's personal ads that day? Maybe he had about given up his quest of finding his special someone. Maybe, he convinced himself that sitting alone on his couch watching TV, while accepting slobbery kisses from his dog was the closest he would get to everlasting, unconditional love. Although Jeanie loved her animals, she knew that she needed more than the love of her furry friends to fill the gnawing emptiness that she continuously felt inside.

The romantic, idealist tried to convince herself that she would be better off alone...especially after breaking up with an emotionally or physically abusive man. No matter how hard she tried, she never could seem to win what it was she sought. If, by some miracle she captured the heart of her dream love, all too often their romance turned into a nightmare.

When Jeanie was young and wild, she thought spreading her seed like a bee spreading pollen was fun. Boy how she changed. She couldn't imagine doing that now. She was even tired of fluttering from one semi-long term relationship to another. Maybe, it was because she realized that despite the numerous mistakes she had made, she saw herself as a worthwhile person. At last…she felt worthy of the love of a good man.

Before Jeanie handed the AD over to the newspaper agent, she read it one more time. Hopefully this well worded, personal AD would attract the attention of the gentleman of her dreams. She smiled serenely with a hopeful heart.

The day the AD appeared in the paper was a joyous time for Jeanie. A few days after it was printed, she enthusiastically checked her P.O. Box. Although the young woman received several responses, there were only two men among the dozen that interested her. One of the men Jeanie chose as a potential mate was a mechanic. The other man who corresponded to her AD that she was interested in, was a businessman.

For the next several days she played telephone tag with her selected gentlemen. Finally she got in touch with Bob, the mechanic and arranged for a brief rendezvous Thursday night. However, the determined lady could tell after talking to him for 15 minutes, that nothing would come of their encounter. After finishing their nonalcoholic drinks, both individuals went their own way. That was a disappointment, the disheartened woman thought to herself.

Early the next morning before leaving for work Jeanie called bachelor number two. She wanted to make sure she reached him before he went out for the day. She had been trying for days to contact him by phone without any success. She was anxious to meet this particular man. They appeared to have much in common. She felt guilty calling him so early, but she did it anyway. He definitely didn't mind the early wake-up call.

After a brief five-minute phone conversation, they arranged to meet at a local fast food restaurant after work. Even though Jeanie dearly wanted to meet with Harry, she almost canceled their date. She had a little mishap with her dentures shortly after she phoned him. One of the front teeth in her dentures broke off while eating a granola bar and she swallowed it. She thought if she could chuck it up, she could clean it up and glue it in her bottom plate. Her attempts at that were unsuccessful, so there was nothing she could do. She was in a terrible bind. Although Jeanie was terribly self-conscious about the missing tooth, she decided to go ahead with the planned rendezvous anyway.

Right after Jeanie left her last client, she drove to the designated meeting place. She recognized Harry through his vehicle description. His truck was passionate purple. It was definitely unique. Hopefully, he was too.

The subconscious lady watched the young man get out of his plum painted truck, and smiled. Harry certainly was quite handsome. He had a well-built body too. Obviously he must take care of himself, she thought. Although he was getting up there in age like she was, he definitely wasn't bald. No, his head was covered by a large array of blonde waves. Jeanie looked at herself in the rearview mirror one last time to inspect her face. Her hair was combed, her make up was scantly applied. Yes, she passed inspection…until she smiled. Oh God, why did she have to lose a tooth now?

Carefully Jeanie stepped out of her blue Ford. Harry approached Jeanie with a ready smile and sparkling blue eyes. When they were in touching distance of each other, rather than extend a hand, he reached around the amazed girl and gave her a big hug. Naturally she reciprocated the loving gesture. Ummm, Jeanie thought, an affectionate man who's not afraid of expressing his inner passions. I like that!

The two of them spent nearly an hour talking over their soft drinks. Confident that this sweet man she had been conversing with wasn't the town's rapist, Jeanie invited him to her place. Her small apartment was just a mile away. Neither of them were ready to end their date. There wasn't much to do during the week in the small town she currently lived in. Jeanie felt their choices of where to go or what to do were limited.

Finishing their date at her home seemed the logical solution. It would be quiet and cozy there. She could put on her favorite soft rock music from the 80s. They could talk and maybe cuddle without any interruptions from Rosa or her rowdy friends. Jeanie's daughter was currently out of town visiting her family, so the whimsical lady knew she would be entirely alone with Harry without worrying over anyone peeking around the corner spying on her. Yes, Jeanie's small, but tidy apartment would do nicely for their little visit.

Harry followed Jeanie out of the Burger King parking lot towards her home. After only five minutes, the two stood outside the little white house where Jeanie resided. The girl readily led Harry into the front door and stepped into the living room. They could continue their conversation there while listening to music. Jeanie mentioned to Harry that she nearly canceled their intended meeting after her tooth mishap. However, she added she was glad she didn't. She was real glad that she didn't.

The man before her was so sweet, so handsome and so cuddly. She really enjoyed his company too. Wow! They talked about life. They talked about their likes and dislikes. The two even shared a slow dance on Jeanie's braided rug. The physical attraction between the two was obvious. The chemical attraction between them was stronger still.

After the two of them shared that sensuous dance together, they didn't want to separate from their embrace. One heartfelt hug led to another. The one soft kiss Harry implanted on her lips following their dance led to more moist, passionate kisses.

It had been many months since Jeanie had any type of physical affection from anyone. She gobbled up the multitude of hugs and kisses that sweet Harry happily bestowed upon her. After a few minutes the lovable lady was nearly breathless. Oh, how she wanted this splendid display of emotion. How she craved the passionate array of physical attention. However, she was not the reckless school girl from the past. She could easily became totally engulfed in his sweet affections. If she didn't exert some type of self control, she would fall victim once again to her own animalistic lust. She could not allow herself to become so swept away that she'd do something that she may have regrets about later.

Jeanie couldn't release her physical love to Harry too soon. She wanted more then just a fast trip in the hay! After several minutes of passionate, mouth exploring kisses, Jeanie pulled away. Before things went too far, she made an excuse to get up. She needed a few minutes to get it together. Jeanie made a trip to the bathroom. While there she checked her composure. Then she proceeded to the kitchen to pour another cola for her and her date. That gave the soulful lady a chance to think about what it was she had to tell Harry.

Jeanie arrived back into the living room with two fresh cans of cola and handed one over to her handsome, mustached man. Rather than sitting next to her friend, she chose to sit in the rocking chair next to the couch. After she took a sip from her can, Jeanie looked deep into Harry's eyes. It was obvious she had something to tell him. Harry placed his drink on the wooden table beside him and gazed up at the sensitive, sincere lady before him and smiled.

"Harry, I really like you. I think we could be good for each other. Although I do enjoy your hugs and kisses, I want much more. I want a long lasting relationship. I'm not into one night stands. You shouldn't expect anything more tonight except hugs and kisses. Are you ok with that?"

Harry just smiled and quietly acknowledged that he agreed to her terms of affection. He did not push her for more than she was willing to give that night. He was a true gentleman. The evening quickly slipped away. Jeanie looked at the clock in the corner. It was already 11:30. Where did the time go?

"It is getting late. I have to get up early tomorrow for work. I need my beauty sleep you know," Jeanie told her new man with a smile.

They made plans to meet again Saturday. Jeanie was ecstatic. The two passionate people shared one more kiss before saying goodnight.

Saturday night didn't get there fast enough. Harry arrived right on time. His blond hair glistened in the setting sun. His blue eyes sparkled as he approached Jeanie's front door. The star struck lady greeted the handsome man with a tender kiss. Yes, there was something special about him Jeanie thought…something very special indeed.

Harry and Jeanie had more going for them than the physical attraction to each other. They were so alike in many ways. They shared common interests and goals. In many ways they even thought alike. After a lovely time out of town, the two of them ended the evening together cuddling on the bed. Although Jeanie's body craved her honey's physical love, she held back. Although it was obvious that Harry wanted all the passions her body could physically give, he accepted Jeanie's limitations.

Early on in their long make out session, Jeanie decided she had to tell him about her past wild life and her health problems. Before their romantic interlude became even more intense, Jeanie pulled back from Harry. She had to tell him now before things got too serious. She had to know how he would handle what it was she had to tell him. After taking one deep breath, Jeanie began to speak.

"I know we just started seeing each other, but there is a whirlwind of emotions stirring around in my heart. I really feel for you and by the way you treat me, I'd say the feeling is mutual. There are so many things you need to know about me. I want you to know them because if you can't deal with anything I tell you, then we can each go our own way. Neither one of us will get hurt that much now, if we choose to part company this evening."

Harry looked at Jeanie with a perplexed expression on his face. He wondered what could his new love have to tell him that was so important. Maybe she was married. Maybe she was bi-sexual. Maybe she was a wanted criminal from another state. Anticipation loomed in the air.

Without hesitating any longer, Jeanie went on to tell Harry everything she deemed was important. She talked about her past, her health problems, her wayward teen…everything. Harry just sat quietly on the couch beside her and intently listened. After Jeanie was through with her talk, she looked him in the eyes and sheepishly asked,

"Are you okay with everything I told you?"

Harry took Jeanie's delicate hand in his and squeezed it tight. He leaned towards her and gave her a long, passionate kiss. Obviously his answer was yes.

The understanding, sweet man who sat beside Jeanie was very accepting of what she had to tell him. After she got through pouring out her guts, Harry told Jeanie about his past as well. He told her the details that surrounded his very recent divorce. The break-up left the guy impoverished financially, but not spiritually. Although his ex-wife put him in debt, he didn't seem bitter about it or her.

"If I'm real careful, I'm sure I can pay off all of my ex-wife's debts in a couple of years," Harry told Jeanie nonchalantly.

Jeanie could deal with that. Besides the settlement money she was expecting from that car accident would be coming in soon, she thought. So he's a little in debt. Since Jeanie considered herself a thrifty little cheapskate, they would be out of debt in no time!

Despite what Harry had recently gone through with his ex-wife, he wasn't a woman hater. Yes, in spite of his recent emotional and financial whipping, the man wasn't angry or bitter concerning his recent divorce and monetary losses. Jeanie could tell he wasn't by the way he treated her.

Harry told the wide-eyed woman more about his family, mainly his three sons. The charming man spoke of his children with great pride. She could tell he was totally devoted to them. The eldest son recently graduated from trade school and was now living with him. However, the two other boys were much younger so they lived with their mother. It hurt him to only see his children every other weekend and during school breaks. However, since his ex-wife moved to a distant city, he was thankful that he was able to see them that much.

Harry's younger children weren't as old as Rosa. They hadn't started acting rebelliously either. Her own daughter currently was in that stage, and it was tough on both mother and daughter. Jeanie couldn't help but wonder how her teen would get along with Harry's kids. It worried Jeanie a little when she thought about all the children getting together. However from what Harry told her, the younger two boys were fairly quiet. They sounded like angels.

Even though Harry himself was far from an angel, he certainly was one to Jeanie. Everything about this gentleman was to her liking. He seemed to be made for her. It was as if God put him on the earth just for her.

Harry and Jeanie continued to see each other almost every night. They shared kisses. They shared many heart to heart talks. They divulged personal information that neither one had shared with anyone. It was so easy for the two of them to fall in love. Jeanie though, hesitated to tell Harry what it was she felt. Although she felt immensely for him, she was afraid she'd get hurt again. She was afraid that her love would just crumble in her hands, like tiny grains of sand…again. Although the love feelings poured from Jeanie's heart, at first she didn't admit to Harry just how deeply she loved him. The words emerged from her throat a bit easier when Harry revealed his undying love for her. The spoken words only confirmed what their actions already showed.

"Carmalita Jean. You are so, so special to me. I love you! I don't care about what you did when you were young and dumb. I love the person you are now!"

"Oh Harry, I feel so much love in my heart for you too!"

Love was indeed a special emotion. If the two were alone, without children, their life together would be far less complicated. However, they both had their little wards. They had to consider what their lives together would be like as a blended family.

Rosa had been back from her New England vacation for several weeks. Even though she had been officially home, she rarely was at the house when Harry visited. Rosa had an active social life, even more so since she had been out of circulation for awhile. What little time Rosa and Harry were together was uneventful and with little friction. She probably just thought that Harry and her mom were just casually dating. She didn't know until the couple planned a big excursion with both families that Mom may be getting serious about this man.

Harry and Jeanie's children were a big a part of their lives. It was important that they became acquainted soon to see how they all would get along. Hopefully, everyone would get along ok. Jeanie was plagued with anxiety over the event scheduled for the following week. She didn't know for sure how everyone would get along. She knew her daughter. Although Rosa wasn't a mean child, she did have her moods. However she seemed to like Harry. She liked the idea of meeting his sons too.

That Saturday, Harry brought Jeanie to meet his parents and his sister. Later on that night she met his eldest son, James. The two of them talked only a few minutes. It seemed that he also had a date. After the teen put on a sweater, he bounced off to meet his girlfriend. Well, that went fairly well Jeanie thought to herself. Jeanie's daughter Rosa would accompany them on their next family excursion. She already made plans previously to go out with her friend that night, so Rosa hadn't joined them that evening. She did talk to her mother about how excited she was about meeting Harry's children the following week. She never had any siblings, so it would be nice to not be the only kid in the house.

The following week Harry and Jeanie acted out their planned family cookout. Everyone would meet each other then. Oh God, Jeanie thought to herself, please let them all get along. After a brief hello, Harry's two younger boys scampered off into the near by field chasing after a baby bunny. Harry's eldest son James, sat around outside eating chips and talking about music with Rosa while waiting for the burgers to finish cooking. Everybody seemed to be getting along quite well. The event Jeanie was so tense about all week went off without a hitch. How wonderful! The group already seemed like a big happy family!

Jeanie's love affair with Harry continued to blossom and grow. They loved each other so much that they couldn't stand to be away from each other for more than a day. Just three months after their first meeting, Harry and Jeanie were talking about marriage. One night as she was laying beside her cuddly man, he turned and looked deep into her brown eyes. He obviously wanted to tell her something. Jeanie just stared back at him. The two automatically smiled at each other.

"You know, I don't think I've ever felt so much love for anyone in my life. I am so happy when I'm with you. Carmelita Jean, would you be my wife?"

"Oh Yes!" Jeanie said enthusiastically. "Yes, I will be your wife!"

The thought of spending the rest of her life with this wonderful person and his beautiful children pleased Jeanie to no end. She was so happy! She couldn't believe that after all those years, she finally found her one true love. A few tears trickled from her eyes. Those tears were not the result of intense pain and disappointment. No, the clear drops that fell from her eyes were tears of extreme happiness! At last she found her soul mate!

They were so much in love, they couldn't stand to live apart much longer. Surely their union would last forever. The following Monday, the couple made arrangements with a local minister to marry them just three months later. A little church wedding followed with a small reception at his parents house was planned. It would be simple, but it would be nice Jeanie thought.

The day before the wedding, Jeanie returned to her apartment to pack up her few possessions she had left in the house. As she boxed up her paperback books, a bookmark fell on the floor. Underneath the scrawled letters, imprinted on the plastic card Jeanie read the Bible quotations on love. "So faith, hope, love abide, these three; but the greatest of these is love."

Yes, Jeanie had the love of God all long although there were times when she thought not. She had the love of her daughter though often it was not shown, and now praise God, she had the love of a good man and his darling family as well. She felt truly blessed.

As tears began to trickle from the sentimental lady's eye, a warm hand tenderly pressed against her shoulder.

"Old Harry honey, I do love you so. I thank God I have you!"

As Jeanie stood up to hug her future husband one more tear trickled out of her eye. Her sweet man looked into Jeanie's water filled eyes and kissed her forehead gently.

"You have been the missing piece to my life," Harry whispered in her ear while he gently embraced her. "I'll love you forever until death do us part."

"Yes, until death do us part," Jeanie echoed.

As they uttered those words, a flash of lightning filled the living room window. The two loving souls looked warmly in each other's eyes. There was no doubt that this union was orchestrated by the great master himself and so it will be Blessed.

# Epilogue

Jeanie did indeed become Harry's wife. They have been married now for over 14 years. Her own daughter Rosa blessed her with three lovely grandchildren. Between her and her husband, they have seven grandchildren and counting. Although not everything is perfect in Paradise, Jeanie finally got what she wanted. She spends her life nurturing and loving her grandchildren and their various furry animals. When she's not with them, she pursues her artistic interests of painting, writing and singing. In between her babysitting and her artistic interests, she maintains a beautiful home with the wonderful, kind, accepting man that she married. God has truly blessed her.

Jeanie's life was extremely turbulent in her adolescence and early adult years. Many times, that troubled lady muddled through tremendous obstacles in her quest to become what it was she was meant to be. Even though she's still an anxious person, she's learning to let go and let God. She accepts the fact that she was not alone in the universe, although at times in the past, she felt she was. She also became very aware of the importance of acknowledging God and living by his Golden Rule. If everyone treated others how they themselves would like to be treated…just think how beautiful life would be everyday for everyone!

Jeanie is a great believer in karma. Whatever a person does comes back to them in either this lifetime or the next. Perhaps, in her previous life, she had some old karma to work through. That's the only way she can come to terms with the soul shattering events that took place in her early adolescent years. Why else would our God of supreme love allow such atrocities to happen to an innocent child? The molestation in itself was hard enough, however the ripple effect created by the relentless name calling that tortured her for years continued on. That long endured bullying altered Jeanie's thoughts, beliefs and life far more than anything that she had so far encountered in her young life. However, all she experienced happened for a reason.

No doubt Jeanie had many lessons she had to learn in this life time before her soul could go on. One of the important lessons she had to learn was forgiveness. Despite what Mr. Martin's actions did to her sense of well being, Jeanie was readily able to forgive him. He was an old man searching for affection. Even though Jeanie was still merely a girl, he saw her as a young adult. Rather than feeling anger towards him, she now feels sorrow. She doesn't understand why he did what he did, but she forgives him.

Forgiving the peers who tortured her with their relentless name-calling and prodding well, that bullying total changed Jeanie's personality, beliefs, goals…everything. She would have had entirely different options presented to her if she was allowed to attend school without the endless bullying. At first their tormenting, name calling turned the girl into her psychological shell. Eventually, Jeanie came to believe just what her peers constantly pounded in her head…that she was nothing but an object to be used and discarded. She became the sex siren. She became the promiscuous girl they already thought she was. She became Sex Pot!

If Jeanie was allowed to continue on in school without the verbal torment she received daily, she would have continued on learning all she could in high school and undoubtedly attend college immediately afterwards. Maybe Jeanie wouldn't have had to go through many of the emotional and financial hardships she endured, but maybe she would have anyway.

Still, the misguided peers who continuously threw those cruel names at her aren't fully to blame. Those growing years were difficult for them. They, like so many others, just wanted to fit in. So when one person called Jeanie those names, many echoed those cruel names also. Jeanie would like to think that those mean words were spoken from unknowing, immature kids who did not know the power of their hurtful words. Since most everyone did stupid, careless things when they were young without thinking of the consequences of their actions, Jeanie does not hold them fully accountable for their actions either. Because of that...she forgives them for the part they played in her difficult, painful journey in life.

Jeanie would have had a healthier self-esteem and probably would have made better choices in her life. If she didn't think of herself as merely as an object...a headless, nameless object to be used and abused by men, her life would have been so different. If she hadn't endured all that she had suffered through, she wouldn't have made many of the past mistakes. Although she hurt people in the past, it was because she was so incredibly hurt herself. Hurt people hurt others. Although she had injured people in her past through her quick tongue and careless ways, the person she had hurt the most in her life was herself.

Jeanie had to learn to forgive the person who murdered her father. For some reason God used him to fulfill her dad's destiny. In some weird way, it also acted as a catalyst for positive change for Jeanie too. For it was shortly after his demise that Jeanie had the courage to leave her long term abusive boyfriend. Lately many more beneficial experiences have come about in Jeanie's life. However those occurred only after she was able to work through the anger and rage that ate away at the sensitive woman's heart.

The men who used her, and forcibly raped her, she had to learn to forgive them as well. Jeanie had spent many hours talking to counselor after counselor trying to alleviate the multitude of inner pain she has suffered because of the indignities that she as a young woman had endured. Through much work, Jeanie has finally come to terms with what happened in her life and has gradually healed from many of the psychological effects of the various abuses.

Although Jeanie's misconceived thinking patterns have abruptly turned around, she is still a work in progress. Once in awhile something would happen in her current life and emotionally she's thrown back to the hurting child of yesteryears. However, Jeanie is the healthiest she has ever been mentally, spiritually and psychologically. She does still struggle with forgiveness issues. For a long time Jeanie refused to forgive the men in her past who sexually molested her, used her sexually and forcibly raped her. She didn't feel they deserved forgiveness. We don't deserve God's forgiveness either…but it's given to us anyway.

It was not hurting the predators at all by withholding her forgiveness from them. Jeanie was only hurting herself holding onto her extreme hate and rage towards those individuals. Holding onto such emotions only poisoned Jeanie's spirit. Her body and soul had suffered enough in this world. Although she could never forget, it was time to forgive even them!

The person who was hardest to forgive…was herself. All the years wandering like a nomad searching for herself was hard on Jeanie. There were many trials she endured throughout her life's path. She developed many inner defenses to keep her from dealing with her present reality. That was the only way she could continue on in life with any amount of sanity.

These defenses helped her to survive, mentally, physically and spiritually. The scarred girl's brain became lost within it's own inner clouds. She didn't experience a total break from reality, but she came real close.

Jeanie was indeed sorry she endured such tragedy and pain in her life. However, she was no longer angry at God. She was still a bit angry at herself…but she's learning to let go of that too. She punished herself enough through the self bullying behaviors of yesteryear (like her bulimia). It was time to let go of the resentment she had in her heart for herself as well.

Jeanie learned to forgive others of the hurt they inflicted on her, but the remorseful woman had to learn to forgive herself as well. Even though Jeanie had made many errors in her life, it was necessary for her to go through those particular experiences. God used those ordeals to help the young woman learn her various life's lessons. Jeanie acknowledges all the trials and pain her hurting heart went through. She understands, she feels, she empathizes and she forgives everyone for their part in her great passion play of life…even herself.

Some days Jeanie is at peace with the harsh life changing events of the past. Other times, she is not. There was so much she wished she could change, but whatever consequences she had to endure because of her past life…she had to live with. Despite everything Jeanie endured, she had to accept her role in the multitude of turbulent life events. She had to accept herself…as she was then and as she is now. The cumulative experiences in the past had made her into the person she is today.

Jeanie is learning the greatest lesson of all "loving others as you love yourself." How can one truly love others if you have such disdain and disgust for your own self? You can't.

So, although bullied and abused Jeanie learned forgiveness and love. Once she learned that…Carmelita Jean Jones became beautiful.

Butterfly Flight

Like a traveling butterfly
the precious child would wander free,
but life's experiences
weren't always good for that entity.

She stumbled and tripped,
on the rocky terrain.
Felt moments of sunshine,
but mostly was clouded by rain.

Despite oppositions
the girl ventured on.
Eventually she would find
where it was she belonged.

With open eyes and magic wings,
God revealed to her
life's important things.

The forgiveness and love
that she for so long sought,
was there all along,
but she thought not.

God led her on
the path she'd need.
He raised her up
and planted a seed.

It's up to her now
to nurture it to grow.
It's up to her now
to let the past pain go.

Forgiveness and love
finally graced this entity.
At last the butterfly within
can truly be free.

Forgiveness and love
finally graced this entity.
At last the butterfly within
can truly be free.

CPSIA information can be obtained at www.ICGtesting.com
Printed in the USA
BVOW06s0531090716

454836BV00009BA/208/P

9 781634 496834